Promises

Wendi Sotis

All rights reserved. No part of this book may be reproduced in any form or by any electronic or mechanical means including information storage and retrieval systems—except in the case of brief quotations embodied in critical articles or reviews—without permission in writing from its publisher and author.

The characters and events portrayed in this book are fictitious or are used fictitiously. Any similarity to real persons, living or dead, is purely coincidental and not intended by the author.

Copyright © 2011 Wendi Sotis
ISBN-10: 1463643063
ISBN-13: 978-1463643065

To my children, Katie, Luke and Maddie.
Believe in yourself and you can do anything you want to do.

To my husband, Matt.
Thanks for always being there.

To my parents, Lillian and Charlie.
Miss you, Daddy.

Acknowledgements

My editing team has offered unwavering support in everything concerning this book and my writing: Gayle Mills, Robin Helm and Jessica Worton. Their encouragement, patience, skill and friendship have been more than invaluable. I can never thank them enough. I must make extra note of Gayle's contribution, who has re-edited this story several times. I thank God for steering me in the direction to meet Gayle while writing *Dreams and Expectations*, and in turn, to Robin and Jess. I could not, and would not, have done this without all of you.

As usual, even with the outstanding assistance of my editing team, I panicked and needed even more opinions on the plot. L. E. Smith and Peculiarlady eased my mind by cold reading this story. I appreciate your time and support.

I would also like to thank barneyrockz, who had convinced me that the "plot bunny" on which *Promises* is based was worth writing, though this story bears little resemblance to the original idea.

To Jan H., I must say that reading your stories first inspired my love for Jane Austen Fan Fiction.

To the entire Jane Austen Fan Fiction community—without your support on my first novel and short stories, *Promises* would not have been written. Thank you for all your comments and the support you have offered on all of my stories.

Of course, I must thank Jane Austen for authoring the fine work that has captured my heart for many years.

Chapter 1

April, 1801 – London

William's distress was evident on his face. So confused was he by the turmoil of emotions churned up by this quest that he no longer knew how to find what he was looking for among the rows of publications on the shelves of the bookshop.

"Excuse me, sir, but you must stop!"

Surprised, the fifteen-year-old boy looked down to find a little girl of perhaps nine or ten years sitting on the floor with an open book on her lap. "I would curtsy, as my mama says is correct when meeting a gentleman, but you are standing on my skirt, sir."

He jumped back a step or two, and the girl rose and curtsied, saying, "Thank you, sir."

The boy bowed. "Please forgive me. If I have damaged your dress, please allow me to ask my father to compensate you."

"Oh, I do forgive you, sir. There is no harm done, only a bit of dust on the hem. Had I been at home, by this time of day my skirts would have been covered with dirt and most likely would have been torn already. I am certain that Mama would be scolding me right about now! I know that a proper young lady should not have been sitting on the floor in a bookshop, especially in London, but after finding the book I had been searching for, I could not wait to begin its perusal!"

They stood in silence for a few moments before she continued, "Do you live in London, sir?"

Taking in this girl's appearance more thoroughly, he realized she was most likely the daughter of a gentleman. Though it seemed she was in an awkward stage of development, there was something pleasing about her looks. She had dark hair that was more aptly described as a tumble of curls framing her face, tied back with a ribbon in an attempt to tame them. The healthy glow about her skin indicated that she spent more time outdoors than did her peers. She seemed more intelligent than her years... perhaps it was the indescribable sparkle in her dark eyes that assured him of this. "I have arrived only just yesterday with my father and sister from our estate in Derbyshire."

"Mama says I should always ask about the weather, so now I must ask you: how does the weather in Derbyshire? Is it as warm there as it has been here in London the past few days?"

Her polite look of exaggerated interest made him smile a little before saying, "It is never quite as warm in Derbyshire as in London, Derbyshire being so far north."

"And were the roads in good condition for your journey, sir?"

He pressed his lips together for a moment to hide the increasing urge to smile. Idle chatter had never been so amusing. "Yes, they were in as good a condition as could be expected after the unusually harsh winter."

"Capital! And had you a pleasant journey south to London?"

"Yes, we did. Thank you."

"I am glad to hear it... and I do hope I have covered the subjects of the weather and your journey well enough because I do not believe I can think of one more question to ask about either. I have heard much of Derbyshire, though I have never been there. Papa has a friend who lives in Derbyshire, and he visited his friend there many times while they attended Eton and Cambridge together. Papa says the area is very beautiful and promises to take me there some day."

Since the death of his mother several months ago, his father had allowed the boy to stay at home, but now it was time to return to school after a brief stay in London, and he was not looking forward to it. His mother's letters from home had always been the highlight of his week, and the idea that there would never be another was making his return all the more difficult. This little girl was very amusing and, it seemed, just what he needed right now to distract him from such somber thoughts. His generally depressed mood of late was lightening considerably. "Do you know where in Derbyshire your father's friend resides?"

"Yes, I believe the estate is called Pemley... no, I am not saying it right, but that is close to the pronunciation."

His eyebrows raised and he said, "Pemberley, perhaps? And what is the gentleman's name, do you know?"

"Yes, I think it is exactly that! His name is Mr. Darcy."

"Well then, I do know your father's friend very well as I am Fitzwilliam Darcy. Mr. George Darcy is my father."

Her smile brightened the room. "How wonderful!" She noticed the black armband he wore, which was similar to the mourning band her father had worn when her grandmother had died. Remembering what her father had told her, suddenly her smile faded, and she put her small hand on his arm. "Oh... then may I say how sorry I am to have heard about your mother's passing, Mr. Darcy."

He looked down to the floor and sighed before saying, "Thank you." It *had* been nice to spend a few minutes *not* thinking on that subject.

A very insightful child, she detected his pain and his need to change the subject. Her hand gently squeezed his arm before letting go. "Since our fathers know each other, I should introduce myself—though Mama would be very displeased with me for doing so, and I must beg that you do not tell her! I am Elizabeth Bennet, but most people call me Lizzy."

He bowed to her again, and she curtseyed in return. "It is a pleasure to meet you, Miss Bennet. I have heard my father mention Mr. Bennet often. You live in Hertfordshire, do you not?"

"Yes, at Longbourn." Elizabeth felt the subject was exhausted. "May I ask what book you were looking for, Mr. Darcy? I have an interest in botany, and since you are searching in this section... I wonder if I could help you find it. This is my uncle's bookshop, and I know where most everything is," she said, beaming proudly.

"I am looking for <u>The Temple of Flora</u>, a book by Robert John Thornton," said William quietly.

"Why does such a lovely book on botany make you feel so sad?"

Something about her made him want to tell her everything that was in his heart, but he restricted himself to saying only, "It was my mother's favorite; botany was her special interest. We have a copy at Pemberley and another in our house in London, but I wanted to take one with me to Eton..." he said, his throat tightened with emotion.

"I understand, Mr. Darcy." He looked up to see such a look of compassion in her dark eyes that it almost overwhelmed him. He blinked back a few tears. "It is just here." She moved past him to take the book from the shelf and then handed it to him. "It has the most beautiful pictures I have ever seen in any of these books. I hope it brings you comfort."

Swallowing the lump in his throat, William said, "What was it you were reading, Miss Bennet?"

She passed the book to him.

Flipping through the pamphlet, he said, "But this is not written in English. I believe it is in German! Are you able to read German?"

"Yes, my neighbor, Baron Leisenheimer, was originally from Prussia and he taught me his native language. I enjoy German more than French and Italian, though I like Latin about the same."

William's eyes widened, "*You* know all those languages? But you are so very young..."

"Papa says I have a special gift for languages. Mama says I should not show off so much, but I am not trying to show off. I just learn easily, and that is all; I am not trying to impress anyone. She also says I should not tell anyone what I can do because they will think I am odd, and that I will never catch a husband. Do you think I am odd, Mr. Darcy?"

He found himself holding back a smile again. "No, Miss Bennet, I do not think you odd. I think you very intelligent."

"Mama says I'm im…impernant. Do you think I will never catch a husband because I am impernant?"

"I believe the word is 'impertinent,' but from what I have seen today I do not think you impertinent. You are honest, and that is a fine trait to have."

"Yes, I am honest, but mama says I must learn not to be too honest because it is rude. I cannot understand this. Do you know how one can be too honest?"

"Well, I am older and can understand it a little better. For example, sharing that your mother is instructing you on how to 'catch' a husband is not an appropriate subject to discuss with a gentleman… or with any acquaintance, really."

"But that is almost the only subject she ever talks of… and she often repeats that if my four sisters and I do not marry well then we will all be thrown into the hedgerows to starve when my father passes. If that is all *she* ever speaks of, why should I not speak of it?"

William's raised his eyebrows, and he blinked a few times before asking, "Perhaps she speaks of it only when among intimate family?"

Elizabeth shook her head.

William did not know what to say to that and changed the subject slightly, "Why would you all be thrown into the hedgerows?"

"Because Mr. Collins is a nasty man who Papa had an argument with many years ago, and they have not spoken since."

"Mr. Collins?"

"Yes, I have no brother and my father's cousin Mr. Collins will take Longbourn when Papa passes."

"Oh, I see."

"Though Mama says he will 'steal' it because she does not believe in entailments away from the girls in the family. Mama insists that catching a husband is the most important thing we girls can do, but I have decided that I do not wish to be married at present."

William almost laughed out loud. "I do not think you will need to decide to whom you will be married for a few years yet."

She arched her brow. "One would not think I am too young the way Mama speaks of it!" She put her book back on the shelf.

"You will not be purchasing the book?"

"No, I have read it already, and so I do not need to."

"That is more of a reference book, is it not? You do not think you might need to refer to it at a later time?"

"I have it here, now." She pointed to her head.

"I do not understand."

"Every time I read something, I keep a perfect picture of it in my mind and can look at it later. It is like the book is in my hand, and I am reading it again."

"How interesting!" He opened his book to a random page, "You have read this book, correct?" When she nodded he asked, "What is on page number five of the book I have?"

She described the pictures and said the names, spelling anything that she could not pronounce.

Shaking his head, he said with a wide smile, "I think you are an amazing person, Miss Bennet!"

"Thank you, sir. I am glad you do not think I am strange. Mama tells me I should not tell anyone about that, either, because when I have, people have thought I was odd, and someday they might have me sent to Bedlam when Papa is no longer here to protect me."

William frowned deeply. "If in the future *anyone* wishes to send you to Bedlam for one of your talents, I beg that you contact me. I will protect you if your father is unable to do so."

Elizabeth smiled brilliantly. "Thank you, Mr. Darcy! That relieves my mind a great deal."

Just then the bell above the door rang, and Mr. Bennet came into view at the end of the aisle of books. "Papa!"

"Ah, there you are, Lizzy." Warily, he eyed the young man standing with his daughter, but his demeanor changed as recognition dawned on him, "And you, young man, are you perhaps related to Mr. George Darcy?"

William bowed and said, "Yes, Mr. Bennet; I am his son. My father is within as well, sir. I believe he can be found in the philosophy section of the shop."

"You certainly look very much like him when he was about your age." Mr. Bennet looked back and forth between the two children. "Has my Lizzy been entertaining you?"

"Miss Bennet is a delightful young lady, sir. She helped me find the book I was searching for, and we have been conversing these past minutes."

Mr. Bennet nodded, "Come, let us find your father. I have not had the pleasure of his company for these several years at least."

They found Mr. Darcy discussing his book purchases with Mr. Gardiner, the proprietor of the shop, while waiting for his son to join him. As Mr. Bennet approached, Mr. Darcy turned and said, "Bennet! What a surprise to find you here in London! It is good to see you!" The two shook hands.

"Darcy, it is good to see you as well. It seems my daughter has been assisting your son in finding a book, and I have just met him. He seems a fine young man. I am a bit shocked to see how much he has grown—when I had last seen you, he was only just walking! I cannot believe so much time has passed! I see you know Gardiner, my wife's brother?"

Mr. Darcy looked surprised, "I did not know you were related. I have been a patron of this superior bookshop for years, and it has only improved since Mr. Gardiner became proprietor last year."

"Yes, I quite agree. If not for the bookshops, London would be intolerable!"

"I see your opinion of Town has not changed, Bennet." Mr. Darcy laughed.

"Not in the least!" Mr. Gardiner replied. Mr. Bennet introduced Elizabeth to Mr. Darcy and then the three gentlemen began to speak of Cambridge. Mr. Gardiner had attended beginning the year the other gentlemen had left it, but they still had much to discuss.

"You said earlier that you attend Eton, Mr. Darcy.... do you like school?" asked Elizabeth.

"I like it very well, Miss Bennet." William felt a pang of guilt because he knew he was not being completely forthright with this very honest girl. He did enjoy learning, but he did not feel comfortable with the social aspects of living at school.

"I wish I could go to school."

"Perhaps if you tell your father, he will allow you to attend a school for ladies."

"I would not want to go to *that* kind of school! I meant that I want to go to the kind of school that boys attend. Girls learn silly subjects like embroidery, netting purses, and how to serve tea... and I already know more languages than they could teach me at a school for *ladies*. Papa says that I could probably teach the instructors a thing or two! I do like to dance and play the pianoforte... but embroidery!" Elizabeth rolled her eyes in such a way that had William attempting to hold back his smile again. "I want to learn about literature and mathematics and science and philosophy! Mama scolds me for reading so much for she says men do not like girls who know more than they do, but I want to *learn*! I am glad that Papa allows me to read anything in his library, and he does not forbid me from studying any subject I wish." She lowered her voice and said conspiratorially, "Well, except for the books on the uppermost shelf by the window on the left, at which I am *never* to look."

This time William could not stop a chuckle from escaping before he said, "It sounds as if you have many diverse interests, Miss Bennet, much like my mother did. She was an intelligent lady, and I applaud your wish to expand your mind past subjects you find silly." Thinking his praise might actually end up getting her in trouble, he thought to add, "Though embroidery does serve a purpose and would not be a bad thing to learn if it pleases your mother for you to do so. Do you enjoy only reading, or do you have other pursuits as well?"

"I love to be outdoors, sir, doing just about everything. I walk a great deal. Charlotte and Jane will walk with me, but they do not like to climb trees, or play army and pirates and bandits with the boys like I do, so they often go home after our walks. They like doing *girl* things much better."

"Are Charlotte and Jane your sisters?"

"Jane is my elder sister by two years, and she is an angel!" Elizabeth's smile was wide as she spoke of Jane, but it lessened as she continued, "I have three other sisters. The youngest two, Kitty and Lydia, are too young to go out with me, but I do think they will not be interested in what I like to do when they are old enough as they are very silly. Mary, the sister who is two years younger than I, is too serious to play at... anything. Charlotte is my friend and neighbor. Her father was just made a knight, and we must call him 'Sir William' now instead of 'Mr. Lucas.' It is mostly Charlotte's brothers that I play with, though there are other boys from the neighboring estates and tenant farms that join us as well."

"And what position do the boys have you play during these games?" William asked, thinking they would have her pretending to clean up after the horses and swab the decks.

"I am not supposed to tell anyone... do you promise not to tell?" William nodded. "I am always the general of the army or the captain of the ship or the leading bandit, of course!"

"Of course!" William said with a grin. "And the boys do not get angry because they must take orders from a girl?"

"No, for I make up much better games than they do, and though they might not admit it to anyone else, they do say it to *me*. None of the boys play chess or read much, but I do, and I believe that is why I devise better strategies in our wars and conflicts. Sometimes we fight real battles as they were portrayed in history books or the newspaper—*not* with real weapons, of course. I am the best tree climber of the lot, as well as the best swordsman!"

At this point, William was not surprised by anything this obviously witty and adventurous young lady had to say. He saw his father looking at him with a small smile that reached his eyes—one he had not seen on his father's face since his mother had died. Little did he know his father was thinking that he had not seen his son laugh, smile or even take an interest in *anything* other than his sister since his wife had died... until now.

William overheard the men making plans to meet at Mr. Darcy's club for lunch the following day and expected them to soon be bidding each other farewell. "I am quite impressed with the many accomplishments already achieved by one so young. But I do believe you should try to work on the *girl* things as well. I know it is difficult to do things that one does not enjoy in the least, but we all must carry that burden. If you think of it as a challenge to improve yourself, as I do, it will make it more palatable." When Elizabeth looked doubtful, he added, "It does sound as if it would make living with your mother a bit easier if you showed her you were putting in a good effort, if nothing else."

Elizabeth made another face that reminded William of her age, and he almost expected her to stamp her foot and have a tantrum. He had been at first surprised and a little amused at hearing her converse with more intelligence than ever he had heard from young ladies twice her age, but soon he had become so comfortable with her conversation that he had forgotten just how young she was. Elizabeth sighed and relented, "Well... it does sound like a better idea when you put it that way. Since you do seem like a sensible young man, I will make the attempt to follow your advice. Perhaps I will ask my Aunt Gardiner to teach me a bit of embroidery while I am still in London. She has more patience with me than does Mama."

William could not help but chuckle. "That sounds like a very good plan, Miss Bennet."

Mr. Darcy approached and said, "It certainly was a pleasure meeting you, Miss Bennet. Your father will be having dinner with us in two days' time. Would you like to accompany him? Your father tells me you are interested in books, and I thought that William could show you our library; I hoped you might enjoy meeting my daughter as well."

Elizabeth looked at her father, and at his nod, she smiled brightly and said, "Yes, sir, I would like that very much. Thank you, Mr. Darcy." She curtsied.

Mr. Darcy bowed to her and said, "I look forward to seeing you again, Miss Bennet."

The Darcys took their leave, both happier than when they had arrived.

~%~

When the Bennets arrived at Darcy House, after the usual greetings Mr. Darcy suggested that William show Elizabeth the way to the nursery so that she could be introduced to Georgiana. After the children left them, Mr. Bennet said, "Good thinking to have my Lizzy meet Miss Darcy *before* seeing the library. We may never see her again after she has experienced the famous Darcy collection!"

"So she takes after her father in this way?" Mr. Darcy laughed.

"Yes, she certainly does, though I think she will surpass my abilities in many areas. I am afraid her mother feels Lizzy's thirst for knowledge is a liability, but I cannot deny her... and it has caused quite a bit of contention between us. Elizabeth is truly one of the most intelligent persons I have ever met, Darcy. She will be but ten years old next month, and she already knows more than do most boys upon entering Cambridge, and all from her own reading. The instruction I have given her is more guidance than teaching. Occasionally there is a concept that she has trouble comprehending, but to see how her face lights up with understanding when all becomes clear is reward enough to brave even my wife's disapproval! I think sometimes my wife is actually frightened of her. There is no doubt she is frightened *for* Lizzy, and at times I have to agree."

"Why would you be frightened for Elizabeth, Thomas?" When they were younger, the two had always switched to first names whenever discussing a serious matter, and though many years had passed since they had seen each other, Mr. Darcy easily fell into this old habit.

"If she were a boy, nothing would be able to stand in her way... but she is not. She will grow up someday, George—sooner than I am prepared for, in fact. To be honest, I do not know how she will manage. There could not be one in a thousand men who could be considered her equal in intelligence, and even fewer who would accept her for who she is and not insist that she pretend that she is something she is not."

From the moment George Darcy had seen his son interacting with his friend's daughter at the bookstore, he had had an idea of what Elizabeth's future would hold, but it was far too soon to bring that subject up with her father. "Do not fret, Thomas. I have a strong feeling all will be well for Elizabeth."

"You always did have a sense of what would work out well. I hope in this case you are correct."

Perhaps, though, he *could* plant a seed. "Actually, from what you have told me and from what I have seen, she reminds me of William at that age, but she seems to have an intuitive sense of other people's feelings that William has always lacked. She has gotten William to talk, and, believe me, that is a feat! He is even shyer than *I* was at his age, if you can believe it possible. Georgiana has been looking forward to meeting Elizabeth because William has mentioned her so often since we met you both at the bookshop."

"Really? No, I would not have guessed it! In fact, I had been thinking that while he *looks* very much like you did at his age, he does not *act* like you did at all, in *that* way at least. But then, I *did* come across them after he had already been speaking to Lizzy for some minutes, from what I understood."

"You always did have that effect upon me as well, Thomas, and I am certain you would have the same effect on William. With you, I always felt comfortable; it was with others that I became reticent. As far as I know, before two days ago the only person outside the immediate family with whom William was truly comfortable was my nephew Richard Fitzwilliam. He has had a difficult time at school and has had no Thomas Bennet to help him through it as I did. The headmaster tells me that while he is accepted due to his name, he does not really fit in with the other boys. Sound familiar?" When Mr. Bennet nodded, Mr. Darcy continued, "I was hesitant about sending him back to Eton after my wife's passing because he seemed so... lost, but I am sure you will agree that keeping him at home will do him no favors. He must learn to find his way in society, and Eton is a proper place to start. I keep hoping that perhaps he will find a true friend there, too. Seeing him the past couple of days has made me feel more comfortable with the decision. I now feel he will be all right."

After discussing a few other subjects, the gentlemen became curious as to what had happened to William and Elizabeth. Mr. Darcy invited Mr. Bennet to the nursery to see what they were about. Upon arriving they found William sketching and Georgiana entranced in Elizabeth's telling of the story, *Beauty and the Beast*. The gentlemen stood by the door, watching and listening for a few minutes before Georgiana noticed them and ran to her father with her arms open. Mr. Darcy scooped her up and gave her a hug before setting her down to introduce her to Mr. Bennet. Georgiana looked up to Elizabeth, who had joined them near the door, and Elizabeth nodded very seriously. Georgiana curtsied as well as a five-year-old could, and Elizabeth applauded. "You learn very quickly, Miss Darcy!"

"Very well done, Georgiana! Your curtsy has certainly improved since yesterday!" Mr. Darcy praised.

"Miss Elizabeth showed her a special way to accomplish it, Father."

"I thank you for your instruction, Miss *Bennet*." Mr. Darcy said with a sharp look at his son indicating that he was correcting him.

In a very serious tone of voice, Elizabeth said, "Mr. Darcy, I know I am supposed to be called 'Miss Bennet,' but 'Miss Bennet' is my sister Jane. I like to be called 'Elizabeth' or 'Lizzy' much better, but your son says *that* would be improper. So, we have decided to compromise and have settled on 'Miss Elizabeth,' if you do not mind, sir."

Mr. Darcy glanced at Mr. Bennet, who was stifling a laugh, and shrugged. "I suppose it is fine with me as long as your father does not object. But William, when you are in public, you should refer to her as 'Miss Bennet.'"

"Agreed, sir," Elizabeth said, "but may Miss Darcy call me 'Elizabeth'?"

"Perhaps when she is older she may, but for now I would be grateful for your assistance in teaching her to respect her elders by having her address you more formally."

Elizabeth's mouth formed into a silent, "Oh," and she nodded.

At a look from Mr. Darcy, the governess told Georgiana that story time was over, and it was time for a writing lesson. The remainder of the group said goodbye to Georgiana and headed toward the library.

As they walked, Mr. Bennet asked William what he had been sketching, and William handed him the pad, blushing. "This is very good!" Mr. Bennet said as he slowed to look at the beginnings of a sketch of Elizabeth. "Have you studied with a master?"

"A little, sir. I enjoy it, but…"

"But?"

"Mr. Bennet, at school the boys tease me, saying that drawing is a girl's activity, so I do not practice when away from home." William blushed again.

Mr. Bennet smiled. "Ah! Lizzy is often told she should not read so much, and that girls should not learn mathematics or science or ancient languages or play chess because they are all things that boys usually do. What is your opinion, Master William? Do you think I should not allow her to learn these subjects?"

William's look could be described as horrified. "No, sir, I would not change anything about Miss Elizabeth."

"What do you think Lizzy would say to anyone who dared to tell her that she likes boy's activities? Do you think that would stop her from doing what she loved to do?" Mr. Bennet said with a smirk.

William tried not to smile while saying, "I cannot imagine what she would say, but I know she continues to do what she enjoys as long as you do not forbid it, sir, and she is proud of her accomplishments. I do admire her spirit, Mr. Bennet."

"One would think that the father has much to teach the daughter, but Lizzy tends to teach me more than I could have dreamed possible. Perhaps you can learn a lesson from her in this regard as well?"

"Thank you, sir."

He clapped William on the shoulder, and the two picked up the pace to catch up to Elizabeth and Mr. Darcy.

When they arrived at the door of the library, Mr. Darcy allowed Elizabeth to enter first. She took a few steps into the room, and all eyes were on her expression. Elizabeth stood wide-eyed and open-mouthed as she looked around the room. She whispered, "*This* is your private *library?*"

"You do not have to whisper, Miss Elizabeth. We are the only people here. This is just a small sample; the true collection is at Pemberley," Mr. Darcy answered.

The eyes that none of the gentlemen thought could open wider, did. "This is but a *small* sample? But... there are more books here than in my uncle's bookshop!"

"I am very proud of our collection, Miss Elizabeth. It is the work of many generations of Darcys. Your father spent many hours ensconced in this room during his youth, as well as in our library in Derbyshire. Do you like it?"

"It is… *heavenly*, sir!"

Chapter 2

July of 1804 – Hertfordshire – Three years later...

After inspecting the wheel to their coach, Mr. Darcy shook his head while addressing the driver, "John, take the lead horse and ride ahead into the next village. I am certain they will have someone able to repair the wheel. If there is an inn at the village, inquire about any available rooms for us."

"Yes, Mr. Darcy. I'll be back as soon as I can, sir," John responded as he unhitched the lead horse from the coach.

"We will need to send an express to Georgiana's nanny in London when we know where we will be staying, William. I trust the delay in our arrival in London will be only a day or two in duration. You will still have plenty of time to shop for what you need to begin your life at Cambridge."

"We could not be more than two or three hours from London by horseback, Father. If it should take more than two days, we could always ride."

"Excuse me, can you tell me if Longbourn is anywhere near here?" asked Mr. Darcy of the laborer who was seen walking down the road towards them. William's eyes brightened. Mr. Darcy remembered his son's disappointment to have missed Mr. Bennet's visits in London several times over the past three years, especially on those occasions that Elizabeth had also been present. William knew that Longbourn was in Hertfordshire, but had no idea where it was exactly.

"Yes, sir. 'Bout a mile back from where I came."

"Thank you." Mr. Darcy handed the man a coin, then turned to William. "What good fortune! I would enjoy a visit with Bennet while we wait for the wheel to be repaired. Would you rather stay with the coach, William?" Mr. Darcy could not resist laughing at the disappointed expression on his son's face. "I was only jesting, son!" Turning to the footman, he said, "James, we are walking ahead to the estate of Longbourn. Please stay with the coach and ask John to follow to inform us of his findings in the village."

The two began to walk in the direction in which the laborer had pointed, but came across a group of boys along the road. They asked the boys if they were headed in the right direction, and the boys obligingly showed them a shorter footpath to Longbourn. As they were walking through the woods the boys had indicated, William looked up, and his attention was drawn to some color that did not belong in a tree, piquing his curiosity. As they approached, he noticed shoes, stockings and a bonnet at the base of the tree. Smiling, he looked up and found exactly what—or who—he was looking for.

At the sound of an embarrassed, "OH!" Mr. Darcy looked up as well. Thirteen-year-old Elizabeth Bennet was standing on a tree branch high above them.

"Good afternoon, Miss Elizabeth! It is good to see you again." Mr. Darcy said with a smile of his own.

"Mr. Darcy... Mr. Darcy, good afternoon. I would curtsy, but that would prove to be a bit difficult at the moment." She flashed the gentlemen a brilliant smile and began to climb down the tree. For a moment both gentlemen were undecided concerning what to do, caught between seeing her safely to the ground and retaining her modesty. William turned his back first, whispering, "Father, I have it on good authority that Miss Elizabeth climbs trees rather often. I think she will be safe without our assistance."

"Oh? Just where have you come by this information?"

"Though it was discussed three years ago, sir, it is of her own words that I speak. From the looks of it, things have not changed much." Both Darcys tried not to laugh too loudly.

"May I ask you both to remain facing that way while I return my footwear to its original state?"

"Certainly, Miss Elizabeth," Mr. Darcy said with a smile in his voice. "May I ask what you were doing up in that tree?"

"Yes, you may, sir. I am the captain of a pirate ship and was standing in the crow's nest looking for the next scallywag from which to plunder booty, of course. May I ask how you came to be in these woods, sir?" Her voice betrayed her struggle with one of her stockings.

"Certainly. We are on our way to London to prepare William for Cambridge, and our carriage wheel has broken. Since we found ourselves not far from Longbourn, we could not pass up the opportunity to visit with your father and you. May I ask where your *crew* is presently, Madam Pirate?"

"Are you both well? I do hope none of your staff was injured!"

"We are well, Miss Elizabeth; no one was injured. I thank you for your concern," replied Mr. Darcy, pleased with her inquiry.

"And the horses?"

"They are fine, Miss Elizabeth." The Darcy men exchanged a warm glance. It could never be said that Elizabeth Bennet was not a very caring person.

"Mutiny, sir!" Elizabeth exclaimed loudly as she put her foot right through the stocking with a little too much enthusiasm. The sound of the cloth giving way caused the gentlemen's smiles to reappear. She glared at her bare foot with ire before shrugging her shoulders. "My crew would insist that the captain should *not* be the one to climb to the crow's nest. I felt that since I *was* the captain that I should be allowed to make the rules, and I told them that if they did not like it, they could walk the plank, and so they did. May I now ask if it was three boys who directed you along this path, sir?"

"Yes it was, Madam Pirate."

Fully redressed, Elizabeth walked around to face the gentlemen, put her hands on her hips and said, "Aye, as I thought. They sent you this way on purpose to embarrass me!" she glared in the direction of the path on which the boys had departed and then looked back to the gentlemen before her. After a moment during which the gentlemen could see a multitude of thoughts pass through her eyes, she smiled at them and said, "But I am glad they did, because if they had not, I might have stayed up in that tree the rest of the day and missed your visit entirely. *That* would have been a shame indeed." Elizabeth's smile changed into another glare as she crossed her arms across her chest, "Now, me hearties, if you wish to escape alive from the Dreaded Pirate Lizzy, you must agree to take a blood oath that you will *not* tell my mother that you found me in the crow's nest, nor may you give away my secret identity as the Dreaded Pirate Lizzy."

As she spoke, William observed that Elizabeth was taller and thinner and even more awkward looking than the last time he had seen her, but her personality had the same special quality that he remembered, and the same intelligent sparkle was present in her eyes.

"May I tell *Mr.* Bennet, Madam Pirate?" asked Mr. Darcy.

"Oh yes, that would be fine, sir—just do not tell my mother!"

Though his son endeavored to hide his amusement, Mr. Darcy could not help but allow a chuckle to escape. Elizabeth held out her hand for the gentlemen to each shake in order to seal their agreement, and so they did.

"Have either of you ever *met* my mother?" Both gentlemen shook their heads, and Elizabeth continued to speak as she began walking, leading the way to Longbourn they presumed, "Aye, me mateys, it is just as I feared," She said with a sigh. "Well then, you should prepare yourselves. If you insist upon a visit to Longbourn, you will be fussed over excessively and may even be witness to a scolding or two of my most unladylike manners while my angelic sister Jane is praised to the skies. Please *do* understand that my Jane deserves every word of praise she receives—more actually. But my mother's praise embarrasses Jane exceedingly, and so my mother's habit of persisting in it, no matter how deep a shade Jane's blush becomes, is not favored by either of us. She might even push Jane towards you, Mr. Darcy," she warned as she turned to look at William, "for she is fifteen years of age and will be out next year. She is the most beautiful girl in all of England, in my opinion! But I give you leave to pay my mother no mind, for Jane and I have sworn an oath to marry only for the deepest love, and *I* will not let her fall into any traps set by Mama to marry a man just because he is rich!" The Darcys exchanged another amused look, and William blushed.

After a brief silence, Elizabeth continued, "I must tell you that I took your advice, Mr. Darcy," looking back over her shoulder toward William again, "and took up embroidery, which did *a little* to quiet my mother's fears of my forever being a hoyden and never marrying. Please note that I did *not* say 'catch a husband,' as you had instructed me to avoid the phrase. I have put much effort into improving my skills at embroidery, though I still do not get on very well at all." She frowned and walked on for several minutes before saying in a more subdued tone of voice, "It is not only for my sake that I ask you not to mention what you saw today, but for your own and for that of my parents. Mother is a very excitable lady and would more than likely need her smelling salts if she *were* to know that two such fashionable gentlemen witnessed my misdoings. Father would certainly need to rush you all off into his study to avoid witnessing a severe attack of her nerves."

Trying to steer Miss Bennet away from giving a full account of *all* their family secrets, William asked, "Perhaps you can show me a sample of your embroidery while we visit?"

"Certainly, if you wish it, sir, but I do give you fair warning that once you see what I have managed, you may soon wish you had never made that request!" She laughed, then continued, "Though I am told I should, I have not yet learned to accept empty praise, gentlemen, and I always know when it is not deserved, so please do not offer any to me." Elizabeth stopped walking, forcing both gentlemen to stop short almost bumping into her, though she did not seem to notice. She cocked her head to the side and furrowed her brow, then turned to them before saying, "Though, on second thought, if you feel you *must* to avoid insulting my mother, I give you permission to do so. I will know the difference." Elizabeth nodded a little and said, "I trust your superior judgment in the matter and will endeavor to accept your compliments gracefully," she concluded with a bright smile and began walking again.

Both gentlemen hesitated a few moments to exchange another amused look between them before following Elizabeth again. William thought that life within her family must certainly never be boring!

The trio trod on towards Longbourn, and before long, they heard someone whistling. Elizabeth's face brightened with another smile, and her dark eyes twinkled with delight. "Baron Leisenheimer?" she called out in the direction from which the tune was coming. The whistling stopped, and a slightly portly gentleman of medium height and with a tuft of blonde hair in a half-halo around his head came from around a bend of an intersecting path.

"Ah, Miss Lizzy! How good it is to see you! I was on my way to visit at Longbourn," Baron Leisenheimer said with a thick German accent and a cheerful demeanor. "I see that you have an escort today, my dear."

Elizabeth introduced the gentlemen, "Baron, allow me to introduce Mr. George Darcy and Mr. Fitzwilliam Darcy of Pemberley in Derbyshire. Gentlemen, please meet Baron Charles Ludwig Leisenheimer of Purvis Lodge, formerly of Prussia." The typical greetings were exchanged. "Mr. Darcy," she said to William, "do you remember I told you of the gentleman who taught me German? This is he."

"Taught? I did nothing of the kind. You *absorbed* the language, dear girl! I barely put any effort into the endeavor at all, and you had more interest than either of my own daughters did," he chuckled, his eyes twinkling with obvious affection for all three girls.

"Are your daughters still at home, Baron?" Mr. Darcy asked as they began walking toward Longbourn once again.

"No, my girls are grown now, Mr. Darcy. My Gwendolyn is married these three years and Cynthia a little less than two… a fine choice of husbands, if you ask me. Both had spent some time every year in London with my wife's relatives while growing up, so the fact that the German language is not very fashionable influenced their choice of learning Italian and French instead. Miss Lizzy was a great help to them there, though they were so much older than she," he explained to the gentlemen. "My preferences, like Mr. Bennet's, are for the country, so we rarely accompanied them to town for long after I sold my business. Miss Lizzy has been almost like another daughter to us and a great comfort to me when she stops by to check up on me every day since my wife is away assisting my Cynthia during her confinement. Mrs. Bennet has commanded that I attend tea every day while my wife is away. There are not many men brave enough to risk displeasing such a woman as she; and I, for one, have never passed on good company. But, I did not know the Bennets had other guests today…."

Baron Leisenheimer looked a little sheepish, obviously wondering if he was intruding on the Darcys' visit. Elizabeth said with a mischievous sparkle in her eye, "The Darcys' coach has had some trouble on the road near here, Baron, and they *happened* upon me in the woods. Papa will be so pleased to have so many good friends today at Longbourn, as am I."

Baron Leisenheimer laughed, "I can tell by the look in your eye that you were up to no good today, little Lizzy." He turned to the Darcys and said, "I often 'happen upon her in the woods' myself during my walks. Did she have you swear a blood oath of silence as well?"

Both Darcys laughed and nodded. Elizabeth answered, "I am surprised at you, Baron! You of all people should know that blood oaths are supposed to be kept secret, sir! I should think that you will *all* keep each other's oaths a secret as well as your own." She looked at the three gentlemen severely. They all nodded. "Good! I see you are all very wise in not antagonizing the Dreaded Pirate Lizzy." When she turned her back to them to continue along the path, the three gentlemen exchanged amused smiles.

After a few moments, Elizabeth said, "Mr. Darcy attended school with my father, Baron. I have met them several times in London, but the Darcys have never met my mother or my sisters." She gave the Baron a pointed look.

"Oh…" the Baron said quietly, and then turned to William. "Young Darcy, if I may… what is your age?"

A little surprised, William judged by the look on Elizabeth's face that he should answer. "I am eighteen, sir, and just about to begin Cambridge."

"Ah ha." He looked warily at Elizabeth and mumbled, "*This* should be an interesting afternoon."

"I tried to warn them about Mama…" Elizabeth said quietly.

Baron Leisenheimer laughed loudly. "Then you are a good friend, little Lizzy. It is always best for the prey to know that they are about to be hunted if they are to succeed in escaping unscathed!" He turned to the Darcys again and said, "Beware, sirs! None of Mrs. Bennet's daughters are yet out, but she can already out-hawk any of the London society mothers! *I* would not wish to be an eligible young man within her sights until all five daughters are married!"

William's eyes opened wide, and he looked at his father, whose eyes were sparkling with mirth. "Well, then, it will give William a little practice. It seems, son, if you can escape from our visit at Longbourn without being 'caught,' you will be well prepared for the *ton*."

The only one not laughing was William.

~%~

After the initial surprise of their arrival was subdued and welcomes made, the scene at Longbourn was very much the way Elizabeth and Baron

Leisenheimer had predicted. Mrs. Bennet made quite a fuss over Jane, who had an almost constant blush on her cheeks throughout tea, and made certain that Jane and William were seated next to each other with the intention of furthering conversation between the two. Elizabeth immediately sat next to Jane hoping she could help draw some of her mother's attention, albeit the attention was negative, as usual. The Baron sat on the other side of William.

Mr. Darcy sat with Mr. Bennet across the room watching the rest of the group, both amused by Mrs. Bennet's maneuvers. How Mrs. Bennet could think that two such shy individuals would get along well was beyond the understanding of both gentlemen.

The Darcys were surprised that the two youngest girls were permitted to attend tea with guests because they were not able to sit still for more than a few seconds together, spoke too loudly to each other, and giggled throughout. When William heard their ages, he was shocked. He had expected that they were much younger than nine and ten since Elizabeth had been about that age when he first met her, and Georgiana was about that age now. Both Elizabeth and Georgiana had behaved much better than these two.

Elizabeth tried to turn the conversation away from Jane and Mr. Darcy's fortune several times.

"Baron Leisenheimer, would you mind telling Mr. Darcy about the departure between English titles and Prussian nobility and titles? I find the differences very interesting." She smiled a slightly mischievous smile.

"Certainly," he said with a glint in his eye, knowing what question would come next and that his story would take a while, putting a crimp in Mrs. Bennet's obvious plan. "Most English think that because I am titled, I was a firstborn son, but in Prussia *all* sons inherit the title from their father. Very much like English families, being a fifth son I did *not*, however, inherit the wealth of my family and thus, had to take a profession."

"I am very interested in how you came to decide to move from Prussia to Hertfordshire, sir," William interjected, but then thought twice about the propriety of that question and blushed. Elizabeth smiled at him because it was similar to the question she was about to ask next. Having him ask in her stead worked out much better since Mrs. Bennet would not be able to interrupt unless she wished to appear rude to the Darcys—something even she would not do in front of a prospective wealthy suitor for Jane.

Baron Leisenheimer answered, "My father wished me to go into the army, but I could not see myself in that profession at all. I would have been a poor soldier! After university I went on a tour of Europe. In Paris, I met a British family who had a very beautiful daughter." The Baron wiggled his eyebrows a bit, and Elizabeth laughed. "Lilias and I fell in love and wished to marry. I had declared my intentions and wished to become engaged to make certain her father did not arrange a marriage for her with someone else while I made my fortune. Her family was not opposed to love-matches, but though she had a nice dowry, her father agreed we should not marry until I had a regular income."

His countenance turned a bit darker. "I returned to Prussia to inform my family of my intentions as well and to receive their blessings, but my family objected to my marrying a lady from England, especially since they had already arranged a marriage with a titled heiress whom I had never before laid eyes upon. They tricked me into meeting her, and may I kindly say we were far from well suited for each other, but still my family insisted we marry. Furious with them, I left Prussia and followed Lilias to England.

Baron Leisenheimer shook his head as if to clear it of unpleasant memories, and then continued, "Soon after, I invested the very meager funds I had inherited from a maternal great-aunt in Mr. Gardiner's father's import business. I also brought in some contacts with a few friends in Prussia who would supply us with items from my homeland. I found I had a talent for trade and opened a very successful shop selling the imports we had brought into the country through Mr. Gardiner's business. Lilias and I married when I had earned enough to support us. As I said earlier, I enjoy the country, and though we visited my wife's family estate at times, I insisted on bringing up my daughters away from the foul air of the city. It took a few years to find something that would suit my particular tastes.

"I met Mr. Bennet in London when he became interested in a certain item in my shop and wished to speak to the owner, me, about it. We got along well and quickly formed a friendship. It was I who had originally introduced Mr. Bennet to Mr. Gardiner, and by extension, the very lovely Miss Gardiner—now Mrs. Bennet." He nodded to Mrs. Bennet, and she giggled loudly along with her youngest two daughters. "It was through Mr. Bennet that I heard that Purvis Lodge was for sale and came to inspect it. Other than the house and grounds itself, the easy distance to London was one of the deciding factors on our settling here, as well as knowing we would have such good neighbors. A few years ago, the son of one of my Prussian friends wished to buy my business, and I happily accepted his offer as I was ready to retire to the country for good."

During tea, the Darcy's driver informed them that the wheel was not repairable, and a new one must be either constructed or sent for from London. Mr. Darcy decided they would stay the night at the inn in the village, continuing to London on horseback in the morning. Mrs. Bennet insisted upon the Darcys staying at Longbourn for the night instead of at the inn, and a cart was sent to collect their trunks. An express letter was sent to Georgiana Darcy's nanny before the Darcys removed to their chambers to change from their travelling clothes.

William was soon ready and decided to take a walk in the garden to avoid Mrs. Bennet, bringing along his sketch book. Espying a pretty little wilderness off to one side, he walked in that direction, sighing loudly with relief when he turned and found he was out of sight of the house. He startled a little when he heard the sound of Elizabeth's laughter, and turned to see her sitting on a bench with a book. He approached and bowed.

"Good afternoon, Mr. Darcy. I am proud that you have survived the first battle, but the war is not yet over!" she laughed.

He wondered what she had been doing since he had seen her last that had made her dress so dirty, but was too much of a gentleman to ask. "Not without help! I thank you for your interference. I do not wish to insult you, Miss Elizabeth; I have nothing against your sister as she does seem to be a sweet girl – it is just that…"

"It is just that you have decided that you do not wish to be married at present?" she said, repeating something she had said about herself when they first met at the bookstore. Elizabeth wondered if he would recognize it.

"Yes, exactly!" he said, glad not to have insulted his friend. He hesitated a moment, his attention caught by the light dancing in her dark eyes, then said, "I remember you had told me about your mother's preoccupation with 'catching husbands' for her daughters when first I met you at your uncle's bookstore in London. I must say, at the time I thought you were exaggerating, but now I understand that conversation a bit better, *and* the one you had with Baron Leisenheimer before reaching Longbourn earlier today!"

Both laughed, and Elizabeth patted the bench next to her. "Will you sit with me for a little while, Mr. Darcy? I would rather stay out of the house as long as possible."

"Yes, thank you." He sat and then looked at the book she held in her hand. "What tome are you reading?"

"Oh, *Philebus* by Plato. Have you read it?"

William chuckled. "I cannot imagine any of the gentlemen my age, other than myself of course, reading Plato unless *forced* to for a school assignment, and here you are a girl of thirteen years reading it in Latin! You amaze me, Miss Elizabeth!"

"I hope in a good way, Mr. Darcy."

"Yes, very much so. You are a very interesting person to have as a friend."

"Thank you, sir. What is it that you are carrying? Is it your sketch pad? May I see it, please?" William turned crimson as she flipped through the pages smiling at what she saw, "You are very good!" Stopping at a certain page, she asked, "Is this what Georgiana looks like now?"

"Yes, or at least as close to her image as my meager talents will allow. Do you remember that I sketched you once?" She smiled and nodded. "Will you allow me to sketch you again today? I enjoy making likenesses of the same people over time. I have several of my father and sister and my cousin Richard." As he flipped through the pages to one of Richard, he decided against telling her that he had also made watercolors of those he held dear, including her, which had kept him company at Eton, and that he was planning to bring them along to Cambridge as well. He would do the same with the one he drew today. Finding the correct page, he said, "This was Richard a few years ago. He is in the army now, and when I do have the opportunity to see him, he is not used to sitting still, so I have no recent picture." Both William and Elizabeth smiled.

"I can understand that sentiment. Unless I am reading, I do not usually sit still for any length of time either."

"Well then, I will have to sketch you while you read. Perhaps you will read aloud?"

"I would be happy to. Would you like to hear it in Latin or English?"

"I suppose since you have a Latin book, I must hear it in Latin."

"Oh no, I can translate it as I read and deliver it in English, if you would prefer."

"Certainly, I would like to witness that if you do not mind." His eyes sparkled with amusement while thinking, *"You do equally well with playing pirate and climbing trees, to steering the conversation in a drawing room, to translating Latin into English within the course of a few hours! Yes, indeed, you are the most interesting person I have ever met, my amazing friend!"*

After a while, Elizabeth noticed the position of the sun. "Mr. Darcy? It is getting late, and I will need to change before dinner. I hope you do not mind if we stop for now. So far during your visit we have been fortunate enough to avoid it, but if Mama sees the present condition of my dress, you *will* have a demonstration of her nerves before long!"

"I do not mind at all, Miss Elizabeth," he said as she closed the book and stood up. "I have the basic shape of your face and features, and I can do the remainder from memory if I have to, though I would prefer to sketch a little more with the subject before me later after dinner. You would not have to be in the same position then."

"Will you walk into the house with me, or would you rather remain outdoors for a little while longer, sir?" she said, that mischievous grin spreading across her face once again.

He smiled back at her. "I think I would prefer to remain and work on the sketch before entering the house once again."

"I thought so. I will see you at dinner, sir." She curtsied and began to walk away, then stopped and turned back toward him. "Sketching *does* involve a great deal of concentration, does it not? I will explain to Mama that you cannot converse while sketching. I should tell you that Mama will direct Jane to sit by you and watch you sketch; please know that Jane does not chatter away like my mother did this afternoon, and she will not bother you. Have no fear; Jane is not interested in 'catching' you, Mr. Darcy." Elizabeth smiled brilliantly, and, not waiting for an answer, she turned away and continued on to the house.

Chapter 3

1 September 1807 – Three years later…

It was a lonely moment for William as his ship docked, since nobody waited to greet him, but then he had become used to being alone. His time at Cambridge at an end, William and some of his schoolmates had chosen to tour Italy. His "friends" turned out not to be friends after all. They were interested in pursuits of a very different nature than was he, and once they arrived abroad, the activities of the other gentlemen consisted mostly of debaucheries and "sowing their wild oats," while William was intent upon enjoying the beauty of the architecture and landscapes as well as the rich culture of art and music that Italy had to offer.

When he first entered Cambridge it had shocked him to find that his moral standards were far above those of most others within his circle. William seemed to be one of the few gentlemen who actually enjoyed his classes and pursued learning in general. Oh, he had some entertainment, but within limits. His reputation for being dull and prudish was formed only because he refused to degrade his morals by participating in activities that he perceived as being beneath a gentleman's honor—though others seemed to have no qualms about indulging in even the most lascivious of these activities.

William felt that he should have been more cautious in planning this trip for he *had* witnessed their reprehensible behavior at school, but for some reason, he had thought that since they had now entered the *adult* world, and since they were of the *supposedly* superior first circle, that they would become more interested in serious endeavors. He censured himself for not realizing that it would only be more of the same or worse once they arrived in Italy. Why on earth they had spent so much of their fathers' money to travel such a distance and end up doing only more of the same, he did not understand. His schoolmates' behavior became even *less discreet* once they were out from under the watchful eyes of the gossips of the *ton*, and he was deeply embarrassed to be associated with them.

No matter what manner of teasing he knew he was setting himself up for from this newest generation of the *ton*, William decided to distance himself from his erstwhile friends. Better to be alone in a strange country than to be associated with *these* gentlemen and their behavior that so disgusted him! He had much time to himself which he spent taking in the culture and history of Italian cities, sketching the landscapes and buildings, and, finally, arranging for an early return home.

He truly did love Italy, but he longed for someone having similar interests with whom to share his experiences—other than his valet. William did not notify anyone in England of his change of travel plans mostly because he expected he would arrive at home before his letter would.

Upon his return to England, his intention was to make an overnight stop at Darcy House in London and then to continue on to Pemberley, where he would surprise his father and sister with his early return. The staff at Darcy House was always at the ready so it was no inconvenience, and they were more than happy to have him returned safely. It was pleasant to sleep in a familiar bed and have well-known comforts surrounding him, but truly, Pemberley would always be considered *home* in his heart. Though exhausted from the crossing, William left the next morning and headed for Pemberley on horseback, with a cart following him carrying his trunks.

As he rode, William had much time to think. From the time he had been a young boy, his father had made him familiar with the running of Pemberley by having William ride with him, sharing his love of the land and his respect for the tenants who farmed it. William had learned the cyclical nature of agriculture by sitting in on some of the frequent meetings between his father and the steward, Mr. Wickham, but after he settled in, *this* would be the time that he truly would begin to train to take over the reins of the estate and all of the many other Darcy holdings —many of which the *ton* had no idea existed.

He reflected on the duties that would become his responsibility. Many of those were familiar to him already, and he suspected there were many more to be added. Knowing how many people would depend on him to make the correct decisions was a little daunting. Would he be able to live up to the demands of the Darcy legacy? He had worried about it for years. His wish to be as good a man and as good a master as his father, in addition to his innate propensity to demand perfection from himself, helped to shape his character. He also hoped to be a good husband and father someday, but those goals would have to wait as he would not have time for giving them proper attention now.

If only the *ton* could understand that he had absolutely no intention of marrying any time soon! William, or rather Pemberley and the Darcy name, had been chased relentlessly since he was eighteen, and even before that age there were some who courted him. The young man chuckled to himself, thinking how much more diligent the ladies would be in their pursuit if the *ton* knew what he would truly be worth upon his father's death! There had been numerous ladies who had offered themselves to him as wife, mistress or lover, and William had lost count of the times ladies had tried to tempt him to compromise them. How many times had his aunts or uncles tried to arrange marriages for him, sometimes without even the benefit of seeing the lady from across a crowded room? All of this, added to what he had witnessed of the behavior of gentlemen at university, undermined his beliefs in the *superiority* of the first circles of the *ton*.

None of these ladies cared for *him* as a man, and not one of them even *expected* him to care for them as a woman. After seeing the love and happiness his parents had shared, why should he settle for anything less? It had been mere coincidence that they had been considered an excellent match socially, but he hoped for the same marital felicity for himself.

He had tried to get to know the ladies of the *ton*, but they all seemed too *well trained* and hid who they really were in favor of displaying the polished veneer they had been taught to present. At first he thought there had to be more to their personalities beneath the superficial qualities that were advertised, but more recently he was beginning to doubt that possibility. The women to whom he had been introduced truly did seem to think that only wealth and consequence were important, and their priorities were all based on selfishness, greed, and jealousy. William could not imagine spending his life with someone as insipid as they were. His hopes of finding a jewel among the *ton*, as his father had done, disappeared. And yet, he would need an heir to the Darcy legacy, so he would need to marry *somebody*. No, he would dwell on those thoughts no longer. At least, in that respect, he had plenty of time.

On the third day of his journey home, William walked out to the stables with a spring in his step which had been missing for far too long. He was almost home, and at his beloved home, he would stay! This time there was nowhere else he would need to return—no Eton, no Cambridge. This time there was only Pemberley.

William did not know if his horse recognized the scenery or if he sensed his master's excitement, but Ares seemed to gain more energy the closer they got to home. When he reached a stone bridge that served as a landmark to a path he knew would take him directly to his favorite view of the manor house, William turned off the public road. He slowed the horse as they approached the crest of a well-known hill, anticipating the prospect he would soon have the pleasure of seeing. There—the view was like a breath of fresh air to a drowning man.

William rode on. As he approached, the stable boy recognized the master's son from afar by his seat and the markings on the horse and raised the alarm among the stable workers, but William was able to stop the news from spreading to the house. He wished his arrival to be a surprise to his father and sister.

"Welcome home, Master William!" the head groomsman called out with a smile as he hurried to take the reins.

"Thank you, Smith; it is indeed good to be home!"

Sneaking in through the kitchen door, all the servants wore smiles as he greeted them. He stood at the door and closed his eyes, taking in the smells of Pemberley's kitchens, and recognized that, by chance, his favorite meal was being cooked. He quietly stole into the office of the housekeeper, Mrs. Reynolds, who had been more like a mother to him than a servant since his own mother had passed six years ago. After a few tears were shed by Mrs. Reynolds, William requested bath water and took the servants' stairs to his room. Once refreshed, he made his way to the school room and found his sister. Amidst her squeals and tears, Georgiana welcomed her brother home wholeheartedly. After a short visit, he left her to her studies and set out to find his father.

From a footman William learned that his father was in the study with a guest but had not asked to be undisturbed, and so off he went. He knocked and was bidden to enter, and was delighted to find his father was with Mr. Bennet. "William!" Mr. Darcy exclaimed with a big smile as he rushed forward to embrace his son, then stepped back holding his shoulders at arms' length, "It is so good to have you home, son! You look very well after your trip. Why did you not tell us you would be home so soon? Georgiana and I were planning to be at the dock to meet your ship, but you were not due for another month complete."

"Father! I am very happy to be home, thank you. There were some minor complications in Italy, and I decided to take an earlier ship. Since I would have arrived before a letter could have reached you, I did not bother to write." Turning to their guest, William extended his hand and exclaimed, "Mr. Bennet, what a pleasure to see you again! How are you? And how is your family?"

"I am well, as is my family, thank you. I am glad we are here when you arrived home; Lizzy was so disappointed that you were scheduled to return to England after we would be back at Longbourn."

"Miss Elizabeth is here as well?" William's grin betrayed his enthusiasm. "This is a nice surprise indeed. I am sorry to have missed her first viewing of the library at Pemberley after seeing her reaction to the one at Darcy House." William looked to Mr. Bennet as both gentlemen laughed.

"Yes, it was a sight to behold!" Mr. Bennet nodded his head and then added, "She is out for a walk at the moment, making full use of the grounds available at Pemberley, but she should be back before tea time."

"What a pleasure Miss Elizabeth is to have as a guest!" Mr. Darcy added with a twinkle in his eye. "Miss Elizabeth and Georgiana have become quite close in the past two weeks; they are almost inseparable whenever Georgiana is not occupied at her lessons. Miss Elizabeth's presence has even somehow sparked an interest in Georgiana for mathematics and French! Miss Elizabeth is quite extraordinary."

Mr. Darcy wondered what William's reaction would be when he saw Elizabeth. Up 'til now, she had been in what seemed to be an overly-long awkward stage, so lengthy that Mr. Darcy had wondered if she would ever bloom. How astonished he had been when she arrived to see that she had become a very attractive young lady in manner as well as appearance.

Mr. Darcy was well aware that William had always had a *tendre* for Elizabeth, being very impressed with her intelligence and sense of humor, and that he spoke of her often. William never failed to ask if Elizabeth had been mentioned whenever he spoke of a letter from Mr. Bennet. Mr. Darcy had seen Elizabeth a few times over the past three years whenever she was in London at the same time as he, but because William had been away at school, he had not. He wondered if William's feelings would change from the sibling-type affection he had felt for her now that sixteen-year-old Elizabeth had blossomed into a beautiful woman, and he was looking forward to seeing William's reaction.

After spending the past two weeks in Elizabeth's company, Mr. Darcy could say with no hesitation that William and Elizabeth would be a good match... when she was a bit older. He looked at Bennet and could see the wheels turning in his mind as he looked at his son. In Bennet's eyes there was a look of part amusement at what was to come and part—was it fear? Was Bennet thinking along the same lines as he and regretting his decision to come to Pemberley now that William had arrived home early?

The three gentlemen discussed William's itinerary, but Mr. Darcy suggested they wait until Georgiana and Elizabeth were present to discuss his trip any further since he was certain they both would enjoy hearing of it. William expressed an interest in riding the grounds before tea.

"You did not have enough riding while travelling from London?"

"If I were anywhere else, I would not hesitate to take a short hiatus from riding, Father, but for months I have longed to ride Poseidon on my favorite paths at Pemberley. Would you mind if I leave you now and join you later for tea?"

"Not at all, William. Mr. Bennet and I have some business to conclude, and we shall do so while you ride. Enjoy!"

"Be on the lookout for Lizzy while you are out there," Mr. Bennet called after him.

~%~

A short while later, William was astride Poseidon, riding through the grounds of his beloved Pemberley. He had chosen one of his favorite paths, especially because of the risky turn that he was approaching. His older cousin Richard had always cautioned him to respect this curve and not to take this turn as quickly as was his wont, but his defense in doing so was that he was only endangering himself. It took a great deal of skill to make this turn successfully, and he knew that he and Poseidon were up to the challenge—they had always made the turn in the past.

As he came around the hedgerow, William saw a flash of color. The whinny of the horse mixed with another piercing sound, unidentifiable to William. Poseidon tried to avoid the obstacle in his path and reared up while executing the turn, causing him to fall onto his side, throwing his rider to the ground. William had no understanding of what had occurred; it was all just a jumble of noise, confusion and pain... followed by darkness.

~%~

Elizabeth Bennet had been walking the grounds of Pemberley for hours, and she still had a bit of time left before she had to turn back to freshen up in time for tea. Being a mature young lady now, she had not climbed a tree in more than a year, but today it was if the shades of Pemberley were calling out to her. Convincing herself that on such a vast estate the likelihood that anyone would see her was slim, she took advantage of the opportunity. Once up as high as she dared to venture, she looked out at the beautiful lands that surrounded her. She had never seen anything more beautiful, more perfect—even though she and her father had stopped along the way north at several locations, nothing could compare. Glancing towards the manor house, she noticed a rider traveling at a fast pace in her direction and decided to climb down as quickly as possible. When she had descended to the lowermost branch, she heard the sound of hooves approaching and chose to jump to the ground so that the rider did not discover her impropriety.

If only she had remained in that tree!

She had badly misjudged the speed of the horse. The moment her feet were on the ground, the horse and rider rounded a turn through a high hedge, and all she saw was a blur of brown flesh and hooves. Her next conscious observation was that the rider was on the ground under the horse. The horse managed to right itself and seemed very upset. Elizabeth realized with horror that the rider's boot was still attached to the stirrup. Quickly surmising that the rider would be dragged if the horse decided to bolt, she set out to calm the beast. As the horse quieted, she was able to reach out and stroke his neck. When he finally allowed her to pet his nose, she knew that he was calm enough for her to survey the situation. She took the lead rein, tied it to a very conveniently located tree branch, and went to ascertain the condition of the rider.

Moving to the other side of the horse, she saw that the rider was William Darcy! He was the *last* person she had expected since he was supposed to be in Italy for another month complete. "Mr. Darcy?" she called out while she carefully removed his boot from the stirrup, causing the horse to move a little. Not wanting William to be caught under the horse's hooves, she moved Poseidon a few trees down while she kept calling out, "Mr. Darcy? Sir? Can you hear me?"

As she rushed back to him, she carelessly tripped on a root. *"Oh, good L-rd! How could I be so clumsy? Now I have hurt my ankle as well!"*

Looking towards William, she saw blood on the ground which she had not noticed from her previous vantage point, and she got to him as quickly as her ankle would allow. Realizing his head was bleeding badly, she tore off a piece of her petticoat and used it to help her put pressure on the wound.

Knowing what she must do next, she attempted to hide her own agitation in case he was awake and so began talking, "Mr. Darcy? If you can hear me, I feel the need to apologize in advance. I must examine you to see if you have any further injuries. It is a good thing I have been such a hoyden and have led many an adventure ending with myself or the boys from my neighborhood sometimes being injured."

She took a stick and ran it lightly along the palms of his hands, which caused his fingers to twitch. *"Thank heaven, his neck is not broken!"* she thought as she ripped off a longer strip of her petticoat and wrapped it tightly around his head, keeping the wadded up piece over the cut to maintain pressure on it. Moving on, she removed the boot on the leg that was out straight to check the reflexes in his foot. *"Nor is his back broken! Now I can move him."* Elizabeth began feeling the bones of his arms.

"I have had much experience with watching Mr. Jones, the apothecary, tend injuries of many different types and often have begun treatment before he was able to arrive at the scene of accidents." Noticing his arm was positioned strangely, Elizabeth felt his shoulder through his clothing and realized his shoulder was out of joint. *"I hate doing this!"* she thought.

She straightened out his leg and felt the soundness of his leg bones. "Mr. Jones always jests with me that if I were a boy, I would do well as an apprentice to him since I learn so easily and already know what to do in many cases of injury. With so many sisters, we have had our share of illnesses, and so I do know how to treat those as well."

Satisfied he had no obviously broken limbs to be tended to, she set about unbuttoning his great coat, his coat and his waistcoat. Somehow, she found the strength to lift his back from the ground and leaned him onto herself, surprising herself that she was able to keep them both upright. She removed the great coat and laid it back on the ground beneath him to offer some protection against the cool ground, then tried to remove his coat and waistcoat as gently as possible. He groaned a little, but seemed to remain unconscious.

Laying him gently back on the ground, she continued, "Your shoulder has become dislocated, Mr. Darcy. Fortunately again, I have experience with setting this to rights. John Lucas has a trick shoulder that often pops out of the joint, and Mr. Jones has taught me how to put it back and wrap it safely. It will be very painful for you, but less painful than leaving it the way it is until help arrives." Just *how* she was going to find help, she could not think about right now. She dared not leave him alone bleeding and unconscious as he was, and with her ankle injured, the task would be difficult indeed.

"I apologize again, sir, but I must move into a very unladylike position to do this. I do hope you continue to sleep through this, for I know it will be very painful. Please, if you can hear me, no matter how much it hurts, do try not to move!" She moved his arm away from his body and put her knee into his armpit, pulling and sliding the shoulder back into the joint as she had done for John Lucas many times. William cried out, but he still seemed to be unconscious when she was finished.

"It is a blessing that you were asleep for *that*, Mr. Darcy, believe me! Now I will wrap your arm." She tore off a much larger piece of her slip and fashioned a wrap from it. Lifting him and leaning him to his good side, she placed the cloth under him and then secured his arm snuggly to his chest. His hand was still pink and warm, thankfully.

"Since there is nothing left of my slip, I hope you give me leave to look through your coat pockets to see if you have a handkerchief. Here it is! I see you have a canteen on your saddle, and I can hear water running, so there must be a stream nearby. I need to clean the wound on your head as best as is possible. I will be back shortly, sir."

Elizabeth got up and when she attempted to take a step, the pain reminded her that she had sprained her ankle. She took it more slowly than she would have liked, but she limped over to the horse, retrieving the saddle bags and the canteen, which was thankfully full, and made her way back again. "I see you have a couple of blankets attached to your saddle bag! That is very helpful, sir, for I worry that you are lying on the cold ground." She rolled him onto his good side again and laid one of the blankets on the ground beneath him before righting him and covering him with his coat and the other blanket. She folded his waistcoat and placed it under his head as a pillow. "I am also very worried that you have not yet awakened, sir. Please, Mr. Darcy... please, will you wake up?"

Lifting his head again, she unwrapped the bandage to check the wound and while she was at it, she unwrapped his neck cloth, thinking she might have need of it later. The wound was still bleeding, but not nearly so much as earlier. She rinsed out the piece of petticoat that had been keeping pressure on the wound and then poured some water to clean off the dirt that was still on his forehead from the fall. Moistening the handkerchief with the water from the canteen, she began to wash the rest of his forehead before re-wrapping his head, but she froze, and she blinked a few times in shock. "I have never noticed before, but you are a very handsome gentleman!" she whispered, blushing when she thought of all the places she had touched upon his body that day, and the memory made her heart beat very fast. He was a very fit man, indeed! She blushed more furiously as she chastised herself for thinking of such things when he was injured so badly.

~%~

William opened his eyes and blinked a few times to clear them. What his now clear vision perceived to be a part of the female anatomy made William believe, if only for a moment, that he had died and gone to heaven, for his companion was quite well endowed in this particular area. He looked up a few inches and saw the most beautiful face he had ever had the pleasure of laying eyes upon. *"An angel!"* he thought.

At the same moment that he realized that *had* he actually been in heaven, he would not be in so much pain, the lady looked away from his forehead to his eyes, and a breathtaking smile spread across her features. "Mr. Darcy! You are awake!"

There was something about the light dancing in her eyes that reminded him of... "Miss Elizabeth?" he said and then thought to himself, *"Good G-d, she has grown! How did the awkward girl I remember come to look like **this**?"*

She continued to apply pressure to the head wound as she answered, "Yes! Oh, I am so glad that you have awakened, sir! Mr. Jones says that a person with a head injury should stay awake until he can be examined, and I have been beside myself with worry that you have slept for so long after the accident."

"Accident?"

She frowned. "You do not remember, sir?"

He tried to shake his head, but her hands were keeping it in place. "No, I do not."

"When you came around the hedges, I was in your horse's way, and he did a fine job of avoiding me, Mr. Darcy... though I am very sorry that you have been injured in the process."

"May I ask... why are you holding my head, Miss Elizabeth?"

"You hit your head, Mr. Darcy, and as a result you were bleeding heavily. I am told that head wounds usually bleed terribly, even if the injury is not a serious one. I have been trying to stop it by applying pressure, and it is working, but you have lost quite a bit of blood. You will probably be dizzy for a couple of days, sir." She moved the cloth and looked again, before observing, "It is slowing considerably now. I can wrap it up again, if you would rather?"

He would *rather* that she stay close to him and hold his head in her hands, but he knew it would be highly improper of him to say this. Instead he said, "That would seem to be best." As he attempted to sit up, the pain in his shoulder and arm exploded on his senses, and he made an exclamation that was unfit for feminine ears, which Elizabeth wisely chose to ignore.

"Oh, sir! Please allow me to help you." She supported his good shoulder and helped him sit upright.

"And just what happened to my shoulder?"

"When you fell from the horse, your shoulder was pulled out of joint." She noticed his frown, but continued, "I have put it back to rights and fashioned a wrap. My memory had just been refreshed on the procedure last month while I was on a walk on the Lucases' property. John Lucas had always pulled his shoulder out easily, which is why I know exactly how to fix that particular injury. He was usually awake when Mr. Jones or I did so, and his screams could sometimes be heard over quite a distance from what I understand. Last month when I happened across him, he had been repairing the fences that surround the Lucases' paddock and pulled his shoulder out again. I replaced it for him as I had done many times in the past. Mr. Lucas, now a grown man, was heard all the way along the road to Lucas Lodge, which alerted the servant that he was in need of assistance. So you see, sir, it was a blessing that you slept though the process. I apologize for getting you into this state of undress, Mr. Darcy, but it was necessary." She blushed, thinking of how she had also checked the soundness of his bones, but did not think it prudent at this time to discuss that aspect of what had occurred while he was asleep.

"I did *not* fall from my horse, Miss Elizabeth!"

Elizabeth tilted her head to one side and raised her eyebrows. "You did not?"

"No! I am an expert horseman and expert horsemen do not *fall* from their horses. I would appreciate it if you would not retell the story using *that* word."

Elizabeth tried to hide a smile. Normally having someone laugh at him would have induced discomfort, but the way her suppressed amusement made her eyes sparkle allowed William to forgive her for thinking his statement entertaining. "Well, I think I owe you that much at the very least after being the *cause* of your injuries."

"Do not take the blame upon yourself; my cousin Richard has often warned me that something like this would happen at that turn one day, but I insisted upon taking it with speed since the risk seemed minimal. What are the chances that someone would be in that particular spot on the grounds at the exact moment I came around the hedge? Now it seems I should have listened to his warnings. So, you see, it is my stubbornness which caused the accident, not your walking in this direction." He hesitated a few moments before continuing, "Are you feeling up to the walk back to the manor house, Miss Elizabeth? I do think we should get started back."

"Sir, I was quite serious when I said you will be dizzy for a few days. You will not be able to walk or ride your horse the distance necessary to return to the great house. I think you will need a carriage or cart in which to ride."

"I will walk. Help me to my feet, please." She helped him up, and he immediately became so dizzy that he faltered and leaned on her heavily as he turned green with nausea. "Oh! It seems you are correct, Miss Elizabeth."

"Mr. Darcy, please sit down again. You will fall and re-injure your shoulder. I do not want to have to do that again, sir! Please?"

Once down again, he found himself too dizzy to even sit, so he lay down on the ground. "It seems I should have listened to you, as well, Miss Elizabeth. I apologize."

"If there is anything I can understand, it is being stubbornly independent, Mr. Darcy. Though it is not a very ladylike trait, it is one I share with you, and so I can forgive you fully." She again flashed that brilliant, heart-stopping smile at him.

"How old could she be? Sixteen? Get hold of yourself, man!" William thought, then aloud he said, "Well, then, you will have to walk to the house without me and send help."

"Well, therein lies our next problem; I cannot."

"Excuse me?"

"I cannot walk, sir, as I have sprained my ankle badly. The last time I tried, I was not able to walk more than the few steps over to your horse, and my ankle has swelled considerably since then. I also cannot ride, Mr. Darcy, so please do not suggest it. I do not believe your spirited horse would do for someone who has never ridden before!"

"No, he would not indeed." William thought it over a few minutes and then suggested, "Do you think you can get to the horse again, Miss Elizabeth? If you set him loose, I will give him the order to return to the stables. I am certain when he returns without me, and they realize that you are missing as well, they will send a party out to search for us."

"You *do* have a well-trained horse, sir! Yes, I believe I could, though it might take some time." She looked around, searching for something to lean on. "Ah ha!" She crawled a bit to a long stick that was lying nearby. "I can use this as a sort of cane."

"Your assessment of my horse was correct, Miss Elizabeth; he is a very spirited animal and does not like very many people. Be careful near him!"

Leaning on the stick, Elizabeth was able to limp very slowly over to the horse. The horse put his head down, leaning it against her shoulder. She whispered into the horse's ear while running her hand down his neck and then untied the rein from the tree. She looked to Darcy to let him know that he should give the order, but he was staring at her in disbelief. "How... how did you do that?"

"Do what, sir?"

"Miss Elizabeth, I was not exaggerating when I said he does not like many people... but he certainly likes you! He acts towards you the same as does towards me, and I have been his master since he was born!"

"Oh, I am told I have a way with animals, sir." She smiled and stroked the horse's neck.

He almost asked if she charmed only *male* animals, but he thought better of it. "But you will not ride a horse? I know it is not a fear of heights after hearing about your tree-climbing experiences and witnessing one with my own eyes. I had suspected a fear of horses, but that is obviously not true. What is it then?"

"I am not afraid of heights when I climb, that is true, but consider what we said earlier, sir. I have a stubbornly independent spirit. *I* am in control when I climb a tree, but though people tell me the horse is *not* in control when they ride, he *can* be if he wishes it. In our case this afternoon, for instance, you did not see me, but your horse did, and he did everything he could to prevent his running into me. He is a thinking being and took control away from you, and though I was not hurt, you *were* injured because of it. I would not mind being injured to prevent another from being so, but what if it was only a rabbit that startled a horse to do something similar? No, I will not willingly hand over control of my fate to another living being if it is in my power to avoid it." She gave him a look that spoke of absolute determination, and he accepted the fact that she would not ride... not for the time being anyway. He smiled when he thought that he was just as determined, if not more so, to get her to love riding the way he did! Suddenly, the presumption of the thought shocked him back to the present. She continued, "You may give the order for him to return to the stables now, sir."

"Home, Poseidon," he ordered in a commanding voice, and the horse nuzzled Elizabeth one more time before walking away, back through the hedge from whence he and William had come.

She tried to hide her smile as she hobbled back toward him and saw what he was doing. With much difficulty, he was arching his body, pulling part of the blanket out from beneath him, and spreading it next to him so that she would have a more comfortable place to rest. It was a perfect example of his own stubborn independence as it would have been much easier for him to wait for her return so she could help him. A few times she had feared he would hurt his shoulder, but he did not—at least as far as she could tell. After she had made her way back to William, she sat on the blanket he had so gallantly spread for her comfort.

Exhausted from the effort, he closed his eyes, but Elizabeth only left him to rest for a few moments before asking, "Are you right-handed or left-handed, sir?"

"I do most things with either hand proficiently, but to write I use my left hand."

"How interesting! I did not think I would ever meet another person who is ambidextrous, as am I!"

"Ambidextrous?"

"Yes, it means that we are able to use both hands equally well. I am predominantly right-handed for writing but can write legibly with my left and can use either for almost anything else. It is good that you are left-handed for writing, Mr. Darcy, for it will take a few weeks before you can use your right arm again."

"A few weeks?! I do not think I have any broken bones. Why should it take a few weeks to heal if there are no broken bones?"

"Do you know much of anatomy, sir?"

He blinked a few times; since waking up, he had been trying very hard *not* to admire the amazing changes in *her* anatomy since the last time he had seen her, and he feared that she had noticed.

Though confused at receiving no answer, she continued, "When the bone came out of the joint of the shoulder, the muscles, tendons and ligaments were stretched beyond what occurs in normal activity. More than likely, they have torn a little and will need time to mend. You are in excellent physical condition..." here she hesitated, looking off into the distance to hide her blush upon thinking about her earlier physical examination of him to check for broken bones, "...and will probably heal as quickly as possible."

"And how do you know so much about this?" William asked. Confused as to why her eyes widened, he restated the question, "I only meant to ask how you know so much about anatomy, the nature of injuries, and how they mend, Miss Elizabeth."

"May I take a look at your bandage again while I explain?" William turned his head toward her to signify his agreement. "I had forgotten that you were still sleeping when I told you earlier—oh, I was talking in the event that you were partially awake." She blushed as she continued her explanation, "I mentioned that I have spent much time with Mr. Jones, the apothecary near my home, and had paid very close attention to what he has said and done. Do you remember at the bookstore when I had told you how a picture of everything I read stays in my mind?"

"Yes… yes, I do."

"The same thing occurs with things that happen to me. Not everything, but for many, many things I retain pictures and also what was said during the event. So as I helped you with your bandage, or as I put your shoulder back to rights earlier, I had the picture of a prior event in my mind first, and then I did the same thing that Mr. Jones had done at the time."

"That is absolutely fascinating!"

She smiled, "It can be a curse as well as a blessing, believe me!"

"A curse in what way?"

"A good memory is unpardonable in some circumstances, sir! For example, it annoys people when I can recall, in perfect detail, a conversation or an event where they did or said something foolish. It is an especially inconvenient when *I* am the person who said or did something awry!"

He laughed and could not hide a wince from the pain in his shoulder. He saw her forehead furrow and was sorry that he had been unable to hide it.

She was thoughtful for a few moments, and then said, "Sometimes the memories occur unbidden when I am reminded of a thing in some small way. If the event was particularly unpleasant, it is not a good thing to be able to live through it again in perfect detail. For example, when I realized your shoulder was out of the socket, it was as if I lived through every time that John Lucas's arm did the same all over again—his pain, his screams, what it felt like to put the shoulder back in," she shuddered. "From what I am told, most people's memories fade, but mine do not seem to… not as of yet anyway."

"Are you saying it is possible you will repeatedly live through today's events in detail any time you are reminded of it?"

She did not wish to answer, so she changed the subject, "I am thankful that the wound on your head seems to have stopped bleeding. I used the plain handkerchief from your pocket for this but would like to use your neck cloth now that the bleeding has stopped. I did not wish to ruin it. May I use it? I might have enough of my petticoat left to make another, but that would necessitate my leaving you to go off into the woods to undress for I cannot reach any more fabric from under my skirts!" She laughed.

"You tore up your petticoat? I wondered where you had gotten all this material." He was getting very sleepy, and his words were not as clear as they were before. At least, she hoped he was only getting sleepy.

"Yes, I did. I often did so whenever someone was hurt, and Mama had a fit every time! May I use your neck cloth, sir?"

"Yes, you may use it. I have many others, and I certainly would not want you to have to undress. It is getting cold."

Chapter 4

Elizabeth shivered from the cold and considered how rapidly the temperature was dropping now that the sun was low on the horizon. She wondered how long it had been since he had been injured and attempted to reconstruct the time in her mind so that she might inform a doctor later. It had to have been at least a half hour since the horse had been sent back to the stable. How much longer would it be until someone found them? She looked through the saddlebag and found matches, and then looked around to see if there was any wood close by that was suitable to make a fire. Mr. Darcy should be kept warm! Looking back at him, she noticed that his eyes were closed again.

"Mr. Darcy, you must stay awake!" she exclaimed too loudly, and his eyes snapped open. "Do you not remember that I told you that Mr. Jones said that people with head injuries should not sleep until a doctor can examine them? Please, sir, try to stay awake."

"I do remember. I just cannot seem to keep my eyes open."

"I need to gather wood to make a fire, sir, but I will not go far. Can you tell me about the weather during your crossing from Italy?"

"Only if I can keep my eyes closed while I tell you." They both smiled a little.

She felt a little guilty since he sounded so tired, but she knew this was for the best. "That sounds like a good compromise, sir. If you continue to talk, you may close your eyes."

"Yes, ma'am." Using her "cane" to help herself rise, Elizabeth hobbled over to some dead wood that she had spotted from where she had sat while he talked. "We had a dreadful storm one night. It had cast a very rough sea, and it had been incredibly windy the day before. Many people were already sick from being tossed about by the wind, but when the storm began in earnest during the night, it was much worse as many more people began to be seasick. The ship rocked as it creaked and groaned, and once the rain and thunder…"

"Mr. Darcy? I regret that I must interrupt for a moment. I find myself in need of my skirt to gather the wood and would be appreciative if you would but keep your eyes closed while you continue."

"Why did she have to tell me that? Earlier, I **wanted** *to close my eyes, but now I want nothing more than to open them. ARGH! She is but sixteen, Darcy! Be a gentleman!"* he thought, and, after a sigh, he then said aloud, "You have my word, Miss Elizabeth; I will keep them closed."

"Tell me more about the storm," she said.

"I made my way above deck to speak to the captain to offer any service that might be helpful. I must say that once I was above deck, the conditions were terrifying. I would have been a hindrance had I remained there, and I felt that I should not even offer—the waves were frighteningly tall and were crashing over the side and onto the deck. The crew was experienced, and we made it through the storm. The remainder of the trip was uneventful other than that people continued to become ill."

"Did you meet anyone of interest on the ship?" Her voice was further away this time.

"No, I knew no one."

"You did not travel with your companions from Cambridge?"

"No, I left them shortly after arriving in Italy and went on alone."

"Why?" She was closer again, and he put his arm over his eyes to remind himself not to open them.

"It turned out they were not… their habits… ah… I am too tired to think of a more delicate way to say this, and what I *can* think to say should *not* be said to a lady." He heard the sounds of wood being dropped to the ground.

"Ohhhh…" there was silence for a few moments, and then she said, "I have enough wood to start the fire, sir, but I would like to gather some more so that I will have no need to do so after dark."

"This is most frustrating. I feel terribly guilty for allowing you to do this, Miss Elizabeth. I should be the one gathering wood and building a fire!" William said with more energy than exhibited in his former conversation.

"I know that you would wish to do this for me, Mr. Darcy, and I do appreciate the sentiment, but you *cannot* do this, and so I beg you to allow me to complete my task before dark."

"But your ankle!"

"I have suffered plenty of sprained ankles in my time, sir," she laughed. "I promise I shall rest after I finish gathering the wood that we need." He sighed audibly. "But that still does not answer my question, sir."

"Which question was that, Miss Elizabeth?"

"Did you meet anyone of interest on the ship?"

"I thought I did answer it…I did not know anyone on the ship."

"Yes, but you spoke to other passengers, I am sure." Her voice came from further away again.

He hesitated a long time—long enough for her to think he had fallen asleep.

"Mr. Darcy, you must not give in to your desire to sleep!" Her voice sounded a bit panicked.

"I am not asleep. I am just…attempting to form an answer."

"It is not that difficult a question, sir." She sounded closer again, and by the tone of her voice, he could picture her brow arching the way it often had done when that tone was used in their past meetings.

"It would not be a difficult question for *you* to answer, I am sure, Miss Elizabeth, but it *is* for me. I am not certain how to explain this… but I – I do not have an easy manner with strangers." He heard her drop some more wood nearby.

"I was a stranger once, and I remember very clearly that you seemed to be easy with me."

"Yes…yes, I was. I have often wondered about that, but trust me, that particular instance was an exception to the rule. I usually do not feel very easy with anyone, Miss Elizabeth…anyone outside my immediate family, that is to say. I cannot explain why I feel so comfortable when speaking with you." With her last statement, he could hear the smile in her voice, and his heart was still pounding from imagining the way the sparkle was probably dancing in her eyes.

"Miss Elizabeth, do you mind my asking how old you are?"

"I will be seventeen at the end of May, sir. Why do you ask?" She was further away again.

*"She **is** sixteen…I must stop reacting to her in this way! She will not be old enough to court for…but Mother was seventeen when she married Father…**stop** thinking like that!"* he thought, and then said, "You seem more mature than would be common for your age."

"It is probably from all of the reading I do. I told you that I love to learn. Also, I think my father missed being a professor at Cambridge. When his older brother died, he inherited Longbourn, and left his teaching position to run the estate. Two years later, he married my mother. When we were old enough, he taught my sisters and me, extending our education in any area in which we were interested…" she laughed, "and since I was interested in almost *everything*, I had the benefit of being taught many subjects that are usually forbidden to girls."

"So you had your own private university in the convenience of your own home, then?"

"Yes, one could look at it that way, but I would have preferred to be a boy so that I could attend university myself. Obviously, many of the interests I enjoyed when I was younger were those of interest to boys."

*"I am very glad you are **not** a boy!"* he thought.

"I do hope you were able to enjoy the trip all alone, sir."

"It was better than it would have been had I stayed with the group I set sail with, that is for certain, but I would have preferred someone with whom to share it," he answered, but thought, *"I will take you to Italy someday. **STOP!**"* William was getting very angry with himself. "Miss Elizabeth?"

"Yes, Mr. Darcy?"

She was much farther away this time, and he moved his head quickly to speak in the direction from whence her voice came, causing a horrible round of dizziness to inflict him. *"Good G-d, she will injure herself! Why do I have to be so helpless?"*

"I am feeling quite woozy. I certainly hope I do not, but if I should say something… inappropriate… I ask in advance that you would forgive me."

He could hear her moving toward him again, and the worry in her voice caused his chest to tighten. "Are you feeling that poorly?"

"To be honest, I am feeling almost as if I were inebriated, which is why I felt I had to warn you. Gentlemen tend to be less… guarded in their speech when they have been drinking too much."

"I refilled the canteen on that last trip; perhaps you should have a drink of water." He heard her drop more wood. "You may open your eyes now, Mr. Darcy. Do you think I have collected enough to get us through the night, if need be?"

"Yes, that should be enough. Thank you." The front of her skirt was filthy, but her complexion and eyes were brightened by the exertion of collecting the wood. He had not thought she could look more beautiful than she had when first he had seen her earlier this day, but she did. She picked up the canteen, limped toward him, helped him to sit up a little, and handed him the canteen.

After she helped him to lie down again, she touched his forehead, and her brow furrowed, "You are burning up with fever, sir. No wonder you feel strange!" She was glad she had washed out the bloody strip of cloth while she had been at the stream because she was going to have need of it to bring his fever down.

"Ah, yes, that would explain it. I am sure it is nothing." He waved her worry away.

She did not look as confident as he felt about his last statement. Continuing with her attempts to keep him awake by talking, she asked, "I have never been on a ship. Can you describe your chamber?"

He tried to make the description of his room and the ship interesting for her as she repeatedly wet the strip of cloth and mopped down his face and neck. As he spoke, the sun set, and the temperature was rapidly falling. It was slow going; his thoughts were not as clear as they had been earlier. He was growing so very tired and was feeling so exceedingly cold. As she placed her hands upon his face to ascertain the state of his fever, he suddenly realized that *she* was shivering. "Miss Elizabeth! I apologize; I should have realized that you would be cold. Please take this blanket." He tried to hand her the blanket that was on top of him, but she stilled his hand with her own and then covered him up again.

"Mr. Darcy, always the gentleman! I thank you, but I will not take your blanket! You are ill, sir, and you will become weaker still if you are not kept warm."

"The blanket and fire are helping, Miss Elizabeth, but I do not want *you* to become ill as well. Please take the blanket as I have my coat. Here in the north, once the sun sets completely, it gets very cold at night, particularly so at this time of year."

"I refuse to take your blanket, Mr. Darcy." She hesitated for several moments, thinking that if she told him her idea, he was going to lose some, or all, of his respect for her... but what other choice did they have? "I have a solution, sir, but what I have to suggest might shock you." He opened his eyes and even in the dim light from the fire, he could tell she was blushing. "We could share the blanket."

Now he was blushing. "How?"

"Mr. Darcy... if I knew for certain that they would find us soon, I would not hesitate to allow you to keep the blanket and forget my own needs, but I think we must be realistic. It could take all night for them to find us. You are correct, it *is* getting very cold, very quickly, and I cannot stop shivering. I will probably become ill as well if I do not warm up soon. I will *not* take your blanket, and I will *not* take the blanket from under you and leave you lying directly on the cold, damp ground. The only other option is for us to share the blankets we have. Yes, we could each use one of the blankets, but they are thin enough to allow the cold from the ground through if they are not doubled, so that would defeat the purpose. I reiterate that I will *not* allow that. But if we share both blankets...if I lie next to you... then we would not only solve these problems, but we would also both actually be warmer from the heat of... from having two people together under the blanket." She was blushing furiously by the end of her speech. "I told you that my suggestion was shocking, sir, and I know that doing this would break many rules of propriety, but I honestly do not see any other option." She bit down hard to keep her teeth from chattering. *"My goodness, it does get cold quickly here!"* she thought.

He had to admit that her logic was sound. She had thought it all through, and he certainly was not able to think of a superior option. If *anyone* else had suggested it, he would have been suspicious that she was trying to trap him into marriage. After dodging attempts to trick him into compromising positions for years now, it was second nature for him to suspect every female of trying to do the same...but he could not believe that of her. *"And besides, it would not be a terrible fate to marry beautiful, intelligent, lively Elizabeth...**STOP** thinking that way! Especially if I am going to lie next to her tonight! I must think of her as my sister...If I were out here with Georgiana, I would not hesitate to share my blanket with her...She is just like Georgiana. I will close my eyes and imagine the awkward little girl she was at ten or thirteen! Yes, that will work."* He found he could not speak at the moment... so he only nodded.

She put some more logs on the fire before lying down next to him and covering herself with the blanket, trying very hard *not* to lie close enough to touch him—but the blanket was not large enough, and they both knew it. He swallowed hard and moved his arm so that it was around her, saying, "Miss Elizabeth, you will have to move closer, right up against me. It is alright to do so; I promise you that I will not harm you." She did move closer, and he gently pushed her head down onto his chest. She was very tense, but after a few minutes, he felt her beginning to relax against him. *"I promised I would not harm her, and I will **not**! Good G-d, her scent is wonderful...The feel of her beside me is...**STOP! Sister**, she is like a **sister**."*

Elizabeth sighed. "I have never heard a heart beating before. Yours is beating very fast."

*"What can I say in answer to that statement? 'My heart is beating so quickly because you are the most beautiful woman I have ever beheld, and I am holding you up against me, and I want to...' **STOP**...sister, sister. Think of the pain in my*

shoulder….*Amazing that no matter how much pain I am in, my body still reacts…* **no***…sister, sister…"*

"You are not sleeping, are you, Mr. Darcy?" she sat up a little on her elbow. He was so hot with fever that she had warmed up almost immediately upon lying near him. Seeing his eyes were open, she wet the cloth again.

Her face was so close to his now that he could lift his head just a little, and those lips would meet his. *"Sister…sister,"* he continued his chant. "No, I am not sleeping." His voice was hoarse, and he cleared it. "Who is your favorite author?" Her tongue wet her lips. *"Argh, I must keep my eyes closed."*

"Oh, I have several, but if I had to choose only one, it would have to be Shakespeare. And you, sir, who is your favorite?"

"The same. Which of his writings is your favorite?"

"Twelfth Night."

He opened his eyes and stared into hers, "Mine as well."

He looked so tired, and she could feel that his fever was not abating. She dampened the cloth once again. "Since I know that you are well versed in the names of flowers, Mr. Darcy, which is your favorite?"

He took a deep breath, filling himself with her scent, and whispered, "Lavender."

They went back and forth a few times asking each other favorite colors, favorite composers, favorite operas, and other such things, before they fell into silence. The next time Elizabeth dampened the cloth, she said, "Tell me about Italy."

He was so tired that he could not even think about what he was saying; he just described what he had seen and admired in Italy—the people, the places, the landscapes, the art, the sculptures, the churches—everything that he had wished to share with someone special. Elizabeth *was* special. She was more than he had ever dreamed it was possible to find in a woman, and she still was not even fully grown. He knew she would grow only more amazing with time… and that he wanted *her* to be the one with whom he shared everything.

They heard voices calling their names in the distance. Elizabeth propped herself up on her elbow once more and looked into his eyes with such sadness that he could feel it prick at his own eyes. She looked at his lips, and his breath caught. "William," she whispered, and she leaned in and brushed his lips with hers.

"Elizabeth," he whispered back, and lifted his head to place another gentle kiss upon those lips.

They stared into each other's eyes for a moment longer. Every fiber of his being wanted to tell her *not* to call for their attention, to place her head back down on his chest so he could hold her a little longer, to hold her there and *allow* them all to find her sharing a blanket, with his arm wrapped around her… but he knew that was wrong.

She got up and started limping toward the opening in the hedge, "Here we are!" she yelled.

Wide awake now, but still exhausted, he knew he had to force himself to think as he watched her standing there, waiting for their rescuers. Her eyes were turned toward him, and he could feel her gaze, but his thoughts turned to more serious matters. Would her reputation already be in tatters, being out here alone with him for so many hours? It was obvious that she had laid her hands upon him to fix his shoulder and treat his head wound. The servants of Pemberley were very discreet; they were trustworthy, and would not gossip, but the tenants would talk if they had been called in to help with the search. It was all so very innocent… well, most of it. Could he convince them all that it *was* innocent? Especially in light of his injuries, they should understand that she could not have been truly compromised. Could his father hush this up? What of Mr. Bennet's reaction?

He would gladly marry Elizabeth, of that there was no doubt. It was strange to remember how his views on marriage had changed so drastically since this morning as he rode to Pemberley. But, would that be what *she* wanted—to be *forced* to marry him—even if she was not so young? Women married at sixteen all the time; it was not such an odd occurrence. Would *he* want her to be forced to marry him and never really know if she would have said "yes" if he *had* asked her? If she was not forced, would she want him? She must care for him, even a little… Why else would she have kissed him? He should have asked her—before she had walked away to call out to the others. He should have asked her!

He could see torches through the hedge. People were moving towards her quickly, and she turned away from his gaze to look at them. He could see Elizabeth's father embrace her and wrap her in blankets, and then he saw his own father approach. "I am here, Father," William called out. The shock on Mr. Darcy's face was obvious to all, and he rushed toward his son. "William! Dear L-rd, what happened?" Elizabeth leaned heavily on Mr. Bennet as they followed him.

Elizabeth could see that William was too tired to speak, so she answered for him, "Mr. Darcy, your son's horse had an accident, and your son has suffered injuries as a result." She looked at him with a smile in her eyes that said, *"I remembered **not** to say that you fell!"* Then she continued, "He has had a blow to the head, and it was bleeding quite a bit at first but has stopped now. His shoulder was out of the joint, but I was able to put it to rights. For the past few hours, he has also had a fever. I have done the best I could do with what we had, sir, but he needs to see a doctor as soon as possible. He is very dizzy and cannot move much because of it—he will not be able to walk or ride to the house. Also, you should know that he *must* be kept awake until he sees a doctor, sir." Elizabeth moistened the cloth again and placed it on William's forehead. He was grateful for her touch; he had already begun to miss it.

"If they do not force us to marry, how will I live without her now that I have had a taste of paradise?"

Neither of the older gentlemen missed the way William had looked Elizabeth as she tended his fever, nor the way she was gazing at him. Mr. Darcy thought, *"Well, it is as I predicted; he is already in love with her, and she with him!"*

Mr. Wickham, Mr. Darcy's steward, came up to the group. "Mr. Darcy?"

"Wickham! Master William is injured. Send a man for a cart to transport him back to Pemberley, and send another on horseback to Lambton for the doctor immediately!"

"Yes, sir." Mr. Wickham rushed off to issue the necessary orders.

"It is a good thing we have a full moon tonight, or we would have had to abandon the search until the morning. I noticed that you are limping. Are you injured as well, Miss Elizabeth?" Mr. Darcy asked while he put a few more pieces of wood on the fire and stoked it with another.

"Yes, but my injury was a result of pure carelessness, sir. I was making my way from the tree where I had tied Mr. Darcy's horse, and my foot got caught in a tree root that was hidden beneath the leaves."

Mr. Bennet insisted that she have the doctor examine it when he arrived.

"I will, but it is nothing compared to Mr. Darcy's injuries."

"Miss Elizabeth is very brave. She did not once complain of her injuries. I apologize that I could not be of any assistance to her," William said weakly.

"How did your accident happen, William?" His father asked one of the questions he had been dreading.

"I should have heeded Richard's advice as well as yours, Mr. Bennet. I am glad that Miss Elizabeth was not injured any worse than she was." His voice was not above a whisper by this time.

"I already told you, Mr. Darcy, I was not injured by your actions at all. And I thought we had agreed not to argue about who was to blame. If you will not abide by that decision, than I shall not either, and I will once again have to blame myself for being in your way. You were on your favorite path, and I was on a walk, and that is all. The rest was pure happenstance. Now, you *will* stay awake, sir, but you will also stop exerting so much energy by talking." She went to dampen the cloth once again, then asked, "Do either of you gentlemen have an extra handkerchief? This one is done for, I'm afraid, and I already used up my petticoat on Mr. Darcy's injuries."

Mr. Darcy handed her his handkerchief. "I thank you for your nursing duties toward my son, Miss Elizabeth, and for putting up with what must have been a very disgruntled patient, as he usually is."

"More like a doctor than a nurse, Father," William said.

She gave him a sharp look that remonstrated, *"Did I not say to stop talking?"* and said, "Your son was perfectly behaved during the whole of the afternoon and evening, sir. The only trouble he gave me occurred at the moment he was not able to have his own way when I informed him that he would not be able to walk or ride to Pemberley himself. He insisted on making an attempt, but that did not work out well at all. It seems that we are both gifted with a stubborn streak." She smiled at William.

"You call it a gift, do you?" laughed Mr. Darcy.

"Well, sir, one may not call it a gift if that person is on the receiving end, but to me, it is a gift. Had I not been stubborn, I would not have been as victorious in disagreements with my mother, and I would be a miserable person, indeed—covered with ribbons and lace and gaudy, uncomfortable fabrics; allowed only to embroider, net purses and make bonnets; and *never* would I have been allowed to set foot in my father's library. In my opinion, stubbornness can be beneficial. But, as Mr. Darcy found out today," she said catching William's eye, "when one's intentions interfere with one's health, it is best to defer to someone else's stubborn ideas of what is the correct thing to do in that circumstance."

"Dreaded Pirate Lizzy," William mumbled.

"Yes, exactly! At the time you met the Dreaded Pirate Lizzy, I was just as stubborn as I am now, but I would attempt to force my will upon the other children and have them walk the plank if they did otherwise! I have matured enough to know that it is wrong to have someone else conform to my ideas of what they should do unless I am certain it would be harmful for them to do otherwise." She refreshed the cloth again, and, with a worried look she met Mr. Darcy's eyes and said, "His fever is rising, sir. Do you have any willow trees in the area?"

"Yes, there are several in a grove nearby."

"Can you have someone collect some of the bark off the trees, sir? Willow bark has been proven to help with fevers. Hippocrates himself used to have patients chew the bark, and it can also be made into a tea. It also helps to alleviate the pain."*

"Certainly." He walked off to have someone collect the bark.

She had William drink a little water. "Father, can you fill the canteen for me, please? I do not think I should walk to the stream again." Mr. Bennet went away in the direction of the stream, and the two were left alone.

He had to take advantage of this opportunity… he *had* to ask her. "Marry me, Elizabeth?" William whispered.

"Sir?"

---

* Willow bark has similar ingredients to aspirin.

"Marry me?"

"Mr. Darcy, you told me not to pay close attention to what you said because you feel as though you are drunk." The fire light was reflecting off her eyes more than ever, and he suspected it was because they were filled with tears.

"I am perfectly serious. Marry me?"

"I am but sixteen, sir. You are a great man, and will be master of all this someday..." she waved her hands around to all that was Pemberley. "I hope not soon, but *someday*. You really cannot mean to take someone like *me* as a wife. This is not a game, nor is it a subject to jest about, sir."

"You will not believe me because of the fever?"

"Correct. Mr. Darcy, I think it is the fever speaking and would not take advantage of you in that way." They could hear a rustling of leaves indicating someone was approaching.

"When my fever is gone..." He caught the hand that was reaching to take the cloth from his head, and brought it to his lips, then released it. "Thank you, Elizabeth."

The servant who was sent for the doctor had realized that they were closer to Lambton than to Pemberley, so the doctor was brought to the place where the accident occurred. Fortunately, the doctor was home and dressed and able to come out immediately. Mr. Smythe was a man in his middle fifties, tall and fit with dark hair and eyes. He was introduced to Mr. Bennet and Elizabeth, and after quick greetings were exchanged, he knelt down next to William and said, "So, Master William, you have gotten yourself into a bit of trouble, I understand. Will you explain what happened?"

"I am so tired...Miss Elizabeth can explain..." he looked to Elizabeth.

"I have been with him the entire time, Mr. Smythe. Approximately five or six hours ago..." Elizabeth went on to describe what had occurred over the course of the afternoon and evening in detail to Mr. Smythe and concluded by saying, "Mr. Darcy has taken some water, but not much. I was unsure whether to give him more since he was not complaining of being thirsty, and he was feeling a little nauseated, sir."

"Well, that is probably one of the most thorough reports I have ever received, Miss Bennet. Are you training to be a midwife?"

"No, sir. I just paid attention when Mr. Jones treated my family and friends as I was growing up."

"You have a good memory, then." He turned to his patient and said, "It sounds as if you have been taken good care of, Master William, but I shall need to take a look at you. I would like to see your shoulder and head, for now, and then when we return to the house, I will do a more thorough examination. Miss Bennet, will you please excuse us?"

"Certainly, sir."

William had not taken his eyes off Elizabeth since she had first begun speaking to the doctor, and when he realized she was leaving, he became very agitated and took her hand, "No... no."

She looked helplessly at the doctor, and Mr. Smythe said, "Well, I suppose you can stay as long as our patient does not mind it! But, Master William, you will have to relinquish the lady's hand once we get back to Pemberley. Miss Bennet will not be able to stay for *that* examination."

After a few minutes, Mr. Smythe said, "I have done all that I can out here. When will the cart be here to transport him?"

"It should be here soon, Smythe," Mr. Darcy said.

"Miss Elizabeth's ankle—she has injured it," William said to Mr. Smythe.

"Of course."

Elizabeth smiled at William, "I do think you will have to let go of my hand for a few minutes, sir. I promise I will be back soon."

Mr. Bennet helped Elizabeth take a few steps to a fallen log, and Mr. Smythe examined her ankle by lantern light. He took one look at her ankle, then looked up to her eyes quickly, locked his with hers, and raised his eyebrows in surprise. She shrugged. Mr. Bennet could see in this man's face that his already high level of respect for his daughter had just increased. There were few women who would be able to function while experiencing that amount of pain, and none of the ones he could recall were gentle ladies. Most ladies would be lying in bed crying from the pain of an injury not even half as serious.

"Well, well, Miss Bennet! Did you run a race after hurting yourself?"

She whispered, "Please, sir. I do not wish Mr. Darcy to know how bad it is—he feels guilty enough that he could not help me. It was getting cold, and Mr. Darcy needed a fire, so I collected wood, sir."

Mr. Smythe nodded, and then said, "This is going to hurt, Miss Bennet, but I need to examine the bone."

Elizabeth looked up into her father's concerned eyes. He offered her his hand, and she took it. She gritted her teeth and closed her eyes as he examined her, but she refused to cry out. When he was finished, he said, "Do you not feel pain, Miss Bennet?"

"If the way she was squeezing my hand is any indication, she felt it, all right, sir, have no doubt!" Mr. Bennet said quietly.

"I did not mean to hurt you, Papa!"

"Oh, no, Lizzy, I am fine. Do not be concerned," he said, cursing himself for his attempt at a jest to distract her from the pain only to have it cause his brave daughter to feel guilt instead.

"It is not broken, but this is a very bad sprain. It is very swollen and bruised. You will have to rest it for a few weeks at least. When you return to Pemberley, I will have the housekeeper put some ice on it, but I doubt that will help to reduce the swelling after this length of time. I am certain it will heal completely with time and rest. Please do not attempt to walk on it."

"As we were scheduled to return to Hertfordshire next week, I must ask, Mr. Smythe, when will Elizabeth be able to travel?"

"Oh, it will be some weeks before she will be comfortable enough, Mr. Bennet. It is possible that she will be able to travel in three or four weeks— but one week? No, it would be too uncomfortable to make such a long journey in so short a time."

"Well, then... it looks like your mother and sisters will have to do without us for a while longer, my Lizzy."

"I am sorry, Papa."

"No, no! Do not be silly, my child. I am certain I can find *something* in Darcy's library to keep me busy during our extended stay." He smiled at his daughter and leaned down to kiss her on the forehead.

She laughed, "I daresay you might find a book or two, Papa. And I am certain that you and Mr. Darcy can find a few more 'old times' to discuss as well. From all I have heard over the past weeks, I feel almost as if I attended Eton and Cambridge with you both!"

"Have we old men been boring you, dear Lizzy?"

"Not at all, sir. I would enjoy listening to all your stories again if you have run out of things to talk about. I could never tire of hearing about those things I have longed to experience myself but will never be allowed to do. Perhaps young Mr. Darcy will share stories about his time in Eton and Cambridge as well as his trip abroad. I heard a great deal about his trip to Italy when I was trying to keep him awake, and I am certain his accounts will be much more interesting once his fever has passed. He was slurring his words quite a bit, but still his thinking was clear when reminiscing—his descriptions were so vivid that I could almost see the things he described." Her expression turned to one of deep concern as she asked, "Mr. Smythe, will Mr. Darcy be all right, sir?"

Witnessing this exchange, Mr. Smythe understood their personalities and relationship to the Darcys better. "I do not think his head injury is serious, and you did a wonderful job replacing his shoulder. Honestly, I would not have done anything differently if I had been here myself at the time of his accident. The fever is the part that confuses me, though, as the head wound does not seem infected. How quickly the fever has come on and risen concerns me, but as long as he gets past the fever, I think he will be fine. He is a strong, healthy young man, Miss Bennet, and that is on his side."

"Is it possible he contracted something in Italy or on the passage home, and the fever is not connected to his accident at all, Mr. Smythe?"

"I knew he had been away, but not the details. When did he arrive home?"

"The way I understood it, he left the ship five days ago, traveled, stayed one night in London, and then arrived here today, sir," Elizabeth answered.

"Well, then! It is very possible he had contracted something else… yes." He smiled at Elizabeth. "Thank you for the consultation, Miss Bennet."

Elizabeth was glad for the darkness because it concealed her blush.

"Mr. Smythe? Miss Elizabeth?" Mr. Darcy called out. They looked over to where William was lying and saw him thrashing about. Mr. Bennet helped Elizabeth over to them as quickly as possible.

Mr. Smythe got there first, and said, "His fever has risen quite a bit while I was examining Miss Bennet!"

"He keeps calling out for you, Miss Elizabeth, and will not calm."

She dampened the cloth again and wiped his face. He opened his eyes a little and said in a raspy voice, "Elizabeth." Settling a little, he took hold of her hand.

"There is no need to worry about me, sir. Mr. Smythe says my ankle will be fine, but I will have to rest it. I fear Mrs. Reynolds will be very displeased with me as I am not a good patient when I am confined indoors! I will ride in the cart with you on the way to Pemberley." His eyes never left her, but he had quieted again. "Mr. Darcy, I just remembered… you said some people were sick on the ship; was it only during the storm or were they sick at other times?"

"Other times, too. Fevers and coughing."

She looked to Mr. Smythe, who turned to Mr. Darcy and said, "We think he might have contracted something onboard the ship unrelated to the accident."

"We?" Mr. Darcy asked.

Mr. Smythe smiled a little and said, "Oh… Miss Bennet and I."

"Poseidon likes her," William said with a chuckle.

Mr. Darcy's eyebrows rose up high. "Poseidon? William's horse *likes* you, Miss Elizabeth?"

"Why, yes. I do not understand why it is so surprising. He seems very pleasant, if a little high spirited."

"Pleasant? Tom, come here a minute." Mr. Darcy yelled out to one of the men who had helped with the search. "This is Tom, who works in the stable. Tom, Miss Bennet would like to know your opinion on Poseidon."

"He's one of the best around for ridin', but one of the most ornery, too. Nobody at the stable can't get near to 'm, ma'am… not even Mr. Darcy. Just me and Master William."

"He put his head on her shoulder," William rasped out.

Both Mr. Darcy and Tom gaped at her. "She's a horse charmer?" Tom asked.

"Males of all species!" William said, glancing at Mr. Smythe.

Mr. Bennet laughed. "Quite!"

"Gentlemen, I *am* right here. I would appreciate it if you would end this contest to see who can make me blush the brightest shade of crimson." The sound of the cart approaching caught everyone's attention. "Ah, I am saved from further teasing!"

Several men carried William to the cart. Once he was as comfortable as possible, Mr. Bennet carried Elizabeth and placed her on William's good side sitting up next to him. She asked for the cloth and canteen to enable her to continue wiping down his face during the ride back to Pemberley. The men all rode around the cart, taking it very slowly to avoid as many bumps as possible. Mr. Smythe said that it was safe for William to fall asleep, but he doubted that would be possible in the cart.

While they were on the trip to Pemberley, William's hand found hers again whenever she was not using it to refresh the cloth. One of the men rode up with the requested willow bark, and Mr. Darcy directed him to Mr. Smythe. Mr. Smythe cut off a piece for William and one for Elizabeth and asked them to chew on it. When seeing his scowl, she said, "I know, it tastes horrible, but it will help the fever and the pain."

"You have a fever?" he asked.

"No, but it helps with swelling as well. Once we are at Pemberley, Mrs. Reynolds can make a tea and mix some honey in so it will taste better." After a while they both took it out of their mouths and threw the rest over the side. He was embarrassed that she took his from his mouth, but she only smiled at him, and then persuaded him to close his eyes and promise to try to sleep. His head rolled to the side, resting against her leg, and he fell asleep while she bathed his face almost constantly.

Chapter 5

Elizabeth was awakened by a panicked Mrs. Reynolds. "Oh, Miss Bennet! I am so very sorry to have to wake you, but it is Master William!" Elizabeth sat straight up. "We have tried everything to calm him, but it will not do! His fever is so high, and he is coughing and thrashing around violently. He keeps calling for you, and Mr. Darcy said that when something similar happened earlier, he only calmed once you held his hand…" She stopped talking as Elizabeth tried to stand up, her injured ankle forgotten, and then cried out, almost falling. Mrs. Reynolds caught her.

"Thank you, Mrs. Reynolds. Can you help me with my robe, please?" With this done, Elizabeth limped out into the hallway, "Which way?" Mrs. Reynolds supported her weight, and they made their way down to the family wing. As she passed, Elizabeth told the footman to wake her father and to inform him of her whereabouts.

When the door was opened, she stopped, taking in the condition of William as he lay in the bed. The arm that was not bound to his chest was flailing around as if reaching for something; his voice, calling her name, was so hoarse that she barely recognized it. Mr. Darcy rushed over to her and noticing how she leaned on Mrs. Reynolds, lifted her in his arms and carried her to the chair by the bed.

"Miss Elizabeth, why did you not have a footman carry you?"

"I did not think of it, sir."

William was plagued with another round of coughing, his face screwed up in pain from the jarring of his shoulder.

Once she was seated, she began to speak, "Mr. Darcy, it is Elizabeth. I am here. There is no need to worry about me; I am safe." His hand reached out toward her, and she took it in both of hers as she leaned closer to him. "Your fever is very high; I will need to bathe your face."

Elizabeth took the cloth from the basin, and she squeezed it out while saying in a very calm voice, "Mr. Darcy, you must rest now. This restlessness is not good for you; it is making your cough worse. You promised you would sleep now." She took his hand in one of hers and started wiping his face with the other. His condition shocked her. He was completely soaked in perspiration—his hair, his clothing, even the bedding. His skin was so hot that she was frightened beyond anything she had ever felt before. Mrs. Reynolds came over and squeezed out another cloth for her to use next so that she would not have to release his hand.

"Elizabeth…" William was calming. Elizabeth heard her father as he entered the room, acknowledging his presence with merely a glance.

"Yes, I am here, sir." One would not be able to tell from her voice that she was in a complete panic.

"Elizabeth?" His eyes were open a little now, and she schooled her features, willing herself to look as calm as she sounded.

She switched cloths with Mrs. Reynolds. "Yes, Mr. Darcy?"

"Why?"

"I do not understand, sir."

"Why will you not marry me?" Mr. Darcy, Mrs. Reynolds and Mr. Bennet turned their heads quickly in perfect synchronization to see her reaction.

Elizabeth blushed and tried not to look at anyone but William. "You are ill, sir. You told me not to take anything you said seriously."

"I did not mean this!" He had found a little strength to project his voice just a bit, which brought on a short round of coughing.

When he quieted, she smiled a little while replying, "I did not say 'no,' sir. I told you that I will not even consider a proposal from a man who tells me his fever makes him feel as if he were drunk. When you are feeling better, if you still wish to, you may ask at a later date."

He started coughing again. She could not even imagine the pain that the forceful movement must be causing his shoulder and his head. Her eyes filled with tears as he groaned.

"I am so very sorry," she said, feeling the guilt of her part in his accident. Why did she have to land in the horse's way?

"*Not* your fault I fell," he whispered as his eyes slit open so he could see her.

She tried to smile as she said, "I told you I would not argue over who should take more of the blame. By the by, *I* have been very careful not to say you *fell* from your horse!"

He rolled his eyes as best he could and nodded slightly. He closed his eyes and began to fall asleep, but then startled awake again, staring at her while she mopped his brow. "Why is your hair down?"

"It is nighttime. Mrs. Reynolds came to get me." She glanced at the lady in question.

William turned his head a little and saw Mrs. Reynolds in the room with them, then noticed movement behind Elizabeth and picked up his head a little to see both their fathers in attendance. He did not notice Mr. Smythe in a chair in the far corner of the room. It was obvious that William had thought they were alone and was surprised that the others were there, but he did not have the energy to be embarrassed that they had heard all that he had said to her. He did manage an, "Oh!" before squeezing her hand slightly and closing his eyes again. "Do not leave me."

"I promise that I will not leave before you awaken."

He sighed deeply and fell asleep, his hand holding hers.

Mrs. Reynolds squeezed out another cloth and exchanged with her again, then moved across the room to get a blanket in which to wrap her. She excused herself momentarily to speak to a footman in the hallway. He returned shortly with a small stool and, at Mrs. Reynolds's direction, he placed it near Elizabeth's chair, and then covered it with a large pillow. Mrs. Reynolds helped her place her foot upon it to keep it elevated as Mr. Smythe had instructed. Elizabeth thanked her and continued to mop William's brow.

The gentlemen said not a word, but only settled into some comfortable chairs near the fireplace. For a long while, the silence in the room was broken only with the sound of William's raspy breathing and intermittent coughing, the crackling of the fire, and the sloshing of the water in the basin as cloths were refreshed.

A few hours later, Elizabeth smiled widely at Mrs. Reynolds and called out excitedly to Mr. Smythe; William's fever had broken.

Mr. Bennet suggested that she return to her bed, but she refused. "I promised him I would be here when he awakens, and I will not break that promise, Papa! I will sleep here."

Her father knew better than to argue with her when she had that determined light in her eyes. "You must promise me that you will return to your bedchamber once William awakes."

Elizabeth nodded her understanding. "Yes, Papa."

Mr. Darcy quietly said to Mr. Bennet, "Go to bed, my friend. I will make sure that William agrees to allow Elizabeth to leave when next he wakes."

Mr. Bennet nodded his agreement and left the room. Mr. Smythe also left to rest in the next room, asking them to wake him immediately if anything changed, though he did not expect Master William to do anything but improve from here on out.

Mr. Darcy turned to Elizabeth and said, "Thank you, Miss Elizabeth."

She was too tired to do anything more than smile at him. She closed her eyes and fell asleep, still holding William's hand.

Hours later, Elizabeth awakened. She felt William's hand still in hers, but her neck was stiff from the attitude she had assumed as she had slept in the chair. She rolled her neck a little before opening her eyes—to see William staring at her. A brilliant smile spread across her face as she whispered, "Good morning, Mr. Darcy!"

He smiled weakly, but the smile reached his eyes tenfold. "Good morning, Miss Elizabeth," he said hoarsely and then began to cough anew. She released his hand and reached for a glass, pouring water and then waiting until his cough abated. She held the glass out for him to take, but his hand was shaking too much to hold it steady, so she stood and helped him to take a few sips.

"You seem much improved over your condition last night."

"Yes, I feel much better... may I ask again now?" Feeling the loss of her touch, William took hold of her hand once more.

She laughed. "Mr. Darcy! Wait until you are recovered! You need time to think about it with a rational mind *not* weakened by illness, injury or fever, sir."

He sighed. Should he tell her he never wanted to wake up again without her face being the first thing he saw? Or that when she had lain next to him last night in the woods, she fit so perfectly against his side that he would never again fall asleep without thinking of her? Or that when they had kissed, it had been the most perfect moment in all of his life? How could he convince her that he was in his right mind? He knew the answer was that he should give her *time*. He needed to prove that his feelings were constant.

"Mr. Darcy, your fever broke during the night, and you are out of danger. I had promised both my father and yours," she nodded toward the fire where his father was still sleeping in a chair, "that after you awoke, I would return to my room."

Though he wanted nothing more than to tell her to sleep here, in his bed, snuggled up next to him, he knew that it was impossible. He nodded, but did not let go of her hand. "Will you visit today? Perhaps bring a book and read to me?"

"If both our fathers permit it, yes, I shall. Mayhap I can come with Georgiana." She smiled, and then could not hold back a yawn.

He swallowed hard and said, "I apologize for keeping you, Miss Elizabeth. Go rest... good night." William squeezed her hand one more time and then reluctantly released it. He watched as she limped toward the door, and as the door closed, he heard her quietly ask the footman to assist her to her room.

His father approached the bed. "It is good to see that you are feeling better than you were last night, William. You gave us all quite a scare!"

"Thank you, Father. I am sorry to have worried you all."

"It seems we have a few important things to discuss when you are feeling stronger..." He raised his eyebrows and glanced at the seat Elizabeth had occupied previously, "...but for now, rest and recover, son. I must get some sleep as well. I will send a servant to sit with you. Do not hesitate to have me summoned immediately if you need me, William." He helped William take another drink before heading for the door.

William nodded. "Sleep well, Father."

~%~

When Mr. Bennet entered the breakfast room, Mr. Darcy was the only one present.

"Good morning, Darcy. How is William today?"

"Good morning, Bennet. He is resting now, but still coughing. How is Elizabeth?"

"The maid said she is still sleeping."

"It appears that we have additional serious matters to discuss, eh?" Mr. Darcy said with a smile.

"While I tend to find amusement in most situations, I am certainly finding it difficult to do so with *this* subject."

"Perhaps we should meet in my study as soon as you are finished with your meal?"

"Yes, I think that would be wise," he said glancing at the servants. "I find I have no appetite this morning but will eagerly indulge myself with your delicious coffee."

Mr. Darcy had a coffee tray sent to his study, and the gentlemen headed there. Once the coffee had been served and the door had closed behind the servant, Mr. Bennet said, "What are your thoughts on this matter?"

"To be honest, Bennet, over the past weeks of your stay here at Pemberley, I have been thinking about how perfectly matched William and Elizabeth would be, and was going to ask you to return to Pemberley soon because I was hoping to have them meet—though perhaps I was not expecting to hear that he had made a decision so soon after seeing her again."

Mr. Bennet's brow furrowed. "Well, now… that *is* a surprise. You have no qualms about the difference in their social status? She is not of the first circle, nor does she have the connections usually required by those of the *ton*. Though I have followed your advice on investing over the years, I had only a small amount with which to start. My girls have a dowry of only five thousand pounds each, part of which is dependent on my wife's death."

Mr. Darcy's ire showed through his usual calm demeanor. "You think I am such a snob that I would deny my son the happiness of a life filled with love because of the anticipated negative reaction of the *ton*? After the purpose of your visit here and all of our discussions on the matter, I thought you would understand my feelings by now."

"Do not become angry with me, George! You should be able to understand that I had to ask—had to be *certain*? My Lizzy is too important to me to simply *assume* that you have thought through everything regarding the match. But I am afraid I cannot just take your word for their being well-matched, George. Remember, I have not seen William in years… I will have to see for myself how they get along. It certainly seems that Lizzy is not against it, no matter what she said last night… but she is so *young*."

Mr. Darcy replied, "Her response to William only made me love her all the more, Thomas, and to see even more clearly that she is perfect for him. William can be very intimidating, though he does not realize it, and she would not allow him to intimidate her. Though he is not uncomfortable with *you*, usually he is very reserved in the company of other than a select few. I have seen how he is with her—he is more comfortable with her than he is with anyone other than Georgiana and me. My son is painfully shy, and I can only imagine that with her by his side, he would do much better in any society.

"In her favor, William accepts her for who she is, and you know, as we have discussed in the past, how that is going to be a rare occurrence for Elizabeth, Thomas. Furthermore, she will be hard pressed to find a man that *she* can respect, who can challenge her in wit and intelligence, but William *can*. He often has spoken of things she has said to him through the years and has always been very impressed with her. She would be guaranteed a life of comfort and security as well as a husband who honestly respects her opinion. I believe they would be true *partners* in life. I would welcome her as my daughter with open arms, and Georgiana loves her as a sister already.

"As for her age—I married Anne when she was seventeen."

"Lizzy is but *sixteen*. I would like her to have at least one season, even if it *is* only in Hertfordshire—to be exposed to a number of men before making a decision about whether she wishes to be engaged to any man—even your excellent William. How can I expect her to make a decision unless she has some experience on which to base it?"

"From what I understand, Elizabeth has more experience with boys than most girls her age. Did she not spend most of her childhood playing games with the boys of the neighborhood?"

"Yes, she did, and perhaps Lizzy does have more of an idea of what traits she would and would not want in a life-partner, George, but to be honest, I doubt she has ever looked at her friends from childhood with that in mind. I want her to have the chance to dance and converse with true perspective matches before giving her heart away to the first man who comes along and offers for her!"

"If she has already given her heart to William—and after seeing the way she looked at William last night, I do not think you have much of a choice but to admit that she already has—would she go out into society and flirt with other men? Though many in the *ton* would, I cannot believe that of *her*."

"I would like her to, at the very least, have the opportunity to make a more informed choice, George. One season, that is all I ask. Once William has recovered, if he is still interested in Lizzy, they can meet again when she turns seventeen on the thirtieth day of May. If at that time their feelings are the same, I gladly will give my consent."

Mr. Darcy laughed, "Are you certain you are not trying to keep her home a little longer in your company, Thomas?"

"Perhaps," Mr. Bennet admitted with a smile, "but I also want them *both* to be sure about this, George. You were fortunate in your marriage to Anne, but I have personal experience with rushing into marriage before truly knowing the person. I would not wish that fate upon anyone, especially my dearest Lizzy."

Mr. Darcy nodded. "What you say does sound reasonable. Though, Thomas, I know I will not be here to see Georgiana marry… I would like to be here to witness William's wedding if at all possible. If our children decide this *is* right for them, please do not insist upon a long engagement. If I am lucky, I might even live long enough to meet a grandchild." Mr. Bennet nodded solemnly, and both gentlemen were quiet for a few minutes, lost in thought before Mr. Darcy continued, "Let us see how things develop here, especially now that you will be with us longer than expected while Elizabeth recovers. If all goes as I expect, we will let them know of your— *our* plan." The two gentlemen shook hands on it, and then Mr. Darcy continued, "William has requested that Elizabeth visit and read to Georgiana and him. Is that acceptable to you? He will not be leaving his chambers for a few days at the very least. Since I understand that Elizabeth is just as prone to being a poor patient when illness confines her indoors as is William, it might help to cheer them both, as well as give them more time to know each other better."

"I know I should not… having them found in the woods after so many hours alone was damaging enough to their reputations. But you say your servants are all reliable and discreet, are they not?"

"They are very loyal and will not gossip about *any* of this, Thomas."

"As long as Georgiana or a maid, preferably both, is present at all times, then yes, I will permit it. I want them to get to know each other better as much as you do."

"All right, then; that is settled."

They were quiet for several minutes until Mr. Bennet asked with a serious countenance, "George, will you share what the doctors told you with William and Georgiana?"

"I was going to tell them as soon as William returned, but now that he is home early, and you are still here, I must think about whether it would be better to wait until you leave or to tell them now. They might want the privacy, but then again, Elizabeth could be a great comfort to Georgiana when she hears what I have to say. William might have questions for you, as well. I will need to think about it further. Meantime, today I must ride out to settle a tenant dispute. Would you like to ride out with me?"

"William's injury will postpone your training of him, but I hope the delay will not be of long duration. I do hope that the doctors are wrong about your condition and nothing comes of it, but if it does happen before he is fully comfortable in the master's role, I will need to know as much as possible if I am to help him. It is the reason I came to Pemberley, as you well know—between having Wickham and me to turn to, William will be fine.

"This puts me in mind of a question, though, George. You have told me much about the character of certain members of the Fitzwilliam family and how you do not want them to be the ones to help William with the estate or to influence his decisions. You have also voiced your fear that they will try to turn him into one of *them*. I know what *I* will be up against if what we are preparing for does come to pass. But all this makes me wonder, how will they react if Elizabeth and William marry?"

Mr. Darcy rolled his eyes and stood to leave, "It will not be a pretty sight, and it is another reason not to delay for too long! If I am *here*, I will do my best to be a buffer between the Fitzwilliams and our children and will continue to do so until my dying breath, Thomas. The Darcys have connections enough in the *ton* to counteract any that might make things... *difficult* for them through the efforts of the Fitzwilliams. Now, I am going to check on William, and then we will go."

"Good, as I would like to look in on Lizzy as well."

~%~

When Elizabeth woke, she rang for the maid. Soon after, there was a knock at the door, but it was the one for the hallway, not the servant's entrance as she had expected. Elizabeth called out and eleven-year-old Georgiana appeared.

"I am so glad to see that you are all right, Elizabeth!" Georgiana embraced her friend and continued, "I hope you do not mind that I asked to be notified when you awoke. I waited to break my fast hoping to keep you company while you did the same. Is that agreeable with you?"

"Thank you, Georgiana! Yes, that does sound pleasant, but I was hoping for a bath first thing today. After yesterday, I certainly do need one!"

"Then I will return to my studies, and I will see you after your bath." Georgiana smiled at her and left the room.

When Elizabeth had completed her toilette, she sent word for Georgiana to join her.

"I apologize for taking so long with my bath, Georgiana. Accomplishing *anything* with my injured ankle will take some getting used to."

Georgiana crossed the room and enveloped Elizabeth in another affectionate hug. After the maid left the room, Georgiana said, "I was so worried about you and William last night, Elizabeth! I knew William would *never* get lost at Pemberley, and your father said you have a good sense of direction, so I knew that something was amiss. I could not sleep until I knew you were both safe!"

"Oh, Georgiana, I am sorry you stayed up so late. We would rather have been at Pemberley with you, believe me." She was not certain that Georgiana knew that her brother had become ill, so she did not mention it as it was not her place to do so.

Servants came in with the breakfast trays and set them up as Georgiana directed. Just after they left, Mr. Bennet knocked at her door and was admitted by the maid. "Good morning, Miss Darcy. Good morning, Lizzy." He went to Elizabeth's side and kissed her forehead. "How are you feeling this morning, my dear?"

"My ankle is feeling a little better, thank you, Papa. Mr. Smythe has already been to see me, and he says that the swelling is reduced a little as well. Have you heard how Georgiana's brother is faring this morning?"

"Yes, Mr. Darcy informed me that William was resting as comfortably as his cough and shoulder will allow. I came to inform you that I will be riding out with Mr. Darcy again today, and we will be back before nightfall. If we are needed, the housekeeper knows our destination. Do not hesitate to send for us." Mr. Bennet gave her a pointed look, wordlessly conveying that he was very serious on this last point.

"Thank you, Papa. I am certain that we both are on the mend and will not require your assistance." Mr. Bennet bid them a good day and left.

"William is coughing?" Georgiana asked, a worried frown replacing her former smile.

"You have not seen him this morning?"

"No, I was told he is still sleeping."

"There is no way of avoiding this conversation now!" Elizabeth thought. "Ah, well, he had hurt his shoulder and his head in the accident, and then a fever began before we were found, but it broke during the night. He started coughing after we returned to Pemberley. Mr. Smythe thinks he will be fine with rest, so do not worry, sweet friend."

"My father stopped by the schoolroom a little while ago and told me we are to have luncheon in William's room today. I asked William's valet to send word when he is ready for visitors since Father said we should go in to keep him occupied. Apparently, you promised we would read to him?"

Elizabeth smiled; had Mr. Darcy been pretending to sleep when she told William that she would? "Yes... yes, I did. Are you reading anything interesting in your lessons right now, Georgiana—a book or a play? Perhaps we can incorporate your lessons into our visit."

"Yes, Lizzy, Shakespeare's *Twelfth Night.*"

"That is perfect! There just happens to be a copy right here in my room. Perhaps after breakfast you can get your copy, and we can work out who will play which parts and thereby entertain your brother for a while. Afterwards, we can discuss the play. What say you?"

"Oh, that sounds like great fun!" Georgiana clapped her hands excitedly. The girls had a pleasant morning and had finished planning their performance just as they received word that William was ready for them.

Mr. Darcy had arranged that Elizabeth should be carried by a footman whenever her father was not available, and no amount of arguing on her part could convince the footman to allow her to walk only with the support of his arm. The staff had come to know her well during her stay and liked her very much, so they would easily forgive her for her stubborn behavior, but nothing was making it easier to convince Elizabeth that the footman must carry her. Elizabeth's maid had called for Mrs. Reynolds who was accustomed to headstrong patients as none of the Darcys were very cooperative when they were ill. Even then, she finally had to dispense with all politeness and tell Miss Elizabeth with a very severe look and tone of voice, "Mr. Darcy is the master of this house, and unless *he* tells me otherwise, you, Miss Bennet, *will* be carried. If you refuse, you will not leave this room!"

Soon after this exchange, Mrs. Reynolds knocked on William's door and upon the valet's opening the door, a parade of people filed into the room. Much to William's surprise, a very stern-looking Mrs. Reynolds was seen leading a footman carrying an angry-looking Elizabeth, with an amused-looking Georgiana following in their wake.

When he first saw the group entering his chambers, he was overwhelmed with conflicting emotions: happiness that he was to spend time with Elizabeth again so soon; gladness to see Georgiana again after being away for so long; jealousy because if anyone should be carrying Elizabeth it should be *him*; frustration because he could not manage that task in his present state; and awe to see that Elizabeth was even more beautiful when angry.

While Mrs. Reynolds made sure Elizabeth was well settled in the chair with her foot elevated, Georgiana and William greeted each other. Georgiana sat on the edge of his bed and held his hand, speaking softly.

Before leaving, Mrs. Reynolds said firmly, "Miss Elizabeth, you *will* call for James before you leave this room! The master's orders *will* be followed—you *will* be carried so that you will not injure yourself further!"

Georgiana saw that William seemed quite confused, so she explained, "It seems Miss Elizabeth is about as compliant a patient as are you, William!"

Elizabeth and William's eyes met and both blushed. Not one to hold a grudge and definitely one to find an amusing side to every situation, Elizabeth giggled and said, "Oh, Mrs. Reynolds, James, I apologize. You are correct; I have always been a terrible patient. I am far too independent and do not do well at relying on others. It is especially ungrateful of me to be so difficult after what happened at Longbourn, James."

The normally stoic James surprised the other occupants of the room by smiling. "I'm flattered that you remember, Miss."

"Of course, I remember. I promise to be more cooperative in the future."

Both James and a now-satisfied Mrs. Reynolds left the room.

"Longbourn?" William asked.

"Yes, you do remember staying overnight at Longbourn a few years ago, sir? I had a bit of trouble, and James helped me."

"Trouble?" Georgiana asked, a little bit alarmed.

"Yes." Elizabeth blushed furiously and paid an inordinate amount of attention to smoothing her skirt, but did not elaborate. She looked up to find both pairs of Darcy eyes staring at her, awaiting an answer. "If you *must* know, it had something to do with a not-so-brilliant idea of attempting to catch a badger to make a pet of it… and I think that is all I will say on the subject at present." She smiled at William and said, "You *do* look much better than you did last night, sir; how are you feeling?"

The change of subject was noted, but he did not mind as long as her attention was centered on him. "I am certain I do not look *well*, Miss Elizabeth. I am feeling a little better, thank you. I no longer feel strange from the fever," he said with a look filled with hope that perhaps *now* she would allow his proposal. She shook her head a little, but tempered it with a small smile. Disappointment showed on his face.

"I did not say you look *well*, sir, I said you look *better*," Elizabeth teased.

William smiled slightly. "Is your ankle any better?"

"It *is* a little, thank you. Mr. Smythe said I will make a full recovery as long as I do not walk upon it." Her expression changed to one of concern as she asked, "Has Mr. Smythe been to see you this morning?"

"Yes, he feels I am out of danger as long as the fever does not recur and the cough does not get worse. Apparently the fever was quite high last night. I remember only a little of what happened after we returned to Pemberley." His thoughts showed in his eyes as he looked at Elizabeth. *"I remember your gentle touch, your looks, my waking to find you nearby with your hand in mine, the aching need to have you beside me once more, the emptiness I felt while watching you leave me…"*

Georgiana was surprised at Elizabeth's teasing of her brother and watched him closely to see his reaction. She was shocked to see that he was enjoying the exchange, but then she noticed a look in his eyes that was something akin to the way he looked at her, but it was different as well. The look changed to… something else, something much more powerful. Georgiana smiled as she thought, *"William is in love with Elizabeth!"*

"I am glad to hear it, Miss Elizabeth. I see that you ladies brought books. What have you chosen to read to me?"

"I am studying *Twelfth Night* at present, and Elizabeth thought it might be entertaining if we acted out part of it for you—from a seated position, of course."

With that teasing sparkle in her eyes, Elizabeth added, "From what I have heard, your behavior when confined to a sickbed would not be much different than mine. So we are determined to keep you entertained!" She paused, and her look turned a bit more serious. "If you agree, we will get through as much as we can before luncheon is brought in. After we eat, if you are feeling well enough, we can discuss Georgiana's impressions of it. If our acting is not *too* badly done, perhaps we can continue tomorrow. However, if it *is* unacceptable, we shall choose something else to read."

"I will reserve the right to decide until *after* I have seen your performance," William said, and then was overcome with a coughing fit. Elizabeth sprang into action and poured a fresh glass of water, holding it for him to take a sip once his coughing had calmed.

Elizabeth's unoccupied hand moved without thought, smoothing a curl away from his forehead, and then she jumped a little with the realization that what she was doing was highly inappropriate. Blushing, she moved away and busied herself with the glass and pitcher on the bedside tray. Once she recovered enough to look at him again, the love and hope in his eyes took her breath away.

"Please do not tell Mrs. Reynolds that I stood up!" she jested, trying to recover her equanimity.

Georgiana was only eleven, but having spent most of her time with adults, she was intelligent beyond her years, and she could see this exchange for what it truly was. Though it made her very happy, she also knew that she should not let the scene continue any longer. Playing the part of the little sister, she asked with youthful energy, "Shall we begin, Elizabeth?"

They made their way through a few scenes with a bit of laughter laced throughout before stopping to eat lunch, and then Elizabeth asked Georgiana a few questions about the play. William was becoming too sleepy to participate in the conversation, but he did not want them to leave him, so he struggled with his heavy eyelids.

Elizabeth noticed he was falling asleep, and she shot Georgiana a pointed look. Elizabeth felt that he would not wish them to leave on his account, but would agree to it more readily if it were on hers. She cleared her throat loudly so that William would awaken and hear. When out of the corner of her eye she saw his eyes fly open, she said, "I apologize for breaking up our little party, but would you mind if I returned to my chamber to rest for a while? I feel in need of a nap."

Georgiana rang the bell for James to collect Elizabeth. "William, you should have a nap as well. Father said he and Mr. Bennet would take trays in here with you for dinner, and I will be doing the same with Elizabeth. Will you have Hughes notify Father when you wake?"

William nodded and asked, "Will you both come for lunch again tomorrow? I enjoyed your performance and would like to see more of the play."

Georgiana saw that Elizabeth would be very happy to do so. "I think we would like that." She looked at the clock and feigned surprise, "Oh! Look at the time! I must return to the school room immediately. I will leave the door open. You will wait here for James, will you not, Elizabeth? I am certain that he will be here within a few minutes." Not waiting for an answer; she kissed William on the cheek and rushed out the door.

Elizabeth's eyes danced with amusement. "Did you bribe your sister into leaving us alone for a few minutes?"

"No, but I am thankful for her perceptive nature. Elizabeth…"

She interrupted, "It seems my father wishes to get to know you better, Mr. Darcy, and so you will be subjected to his attentions for dinner this evening. I must warn you that last night while you were at the height of fever, you declared your intentions in front of him, your father, Mrs. Reynolds, *and* Mr. Smythe."

He blushed and said, "I would not mind at all if you had given me a different answer."

"Actually, I gave you the only *sensible* answer at this time, sir. From the moment we have been reacquainted, you have been under severe duress. One should not make life-altering decisions at such a time."

"I am a very patient man, Elizabeth. Though I would rather not, I will wait as long as it takes to prove the constancy of my feelings for you. I am absolutely certain my feelings are not the result of 'severe duress,' or infatuation. I am not afraid of your father's interrogation other than I am not at my best right now, of which I am sure he is aware."

"Well… I should wait in the hall for James so that Georgiana's abandonment is not discovered! My father might not allow me to visit with her tomorrow if it is… and *you* will need a nap before you meet with him to ensure that you are closer to your best!"

She stood, and as a result she was close enough to the bed for him to reach her hand. He brought it to his lips, brushed them over the back of her hand, and then released it. "Feel better soon, William," she whispered and then limped out to a hall chair to wait for James.

Chapter 6

Perhaps William had not felt nervous about speaking to Mr. Bennet when he spoke to Elizabeth of the meeting, but by the time he had awakened and prepared for dinner, he was quite anxious. It was all in vain, though, because Mr. Bennet did not interrogate him as he had expected. William, his father and Mr. Bennet had an agreeable time talking together.

When Mr. Bennet excused himself for a few minutes, Mr. Darcy and his son talked about his tour, the cities that he had seen, and the galleries he had visited. As Mr. Bennet was returning, he overheard Mr. Darcy asking his son why he had separated from the gentlemen with whom he had been travelling, and Mr. Bennet decided not to enter the room but instead to listen from the doorway. He was slightly ashamed of himself for eavesdropping, but had been wondering the same thing and wanted to know more about the character of the man with whom he suspected his daughter was forming an attachment. If eavesdropping had to be resorted to in order to protect his daughter, then so be it.

William became angrier with every word, "Father, they were not of a moral character with which I would wish the Darcy name to be associated, *even* in a foreign country. At school they had never taken their studies seriously and had been involved in many activities of which I did not approve, but apparently I had missed much of what was happening while I was studying. I did not consider these men to be my friends—truly the only reason I travelled with them was because they were going to Italy, and I had always wished to see it—I did not think so badly of them as not to travel with them. Sir, these men had only debaucheries and vices on their minds. They did not travel because they were interested in Italy; they travelled to escape the gossips of the *ton* so they could act in a wilder manner than they had at Cambridge! Through their boasting I learnt that it was not much different for them when in England; they had only been more discreet about their activities! Their main activities were drinking themselves into oblivion, betting on who could lift the most skirts, carrying out these activities, and over breakfast, boasting about each encounter in lurid detail! Gentlewomen, servants, peasants—it made no difference to them, for they had absolutely no respect for any woman they met and, while promising the world to each one, they cared not what consequences they left behind."

"My experience with 'gentlemen' was much the same as yours, William," Mr. Darcy admitted. "It is the way of many men, son, and you will have to accept it. Within the *ton* especially, they marry to have a legal heir, but many will participate in other *activities*. That is the reason I became so upset that time your uncle took you to a courtesan. I did not wish for you to turn into one of *them*."

"Father, that was the only time I have ever done such a thing. After your reaction and our discussion, I would not go again. Now I am glad that I did not." He did not feel comfortable saying that now that he was in love with Elizabeth, though he was somewhat relieved that he knew what to do when they would be together in the future, he was also glad to have saved the rest of himself for her.

"So, you were alone for most of the trip?"

"Their behavior was absolutely sickening and, after less than a week in their company, I went off on my own. I am disgusted that *these men* who have absolutely no morals are the future for the House of Lords, and will be deciding policy for England!"

"I am happy to hear that you were strong enough to stand by your principles and not give way to others' criticism of you, William. You will find there *are* good men with similar principles to your own, and they will become your allies."

"If Bingley had not been two years behind me, I would have been happy to have travelled with him. There were a few of my friends who left Cambridge over the past two years that I had found to be good men as well."

Mr. Darcy was thoughtful for several minutes before responding. "It is good that you are not too proud to be friends with Bingley; I like him very much." He hesitated for a few moments and then continued, "Mr. Bennet is a true friend whom I had found while at school, but we both became so busy with our lives, and Pemberley and Longbourn are far apart, that we lost contact for a while. When we met up again at the bookstore many years ago, I learned a great deal about life and about myself. Spending time with him again was like a breath of fresh air after spending so many years involved only with the *ton*. I had forgotten what it was like not to have to second guess a man's every intention. Mr. Bennet is who he is, and that is all; there are no ulterior motives, no schemes. Though his wife is a bit mercenary, she is truly concerned for her daughters' welfare—and she is certainly *honest* about it. Do you remember our visit there three years past? There certainly were no hidden agendas; she nearly threw her eldest daughter in your lap! It was refreshing!"

William looked horrified, and Mr. Darcy laughed. "Do not look at me like that, William, you have experienced the subtle intrigues of the *ton's* marriage-minded mamas, but you will *not* see them at their worst until you are in control of Pemberley and the Darcy funds. I had this problem before your mother and I married—actually Mr. Bennet had helped me in many ways even back then—but I had forgotten how bad it was until I came out of mourning. Any time I am in London, I have women making all *sorts* of offers, and others contriving ways to have me compromise them or even their young daughters! Whoever said that women are no good at strategy did not know the ladies of the *ton*! They only need the right inducements to make up plans that would rival those of our most stalwart generals. Right now *I* am in control of the estate and so their focus is on *me*, but you will see what I mean when it is your turn. I might sound cynical, but I warn you to protect yourself, William, or you will end up married to a woman not of your choosing—a conniving witch who would take advantage of your sense of honor and duty to get her greedy hands on your money and the power of the Darcy name."

Mr. Darcy let that hang in the air for a minute before continuing, "Back to the original discussion... the valuable lesson I learned when becoming reacquainted with Mr. Bennet was this: Do not allow yourself to lose contact with those you trust now, William. Sometimes ruts appear in the road, sometimes the road is washed out, but if you find yourself on a detour, do not lose sight of the primary road. Always make certain you find your way to it again."

Mr. Bennet did not give away that had he heard every word of what had been said during that discussion, but he had to admit to himself that it eased his mind a great deal. He waited a minute or two after the room had become silent to "return."

The older gentlemen left William to sleep and reconvened in the study for brandy and cigars and to discuss Mr. Darcy's decision to disclose his secret to his son only after Mr. Bennet and Elizabeth had left Pemberley; he and William would decide together when to speak to Georgiana. The two old friends further discussed having their daughters correspond. Mr. Darcy would let Mr. Bennet know in advance when he would be explaining his illness to Georgiana so that Elizabeth could be told before she received Georgiana's letters concerning his illness.

William continued to improve a little each day, and that first day of convalescence had set the stage for the temporary routine at Pemberley until he was finally given permission to leave his bed. The ladies would spend some time with William in the late morning and early afternoon, reading, playing chess or discussing his trip, and the gentlemen would spend the dinner hour with him. He had Hughes to retrieve the books he had read before he had gone to Italy so that he and the ladies could read together about the places he had been. He showed them the sketches he had made, and Elizabeth was impressed with his talent.

Beginning the second day after Elizabeth was injured, she would go downstairs each morning to break her fast with Mr. Bennet, Mr. Darcy, and Georgiana; in the afternoon, after visiting William, the ladies would practice together on the pianoforte. William had asked that his door and the door to the music room be left open when they left his room so that he could listen to their playing, and especially to Elizabeth's singing. The ladies agreed to this only for part of the time; when they were learning a new piece, they insisted on closing the door to the music room.

James continued to carry Elizabeth when she needed to move about the house. Much to Elizabeth's relief, after a few days she was given leave to walk a little each day, excluding climbing the stairs, and the amount of walking she could do increased as time passed. William was relieved as well not to have to see her in James's arms when she entered his room. No matter how well he controlled the outward display of his jealousy, he could not control his thoughts every time he saw Elizabeth in another man's arms, even though he understood completely why it was necessary. Elizabeth saw it in his eyes, though. Little did William know that the jealousy he was so ashamed of, and his success in controlling it, was helping his suit considerably, as was the relief he had no qualms about showing every time she paid the slightest bit of attention to him. Instinctively,

Elizabeth reassured him with subtle looks and smiles only for him and stolen touches in the form of hands brushing when a cup or book was passed between them. If Georgiana noticed any of this, she acted as if she had not.

Mr. Smythe finally gave William permission to leave his room on the last day that the Bennets would be at Pemberley. As he headed downstairs to meet the family in the drawing room, he heard Elizabeth's laugh coming from the stairwell and smiled. As he arrived at the top of the stairs, James had just begun to descend with Elizabeth in his arms. A dark look passed across William's face, and his hand gripped the banister so tightly that Elizabeth could hear the wood creak. Her eyes locked with his, and he willed her to look only at him. As soon as Elizabeth reached the bottom, she said something to James that William could not hear. James returned her to her feet and stepped away against the wall. She waited there for William to descend, which he did without breaking their gaze. When William was beside Elizabeth, he extended his arm, she took it, and they walked toward the drawing room to go meet Georgiana.

Out of James's hearing, Elizabeth whispered, "It is not his fault, William. Your father assigned James to help me because James is his most *trusted* footman."

He stopped and leaned his back against the wall with his eyes closed. She could see his jaw muscles clenching as he struggled to control his temper and took a deep breath to calm himself. He then admitted, "I do not want you to leave me, Elizabeth. If your ankle must be injured, *I* want to be the man to carry you everywhere! I want you in *my* arms. I *never* want to see another man touch you again."

She reached up and laid her hand on his cheek; his eyes flew open and met hers… and he gasped at what he saw there. "I do not *wish* to be touched by any man other than you, William… ever."

His eyes glistened suspiciously from the light of a candle a few feet away, and he took another deep, shaky breath. "I love you, Elizabeth. Please tell me that you will marry me."

"I love you, my William, and would be most honored to become your wife."

He leaned in and kissed her gently before whispering, "My Elizabeth ..." and slow smiles spread across their lips as he turned them to continue toward the drawing room.

Georgiana noticed they were each caught in a sort of dream-like state before luncheon was served. Once they were in the dining room, they both made more of an effort to converse with Georgiana, and after luncheon they went to the music room, as was the ladies' routine, but this time, he followed. William was entranced by Elizabeth's playing and singing, and Georgiana had no doubt in her mind that they were in love. She wondered if Elizabeth was soon to become her sister.

Before dinner, the entire party was assembled together for the first time in many weeks. William brought down some books that he had bought in Italy and began to tell them all about his trip. Elizabeth especially was interested in seeing his drawings again and expressed an interest in seeing Italy herself one day. With a look, William promised her she would, an assurance which was not missed by either of the older gentlemen—nor were any of the other looks exchanged by the lovers unnoticed. After dinner, surprising William, his father called for separating.

Once the gentlemen were settled, Mr. Bennet said, "From what I have seen tonight, I take it my Elizabeth has accepted your proposal?"

William could not hide his shocked expression for a few moments before he schooled his features. He cleared his throat and said, "Yes, sir. I was going to ask for a few minutes of your time tonight..."

"That will not be necessary. Your father and I have already discussed this possibility and have devised a plan."

William felt as if his whole world was falling apart. "A plan, Mr. Bennet? Father?"

They had previously discussed, and hoped, that if Mr. Darcy led this conversation, William might listen more carefully. "William, there are several reasons why we think it too soon to discuss a betrothal between you and Miss Elizabeth. The first being her age... she is but sixteen."

"Mother was married at seventeen, and Elizabeth mentioned that her mother was a bride at seventeen as well."

Mr. Darcy looked at Mr. Bennet for confirmation, and Mr. Bennet nodded. Mr. Darcy continued, "Yes, that is true, but Elizabeth will not turn seventeen until the thirtieth day of May of next year. We think it would be better if you separated until then."

"But… well then, may we become betrothed *now* and have a long engagement?"

"Miss Elizabeth has only just come out. Mr. Bennet would like her to have one season without any obligations restraining her from meeting other gentlemen. He wants to be certain that she has not been influenced while spending time here at Pemberley by… materialistic concerns."

"Do you honestly think her materialistic? Do we speak of the same *Elizabeth?*" William paused for a moment before continuing, "You both know very well that Elizabeth is much more mature than her age implies and has a better understanding than most *men* twice her age! You do not trust that she knows her own mind?" Turning again to his father he said, "Or is it that *you* do not trust your son's judgment and object to my choice, Father?"

"We trust both of you to make the correct decision, but you must also trust that Mr. Bennet has his daughter's best interests in mind. We can plan a reunion when Miss Elizabeth turns seventeen, and *if* you both still feel the same way about each other, you can ask her again at that time."

William's tone reflected his pain as he said, "*If* we feel the same way? Father, I *love* her! I have always had a special feeling for her, well beyond friendship. I believe my heart was just waiting for her to be old enough for it to blossom into love, but now that it *has,* I do not wish to be separated from her. If she did not care for me, I could understand this plan, but I have been fortunate enough to gain her love! *That* is not going to change no matter how much time and distance you put between us and no matter how many men you force her to accommodate as dance partners; I do not believe her to be as inconstant as you both obviously do! Why would you wish to put us both through a separation for eight months with no promise of a future together, not allowing us to so much as visit? Without an engagement, we would not even have the benefit of hearing a *word* from each other in all that time. If you want us to wait to marry, I will wait as long as you wish, but I cannot understand why you would have us wait for an engagement."

William turned to Mr. Bennet. "Have I done something to make you feel I am not a good enough match for your daughter, Mr. Bennet? Are you *hoping* that she will change her mind?" The last was said with such pain in his eyes that Mr. Bennet almost gave in. He did not want the boy to misunderstand him, but Mr. Bennet did not have a chance to respond.

"That is *enough*, William! Mr. Bennet will *not* give his consent to the marriage at this time, and therefore, neither will I. Since Elizabeth is not yet of age, you both will have to abide by *his* wishes in this matter! We *will* honor Mr. Bennet's wish that Elizabeth will have her season to be sure of her decision. You will spend that time preparing to become master of Pemberley. Time will pass quickly enough."

Too overwhelmed with emotion to speak lest he lose control, William left for his chambers.

~%~

The young man paced his rooms until he could no longer stand the infernal waiting. William knew that it was wrong in the eyes of society, but he felt that he *must* go speak to Elizabeth! She was leaving in the morning, and he would not see her again for eight months. That this was their only chance made him despair! As he looked down the hall toward his father's room he thought, *"You have made me desperate! I would not disregard propriety in such a manner if not for this* **plan***!"*

He walked into the corridor and quietly made his way to the guest wing, barely tapping on the door to what he hoped was Elizabeth's chamber. Georgiana had told him that she had been placed in the blue room, and as he waited for her to answer, he prayed that his sister had been correct.

Elizabeth opened the door and whispered, "William!" She stepped aside to let him pass through, and then looked both ways down the corridor before closing—and locking—the door. Once the door was closed, she placed her hand on his cheek and caressed his skin. "What has happened, my love? You do not look well at all."

She looked very well indeed. She was absolutely beautiful, her hair down, clad only in a nightgown and a thin robe. She truly was an angel! He gathered her to him and pulled her closer against him, lowering his face into her hair and allowing her heavenly scent and the feel of her body pressed against his to overtake his senses. *"This is home! This is where I belong!"*

he thought. *"How will I survive eight months without her?"* Aloud he said, "If only my other arm were healed so that I could hold you properly!"

She pulled away slightly and looked into his eyes, her face showing her concern, "Tell me, my love. What troubles you so?"

"Elizabeth, I... what will you think of me? I apologize for having the presumption of coming to your room, and normally I would not have done so, but this will be the only opportunity we will have to talk for a very long time. I could not bear to have you leave without spending time with you once more." He looked into her eyes wishing he could lose himself within them as he had done earlier in the day, but he needed to tell her so many things. "Neither of our fathers will even consider giving their consent to our engagement until your birthday. My heart is battling with my mind— one is telling me to beg you to come away with me this moment for Scotland, but the other would never allow it. I *know* that neither of us would ever feel comfortable with what we had done if we did not honor their wishes. But when I think about how we will not be allowed to contact each other in any way until you are seventeen—never to see each other, not even letters—I do not know how I will get through it."

Elizabeth was stunned. She knew that her father would never force her to marry anyone she did not *want* to marry, but she had never thought that he would prevent her from seeing the man she *had* chosen. "What were their reasons?"

She could feel his whole body stiffen before he said, "Your father wants for you to have a season in order to have the opportunity to meet other men before making a decision about whether you really wish to marry me or not. That means he wants you to feel free to dance, converse, laugh, walk out, and flirt with other men without any prior attachments." He closed his eyes. "*I* have not even danced with you." He was quiet for a few moments, trying to collect himself before continuing, "I think I will go quite mad over the next few months knowing that you will be doing those things, Elizabeth. But since letting you go temporarily is the only path currently available to attain their approval, I will find a way through it... somehow."

He looked so dejected as his voice dropped to a whisper that her heart almost broke. "I do not know what it is about me that your father finds so objectionable." She wanted to say something, but she instinctively felt he had more he needed to say before she spoke. She felt him shudder before saying, "I want you to be happy above all things, even if that means I cannot have you. Elizabeth... do *you* feel that I pressured you into this decision? That you were not ready, or really able to make the choice to marry me? Do *you* feel as if you did not truly make an informed decision or that you were rushed?"

He looked at her with such pain in his eyes and seemed so vulnerable that she laid her hand on his cheek to reassure him with her touch. He leaned into it a little and looked deeply into her eyes as she answered him, "My William, I have not felt pressured by you in any manner; you only showed me in no uncertain way that you were absolutely sure that I was your choice, no matter what I said to you. You never made me feel that I needed to rush—you accepted my delays in answering without question. You have been completely honest and have never hidden anything from me.

"I can understand my father's wishes a little better than you can, I think. The only reason *I* delayed my acceptance was that I wished *you* to be certain of your choice in me. I could not believe that a man such as you would choose someone like *me* when you could have your choice of any beautiful, accomplished, elegant, and sophisticated woman of the *ton*. I was afraid that by assisting you when you were injured that you might have confused gratitude with love, and I wanted to make certain that this was not the case… only because I wished *you* happy; I did not wish to eventually make you miserable by selfishly accepting you." She arched her brow before saying, "I have seen marriages like that—I live daily with the consequences of a marriage like that. I did not wish to end up like my parents, William, with my father, on a daily basis, regretting his decision to apply for my mother's hand, unable to respect her, unwilling even to spend time in the same room with her when it is not absolutely necessary.

"With time, I recognized the qualities of my character that you enjoyed the most when you spent time with me were the very same qualities that make me *different* from the ladies of the *ton*. That being the case, I could see that if you had married a lady from the *ton*, you would be just as unhappy and dissatisfied as is my father with my mother." Her tone turned playful as she added, "And so I decided to save you from that fate and accept you!"

"Knowing this about your parents does make your father's wishes a little easier to understand. I can see why he would not want his fate for you, Elizabeth. You are too precious to be made to live an unhappy life." He looked down at their hands that were entwined between them. "However, it does not cause me to *like* this plan of his, and knowing his reasoning will not make our time apart pass any more quickly…or more easily."

"William, do you doubt my acceptance of your offer or fear that I do not really love you? Did you not believe me when I said that I would never wish for another man to touch me? Do you not trust me?"

"I can see in your eyes that you love me, Elizabeth, and I *know* it deep within me." He smiled. "It is why I was so persistent." His expression turning serious again, he said, "I do trust *you*... it is the men with whom you will be dancing and walking out that I do *not* trust. I will not be there to protect you, and you will not have the public acknowledgement of our betrothal to protect you in my absence." She saw his jaw muscles working before he said, "Thoughts plague me that other men will have the opportunity to brush against you while they dance with you, to feel your hand on their arm as they escort you, or to try to steal a kiss while they walk with you... or that they will try things even worse."

She smiled widely, "Ah, and do you think that growing up as a hoyden did not have *some* benefits toward learning how to defend myself against unwanted advances, then? I can belay your fears and tell you that it most certainly did—mostly by accident..." she blushed, "but then as we got older... well I think that when John Lucas returned home from school last summer, he was taken very much by surprise at certain... shall we say, *developments* that had taken place while he was away." She blushed and laughed when William's eyes were drawn to those shapely developments, and he then blushed at being caught. "Being a very protective older brother to Charlotte and feeling as if I were his sister, he taught us a few extra additional tricks. I hope you do not mind but because I believe that *no* woman should ever be put into the position of feeling helpless, I have even had the audacity to show what I have learned to Georgiana. If my assurances do not make you feel comfortable enough, sir, I suggest that *you* teach me how to defend myself."

He responded in the same playful tone of voice that she had used, "A good teacher first reviews what his student already knows. Tell me what you would do if someone did this..." and he kissed her. Truly he was not expecting her to react to his stolen kiss, and so it took him by surprise when her hands wrapped around his neck to pull him closer to her, and she continued to kiss him. He could not resist her advances, nor did he want to, and he slowly deepened the kiss until they had to break apart for lack of breath. He leaned his forehead against hers and whispered, "Though I do not mind for myself, if *that* is how you would 'defend' yourself, Elizabeth, it is not at all encouraging to me."

She smiled and whispered, "My defenses are only for *unwanted* advances, my William. *Your* advances are most welcome."

In an attempt to maintain his control long enough to teach her how to protect herself, he changed the subject. "Tell me what you would do if the advances *were* unwanted, or I shall not know where your education is lacking and therefore, cannot teach you anything new."

She moved closer to him, brushing his lips with hers while saying, "Oh, but I think you are teaching me quite a bit that is new, William."

His head was swimming at her closeness and her scent; his lips were tingling with the feel of hers being brushed against them… but the fear was still nagging at him. "Please, my love, I cannot be easy until I know that you are safe when you are apart from me."

Her eyebrow arched, and she whispered, "Perhaps a slap."

"And what about this?" he nuzzled her neck and began to trail feather kisses along it, tasting her sweet skin along the way.

"Mmmmmm…"

"What would you do?" he whispered in her ear, causing her to shiver with pleasure.

"Will you do that again if I tell you?" she rejoined, one eyebrow seductively raised.

He chuckled lightly into her ear then whispered huskily, "I would be very happy to reward you for the correct answer."

His whisper caused her to shiver again, and she became lost in all the sensations that were consuming her ability to think.

"Elizabeth?"

"Oh, um… knee." He rewarded her as promised.

"And this?" his hand caressed her waist as it inched higher, until his thumb grazed the side of one of her *developments*.

She gasped and pulled his head closer for another kiss, but he pulled back a fraction of an inch… he would not submit until she answered. In a voice filled with desire, she said, "Pull the middle finger backwards." She was rewarded for her answer.

After a few moments, a soft, sensual moan escaped her while she instinctively pressed herself against his hips. His moan matched hers, and then suddenly he pulled back and turned away from her.

Taking several minutes to compose himself, he finally said, "Elizabeth, you do realize that you are probably in a more dangerous situation at the moment than you have ever been in before, particularly if we continue in this manner… with you… looking at me like that… and especially in your bed chamber?"

"I am not afraid of you, William."

"I am very glad of that, but if we continue, perhaps you should be. You cannot realize how tempting you are to me in *any* situation, but right now the temptation is tenfold, and I am very close to losing all control. I have never wanted anything more than to have you as my wife, Elizabeth, and especially at this moment, to *make* you my wife. I do not want to do anything to hurt you; I would regret it the rest of my life. I *should* quit your room immediately, and if you were not leaving in the morning I would— but I cannot bear to relinquish the time we have left! Please… just talk to me for a while."

He turned toward her to say the last, and his heart wrenched when he saw her face was tearstained, her eyes averted to the floor. "Elizabeth?"

"I apologize, Mr. Darcy… I – I did not mean to act in such a wanton manner. I am ashamed of myself."

"Mr. Darcy? No longer 'my William'? What have I done?" He stepped closer to her and dried her tears with his caresses. "Please, my sweet Elizabeth… I did not mean to make you feel as if you should be ashamed of your actions. It is only that I never wanted to stop, and I knew that I *had* to just then or I would not have until…"

He closed his eyes and sighed. *"How do I explain this?"* he thought, then opened his eyes and said aloud, "I never wish for you to be ashamed to express what you are feeling or thinking to me… or *with* me—not ever. You are the most amazing person I have ever met, and I would never wish to stifle any reaction you may have or make you feel as if you should suppress... anything—any thought, any feeling, any action—when we are alone. But trust me if I say we must stop when we are physically expressing ourselves *before* we are married. There are certain things that will cause the *man* in me to overtake the gentleman who wants to protect you... and the way you moved just then was one of them! What you did... it felt *too* good to me before we are wed, Elizabeth."

"And after we are wed?"

"Believe me when I say that I will *never* tell you we must stop *after* we are married." He pulled her into an embrace and silently cursed his injured arm once again for preventing him from holding her properly. After a minute or two he asked, "Do you understand all that I have said?"

"Yes, I think I do."

"Other men do not love you the way I do, Elizabeth, and they will not feel the need to protect you. The man in them will *not* stop, even without any encouragement. That is why we were speaking of your learning how to defend yourself."

Elizabeth nodded and told him what other defenses she knew of. Some he was quite surprised she was aware of, and some even *he* did not know... but then she explained that she used to wrestle with the boys.

"Good G-d, Elizabeth! Do not tell me such things! You *wrestled* with the boys in your neighborhood? Thoughts like that will prey on my mind while we are apart, and I will come to Hertfordshire and challenge every male that lives within ten miles of Longbourn!"

She tried not to laugh. "William, at the time I wrestled with them they were mere boys. My physical attributes were not that different from a boy's and neither was my behavior! None of them thought of me as a girl at all, which is *why* John Lucas was so surprised when he came home from school that summer."

"And all these 'mere boys' are now *men* who *do* think of you as a *woman!*"

"Right, they now all think of me more along the lines of a sister, not truly a woman." She saw a distraction was necessary. "By the by, I fence."

"You fence?"

"Yes, do you?"

"I am a gentleman, madam. All gentleman fence!" he said with mock insult. "And just how well do you fence?"

"I usually thrash everyone that I ever challenge to a match."

He looked at her doubtfully. "I would think that not many men would accept that challenge, Elizabeth."

"They do before I am through teasing them about being afraid that they might be defeated by a girl, sir."

He laughed. "And then you go about besting them! You are cruel."

"It serves them right for teasing me about fencing's being a man's sport."

"So you play chess, wrestle, and fence. What other *male sports* will I have the pleasure of passing the time playing with you once we are married?"

"No, I will not give *all* my secrets away. You will have to learn some of them when the time comes."

He smiled, "It seems we will not be bored during the long winters in the north."

"Of that, I have no doubt," she said while winding her arms around his waist and pulling herself against him. The position reminded him of when they were in the woods and the longing he had felt to repeat it every time he lay down to go to sleep. *'I can do this without losing control; I know I can!'*

"Elizabeth? Tell me if I am too bold. May I ask if I can hold you the way we did to stay warm in the woods? I…"

"I have often longed for you to hold me that way again, William. I tried snuggling with a pillow—but it was not the same." She smiled playfully.

"I am happy to hear that I cannot be replaced by a mere pillow!"

Taking his hand, she walked over to the bed. He got onto the bed, awkward as it was with his arm in a sling, and pulled the covers back. She slipped in, and then he covered her up again. "Why do you not get under the covers with me?"

"I cannot trust myself, Elizabeth."

"You will be cold," she said.

"Actually, I am feeling rather warm at the moment," he answered, but he could tell she would not be easy, so he pulled the counterpane from the other side of the bed and covered himself with it.

She settled in beside him with her head on his chest. "I love listening to your heartbeat." After a few minutes, she looked up into his eyes and said, "William… my heart is completely yours, my love. Would you like to hear it?"

"I can do this without ravishing her! I can!" he thought and nodded. They repositioned themselves, and she placed his head on her chest, only the thin cloth of her nightdress separating his lips from her skin. His hand slipped between her body and the mattress. Her breath was quick and her heart was beating as wildly as he felt his was. Closing his eyes so as not to be tempted any further than he already was, he was thankful that his other hand was bound to his chest because he knew if it had not been, there would be nothing to stop it from exploring her body instead. Her right hand explored the solid muscles of his back and shoulders as her left played with his hair. *"This is heaven!"* He reveled in all the sensations of holding her this way as he listened to her heart and breathing gradually slow to a normal pace. Her hands slowed their ministrations, eventually stopping, and her breathing became deeper, and he knew she had fallen asleep. *"She loves me! Everything will be all right."* Before long, listening to the even rhythms of her slumber lulled him to join her.

A few hours later, William awakened, and his first thought was, *"Why is the bed shaking?"* He took a deep breath and was filled with lavender scent and, at the same time, he felt a hand rake through his hair and an arm tighten around his shoulders. He whispered, "Elizabeth!" Lifting his head to look at her, he found Elizabeth crying.

"I did not mean to wake you."

"What is it, my love? Are you upset because I fell asleep? I did not mean to…"

"No!" she interrupted, "it was truly wonderful to wake with you..." She began to sob uncontrollably and could no longer speak.

He shifted onto his back. His good arm had been beneath her all this time, and he pulled her to him. She clung to him as if her life depended on never parting from him—and then he knew what this was about. It was almost morning, and he would have to leave her room very soon before the servants began their day... and then she would go home. He pulled her even closer, his eyes prickling with his own repressed tears. "It is not forever."

"What if they do not give consent in eight months?"

"If they go back on their word, I *will* take you to Scotland, Elizabeth, and I would feel no remorse about it."

"Do you promise, William?"

He lifted her chin so that she was looking directly into his eyes. "Elizabeth, I promise you that I will marry you in eight months as long as you still wish it. In my heart we are already betrothed, consent or not! We belong to each other. If for some reason you change your mind..." he swallowed hard to clear the tightness that had formed in his throat, "I will not stand in your way. But know this—my heart will always be yours, no matter what happens. I will always love you, Elizabeth."

"I will not change my mind! You *must* stop thinking that way." She propped herself on her elbow, her hand cupping his cheek. "I promise you that I will always love you, William. Do not ever doubt it!"

She could feel his jaw muscles working under her fingers as he was fighting back his tears. He almost sobbed, "I do not know how I will get through the next eight months without even a word from you."

Elizabeth blinked a few times before saying, "Georgiana made me promise to correspond with her while we were in the presence of both our fathers yesterday. Ask her to read you the letters. I will find a way to send you messages in what I say to her."

He nodded. "I will tell her to pass along my regards to you in every letter. Know that when I say those words, I am truly saying that I love you, and that I miss you. I miss you already, Elizabeth." His hand caressed the tears from her face, his thumb tracing her lips as she leaned over to kiss him.

This kiss was filled with all the passion that would be denied for months to come. The clock on the mantle chimed the hour and brought them back to reality before things went too far. He looked to the window and saw the first light of dawn breaking over the horizon. "I must go. If someone should see me leaving your room…"

They stared into each other's eyes for a few moments, and they knew their thoughts were the same. Yes, if he was caught in her room, they would *have* to marry! It was so tempting. He closed his eyes as she said, "We both know we should not begin our life together that way, William." She waited for him to open his eyes again. His breath hitched at the look in her eyes as she said, "Besides, I would actually wish to *experience* becoming your wife before being accused of having done so."

"We have done enough here tonight to be forced to marry, even if we have not… but you are correct. I would like to gain consent because your father *approves* of me, not because he is afraid of the consequences if we do not marry."

He pulled the covers off her, and she got out of bed. She giggled a little as he squirmed his way over to the edge and sat up. "It is not easy getting out of bed with only one arm," he said defensively but then chuckled. "I feel foolish even when I am alone; I can only imagine what I *look* like doing that!"

She stepped forward, and they were the same height for once. She wrapped her arms around him and kissed him lightly. "I really should leave, Elizabeth," he said between kisses.

"I need more memories of your kisses to last the next few months, William," she said. He was only too happy to comply, pulling her onto his lap.

"I thought you said you had to leave, but are you not getting comfortable again?" She laughed as he tickled her neck with his lips.

"*I* want to remember kissing you *this* way, my love. How I love your laugh! I love the thousand different lights in your eyes that reflect what you are thinking, but most of all, I love the way you look only at me." His eyes drank in the sight of her, memorizing every inch of her face, and then he nuzzled his face into her hair, "And your scent! I think I will have lavender in my room at all times from this moment on." The clock chimed the half hour, and he pulled her closer for a moment. Then he helped her to her feet.

She walked over to the dressing table, which had been mostly packed except for a few items. Opening a drawer she removed a handkerchief and took a vial out of the reticule she had planned to take with her in the coach. "I embroidered this handkerchief myself, here at Pemberley." She poured several drops of liquid from the vial onto the handkerchief and then handed it to him.

He held it to his face and inhaled, closing his eyes. "Not quite the same, but it will have to do. Thank you." He ran his thumb over the embroidery and smiled. "Your skills are improving."

"Georgiana is a good teacher. I truly love her as a sister, William."

"I think she feels the same toward you. I am glad."

He took her hand, and they walked toward the door. As they neared it, they stopped, facing each other.

"I do not want to go."

"I do not want you to go."

She kissed him once more and then opened the door, looking out to make certain the hall was clear. She turned back to him, and he whispered, "I love you," before walking out into the hall.

She could not watch him walk away; she knew she would run after him, so she closed the door and leaned against it trying to hold back her tears.

Chapter 7

Mr. Bennet had arisen early, too restless to stay abed, and decided to go to the library before breaking his fast. As he opened his door, he stopped short upon seeing Elizabeth's door closing and William walking away from it. Mr. Bennet cleared his throat loudly.

William stopped, exhaled sharply, and closed his eyes in disbelief. *"Good G-d! What do I do now?"* He turned around slowly and faced a decidedly unhappy Mr. Bennet. "Good morning, Mr. Bennet."

"Perhaps it was for *you*, but I have other feelings on the matter." He motioned toward his open door and said, "You *will* join me in my chambers—now." William squared his shoulders and walked past him into the room. Mr. Bennet closed the door, then took a few steps into the room and crossed his arms over his chest, waiting.

"Sir, I know how it must seem to you, but that is *not* what happened."

"I should demand that you marry her immediately!" Mr. Bennet growled, and for some reason he was surprised when his harsh tone was met with a wide smile from William.

"Mr. Bennet, I would be a very happy man if you did. It is *not* my choice to wait, sir, nor is it Miss Elizabeth's. It is yours, only yours."

"You say you did not... then why were you in her bedchamber?"

"I went to explain your decision to Miss Elizabeth and to assure her that I *will* wait for her. I also wished to say goodbye until we meet again in May. If she were not leaving with you this very morning, I would have found some appropriate time during the day to speak privately with her, but that is not the case, sir."

"You did not trust that I would allow the two of you a few moments of privacy this morning?"

"Can you not see why I would doubt it, sir? You will not allow us to visit each other for eight months, and by not allowing us to become engaged, you are, in essence, forbidding us to even *write* to each other. The likelihood of your also forbidding us to speak to each other this morning was too great. I could not depend upon your explaining what was in my heart to the woman I love with every fiber of my being when you have said that you *expect* me to change my mind over the next few months. I have no reason to think that you even believe that I feel the way I do about Miss Elizabeth. I cannot bear to think about the years ahead without having her beside me, sir, and I simply could not risk having her leave Pemberley possibly thinking that I had reneged on my offer and abandoned her. I had to be certain that she understands exactly how I feel beyond any doubt and that the delay is *not* of my choosing."

*"I have given him the impression that I do not approve of **him**! Perhaps I have **not** taken his feelings for Elizabeth seriously enough?"* Mr. Bennet thought as he searched William's eyes. *"Am I doing wrong by both of them by separating them now?"*

Mr. Bennet nodded and said, "William, I have nothing against *you* as a match for my Lizzy. I do not wish to risk that she has been charmed into thinking that this is the perfect life. I am worried that she has been influenced by the grandeur of Pemberley and the reputation of the Darcy name. This has all happened very quickly; I cannot help but think that Lizzy has been swept off her feet by a handsome prince as if she were living in a fairy tale! Whether you are perfect for each other or not, life is *not* a fairy tale, as I have daily proof! I want to give her time to reflect upon her choice and, in the meantime, to meet other young men so that she can compare her feelings for you to her feelings for them in order that she can be *certain* that she knows what she wants before entering into an engagement." He hesitated for a few moments before continuing, "You may have ten minutes alone to say goodbye to Elizabeth before we leave this morning."

William smiled. "Thank you, Mr. Bennet."

"Will you assure me that there will be no... *consequences* of this assignation from which you have just come?"

"Sir, I give you my word. Even if I *were* the type of man to do such a thing, which I am *not*, I assure you, I love and respect Elizabeth too much to dishonor her in such a way," he said with conviction, and then thought, *"I am very glad he did not ask just how long I was in her room and what exactly we* **did** *do!"*

"No one else knows you were in her bedchamber?"

"No, sir."

"Very well, then. I will see you downstairs for breakfast," Mr. Bennet said.

"Thank you, sir." William bowed before leaving the room.

~%~

After seeing that the last of her things were being packed, Elizabeth made her way to the breakfast room. Upon entering the room, she noticed a decided tension between William and her father. The two gentlemen were sitting across from each other on either side of Mr. Darcy, who was at the head of the table. Georgiana was sitting next to William, and Elizabeth felt somewhat relieved that she did not need to choose a seat beside only one of the men she loved.

Elizabeth and Mr. Darcy assumed the disquiet they felt emanating from the two was a result of the refused consent of William's proposal. Elizabeth attempted to catch William's eye to provide some comfort and was a bit concerned when she could not.

In the meantime, William was concentrating on his own meal with such careful consideration that it seemed that he was attempting *not* to look directly at Elizabeth. In truth, he *was* avoiding her eyes, afraid that if he did look at her, he would make the remainder of the room aware that his feelings for Elizabeth had, in fact, become even stronger after the intimate time they had spent together during his protracted stay in her room.

Georgiana, knowing nothing at all of what had passed since dinner the previous night, seemed quite uncomfortable and directed confused looks at all of the other occupants of the room, watching them carefully for some clue as to what had occurred to put such a somber mood on their usually lively company. In the end, she decided the cause must be the anticipated gloom that would descend with the Bennets' imminent departure, and in an attempt to break the silence that accompanied their breaking of their fast, Georgiana *again* extracted a promise from Elizabeth that she would correspond with her. "I will write to you as soon as you leave and post it so that you will have a letter waiting for you when you arrive at Longbourn, Lizzy!"

"That would be lovely, Georgiana. I will write the day we arrive at Longbourn so that you will know that we are safely at home. It should take no more than three days for the post between Pemberley and Longbourn, so we can each have a letter a week. You must tell me all about your studies in detail, and we can discuss whatever book you are currently reading. Do not be surprised if I write a letter or two in French, so you must be diligent at your French lessons with Mrs. Brooks! I am certain she would help you with any words you cannot translate or understand from their context. And please do not fail to give me news of your family." Elizabeth smiled brightly at Georgiana, hoping to hear much about her brother in her letters as well.

After her speech, William's eyes became caught by Elizabeth's gaze. They held so much affection that he could not look away until Mr. Bennet cleared his throat. Glancing at Mr. Bennet, William found himself on the receiving end of a stern look, and he reluctantly turned his attention to eating his meal in as dignified a way as one *could* when one had only one hand to accomplish this task.

After a few minutes and several attempts by Mr. Darcy and Georgiana to introduce topics of conversation, Mr. Bennet excused himself, stating that he must make certain his valet had finished packing his trunks. The eldest and youngest Darcys also excused themselves, making certain Elizabeth understood that she would see them outside when the coach was ready to depart.

"Miss Elizabeth, I have found the book we had discussed. If you would care to view it before you leave this morning, this is probably the best time. It is in the library," William said for the benefit of any servants who might be overhearing the conversation.

"Yes, I would like that very much; I thank you, sir." He helped her with her chair, and the two removed to the library.

~%~

Why William was so anxious, even he did not understand, but the fact of the matter was that he was more than a little timorous. That he must tell Elizabeth of his meeting with her father earlier caused a feeling of unease… but no, *this* intense feeling had begun the moment he had retrieved his mother's ring from its place in his father's vault—the ring that had symbolized the lasting bond of the betrothals of the past five generations of Darcys. His fear did not stem from the offering, for he had never felt more certain of anything in his life than that Elizabeth was the only woman who could ever become the next Mrs. Darcy. It was that she might *not* accept it that caused his nerves to come undone.

Though he had been fully truthful when he told his father and Mr. Bennet that he had absolute confidence that Elizabeth knew her own mind, that she loved him, and that the separation would not make a bit of difference in their feelings for each other, in actuality he wondered if she would accept the ring *against* her father's wishes.

Many promises had been made between them, and she had said that it would not make any difference to her whether the betrothal was publicly acknowledged or known only between themselves for now—but the acceptance of this ring made it all *permanent* in his mind—as permanent as if a formal contract had been signed. It was of vital importance to him that she accept the ring so that he could achieve some peace of mind over the next eight long months when they would be apart.

So, as he led Elizabeth into the library, William found himself in an extremely troubled state of mind. He followed her into the room, glancing around to ensure that they were alone and then took the precaution of locking the door behind him so they would not be disturbed.

Elizabeth rushed toward him and into his welcoming embrace. He pulled her closer and buried his face in her hair, taking a deep breath—her scent and the feel of her body pressing against his were a balm to his tortured soul.

"There is something of which I must make you aware, my love. Your father gave us permission to say goodbye this morning. I – I came upon him in the hall as I left your bedchamber."

She gasped and looked up into his eyes. "What happened? Did he know…?"

"Yes, he saw your door close. I think he believed me when I told him… that your virtue was not compromised. I do not think he would have allowed us this time alone if he had not. I explained to him why I was there, that since he did not approve of me, I could not trust that he would allow you to speak to me privately before you left…" he took a deep, trembling breath. "I know what you told me, Elizabeth, but after what *he* had said to me last night, I could not help but feel that he does not approve of me as a partner for someone as amazing as you are. Not that I disagree—I am *not* worthy of you, my love—but since I *have* gained your love, I will not cast it away.

"I love you so much, Elizabeth. I do not know what I would do without you. Which is why I wish to give you this." He took the ring from his pocket and continued, "This ring has been handed down through the Darcy line for many generations. It is the ring that is always used to seal the betrothal with the next mistress of Pemberley. My mother wore it every day of her betrothal and subsequent marriage to my father, and I would like you to wear it every day of ours. I must ask you again—properly this time…" He knelt before her taking her hand in his, so much emotion shining from his eyes that she felt as though she could not breathe. "Elizabeth Bennet, I love you with all of my heart and all of my soul. Will you agree to spend your life by my side as my friend, my partner, my lover—my wife?"

Her eyes were filled with tears as she said, "Fitzwilliam Darcy, I have always been and always will be your friend; I would be honored to be your partner in every way. You already are my only love, and I can think of nothing I wish for more in this life than to become your wife."

They both smiled brightly—William displaying the dimples she loved dearly, and the light of love he treasured shining from Elizabeth's eyes. William slipped the ring onto Elizabeth's finger. "Oh, it is beautiful, William! I thank you for this wonderful gift! I only wish I had a token to give to you."

"I would very much like to have a lock of your hair, my love. A part of you to keep close to me while we are apart would make me very happy."

"I would be very happy to part with a lock of my hair for this purpose, William. Do you have scissors at hand?"

"Yes, there are some in the drawer just here." He began to walk in that direction, but then turned back to her and said, "Elizabeth, I know you cannot wear the ring, but may I ask… will you keep it on your person at all times? It would mean a great deal to me if you did."

"I already have a plan in mind to do just that. Do you see this chain I wear in addition to the one with my cross on it? The chain was inherited from my Grandmother Bennet. It is a very long chain, and for some reason the longer portion always ends up inside my gown no matter what I have tried to keep it on the outside." His look showed that he had definitely noticed the chain disappearing under the neckline of her gown, always pulling his eyes downward and setting his imagination afire. She blushed at the intensity of his expression, smiled, and continued, "I can place the ring on Grandmother Bennet's chain. When I remove the necklace at night, I will wear the ring on my finger. Nobody will notice the addition—only we two will know that I am wearing your ring always next to my heart. The only exception is that Mama will not allow me to wear the chain for formal events for she says it is not fine enough. But I will find a way to continue to wear it near my heart, William… until the day I can wear it openly on my hand."

His eyes shone a little too much to hide the fact that they had filled with tears, and his smile told her that he was very pleased with her plan. He turned back to the drawer and removed the scissors, returning quickly to her side.

"Will you help me take this ribbon from my hair? Poor Hanna worked so hard putting it in, but I think you will need something to tie the lock of hair so that it does not scatter."

"Yes, and since I am such a sentimental fool, a ribbon from your hair would be cherished by me as well." She got up on her toes and brushed her lips against his, then turned, reaching for the ribbon. As he helped her remove the ribbon, William examined each long curl of her hair thoroughly before declaring, "I think I will take this mischievous and most fortunate curl here, as I have spent much time observing and admiring it. It is very much like you in some ways: it is beautiful, as are all your locks; it is 'stubbornly independent,' as you are so fond of describing yourself as being, always wishing to escape the pins and go its own way even when it is most carefully arranged; it does not wish to conform to what the others are convinced should be the correct thing to do; and it is constantly tempting my hand to reach out and touch it every time I see it. This curl is also the most fortunate of all because, when it does escape, its placement allows it to caress your soft skin, and sometimes the way it bounces makes it seem as if it is kissing the curve of your neck—making me quite jealous for the liberties it takes. Yes, I would wish to have this curl... with your permission, of course, madam?"

Elizabeth was nearly giggling when she agreed, and with her help, William carefully snipped the lock off. She tied it and then folded it into the handkerchief she had given him earlier. He put it away in the pocket over *his* heart and pulled her into his embrace again. First tenderly caressing the spot on her neck where the curl had been, he leaned down to kiss it, tasting the sweet, delicate skin in the place where he had seen the curl doing the same on countless occasions. Finally, he laid his cheek against it while taking a long breath, inhaling her scent deeply, and then moved to whisper her name in her ear.

She turned to kiss his lips softly, and they deepened the kiss slowly until he needed to end it, pulling away to trail more tender kisses across her cheeks and neck, returning to her ear again.

He was surprised when she turned her face toward him and did the same to him, trailing her silky lips across his jaw line and cheeks, tasting his skin with her velvety tongue and running it along his neck where the cravat did not cover his skin. Avoiding his lips, she eventually ended her journey at his ear and took his earlobe into her mouth, taking it between her teeth and suckling it. He gasped when she whispered his name.

William could not trust himself after such a physical declaration of her love, and told her, his voice full of regret, "Ohhhh, Elizabeth! We must stop now, my love. The gentleman in me must protect you from the man."

There was no doubt in William's mind that Elizabeth had recovered from her shyness of the night before as he pulled back and looked into her eyes—the look there was so different than was the one when he had stopped them the last time. Now there was a mixture of love, longing, mischievousness, and pleasure... but suddenly these were joined by sadness, and she rested her head on his chest, listening to his heart beating, every beat echoing his love for her.

"I love you, my William, so very much. I do not wish to leave you."

"I do not want you to go, and if you *must* go, I wish it were on different terms. I also do hope your father will approve of me eventually. I do not know how he can learn to like me if I never have a chance to see him. Elizabeth, I will not renege on my promise, but I also do *not* want to go against his wishes. I would rather not be forced to keep my promise of taking you to Scotland if he does not approve of me once you are seventeen."

"William, he has always been very impressed by you and thought very highly, even fondly, of you."

"That was *before* his beloved daughter fell in love with me, my heart. The world is a very different place to me now that you love me, and I cannot imagine that it would be the same to him, either. You are his most precious child and have been his companion for many years. I am the man who will take you away from him forever! I cannot believe he would view me as anything but a threat to his happiness, and I am afraid that over time, he will come to dislike me even more than he does now, perhaps even to despise me. It truly frightens me because I have grown to highly regard him."

"I respect your fears, William, and I am not offering empty comfort to you when I say that I do not believe it will happen in that way. I think he is only being cautious for my sake. He wants to be certain that I will live a happy life. That is all. But I can see there is no sense in discussing this any farther. If we had hours to do so, maybe I could convince you, but we do not and I, for one, do not wish to spend the short time we have remaining speaking of *this*. You shall see in eight months that *I* was correct!" Elizabeth said with the brilliant smile that always made his heart skip a beat. "Now, will you give me a suggestion for a book that perhaps I have not yet read but that you think I would enjoy to occupy my thoughts on my journey to Longbourn?"

"Any preferences as to which subject, or even which language you would like to read in? That might help me to narrow the list of choices a little."

"I do not care, as long as it is something new to me that will absorb my interest and make the time pass more quickly, and, I hope, distract me from the thought that with each passing moment, I am travelling further away from *you*. The subject, I will leave up to you, even if it is farming or animal husbandry, as long as it is something *you* enjoyed reading. As for languages, it must be written in English, French, Italian, Latin, Greek, or German… unless, of course, it is a book that will *teach* me a new language! I have often thought of learning Spanish." They both laughed.

William mentioned the titles of quite a few books, with Elizabeth dismissing them all as "already up here" pointing to her head, until finally his face brightened and he said, "I think I have just the book we are looking for." He searched a few bookcases down from the place where they had been standing. "Have you ever read this?" he asked, handing her a thick volume.

Her smile told him all he needed to know, but she answered anyway, "No, I have not. And you have read this particular book?"

"Yes, I have. Look inside the cover."

Elizabeth did and found the bookplate carried his own name, not one of his ancestors as many of the others did. "Then this is perfect, my love! I wanted to hold a book that you have held, and read it knowing that your eyes have absorbed the same words that mine will, but having your name on the bookplate and knowing that you selected this volume to add to the collection here at Pemberley is even better!"

Elizabeth asked if he would accompany her on a short walk in the formal garden close to the house. She absolutely despised long carriage rides and needed to walk before leaving. William was only too happy to comply. He knew of at least two places in the garden in which they could steal a few moments of privacy again before she left Pemberley.

~%~

Mr. Darcy, having made the excursion to London often and knowing the value of a good book to pass the time, had suggested that both Bennets select a book from the Pemberley library to read on their journey home. Mr. Bennet promised they would return the books by post later, but Mr. Darcy insisted they hold onto them until they saw each other again. And so, that was the *reason* Mr. Bennet had been in the library behind a tall bookcase far away from the door, searching the stacks when William brought Elizabeth in to say their goodbyes.

At first, Mr. Bennet did not notice they were in the room with him, and when voices began to echo through the vast room, he honestly did not pay them any mind. Absorbed in making his choice, the thought crossed his mind that Lizzy had been on the same errand as himself. During the times of quiet, he assumed she was reading some of her selection to see if it was something she would like to bring along, just as he had been doing.

But when he moved down the stack to search for a tome in a different location, he soon found that, because of the acoustics of the room, he was able to understand their murmurings when standing there. His eyes widened in alarm when he heard William moan and say breathlessly, "Elizabeth! We must stop now, my love. The gentleman in me must protect you from the man." He was about to rush out to stop whatever had been occurring while he had been unaware, but then he heard them begin a conversation.

Knowing they would not be engaged in improper activities now, and that all he could do at this point was insist they marry—which, he was sure, would only end in a repetition of the conversation he had had earlier in the day with William—Mr. Bennet decided that since he had little chance to observe the two of them together over the past weeks, he should take advantage of the opportunity to eavesdrop once again. The fact that he absolutely loathed this particular behavior pulled at his conscience. *"But the last time, I gleaned good information which put my mind at ease,"* he thought. *"It is being done in the name of protecting my daughter, and so it is for the best! I will soon make my presence known."*

After a little while, Mr. Bennet was mortified at witnessing such a tender scene, and now he did not wish to come out. He did not want to embarrass either of them, especially after overhearing William's concerns about his own approval of him, not to mention his discomfort at the thought of exposing himself to the censure of engaging in this disgusting behavior of eavesdropping in the first place.

Mr. Bennet moved further down the stack back so that he could not make out what they were saying, swearing to himself that he would never eavesdrop again even if it *were* for a good cause! He was not certain if he would be able to look at his daughter again without blushing.

The positive side was that Mr. Bennet came away from the experience with the absolute knowledge that the two were deeply in love, and that William was as good a man as his father ever was. William could have easily overpowered Lizzy and forced himself upon her, as she stood about foot shorter than did he, but from what he had heard, William had stopped events from progressing too far, and he was honest about it without frightening Lizzy.

While he was trapped in the alcove waiting for the lovers to depart, Mr. Bennet had had time to think. The journey home would probably be the last opportunity of spending any length of time alone with Lizzy for a long while, and he planned on taking full advantage of the trip. *"I will have to speak to Lizzy… mayhap I will allow a visit in a few weeks. But to take William away from Pemberley again when he still has so much to learn? I will write to Darcy about it and ask for his opinion before making my own known to Lizzy or William."*

Upon exiting the library, Mr. Bennet asked a footman for the whereabouts of his daughter. He was told that she had expressed a wish to take a short walk in the garden before leaving this morning.

~%~

Mr. Darcy allowed William to go off on his own for a while after the Bennets departed, knowing that he would need a few moments alone, but after an hour, he had William summoned to the study.

"William, there is no time like the present to begin to learn what is involved with the running of Pemberley. Up until now, you have seen only some of the outdoor work, but much of the work is on paper and done here in my study. I would like for us, at the very least, to discuss the work I do today as I go along. When you are fully recovered, you will sit behind the desk, and I will answer your questions."

"Yes, sir," William replied.

Mr. Darcy could tell his attention kept wandering. "William, are you as yet feeling ill?"

"I am sorry, Father. I cannot seem to stop thinking about Elizabeth. I do not know how I will get through the next eight months without her. I feel … lost."

"It is for the best, William. I need you to *concentrate* on spending as much time as possible training to take over Pemberley and all the other family holdings, son, especially since this injury will keep you from riding for such a long time! Every minute is critical now. The last thing we need is for you to be distracted by a betrothal or, worse yet, by a new wife. Though you will have help, you must be prepared for the inevitable!"

"You are holding something back, Father, I can tell. You have always put off teaching me the details… you have always said that we would have plenty of time for particulars after I graduated and took my tour. Why do you seem anxious to start *today*? What is critical about *now*, sir?"

Closing his eyes, Mr. Darcy took a deep breath and studied his son before saying, "I have a… condition. It will be a while yet, but there is no doubt…

I am dying, William." He let the words sink in for a few moments before continuing, "I have seen all the best doctors, and they are unanimous in their opinions – there is nothing to be done. I have some time, but eventually I will become too ill to be of use to you.

"I cannot put this request in my will, but it is my wish that if anything happens to me before you are completely prepared for your responsibilities, that you turn to Mr. Bennet and Mr. Wickham for assistance. Mr. Wickham has been my steward here for years and knows much of what occurs on a daily basis, and I trust him to do well by you. While Longbourn is smaller in size, I trust Mr. Bennet's sense and experience much more than that of others. It was the reason he came to Pemberley; as a favor to me, he has been riding with me these past weeks and sitting with me while I do business so that he can help you if need be.

"Your Aunt Catherine and Uncle Robert will do everything in their power in an attempt to influence you so that they can have some level of control over the Darcy legacy, but you know that I have never agreed with them on… well, on *anything*. Even your mother did not wish them to be a major influence upon your life nor Georgiana's. Their opinions and morals were not hers, and they are not mine, and we would not wish either of you to follow their example.

"We will discuss this in further detail soon, but you must know that time is of the essence. I do not wish to leave you unprepared, my son—too many lives depend upon the decisions made by the Master of Pemberley."

~%~

My dearest Elizabeth,

I know that I can never send this letter to you, but I have a desperate wish to tell you everything that happens in my life while we are apart, to speak to you as I would if you were here. Since I will not be able to do so for many months, I will write to you here, in this book, as if you would read my letter within a few days.

It is strange what one thinks about when one is very ill. When my fever was high and you were bathing my face, it occurred to me that I must begin a new journal as soon as I was able. I had thought back to the last time I had written in my journal and realized that I was a completely different man from what I had been when I made that last entry. In truth, the change did not take place over days or hours or even minutes. Within moments after I saw your lovely face once again, my thoughts and plans for the future were so vastly different from the ones I had envisioned even while riding on the grounds of Pemberley. The differences astound me!

And so, today I begin this new journal in the form of letters from my heart, addressed to the owner of the same—my beautiful Elizabeth Bennet, who has promised to become my bride. That day cannot come soon enough, my love.

You left Pemberley only a few minutes ago, yet I feel as if my very heart has gone with you. I took out your handkerchief to feel closer to you, but I think I had mentioned that the scent is not quite right... there is an essence that is distinctly your own that is added to the scent you wear but not present on your freshly laundered cloth. I am not embarrassed to tell you that I have just returned from the rooms that you had occupied. I took the pillowcase you laid your head upon last night. If I had been able to have used two hands to remove it from the pillow I would not have been caught, but Hanna, the maid who was assigned to you during your stay, came in just then to remove the sheets to be laundered! I can hear your laughter as I write; I do not think I have ever blushed as deeply as I did at that moment—but being caught did not dissuade me from my purpose. I will cherish your scent for as long as it lasts, and I hope it does not fade too quickly.

My father summons me to his study, and so I must continue this at a later time.

You departed from Pemberley barely two hours ago, but it seems as though a lifetime has passed since you were here. I know of no easy way to say this, and your speeches about honesty came to mind when I tried to think of a more agreeable way of wording it, so I will get right to it. My father has told me that he is dying.

It seems that this is the reason he agreed so readily with your father's idea of putting off the engagement until your birthday. He regrets that, though I had ridden the grounds with him many times and as we came across problems we would discuss them, never in the past had we gone over the detailed workings of Pemberley and the other Darcy holdings. Instead, we spent the time while I was home from school in more enjoyable ways. I never have seen this emotion from him before, but if I had to put a name to it, I would say that he seems panicked because I will need to learn everything very quickly instead of over the course of time I would have had if events had occurred as we had thought they would. It seems that his condition will slowly rob him of his abilities over time. He spoke of looking forward to attending our wedding, so I believe he expects to live at least that long, but there is no way of knowing for certain.

He has planned for the possibility that I will not have learned all I need to know before he dies. This is why you and your father were invited for your visit, and why Mr. Bennet was shadowing Father. We had so little time alone together, and I had wished to ask you if you had noticed this and what your opinion of it was, but I never did. Now I have the answer. Your father has agreed to return to Pemberley upon the notification of Father's death. Longbourn may be smaller, but your father has a much more extensive knowledge of estate management than I do at present, and even more importantly, my father trusts him. Father feels that between Mr. Bennet and Mr. Wickham's assistance, I will learn all I need to know that I do not already know by that time. I only hope that my father will live longer than he expects at present.

After our talk, my father and Mr. Wickham departed for a neighboring estate to speak to the owner as to some confusion over our shared border. It seems they had a new survey done, and it shows that the Pemberley border should be in a different place than in the location that our maps display, in the neighbor's favor of course. I felt a great need to attend the meeting, but Mr. Smythe still feels that traveling by coach or horseback would set back the healing of my shoulder. My father assures me that we will work on going over his papers and accounts while my shoulder heals, and then he will begin to take me out to meetings of this nature.

Elizabeth! It has been more than a full day since writing the above... something has happened of a most serious nature. Oh Elizabeth, I need you here with me, and Georgiana needs you as well. I try to comfort her, but I, myself, am so grieved I do not know how well I do. She has just stopped crying for the first time since the tragedy we have suffered as she fell asleep with the help of laudanum from Mr. Smythe. I can only hope your father will bring you with him when he returns as I have requested—no, begged him to do—in the letter I have sent! Father had me send it regular post as he did not wish to upset your mother if she read it before your father arrived home. Your father had told him she reads his letters while he is away to see if there is anything that should be forwarded to her husband.

The heavy rains had damaged a bridge leading to the neighbor's estate that I told you about in the above paragraph. Your friend James, the footman, had gone with them, and he has since explained that the bridge looked perfectly sound before they attempted to cross it. They assumed it had been inspected, but obviously, Mr. Walsh is not as attentive to these duties as my father is... or was. The bridge collapsed with the coach atop it, and the stones from the bridge crumbled onto the broken coach. Mr. Wickham and the driver were killed instantly. James leapt from the coach onto the shore as the collapse took place. He, with the help of the driver of the farm cart that was travelling behind them, were able to move some of the stones and broken coach and to pull my father from the rising waters... but his injuries were extensive.

Father survived about half a day after being brought to Pemberley by the farm cart. Georgiana and I were able to speak to him before he passed on. He acted as a man who was driven, Elizabeth, hastening to tell us so many things in such a short time... especially to me. He spoke constantly until his last breath—his voice was but a hoarse whisper the last few hours, attempting to crowd a lifetime of knowledge and experience and to convey his love for us into the few hours he had left.

Father had repeatedly asked me to tell you that he loves you as if you were his own daughter, and he has every confidence that you will be a wonderful wife, mother and mistress of Pemberley. He thanked G-d that you and your father would be here for Georgiana and me. He asked me to send his thanks to your father as well, for all he had done for him in the past and for all he is about to do in his memory.

I asked Mr. Smythe if Father's illness had influenced the outcome of the accident, weakening him enough so that he was not able to survive his injuries. He did not believe so, but he also said this accident was a much less painful way for him to die than had he lived through the usual course of his illness.

I have sent letters by express to my mother's siblings. I know that they will arrive before you and your father do, and I do dread their being here at all now that Father has told me what he has about them; but out of respect, I did not have much of a choice. My father has warned me that they have always attempted to influence his way of handling Pemberley, and he was afraid they would try to influence me. He was quite adamant to wait for your father's assistance and not take my uncle's advice. He explained his opinion of my mother's family, and though I have fought with my own feelings on the matter for years, afraid that even to think such things was an act of disrespect, I was surprised that his opinions of their characters and actions coincided with my own. I was even more shocked that he said my mother had agreed with him fully, and that neither of them had wished for my Uncle Robert or Aunt Catherine to have any influence in our upbringing.

Father also told me that Mr. Bennet knows of all these things and more, and will help to keep them from overwhelming me with demands while I try to make my way. I do not expect that Mr. Bennet will be able to return for at least a week, perhaps longer if there is urgent business to attend to after such a long absence from Longbourn, but I cannot tell you how I have been praying that it will be sooner. I have asked your father to send an express stating when we can expect you both.

The last time Father spoke, he told both Georgiana and me once again that he loved us, and then he told me, "You are now Master of Pemberley, William,"... handing over the reins officially — as he slipped away. It seemed as if he had but fallen asleep, but we knew he had not. He was gone.

As I sat next to his bed, I felt as if I was not a man, but the frightened young boy I was while I was waiting for my mother to die. All I wanted to do was to cry, but as I looked down at my sister as she clung to me, at Mrs. Reynolds across the room weeping into her husband's shoulder, at the maid sitting in the corner crying, at my father's valet, at the doctor wiping the tears from their eyes, and at the minister praying as his tears flowed down his cheeks, I knew... when my father had left us in the morning, I was but the son; now I am the Master. I have to remain strong for them... for all of those who depend on me... for Pemberley.

Though I had already felt the burden before, the weight of his statement was staggering. It always had been an event that was far in the future, but now it is reality. How many families, how many individuals now depend solely upon my making the correct decisions and taking the correct actions? How can I possibly accomplish the monumental tasks laid before me with no knowledge of what awaits me?

I am not prepared for this, Elizabeth.

I have not slept a night through since doing so in your arms, and that is where I wish to be now. Will it shock you when I say that the one thing I have longed for so urgently these past hours is to rest my head upon your breast and listen to your heart beat?

I need you, my heart. I am desperate to take you in my arms, bury my face in your hair and weep for the loss of my father – it is the only place I will ever allow myself to show this weakness. You would not judge me; you would not think me less of a man if I did so.

I have promised Mr. Smythe to make an attempt to sleep now to prevent my illness from recurring. Exhausted, I had tried earlier, *but I could not even close my eyes before sharing with you all that has occurred and all that is in my heart.*

Elizabeth, I need you. I am lost. Please come home to me soon.

With all my love,
William

~%~

Considering the condition of the roads after the rains, and the many detours they had encountered, the Bennets had made good time on their way home from Pemberley. They had had a long talk about Elizabeth's feelings for William, and Mr. Bennet was convinced that he would, at the very least, agree to a long engagement, though he did not tell her of his decision since he first wished to hear Mr. Darcy's opinion.

There was a letter from Georgiana waiting for her when she arrived at Longbourn, and Elizabeth wrote to Georgiana after spending some time with her sisters and mother, giving them the gifts that she and Georgiana had chosen for them in Lambton before she had been injured. Her father wrote a letter to Mr. Darcy as well, telling his friend of his decision to consent to their children's engagement. First thing the following morning, Elizabeth and Jane walked to Meryton as Elizabeth wished to post the letters herself at the local post office.

~%~

Mr. Jaresberry had been the Postmaster at ----- Sorting Station, located several miles away from Meryton, for forty years. After so many years of sorting, he had come to know the handwritings of the postal patrons he served most frequently. Miss Elizabeth Bennet's script was among the ones he had come to recognize, and it never failed to make him smile.

Mr. Jaresberry had enjoyed the great pleasure of meeting Miss Bennet on several occasions. A bright and curious girl, she had begged of her father years ago to learn how the post worked. Mr. Bennet had petitioned Mr. Jaresberry for a visit to the sorting station, and a friendship had begun. It always made him smile when he saw Miss Bennet's writings, because she had told him about her plan to put a mark in the corner of every envelope she sent through the post as a secret "hello" to him. Mr. Jaresberry ran his finger over the mark on the envelope before him—it warmed his heart to know that through the years she had never forgotten him! He had always made certain the Bennets' letters were handled with great care.

Unfortunately for all concerned, especially poor Mr. Jaresberry, the gentleman's time remaining on this earth had been extremely limited. Upon the expiration of Mr. Jaresberry's life, an oil lamp was overturned directly onto the letters posted from the Bennets to the Darcys informing them of their safe return home, as well as those being sent through the station from the Darcys to the Bennets containing the news of Mr. George Darcy's passing. They were all completely destroyed in the resulting fire.

This was the first in a chain of events that would change the course of several lives—especially those of our dear couple.

Chapter 8

16 October 1807

As early as the day after his father died, the staff began to treat William differently, and as time continued to pass, the difference became more apparent. It was three days after his father's death when he was sitting at his father's desk with piles of papers strewn across it that Mrs. Reynolds came in and called him "Mr. Darcy" instead of "Master William" for the first time. He had stared into her eyes for some minutes before nodding. Her message was clear... *you* are the master now, and you must accept that fact.

Now, a full two weeks after his father's death, William was a little more accustomed to the staff's change in attitude. He waved his open hand over the desk and said in mounting exasperation, "Mrs. Reynolds... I do not know what to do with all this. Mr. Bennet and Mr. Wickham were supposed to be here to help me make sense of all this, but now I find myself completely alone."

"Your uncle would be happy to help you, Mr. Darcy."

"NO! Father was most adamant—he did not wish my mother's sister or brother to have any hand in managing the Darcy assets." He looked past her, seeing nothing. "I must find another steward, and I must learn how to do all this. I am depending on Mr. Moore, Father's—*my* solicitor, for his assistance in the search for a trustworthy steward. I know Father would not have wished Uncle Robert to recommend someone, thinking the earl would then have access to information about Darcy holdings." He sighed and passed his hand over his brow. *"Why do my Uncle Robert and Aunt Catherine not just leave us alone instead of making things more difficult?"* Sighing again, he continued, "Father told me that there are many who depend upon the Master of Pemberley, and now whether I am ready for it or not, I am he. I hope I do not make too many mistakes, Mrs. Reynolds. I will depend upon you and Mr. Reynolds to be honest with me; no matter how harsh it might seem, if you see I am doing wrong, please let me know *discreetly*. I will have to leave the day-to-day running of the household to you for now, as you have been doing these two weeks past. I cannot take that on as well—*not now*—not even a menu; I trust you to manage without me.

"I am thankful that Richard is to be co-guardian for Georgiana so that I can share those decisions at least, but again, if you think that there is anything concerning her that two young men would not understand, please tell me." Shaking his head, he thought of how his aunt had continued to harp on about her intentions to remove Georgiana to Rosings to rear her there and his ensuing discussion last night with a panicked Georgiana in which she begged him not to allow Aunt Catherine to take her away from him.

"Mr. Darcy, I have faith in you. You will be just like your father—the best master and the best landlord. Your sister will already attest to your being the best brother, and your father had often said you were the best of sons. Trust yourself, sir; the entire staff already has faith in you."

"Thank you, Mrs. Reynolds. Please summon Mr. Moore to the study; I must speak to him about his progress in the search for a new steward." He took her hand and squeezed it gently before turning back to his work at hand.

While he waited for Mr. Moore, William did try to concentrate on his work, but his mind kept turning back to thoughts of Elizabeth and how desperately he needed her calming presence. He knew he would have been able to speak to her of his sorrow at his father's passing and his fears of failure, and he knew she would have been able to support him as no one else could.

It had been more than two weeks since she had left Pemberley. *Two weeks!* He had sent two letters and Georgiana had sent three to Longbourn—why had they heard *nothing* from either Mr. Bennet or Elizabeth? Why were they not already at Pemberley if all was well? If they could not come, why had William not received an express from Mr. Bennet?

After what had already occurred as a result of the heavy rains the day before they had journeyed home—namely the accident which caused his father's death—both he and Georgiana were understandably concerned. William had tried to belie Georgiana's worries, but even as the words were uttered, he found the reassurances truly difficult to believe. Every day of silence from Longbourn added to the level of anxiety he felt over their safety.

He tried to convince himself that perhaps Mr. Bennet had become angry with him for going to Elizabeth's room after all and could not forgive William at present. Ignoring the letters for now would be his punishment. After recalling stories from his father about Mr. Bennet's habit of being a poor correspondent, William thought that perhaps he had not even read the letters as of yet.

As for *Elizabeth*, though... what of Georgiana's letters to Elizabeth? Mayhap Mr. Bennet had kept them from her? Surely he would not continue in this way for long. Mr. Bennet would not ignore the friendship he had enjoyed with his father, and the promises that had been made.

William decided that Mr. Bennet was just trying to teach him a lesson by delaying, and that was all. He *had* to believe Elizabeth was safe—and that she would come to him soon.

~%~

Mr. Moore, who had arrived earlier in the day for the purpose of the reading of Mr. Darcy's will, met with William in the study as requested. They spoke of the letter that William had sent to his London office requesting his assistance in finding a suitable steward, and Mr. Moore had a list of the men whom either he had already interviewed, or he would interview upon his return to London. After they were finished with that business, and William had chosen two men from the list to have investigated further, he had another request of the solicitor.

"Mr. Moore, do you know whether my father had an investigator for private matters?"

"Yes, he employed someone that I had recommended who did work for him when needed." Mr. Moore told William the man's qualifications, and William was satisfied.

"I cannot go to London myself at the moment for obvious reasons, so I would like you to pass on the specifications of the investigation to him. Of course, as is all my business with you, this matter is strictly confidential." William passed along the particulars of the investigation he wished to be carried out.

"This is not complicated at all, Mr. Darcy; it should be no trouble. I would think you will have a report within a few days of my return to London."

"It may not be complicated, but it is quite important to me personally, Mr. Moore, and urgent. I want him to be very discreet—there should be no association known between him and myself, nor should he allow it to be known that he is an investigator."

"I understand, sir. Mr. Robinson is an expert in his field."

"Thank you, Mr. Moore." William's expression changed to a more solemn one. "Tomorrow after breakfast would be the best time to schedule the reading of the will, if the time is agreeable to you."

The gentlemen shook hands, and Mr. Moore left William to himself.

~%~

Mr. Wickham's son, George, had been Mr. Darcy's godson. As a gift to his steward who had worked diligently and treated Pemberley as if it were his own, Mr. Darcy had sent George through school with William, with the hopes that someday George would take over his father's position as steward of Pemberley. William had not wanted to tell his father that George had been one of the worst behaved young men at school. Any debts George ran up, William paid so that his father would not be ashamed of his godson. Though it never took place in William's presence, there was much talk at school naming George Wickham as Mr. Darcy's illegitimate son, which, to the gossip lovers of the *ton*, explained why George was treated in such a favorable way. Any other difficulties that George's wild behavior created were smoothed over by this assumed association with Mr. Darcy, which misconception George did not correct.

While the two had been friends as young boys, the growing differences between William and George had prevented a continuation of that friendship into adulthood with William taking the good and honorable path and George taking the path pitted with vices and debaucheries. By the time they had left Cambridge, George Wickham was one of the last men on earth with whom William would ever wish to be associated.

When the reading of Mr. Darcy's will was completed, George Wickham was quite dissatisfied. Since Mr. Wickham was also deceased, the money that had been left to the steward went to his wife as specified in Mr. Darcy's will. Mrs. Wickham was George's step-mother, and, knowing of the disreputable ways of the son of her late husband, she wanted nothing more to do with her step-son. George himself was left one thousand pounds in Mr. Darcy's will, and *if* he decided to take orders, Mr. Darcy promised that William would give him a valuable living. William was quite taken aback since he knew very well that the last thing George Wickham should *ever* become was a clergyman. He was, therefore, relieved when George asked for a cash sum instead of the living, stating a preference for the law over the clergy. William called in Mr. Moore, who quickly wrote out a bank note for a total of four thousand pounds and drafted an agreement stating in short that Mr. Darcy's will had been fully discharged with respect to George Wickham. The two young men signed three copies of the agreement, and George left Pemberley. William hoped that he would never see the man's despicable face again.

~%~

28 October 1807

Ten days after Mr. Moore's return to London, William received a simple report from Mr. Robinson, the investigator, which read as follows:

"Father and daughter are safely arrived at their home."

It was a relief that Elizabeth was safe, and at least he could reassure Georgiana of it with complete conviction. But the report also left many questions unanswered, all beginning with "Why?"

~%~

Jane Bennet looked out the window to see her sister Elizabeth pacing the garden, anticipating the arrival of the post again—a recurring activity since she had returned home from Pemberley. Jane put down her sewing, collected her spencer and bonnet, and joined her sister outside.

"Lizzy, this behavior is worrying me. I am beginning to think that you have acquired mama's affliction of severe nerves!" Jane's attempt to tease Lizzy into a better mood did nothing toward achieving that goal.

Elizabeth sighed, "Oh Jane, I do not understand what has happened! Since my return to Longbourn, the only letter I have received from Georgiana is the one that had arrived before I had returned home. I wrote that same day and delivered the letter to the post the next morning, along with Papa's letter to Mr. Darcy. You accompanied me into Meryton that day, do you not remember?" Jane seemed confused and Elizabeth continued, "It was the day you were so unsettled by the disagreement I had with Mr. Wells. He refused to begin Papa's newspaper delivery again once Papa was home, requesting a note from Papa instead of taking my word. Papa was upset for he had already missed quite a few days of news while we travelled. He was further unsettled when he heard that Sir William and Uncle Phillips had already discarded their newspapers and so he could not borrow them."

Jane nodded. "Yes, yes, I remember now."

"It should take three days for the letters to travel that distance, but that would account for only six days. Today it will be three *weeks*, and I have heard not a word in response! Why would Georgiana not have replied to any of my letters? Why has Mr. Darcy not responded to Papa's? We both know that Papa might not always answer his letters in the timeliest manner, but Mr. Darcy has always been the best of correspondents."

"Have you asked Papa?"

"Yes, I have. He says he does not understand the silence either… but there is something in his expression that makes me wonder if there is something he is not telling me."

"What do you think it could be?" Jane asked, her concern evident in her voice.

"I am concerned that Papa had mentioned something in his letter that caused Mr. Darcy to become angry, no longer allowing Georgiana to correspond with me."

Jane said, "There must be some sort of misunderstanding, Lizzy. I am certain that Mr. Darcy would not forbid his daughter from writing to you even if he *were* angry with Papa."

Elizabeth blushed knowing full well that it was *she* who Mr. Darcy was likely angry with and refrained from meeting Jane's eye, exclaiming, "Oh, Jane! I do not know what I will do without hearing any word from them at all!"

"Lizzy, I think there is something *you* are not telling *me*. Is this only about Miss Darcy, or is it something more?"

Elizabeth thought about it for a few moments. She had been tempted many times since her return to confide in Jane—she knew she could trust Jane, but she did not wish to burden her with her secret. Now it was obvious that Jane had guessed there was something, so she said, "Mr. Darcy has proposed, Jane, and I have accepted!"

Jane looked horrified. "But Lizzy! Mr. Darcy is the same age as Papa!"

"No, Jane, no!" Elizabeth laughed for several minutes before she could speak again, "Not *that* Mr. Darcy—his son, William. I think we should refer to him as 'William' from now on so that we do not become confused again! Do you not remember him from a few years ago when their coach wheel broke, and they stayed with us at Longbourn? William is fewer than five years older than I." Her eyes were sparkling with her love for William as she spoke of him.

"Why has not Papa announced your engagement?"

"Well, therein lies the problem. Papa has forbidden us to become engaged just yet. He wishes me to have a season 'out' first, and then we can meet again on my seventeenth birthday. Papa says if our attachment persists, he will give his consent. But Jane, *this* you must not tell anyone..." she waited for Jane to nod and then continued, "William has given me this." She pulled a long chain out from the bodice of her gown and showed her the ring. "This was his mother's engagement ring. He wanted me to have it as a symbol of his promise to me."

"OH! Lizzy, it is so beautiful!" The two girls smiled at Elizabeth's obvious happiness and then Jane said, "Papa does not know that William has given you the ring?"

"No! Perhaps it is wrong, but I did not want to risk his taking it from me, Jane. Papa will not allow me to see William or exchange letters until my birthday, so I did not think he would allow me to keep this. Oh, Jane, I love

William so much—I am so glad to have something of his to hold until I can see him again."

Her expression turned to one of worry as she continued, "But, I am concerned that Georgiana and William's father have not written. Georgiana is a sweet girl, and I truly love her as if she were another sister, and I am very fond of Mr. Darcy as well. William would not allow her to forget to write to me. I am afraid something has gone wrong…"

"Lizzy, what could have gone wrong?"

"Well… Jane what will you think of me if I tell you?" Elizabeth placed her hand on her sister's. "Oh, I have gone too far for concealment, I must tell you all. William came to my chamber the night before we left Pemberley."

Jane's eyes opened wide in shock.

"Jane, it was not like that! I had only just accepted William's proposal that day, and there was no time to ask Papa for consent until after I retired. Since we were leaving early the next morning, William came to tell me of Papa's decision to have us wait and to reassure me that he loved me, and it was not *his* choice to put off the engagement. He did not understand Papa's reasons, and I tried to explain that he did not want a repetition of his own marriage for his daughters."

Jane blushed but nodded. "I understand what you mean, Lizzy."

"William is a gentleman, Jane, and he loves me. He did not… we did not…" Elizabeth could not finish the sentence, but Jane understood. Elizabeth did not wish to tell Jane what they *did* do… that was only for her and William to know. Jane took Elizabeth's hand and gave it a squeeze.

"Papa saw William leaving my room."

Jane's eyes widened again and she gasped. "And now you believe that Papa might have written to Mr. Darcy about it? That Mr. Darcy would no longer approve the match? That he will not allow Georgiana to write to you?"

"I do not know!" Elizabeth cried in exasperation. "Papa seemed to believe the truth after speaking to William—he even *told* me he believed it! He allowed William and me to have a few minutes alone to say goodbye before we left that morning, and I do not think he would have allowed it had he believed the worst. But why else would Georgiana and Mr. Darcy not have written by now, Jane?"

Elizabeth closed her eyes and shuddered. "Though I already miss Georgiana, it is not the same as the way I miss William. I feel empty inside without him, Jane. I just cannot imagine not hearing word of William for an entire eight months. You see how I am now, after only three weeks! But I do not know what else I can do except to wait."

"So you think that William will marry you even if Mr. Darcy disapproves?"

"He promised me that even if Mr. Darcy *and* Papa did not give consent after my birthday that we shall still marry. If we must, we will run away to Scotland!" she smiled slyly and said, "To be honest, Jane, I would have left with him for Scotland that night had he asked me! I do not believe he would have given me his mother's ring if he was not certain of his choice. Do you?"

"No, I do not Lizzy. Do not worry; I am certain that you will receive a letter soon." She hugged Elizabeth and when she pulled away, Jane looked confused again and asked, "But what will you do during the season, Lizzy? Will you dance with other men?"

Elizabeth sighed, "I think I must, Jane, to make Papa happy. Papa was very specific in that he wants me to make an *effort* to meet other young men so that I am certain I am doing the right thing before accepting William. To be honest, I will not be thinking of anyone but William while I am away from him, but I do think I could at least put on a pleasant expression while dancing with the young men with whom I grew up and whom I consider to be my friends. William was worried about young men making advances without his being here to protect me, so he gave me lessons on how to defend myself. I will show you what I have learned that you do not already know."

Just then the post arrived and both girls walked briskly to collect it. Elizabeth shuffled through the letters, and Jane could tell by her expression that there were none from Pemberley.

~%~

12 November 1807

Six weeks after William had taken over as master, Mrs. Reynolds entered his study to make William aware of the interference that his Uncle Robert, the earl, and his Aunt Catherine were attempting with regard to the staff. It was bad enough that they both were relentlessly needling him to accept their assistance, but attempting to change the way Pemberley was run by ordering the staff to conduct themselves against William's orders was too much!

"Thank you for bringing this to my attention—they have gone too far this time, Mrs. Reynolds. I did not wish to do this to my mother's siblings, but I fear if they do not begin to behave themselves, I might have to remove them from the property to end this... siege! Please have Mr. Reynolds come to me. If it comes down to expelling them, I will need the support of all of the footmen."

He did not dismiss her, so she stood in place while William sat silently looking at her, lost in thought. After a few moments, Mrs. Reynolds cleared her throat bringing him back to the present.

"I cannot understand why Mr. Bennet has not responded to my letters." Waving his hand across his desk, which was almost covered with piles of paper, he continued, "I had delayed some of this because they were not urgent matters at the time, but it is now *all* urgent. If Mr. Bennet will not help me, then I will need to puzzle it all out on my own. I will not act against my father's wishes and seek help from my uncle."

"It is possible, sir, that you could make use of additional support staff, a secretary perhaps? You cannot research these matters or ride out to the tenants if you are too busy with all these papers, and the opposite is true as well."

"How did my father manage all this without any additional help other than a steward, Mrs. Reynolds?"

"Mr. Darcy, you must remember that you have come into managing Pemberley suddenly, being unprepared to do so, and with a steward who had never even seen the estate the day before he took the position. He has been learning the job as well as learning your preferences for running the estate—preferences that *you* are only now discovering as you go along. If Mr. Wickham *had* survived, it would have been much easier for you. You were required to resolve a property line dispute and assess the damage from the floods when the rivers rose over the first few weeks following the death of your father. During that time you were also without a steward." Mrs. Reynolds pointed to the papers on the desk. "Much of *this* accumulated while you were tending to much more urgent matters.

Mrs. Reynolds' expression softened as she shook her head. "You have not even given yourself time to grieve your father's loss. Sir, no *rational* person who has seen how hard you have worked the past weeks could possibly criticize you."

William smiled at her emphasis on the word "rational" since she knew very well that his aunt and uncle were not accepting at all of the way he was running Pemberley. "I will write to Mr. Moore to inquire after obtaining a secretary. I assume a secretary would not be under your or Mr. Reynolds' authority, but directly under mine?"

She nodded.

"Mrs. Reynolds, I thank G-d for you and your husband every day. I do not know what I would have done without you throughout this difficult time."

"Mr. Reynolds and I are quite proud to be associated with you, Master William," she said, reverting back to her previous, more personal way of referring to him. A teary-eyed Mrs. Reynolds left the room.

Once alone, two questions that had not been far from his thoughts these six weeks entered William's mind once more. "*Why did Mr. Bennet not respond to any of his letters? Why had Georgiana not heard from Elizabeth?*"

He cleared a portion of his desk. First he wrote to Mr. Moore about acquiring a secretary, and then as an afterthought began to write another letter.

Dear Mr. Bennet,

After six weeks, I can no longer make excuses for why you would completely ignore all of my letters. I know there were issues that we had not agreed upon, but I felt we had worked them out satisfactorily before you had departed. I wish that you would explain to me what has changed so drastically since your removal that you would blatantly ignore the promise you had made to my father to assist me if he passed before he felt I was ready?

I am left here without your guidance and without that of Mr. Wickham since he passed in the same accident that took my father from us. I am floundering in an attempt to do what is right by everyone associated with the Darcy name, but I am unsure what exactly I must do to accomplish this. My father told me that I could trust you as he did, and yet I have heard nothing from you since you left here that fateful day.

My uncle, the Earl of Matlock, and my aunt, Lady Catherine de Bourgh, have descended upon Pemberley, demanding that I allow them to assist me. I refused, as was my father's wish, but they continue to stay on here. I can only imagine they are thinking that I will eventually be so overwhelmed that I will give in to their machinations. My father feared that they would attempt to take control of the Darcy holdings, and his fears have now become reality. They will not relent — every free moment I allow myself is inundated with their complaints and demands. I cannot turn my mother's siblings out of the house without making a public display and disgracing all of our names, so I have not. My father told me that you were prepared to assist me with "beating back the wolves from the door" as he said you put it. But you have not; and so I do this alone as well.

My aunt's constant attempts to convince me to release Georgiana into her care are most distressing. My sister is grieved by the death of our father, but she is terrified that we will be separated. Legally, I am told by my solicitor, my aunt cannot remove my sister, but I fear that if I do not accomplish everything related to the estate in a perfect manner, she will find a judge who will declare me to be incompetent and overwhelmed by responsibility, providing a legal way of removing my sister from my care. I do not put the possibility of bribery beyond her machinations. She divides her time in my presence between harping on this subject and her offering to end this constant pressure by having me agree to marry her daughter. My uncle is behind her in this; he says that if I marry Anne, they would have no qualms about leaving Georgiana with us.

Do not allow Miss Elizabeth to fear that I will marry my cousin Anne; I would rather endure listening to my aunt's rants every day for the rest of my life than to marry anyone other than Miss Elizabeth.

Of all that has occurred since my father's untimely death, Mr. Bennet, your and Miss Elizabeth's silence is what bothers me the most — I cannot believe that Miss Elizabeth is ignoring Georgiana's letters, so I can only assume that you are keeping Georgiana's letters from reaching her. Please, sir, if you are angry with me for what occurred the morning you left Pemberley, which is the only conclusion to which I can come, I beg of you to allow Georgiana the comfort of at least corresponding with Elizabeth. She lost her mother at a very early age, she has just lost her father, and though I try to protect her from her aunt's and uncle's ranting, she knows of their threats to take her from me, her brother. Must she lose her friend as well? This is too much for an eleven-year-old girl to be expected to bear, sir, and I do not understand your thinking.

Once again, I beg some sort of answer from you. Even a note with the word "NO!" written across it would be better than this deafening silence.

Fitzwilliam Darcy

William sealed the letter and walked out into the hallway to the silver tray meant for outgoing mail, placing the letter to Mr. Bennet on top of two others, and then returned to the study.

A few minutes later, Mr. Reynolds, the butler, retrieved the letters off the silver tray, handing them to the runner who would take them to the post station. "Roger, there are only two letters today; come to my office, and I will give you the funds to post them in Lambton."

Roger would always be grateful for the master's kindness the previous day and wanted to do everything perfectly from then on. "When I come back from Lambton, I put the post on the gold tray; right, Mr. Reynolds?"

"Yes, as I showed you yesterday, Roger, and then inform me immediately that the post has arrived. *I* will bring it to the master when it is convenient for him. Do *not* bring it in to the master yourself." Mr. Reynolds gave him a pointed look; he did not wish the mistake of Roger's first day to be repeated. Mr. Darcy had been very understanding the day before when Roger had made the mistake of walking into the study unbidden with the post, and was quite generous in allowing Roger to continue in his position after such a glaring error.

"Yes, sir! Thank you, sir!" Roger took the money to post the two letters and headed for Lambton.

~%~

The Earl of Matlock knew from the moment he had read the letter informing him of his brother-in-law's demise that his nephew was not going to accept his assistance easily. The express stated that George Darcy lived at least half a day after the accident, giving him plenty of time to advise his son against it. At first, he did not have any intention to rush to Pemberley, but after the meeting with his informer in which he was told of the events lately at Pemberley, he made arrangements to leave his estate at Matlock as soon as possible. The earl did not want the country squire that his brother-in-law had trusted, Bennet, anywhere near his niece and nephew again!

At the time of passing on the information, which happened to be just after receiving Fitzwilliam Darcy's express, his informer—the son of the steward at Pemberley, George Wickham—had been quite put out when he was told that the earl would need to find someone to replace him since his father, the unwitting source of all the information he gathered for the earl, had also died in the same accident. Wickham's momentary shock at the news of his father's passing gave the earl great satisfaction, but Wickham did not hesitate for more than a heartbeat or two before continuing on as if he had *not* just been told that his father was dead.

The truth of the matter was that the earl knew Wickham was very persuasive and more than likely could have found a maid to seduce into passing him information at regular intervals, but he also knew that now that Fitzwilliam was master and the elder Wickham was dead, it would be much more difficult for young Wickham to have an excuse to be on the grounds of Pemberley at all. The earl had heard from another attendee at Cambridge that Fitzwilliam did not like young Wickham's *extracurricular activities* while at university. The fact that Wickham had been raising the price every time he provided information to the earl did not help Wickham's argument for continuing his employment. The problem with this part of plan was that Fleming, the earl's footman who helped him with all of his less than honorable dealings, could never seem to find a Darcy servant willing to talk, even after seducing several of the maids at Pemberley! Fleming would have to continue his search for the right maid. *"Poor man—the sacrifices he makes for his employer!"* The earl laughed to himself, and then his smile widened as he thought about the possibility of making the same sort of *sacrifice* to the cause.

The earl's countenance soured quickly, though, when his thoughts returned to the information revealed by young Wickham about the Bennets' visit. Truly, the elder Wickham was a fool for trusting his son with *any* information. The father wrote in his letter that he was certain the future Mrs. Darcy was presently staying at Pemberley, and gave his impression of her—which was all good, of course, but what lady would *not* attempt to put up a good front for the Darcys?

Through his own dealings with Bennet during their shared time at Cambridge, he knew that he was an extremely intelligent man, and the earl was convinced that Bennet had used his years of what he believed to be a *false* friendship with the elder Darcy to subtly manipulate George's views on the *ton* and to gather information on his son's preferences. He was also certain that Miss Bennet had been carefully instructed as to how to behave in company with all three Darcys. If Miss Bennet was as intelligent as Wickham's father asserted, she would have no trouble duping the Darcys into thinking she was precisely what they wished for in the next Mistress of Pemberley—which was as much like the former Mistress as could be possible.

He had to break the Bennets' hold on them!

If he could somehow manage the illusion of the Bennets abandoning Fitzwilliam and Georgiana upon George Darcy's death, Fitzwilliam would have no one to turn to for assistance with the estate since the elder Wickham was also dead. The earl thought the chances were good that Fitzwilliam would eventually turn to him for help after he had failed in the management of Pemberley.

Upon reaching Pemberley the earl heard that a letter had already been sent to Mr. Bennet informing him of the loss, seeming to make his plans much more difficult to execute. He had decided that he would stay, and if Bennet returned—he would decide later what to do. Perhaps Catherine could assist him in that, but he felt that all depended on how circumstances developed.

Meanwhile, he put into effect his idea of making it look as if the Bennets had abandoned the Darcys. Surprisingly, it had been an easy task to achieve! Since the Darcys never had reason to doubt the loyalty of their servants, they never felt the need to be very careful with their correspondence and actually left it lying on a table in the hallway outside of the master's study! Fleming easily gleaned the post schedule for the house and would confiscate all outbound or inbound letters between the Bennets and the Darcys.

The moment that his sister Catherine arrived, he had discussed his plan with her, and she agreed fully to all he had already initiated, and then added to it. They would pressure Fitzwilliam either to turn Georgiana over to Catherine, which they knew their nephew would never do, or to finally agree to marry his cousin Anne de Bourgh—to provide the proper female guidance that she had so sorely lacked since her mother had died, of course.

Since they expected him to refuse, Catherine had already ordered her solicitor to begin to research ways of having Fitzwilliam removed as Georgiana's guardian so they could threaten him with that alternative. Knowing their nephew would never release his beloved sister to another's care, they anticipated he would eventually relent. It would not be long before both the earl and Lady Catherine gained an increasing amount of control over the Darcy holdings, name, and connections.

With the Darcy name fully behind them, the Fitzwilliam family would regain the grandeur that the shame of scandal had stolen from them years ago—and they would once again become an unstoppable force!

Now that their scheme was progressing nicely, the earl and his sister knew they had reached the point at which their nephew would soon send them packing. It was time to put the next phase into effect. Since their arrival, Fleming had spent many evenings in Lambton to discover who would best suit their needs. Finding a man named Booth, Fleming had befriended him, convincing him to spend some time every day after work engaging in manly pastimes—mostly drinking and playing cards at the tavern. It was *not* a coincidence that Booth kept losing to a man who was actually Fleming's brother.

All said, Booth had promised and lost more than a whole year's worth of his salary as an employee of the postal office at Lambton. When the stranger insisted on being paid immediately, Booth, the sole support to a number of younger brothers and sisters, was desperate to find a way to pay his debt and still be able to care for his siblings. Conveniently, his new friend Fleming had a proposition… if Booth would use his position at the postal office to do Fleming a few *favors*, he would buy his debt from the stranger, and they would call it even. Booth agreed to the arrangement immediately.

He was instructed to burn *all* letters between Pemberley and Longbourn in Hertfordshire, and all letters between anyone by the names of Bennet and Darcy, sent through regular post or express riders.

In addition, he was told to prevent *any* letter from the county of Hertfordshire from reaching Pemberley—in the event that the Bennets sent a letter through a friend. Booth was told to forward these letters to Fleming and await instruction.

It was not a perfect plan by any means. The earl and Lady Catherine could think of three scenarios where it would not succeed, but since to date they had not been able to coerce anyone within the Darcy household to aid them, it was the best chance they had at carrying off the illusion of abandonment.

It was a possibility that the Darcys would travel away from Pemberley and then their letters would go through a different postal office, but they were confident that the Darcys would not be able to leave any time soon and by the time they did, they would have given up all attempts at communication with the Bennets.

The second was that if the Bennets sent an express letter to Pemberley, the express rider would most likely *not* stop at the postal station in Lambton before delivering it to Pemberley, but as long as the Bennets sent their letters through regular post, the Darcys would never know they had written. Any express sent from Pemberley *would* be stopped since they had to be sent through Lambton postal station.

The last was that if either party sent a message through a private messenger, Booth would not be able to stop it—but since all other posts would be delivered without interruption, the earl did not expect that either party would suspect a problem with the post, and therefore, would not take on the added expense of hiring a private messenger.

~%~

"Mr. Cassidy, the jeweler from Lambton, is here to see you, Mr. Darcy. He states that he will not hand his package to anyone other than you, sir," Mr. Reynolds stated—his voice colored with a touch of annoyance at not being deemed trustworthy enough.

A quite haggard-looking William ran his hand through his hair to settle it and straightened out his coat, saying a bit nervously, "Send him in directly, Reynolds."

Mr. Cassidy was announced and entered the study. He came to a stop before William's desk, gingerly holding a medium sized parcel in both hands.

"May I see the results of our endeavor, Mr. Cassidy?"

"Yes, sir, Mr. Darcy." He carefully handed the parcel to William. "The piece you had designed is in the blue box, sir. I must say, though it was a pleasure to fashion your mourning jewelry as well, it was a pure delight for me to construct the ring according to your design, sir. Would you mind if I used the pattern for other jewelry?"

William opened the package as Mr. Cassidy spoke and opened the blue box first, removing his new signet ring. The ring opened as if it were a locket, revealing the precious hair of his beloved Elizabeth set in glass beneath it. He did not wish his gaze to linger for long—there would be plenty of time for that later. The ring closed perfectly and William placed it on the smallest finger of his left hand. Not that he had doubted Mr. Cassidy's work, but he was pleased that it fit perfectly, for to him it meant as much as the ring that he had given Elizabeth upon their engagement. He then moved on to open the other boxes which contained his and Georgiana's jewelry in memory of their father's passing, saying, "You are certain you used the correct lock of hair, Cassidy?"

"Yes, sir; I was extremely careful not to confuse this hair with your father's! Besides, the scent would have given it away had I been in doubt."

William colored slightly while saying, "Good. It is perfectly constructed, and I praise your talents." He hesitated while he inspected the other pieces and then said, "And for the rest, as well. Very nicely done, Mr. Cassidy. I thank you for your efforts."

Somehow wearing the ring helped him feel a little more at peace... at least part of Elizabeth would always physically be with him.

~%~

25 December 1807

My dearest Elizabeth,

Happy Christmas, my love. It has not been a happy time for the Darcys, I am afraid. Georgiana and I have attempted to put on a good front for each other's sake and for that of the servants, but we both are highly aware of all that we have lost in the past three months, and I seriously doubt that we are fooling anyone.

Three months... yes, the last day of this year will mark that amount of time since you have left us; the first of the new year will mean the same time has passed since the death of our father.

I had been making a fine attempt at viewing each sunrise as being one closer to seeing you again, but I admit this has been difficult to accomplish during the past few days. I cannot think of the day that I dream of — the day I will be seeing you once again — as the thirtieth day of May. It seems too far away when I see that the calendar is still turned to December.

I will not abandon you as your father has done to Georgiana and me. I will come to you on your birthday and, if he is still set against me, G-d help me, I will take you away from him to Scotland as I have promised you. I swear it, Elizabeth. At times, it is only this thought that spurs me on in doing what I must to get through the day. I must keep all running as smoothly as possible here so that our future together is secure.

Did you receive the gift that Georgiana and I chose for you in Lambton, I wonder? I wished to send you so much more than a set of handkerchiefs and have actually purchased several gifts for you, but I could not imagine that your father would allow you to receive any gifts from me, so I will give you the gifts when I see you again. I am not even certain he will permit the one gift from Georgiana. I understand it is not likely, but I am nursing a small hope that he did not tell you they were from Georgiana and gave them to you under the guise of a gift from himself. You would then recognize Georgiana's embroidery work — or you would instinctively know from whom they came. Perhaps this hope is silly, but it has helped me through my days of late.

Georgiana has given me a detailed account of all she has written to you — the letter she sent today was one that she had begged I read before posting. She is worried that she has offended you in some way and that her unintentional slight is the reason why you have not written or come to Pemberley, but I have assured her that is not the reason. I do not know that I have convinced her; the current generation of Darcys seems to have a tendency to predict the worse possible outcomes of any situation and to blame themselves for being the cause of it.

My time spent writing to you here in this journal has been decreasing as I have little to say other than to repeat my longings for you, and I have found another way in which to express my feelings that does them more justice than any words could ever do, of which I will tell you in a few moments.

I could share with you what has transpired during my days as I would if you were here, but it seems pointless for two reasons. The first is that you will probably never read this journal since I will someday have the honor of telling you all that has been written within with my own voice. The second is that I have found it helpful to keep several, more formal, journals in addition to my ledgers for such things. I have made separate journals for each type correspondence: tenant business, notes I have made for the spring plantings, and a few others for miscellaneous business and personal dealings. I began them because I was so overwhelmed at first, trying to remember every detail so that I could repeat it when necessary, and this practice became so helpful that I have continued it. My steward and secretary find them useful as well. However, I do feel the need to update you on several subjects since my last entry.

I am embarrassed to admit to this, but since I sleep very little, I spend the time I have to myself sketching you. As if you were here, I can hear you laugh and ask why that would be a problem since you had given me permission to make drawings of you many times in the past. My answer would have to be that it is not merely the fact that I am making sketches, Elizabeth, it is the sheer number of them... I have made several dozen and have absolutely no intention of restricting this indulgence since it provides me with some little bit of solace. My dreams are filled with you and many times when I awaken without you near, I am filled with an ache of overwhelming loneliness and despair. The best way I have found to feel closer to you is to sketch your likeness.

One might say I am a man obsessed! As you once said, although your memories do not, most people's memories fade with time. To be honest, that statement has made me terrified that this will happen with my memories of you. Consequently, I have begun to recreate your stay at Pemberley as I remember it, depicting you in each circumstance in which I had found you, or vice versa since I was less able to move than you. I have found that each situation provides me with an endless number of memories of your expressions that I had grown to love, even some that I would dread to have repeated upon your lovely face.

I can only wish that I had better skills, for I cannot do justice to your beauty, but it will have to do for now. I certainly hope I will not have a chance to make many more before I can again see the original, my dearest Elizabeth.

I cannot put into words how much I miss you. I cannot suppress my constant urgent need to know what you are thinking and feeling — I thought I would hear from you at least through your letters to Georgiana. Sometimes I think I shall go mad without knowing what is occurring in your life.

I cannot imagine that you could know all that I have written to your father and all that Georgiana has written to you, and that it does not affect you. At all times I have two opposite wishes — one is to find that you do not know of the happenings here, that your father has kept this news from you and has kept Georgiana's letters from your hands, so that you are not pained by our suffering without any way to relieve it. But, I also feel a desperate need for you to know, so that I can be assured that your affectionate heart is feeling something of what we are experiencing. I know the latter is selfish and cruel, but I cannot help myself.

I confess that there is a very small part of me that, at the worst of times, wonders if you ever truly cared for me at all, but then I remember the way you looked at me, the way you melted into my embrace as if you had as great a need for my touch as I had for yours, and my doubts are quelled.

Perhaps this is the reason that many of the drawings I have made are limited to your eyes and brows alone. I am driven to attempt to catch on paper the exact look of love that I recall seeing in those eyes that have so bewitched me. I have always marveled at the way your eyes seem to articulate your thoughts and emotions—they are so revealing! I cannot get the look of love in your eyes just right, and I am desperate to see it again.

I do not understand your father, and I am afraid that my disappointment when he did not answer my letters at first has now turned to bitterness toward him. Though you had almost convinced me that your interpretation of his response to my proposal was correct, I now know all that you had thought about him was wrong, and that my father was mistaken to trust him. How could he blatantly disregard all of his promises to my father?

It must be because we fell in love, but why does he feel I am so wrong for you? On what grounds does he reject me, Elizabeth?

The Darcy line is respectable, honorable, and ancient—though untitled. On my mother's side, I am descended from a noble line. I am the grandson of an earl! I am wealthy and in sole control of the Darcy legacy. He could not have doubted that I could provide for your material needs. I have made every attempt at being a good man and have rejected following my peers when their activities went against my values.

Could he have doubted that I loved you enough, even after all that I said to him? I believe I treated you well... did I not, Elizabeth? Does he believe that I did persuade you into my bed, and, therefore he feels he cannot trust me? Does he feel I would not respect you if we married and would not honor every aspect of the vows I would make to you — that I have already made in my heart?

I wish that I had got down on my knees and begged your father for as long as it took to gain his consent. Would that have done any good? I go over and over everything in my mind — what could I have done differently? I do not believe I could have changed any of my actions, except for that last night. Knowing what I do now, that he would have allowed us a few minutes the next morning, I understand that I should not have gone to your room... but there was no way of foreseeing that. Perhaps he would not have allowed it if not for what I said in his rooms that morning, and you would have left without the reassurance of my love for you! I could not risk it, my love.

I am finding myself praying often the past three months. Every time this rancor enters my heart, as well as when I become angry at my father for dying, I ask for His guidance and forgiveness.

Ah, I have reviewed my letter and realize that I have not told you of the anger as of yet. You see, Father was supposed to begin to hand over the responsibilities now, not leave me with the whole all at once. He was supposed to be here to give his guidance to me, to approve of my plans before I put them into effect. This transition was supposed to happen <u>slowly</u>! And I was not supposed to have the added responsibility of suddenly having to be a father to my young sister at the same time!

I know he did not wish to die! I know my anger is completely unreasonable! I feel incredibly guilty for feeling this way, Elizabeth, but still I cannot stop myself, and I feel as if I am very weak. Perhaps being deprived of your support is G-d's punishment?

Will I lose your love as well, Elizabeth? I could not survive if I did! Please, please do not stop loving me!

Though I wish you were here, I truly do hope that you had a happy Christmas, my heart.

Yours forever,
William

Chapter 9

27 May, 1808

Five months later

Colonel Richard Fitzwilliam's horse came to an abrupt stop in front of the main entrance of a damaged Pemberley Manor. As he had approached, he could not miss the acrid stench of smoke that still hung heavy in the air—a telltale sign that the fire was still smoldering somewhere within. Dismounting before his horse had completely stopped moving, Richard handed off the reins to a servant and rushed up the steps and through the front door. As he entered, he recognized the older man walking toward him and called out, "Reynolds! Is he in his chamber?"

"Yes, Colonel Fitzwilliam, he is," Mr. Reynolds answered while helping him off with his coat.

"Any change?"

Mr. Reynolds followed as Richard began to walk toward the staircase. "You should brace yourself before seeing him, sir; the only change since the express was sent to you has been for the worse. I should tell you before you are in company with Miss Georgiana that Mr. Smythe is not very confident of a positive outcome, Colonel."

Richard stopped walking for a moment, closed his eyes, and said a silent prayer. Taking a deep breath, he began walking again as he noisily blew out a rush of air. "I appreciate the warning, Reynolds, but I have every confidence in William's ability to win this battle with his stubborn determination! He *will* refuse to leave Georgiana alone—I guarantee it!"

Taking the stairs two at a time, Richard quickened his pace even further when he neared the third floor and could hear the screams of his cousin. Not bothering to knock, he opened the door to the master's suite and stood in shock for several moments, staring at the scene he found within.

William was in bed, propped up with pillows, completely drenched with sweat, his left arm flailing about frantically as if reaching out to someone who was far away, and he was screaming a woman's name in a hoarse voice, repeating it again and again. He surmised that William must have either already fallen from or had tried to remove himself from the bed, because a footman, James he thought, was posted close by—ready to spring into action if required. Georgiana had collapsed into a chair near the bed and was sobbing quietly. Mrs. Reynolds was endeavoring to tell William that *she* was the woman he sought while mopping his face, left arm, and the undamaged part of his chest with a wet cloth, Richard assumed in an attempt to lower his fever. There was a maid who seemed to have the duty of making certain that clean cloths were available for Mrs. Reynolds' use. Richard recognized Mr. Smythe, the doctor from Lambton, and saw that another maid was assisting him in preparing a salve, most likely to apply to William's wounds. A fire was blazing in the fireplace, keeping the room as warm as possible.

Richard kneeled at Georgiana's side and took her into an embrace. "Richard! Oh, Richard!" she sobbed into his shoulder. Mrs. Reynolds caught his eye for a moment, and she gestured toward the door to the master's sitting room. Taking the hint, Richard stood, pulled Georgiana with him, and supported most of her weight as he moved her out into the sitting room. As he passed the table at which Mr. Smythe was working, his eyes silently begged the doctor for more information as soon as he was able.

Mr. Smythe approached and said so that only Richard could hear, "Miss Darcy has not eaten in two days."

Richard nodded. When he had moved Georgiana to a sofa in the sitting room, Richard walked to the door joining the two rooms and closed it, ringing for tea while returning to her side. "I must return to William!" Georgiana sobbed and began to rise from the sofa, but Richard held her in place by the shoulders.

"Georgie, you need to eat and get some rest first."

"NO, Richard! William needs me!"

Richard could see that he was going to have to use what William and Georgiana referred to as his *colonel voice*. "Georgiana Darcy! I am your guardian, and you *will* follow my instructions on this." His tone softened as he continued, "The doctor said you must eat, and so you shall. You cannot be strong for your brother if you fall ill yourself, and I will not have both of my favorite relatives needing nursemaids. Besides, everyone is so busy with your brother that the job would most likely fall upon me! I do not think you would like *me* as your nursemaid, Poppet."

Her crying had quieted, and she tried to smile. "I would think you would do better as nursemaid to William. Perhaps that would help to cheer him."

A knock on the door was followed by the entrance of a maid bearing a tray with tea, cold meats, and cheeses, which she set up on a table nearby before quickly exiting the room. Richard made a plate and tea for Georgiana, bringing it to her. "You see, I am already serving tea; nursemaid may not be far behind!" Again Georgiana made a weak attempt at a smile. "Eat!" Richard commanded, and then returned to make up his own plate.

Once seated, Richard saw that Georgiana must have found that she was hungry after all—her plate was more than half cleared already. They sat in silence as he attacked his own plate, both lost in thought. When Georgiana returned her plate to the table, she said, "Thank you, Richard, I do feel a little better. I do not remember how long it has been since I have eaten."

"Mr. Smythe said it was two days ago. I can only assume it was before the fire."

"Oh."

"Georgiana, who is Elizabeth?"

"Miss Elizabeth Bennet. I am certain you have heard us speak of her." Richard nodded and Georgiana continued, "Elizabeth and her father stayed with us last summer and into the autumn. Do you remember when William was ill at the beginning of September? Elizabeth had been walking near William's favorite riding path, and his horse reared to avoid her, which is how he was injured. She had injured her ankle as well and while William had a high fever, he was acting in much the same manner as he is now. Mrs. Reynolds tells me he wanted to make certain Elizabeth was safe so Father had her brought to William's room. She sat with him until his fever broke. We are assuming he thinks she is still here and wishes to make certain she was not injured in the fire. He has been calling for her almost constantly since he was injured."

"Are you saying he has been like *this* for almost two days?"

She nodded and tears began to form in her eyes once again.

"Can you send for Miss Bennet, Georgiana?"

Richard could see he had touched on a sensitive subject when the torrent of tears began anew as she said, "She and her father have not written since they left here. William believes her father has kept our letters from her and will not allow her to write to us."

"Why on earth would he do such a thing?"

"Well… William only told me his thoughts on that subject a few days ago when he told me of his plans. He proposed marriage to Elizabeth last September, and Mr. Bennet did not consent. William feels that her father does not approve of him. Brother had promised to stay away until Elizabeth turned seventeen, which will be in a few days. He was about to leave here and go to her; they had planned to elope to Scotland if Mr. Bennet continued to deny his consent, but he will not be able to go now…"

"Not approve the match?! Is the man daft? William is every father's dream! What could he possibly *object* to?"

"I do not know, Richard. I cannot understand it."

Richard was thoughtful for a few minutes before saying, "Perhaps if *you* wrote a letter directly to Mr. Bennet, begging him to allow Miss Bennet to travel to Pemberley. Appeal to his fatherly sensibilities. Offer him anything he could want, Georgiana. William cannot survive like *this*! Something must be done to calm him."

Happy to be able to *do* something to help her brother, Georgiana replied enthusiastically, "Yes… yes! I will write directly to Mr. Bennet. I will go to my room now and send it express. Meanwhile, we shall have to continue to try to convince him that Elizabeth is well. After all, he did have the investigator check on her twice to be certain."

"Good to know, Poppet. I will go in to William now and try to quiet him."

~%~

27 May, 1808
Pemberley, Derbyshire

Dear Mr. Bennet,

I respectfully request that you put aside whatever quarrel you have with our family while reading this letter. I myself have many pleasant memories of our time spent together, as does my brother, and we have both been saddened and confused by the recent lack of communication between our families.

There has been a fire at Pemberley. It pains me to write that my brother William was burned about the arm and a portion of his chest when a beam fell upon him while he was entering the house to free several members of our staff who were trapped within.

Infection has now set in, and William has developed a very high fever in addition to the great amount of pain he is suffering from the burns. Mr. Smythe, the doctor from Lambton, tells me that, unlike his reaction to a previous high fever in September, William is not truly aware of his surroundings. William seems to think that you and Miss Elizabeth are still presently visiting Pemberley. He is calling out for her, much like he did almost eight months ago, but this time Miss Elizabeth is not here to show him that she is safe, and we have not been able to quiet him. He thrashes about and calls for her for hours at a time, sir! My brother is only becoming more agitated as time passes, and Mr. Smythe is extremely concerned as he feels that if William does not rest, there will never be a chance for his fever to abate, and in that case he will soon die.

Please, Mr. Bennet! I must beg that Miss Elizabeth be conveyed to Pemberley the moment you read this letter.

I will arrange for horses to be brought to the post stops between Longbourn and Pemberley so that your driver can continue straight through without stopping to rest your horses. I would have sent one of our coaches, but it was much faster to send an express.

If you do not wish to send Miss Elizabeth for William's sake, please do so for mine, sir. Pity me, sir, if nothing else since I have only my brother and my cousin Richard remaining to call my family. I appeal to your sense of Christian charity if pity is not enough to bridge the breach. I promise to do anything you ask, sir — anything — if you would just assist me so that I will not lose William, too!

I thank you, Mr. Bennet, for I have faith that you will come to my aide at this most desperate time of need.

Sincerely,
Georgiana Darcy

A few tears fell onto the paper as she sealed it, but Georgiana had not the time to write her letter again. She asked her maid to give it to Mr. Reynolds to be delivered to the postal station in Lambton to be dispatched express immediately, and then joined Richard at her brother's bedside.

Several hours had passed, and William had rested for limited periods of time between bouts of screaming. Georgiana had fallen asleep on a couch during one of William's short slumbers, and Richard had gently lifted and carried her to her room, hoping she would sleep for many hours. There was nothing she could do, and Richard had left orders with the staff that she should be awakened if there was any change in her brother's condition.

The doctor lay down upon the couch that Georgiana had previously occupied, and Richard ordered Mrs. Reynolds, the other maids, and James to retire as well when reinforcements had arrived. For a few minutes all was quiet, and Richard began to look about the room for something with which to occupy himself lest he fall asleep himself.

His gaze was caught by the writing desk since it had the corner of a piece of paper protruding from one of the drawers. He was curious about this oddity... his cousin was always so fastidious! Richard opened the deep drawer to straighten the page but what met his eyes mesmerized him. It was a half-finished drawing of a truly beautiful lady. He lifted it out of the drawer to get a better look at it, and saw another; beneath that one he found another... and another... and another... and another! Lifting a handful from the drawer he found that *all* the drawings were of the same woman—she was employed in different occupations and drawn from different angles. There had to be hundreds of them! Richard opened the drawer above this one which was about half as deep and found drawings of eyes, many of them had several sets of eyes per page.

This had to be William's Elizabeth, and he was obviously madly in love with her. Choosing one of the first few sketches he had seen, Richard approached the bed and sat down, hoping to be able to catch his cousin's attention by the drawing when he awakened.

~%~

Hearing the clock chime four, Georgiana awoke and saw that it was the middle of the night. It took a few moments before she remembered what had been occurring the past few days, but those blissful moments of ignorance were short-lived. Sorrow and worry came crashing down upon her when she heard her brother's screams echo down the hall as they began again. Where he found the strength to continue on this way, she could not understand.

Still dressed from the previous day—or was it the day before that—she rose and pulled out the hairpins which were no longer doing their job and twisted her hair into a simple knot as she walked toward the door.

Upon entering William's room she could see that there was no change in William's condition; though at the moment he was quiet, he was still moving around restlessly. Richard was sitting in the chair next to the bed, bathing his face with a wet cloth. *"He is playing nursemaid after all!"* she thought as she looked upon the scene so full of brotherly love.

Georgiana then started when William began to scream again… or as close to a scream as he could get with his voice so raspy after the past few days.

Richard's voice boomed out much louder than William's, "I have had *ENOUGH*, William! Stop this nonsense at once! *YOU MUST REST!* Georgiana is depending on you to be alive and well! You *WILL NOT* leave her alone in the world. Do you understand me? Being in the army, I cannot always be here for her.

"*I* am depending on you, blast it! You have always been my best friend and confidant; I am closer to you than to *anyone else*. You and Georgiana are the only two people that I truly consider to be family in every sense of the word.

"Miss Elizabeth is well! *I* was *not* here when Miss Elizabeth was at Pemberley, which is proof enough that Miss Elizabeth is safely away from here. You have confirmed that Miss Elizabeth is safe through an investigator. You *must* become well before you can go to her. Miss Elizabeth is waiting for you to marry her, William. Do not disappoint her!

"If you die, my father will come and take over Pemberley, stating it is for Georgiana's sake! He and Aunt Catherine will ruin everything your father had achieved and all that you have strived to maintain.

"Do not break the hearts of all those you love! YOU **MUST** RECOVER!" The last shout echoed throughout the room.

Georgiana noticed that William had stopped screaming at the beginning of Richard's rant and had remained silent through all of the rest of it, but did not seem to be awake. Did a small part of his mind hear it? Did he understand?

She walked to Richard's side and placed her hand on his shoulder, startling him a bit. He looked up at her sheepishly, but his countenance changed to one of relief when he saw the hint of a smile in his cousin's eyes as she squeezed his shoulder. Clearing his throat, he said, "I have seen too many young men die for crown and country… for *good* causes. I could not watch him die for no reason at all. I had to try *something*. I hope you can forgive me for shouting at your brother when he is so ill."

"We have tried everything else, Richard. I do not believe it could harm him." Moving her eyes to William she gasped, "Richard! I do think you have done some good."

Richard looked back at William and saw his face seemed more relaxed, as if he were sleeping soundly. He took a trembling breath and let it out slowly in an attempt to hold back the tears that had filled his eyes.

~%~

It was Richard's turn to sleep on the couch while Mr. Smythe and Georgiana stood watch over William. After sleeping for he knew not how long, he was awakened by Georgiana's cries. Fear gripping his heart, Richard jumped from the couch and rushed to her side. The young girl buried her face in his chest, sobbing uncontrollably. He did not wish to look at William but knew he must. Mr. Smythe was leaning over him with his ear to William's chest listening to his heart, blocking Richard's view of his cousin. When Mr. Smythe moved aside while he examined William, Richard saw why Georgiana was so distraught—William's skin was so very white, and he was lying perfectly still. It looked as if he were…

Mr. Smythe straightened up, a wide smile spreading across his face. "The fever has broken! The chances are good that he will live!"

Richard exhaled with a howl. He looked down and saw Georgiana's smile had probably outdone his own and now her tears were tears of joy; Richard could not stop the few that fell from his own eyes as well. He picked up his cousin and twirled her around. Georgiana laughed, which made him laugh along with her.

The relief that the Master would live and the sight of the two cousins giggling like school children caused Mr. Smythe, Mrs. Reynolds, James, and the maids to join in as well. Mrs. Reynolds called out to one of the maids to spread the news among the other staff.

"You did it, Richard! You saved him!"

"No, Poppet, William saved himself—he just needed a bit of a reminder of all he had to live for."

~%~

William slept for several hours, and when he woke, the only thing that he noticed was that the pain in his arm and the right side of his chest was much worse than it had been when his shoulder had been injured, though he could not remember why. He opened his eyes and blinked a few times, and when his eyes cleared, he saw both Richard and Georgiana asleep in chairs next to the bed. Looking to his arm, William saw that it and part of his chest were covered with some sort of salve and a cloth was draped over his stomach and left arm. The cloth was tickling his chin and when he tried to move his right arm to scratch it, the arm would not respond. His eyes widened as he concentrated on moving his arm again, and it did nothing. William tried to ask what had happened to him, but his throat was very sore and his voice failed him. The resulting cough woke Richard and Georgiana. Mr. Smythe came into view as well, looking rather disheveled, as if he had been sleeping. The doctor moved quickly to the water pitcher, poured William a glass, and helped him to drink a few sips.

"William!" Georgiana said with a wide smile, eyes bright with tears. She leaned over to kiss her brother's cheek.

"You gave us quite a scare, cousin! It is good to see you awake and aware again."

"What happened?" William croaked out.

"You do not remember the fire, Brother? Pemberley's guest wing has burned, as well as part of the servants' quarters. Some of the servants were trapped, and you went in to rescue them."

"Did anyone..."

Georgiana shook her head. "No one was lost; there were no major injuries other than yours. You saved those who were trapped before a beam fell upon you. James and another footman had gone in with you, and they lifted the beam and were able to carry you from the house. I am not sure who the other footman was; I will have to enquire so we know who to thank. I am afraid I have not been thinking very clearly the past three days!"

"Elizabeth?"

"She is at Longbourn I believe."

"Dreamt Elizabeth died in a fire!"

"Yes, thank G-d they were only dreams! She has not been at Pemberley for eight months."

Georgiana helped him take another drink and then William's brow furrowed. "Eight months? Her birthday... what is the date?"

"Today is the eight and twentieth day of May."

William's eyes widened again, "I will be late!" He tried to sit up and failed miserably, moaning at the pain.

Mr. Smythe placed a hand on his left shoulder and applied a little pressure to have him lie down again, "Do not even *think* about travelling!"

"But I must be in Hertfordshire by the thirtieth day of May!"

"You are *not* going anywhere for quite a while, Mr. Darcy! You have burns to a good portion of your arm, part of your wrist, and part of your chest. Your fever was very high for more than two days and the infection is just beginning to retreat. To be honest, sir, I did not think you would be with us today. You will rest and recuperate until *I* tell you differently or you will have a relapse. You are not strong enough to survive another few days similar to those you have just experienced!"

"William, I wrote to Mr. Bennet yesterday begging Elizabeth to come to Pemberley and sent it by express. He should have it by now—Elizabeth might even be on her way here."

A dark look clouded his face. "He would not tell her even if he thought I was dying... he would not allow her to come to Pemberley, Georgiana. If anything, he is rejoicing at the news."

"Now, William, I do not think Mr. Bennet could be that bad!"

"Do not depend upon it, Georgiana. Though it might be better this way; the scarring from the burns will be horrendous will it not?" he said the last to Mr. Smythe.

"You are alive, sir. The salve may help the scarring."

"Mr. Smythe may I ask... with burns... is it normal not to be able to move my arm or hand?"

Mr. Smythe performed some further examinations of his hand at least, not wishing to touch the burnt skin. "It seems you have some damage to the nerves of your right arm in addition to the burns. It will take quite a while and much work for you to regain use of your arm and hand. Time will tell if the recovery will be complete or partial. That you can feel pain in the arm is bittersweet—I realize burns are very painful, but it is a good sign for recovery."

William closed his eyes and sighed. "It is not as painful as it probably should be judging by the way it looks."

"You might not be able to understand this, but if the nerve damage is lessening the pain, it is a blessing right now, Mr. Darcy."

"I am very tired." William said.

"We all need to catch up on some sleep as well, cousin. I will ask James to come sit with you."

William's eyes snapped open and he asked, "Before you go, where is my ring?"

Georgiana, Richard, and Mr. Smythe said they did not know.

The maid answered, "Beggin' your pardon, sir, I do. We took it off when you were first brought up." She walked over to a table and retrieved his signet ring.

"Thank you. Georgie, can you put it on my hand, please?"

Georgiana did as she was asked as Richard had James come in. William relaxed against the pillows and fell asleep almost immediately. The remainder of the party left the room.

~%~

30 May 1808

Two days had passed and William regained a little strength each day, but his spirits were considerably depressed, even more so on Elizabeth's seventeenth birthday. Both Richard and Georgiana had expected this development, so they had made up a plan for one or the other to stay with William at all times and distract him. Richard entered his chamber as soon as Hughes had informed him that the Master was awake. "Good morning, cousin! Are you feeling any better?"

"Yes, yes… better. Now, please leave me alone!"

"Ah, you must be feeling stronger at least to expend so much energy on being ornery!" Richard quipped.

"I am in no mood for company."

"I know exactly why you are not, and that is precisely why Georgiana and I have conspired against you. We will not leave you alone all day today."

William rolled his eyes. "Just go away, Richard."

"No." Richard hesitated before saying, "I have a confession to make, William. There was something protruding from one of your drawers, and I opened it to place it in correctly. I found the drawings."

"Which drawings?"

Richard walked over to the desk, took out the drawing on top and brought it back to the bed to hand it to William, watching his expression soften when he saw it. "I am assuming they are of Miss Elizabeth."

"Yes."

Silence prevailed for several minutes before Richard asked, "Will you tell me about her?"

"What do you know?"

"You all have written of her several times over the past few years; I think before last year your father wrote of her most of all. He was considerably impressed with her. Georgiana has spoken of her a great deal over the past few days, but it seems there is more I can learn only from you, if you are so inclined. You should know that you did not stop screaming her name while you had a fever."

William, who had not taken his eyes off the sketch since it had been handed to him, looked at his cousin in surprise. "I called for her for three days?!"

Richard nodded.

William closed his eyes for a moment and then said, "My ring is also a sort of locket... with my arm like this I cannot open it. Will you do it for me?"

Richard did as he asked and found a lock of hair set under glass. "Miss Elizabeth's?"

William nodded. He had Richard to bring all the drawings of Elizabeth to his bed and he handed at least one to him for each scene he described as he went on to tell Richard everything he could remember about his time with Elizabeth—or at least everything he cared to share—beginning with the first time they met through the day she left Pemberley. Richard sat in awed amazement. The sketches were like a picture book, some even had the words she had said printed beneath the drawing. Then William explained to Richard what he felt had happened after the Bennets left.

"So, you think Mr. Bennet has something against you personally and is keeping the letters from her in an attempt to have her think Georgiana— and especially *you*—have abandoned her? I do not understand why!"

"Neither do I, Richard. I think Elizabeth does not even know that Father has died. But Mr. Bennet *does*, and he has completely disregarded all of the promises he made to Father by not coming directly to Pemberley after he received word of his death. What else could explain it other than that he does not approve of me for his daughter? He was quite willing to do so *before* his daughter and I fell in love!"

"And now?"

William sighed and with a pained look on his face he said, "I fear that she will begin to believe him now that I have not come to see her for her birthday."

"Why do you not send someone to contact her—tell her what has happened since she has left? I would be happy to make the trip, if you would like. If she cannot make the journey here without her father's permission, at least she would know that you have not abandoned her!"

"I have had the same thoughts over the past two days... but I cannot—*will* not! She cannot know anything about my injuries, at least not until I have recovered the use of my hand and arm, Richard. I forbid both you and Georgiana to attempt to contact her! I have seen adoration and love when I have looked into her eyes; I refuse to look now only to see pity, sorrow, and disgust in them. She will *not* know until I am able to hold her in my *two* arms. We will not even attempt to contact the Bennets again until I can; no more letters at all. Please do not go against my wishes on this, Richard—it would end in disaster."

"If she is as wonderful as your father, your sister, and you have described, then I think you are a fool, William. She would not react in the way that you anticipate."

"I can only say that, though I would hope she would not, I dread the possibility that she would. I will work especially hard to regain the use of my arm, of that you can be certain."

"But William…"

William interrupted, "NO, Richard!"

"I promise I will not attempt to contact her. If I do happen to come across her at some point, I will not tell her anything of you."

"I doubt very much you will ever meet her until I have recovered, and we are either engaged or, more likely, married. She moves in very different circles than your parents do. I will love her forever, Richard, and she has vowed to love me for the rest of her life. All will be well… it will only be a little delayed—and different as well." William thought about the scarring and how he had often longed to hold her bare form against his own and feel her hands explore his skin. That would never happen now—he could not allow it. He could never remove his shirt in her presence for she would be too disgusted by the sight of him. William shuddered at the thought.

When he heard clock in the hall chime eleven bells, his eyes were drawn to the clock on the mantelpiece in his room. "What is she doing right now, Richard? I have a clear image in my mind of Elizabeth sitting by the window in the drawing room at Longbourn—she would be able to see the drive from there. A book lies open on her lap, one she had been attempting to read to distract herself, but she had been unable to tear her eyes from the window, waiting for me to appear." He took a shaky breath. "But I will not appear. What will she think of me, Richard?" William's breathing came in starts as he quelled the tears from spilling from his eyes. "I am tiring again…" he saw Richard's doubt clearly displayed on his face. "Truly, I am in need of a nap. I will have Hughes let you know when I have awakened. Thank you for listening. It was helpful."

Chapter 10

25 May 1808

Early one morning in the days leading up to Elizabeth's seventeenth birthday, Mr. Bennet sat alone in his study pondering all that had transpired over recent months. His concern for his favorite daughter had escalated with each passing week of the past eight months as he had watched her sink deeper into melancholy. Although during the past few days Elizabeth had become more animated than he had seen her since they had left Pemberley all those months ago, this behavior actually increased his worry for her.

A knock on the study door interrupted his solitary reflections, and Mr. Bennet sighed and bid the intruder to enter. He was relieved to see Jane step into the room, for he had been thinking of speaking to her about Elizabeth, and this happenstance decided it for him.

"Good morning, Papa. May I speak to you?"

"Of course, Jane, come in and have a seat."

She closed the door firmly behind her and sat in one of the chairs in front of his desk. "Papa, I am afraid for Lizzy. Though she has attempted to behave normally and conceal her feelings over the past few months…" Jane's brow furrowed deeply as she exclaimed, "Oh! I fear I will be betraying a confidence by speaking of this, but I am so deeply distressed that I must speak to *someone*, Papa!"

Mr. Bennet moved from behind the desk and settled himself in the chair opposite Jane. He put his hand upon one of hers which was gripping the arm of the chair firmly, convincing Mr. Bennet that her discomfort was greater than was betrayed by her countenance. "My dear Jane, I will keep Lizzy's confidence; I promise. If this involves William Darcy, you are not betraying Lizzy by speaking to me. Lizzy and I have had several discussions about the Darcy family over the past several months."

Jane nodded in relief and continued, a little more relaxed, "I am certain you have noticed that Lizzy has become increasingly discouraged at the lack of correspondence from Miss Darcy and Mr. Darcy. She told me all that had occurred during your visit soon after your return from Pemberley." Jane gave her father a pointed look, "As her birthday nears, her spirits have grown higher every day in anticipation of that special day. I fear what her response will be if her expectations do not... well... if she is disappointed, sir."

"You mean if William does not come to Longbourn. Yes, yes, I fear this as well."

"Papa, do you know what has caused this rift?"

"I do have an inkling, but I cannot be certain until I speak with Mr. Darcy again, or receive word from him. Even if my suspicions are correct, William may come without his father's approval. I do *not* find it encouraging that there has been no letter announcing his intent to visit, but perhaps William feels he does not need to write since he made a promise to Lizzy.

"I must say, Jane, that Mr. Darcy's lack of communication has wounded our friendship. There will have to be a very good explanation if I am to forgive this behavior, especially toward Lizzy. Denying her correspondence with his daughter after approving of it wholeheartedly when we were at Pemberley is inexcusable. I can only imagine that his wish was to break off completely the connection between the families since he refuses to correspond with me as well. If that is so—if William disobeys his father by coming to Longbourn—I fear he will be disinherited. If so, William would be penniless, and I could not give my consent for their marriage."

Mr. Bennet hesitated for several moments before continuing, "Jane—I overheard them speaking the day we left. William and Lizzy agreed that if they did not have my approval, they would go to Scotland. I hoped to forewarn you of this possibility so that you would talk to Lizzy about this subject and have her see sense. If William had no income, life would be very difficult were they to marry. Contrary to what they may believe, love is *not* enough to live on."

"Oh Papa, Lizzy is such a sensible person, she would never do such a thing…" Jane's expression turned a little bashful as some fairly insensible things Lizzy had done in the past came to mind, "… well, at least *not* under *those* conditions! I am certain that Mr. Darcy would not disinherit his son. This breach is all some sort of strange misunderstanding between the families, and reconciliation would be easily obtained if each was given the chance to explain his own situation. What *I* worry about is that, given that the breach exists, young Mr. Darcy will not come at all. What would that do to poor Lizzy? She had a terrible nightmare last night, sir. I fear for her disposition if he does not appear."

"Well, my dear, since we are not fortune tellers and cannot predict what will happen, we can discuss this for hours, and it will get us nowhere. I do not know what Lizzy's reaction will be if he does not come, though I can anticipate two possibilities—anger or a deeper melancholy—and I do hope we will never discover which it would have been. Either way, we do not have much choice in the matter, do we? We will only be able to help her through it as best we can if the worst does come to pass."

"Yes, Papa."

~%~

30 May 1808

Elizabeth was unable to sleep but stayed abed until a few minutes before dawn, powerless to contain her excitement—or her fear—any longer. Thinking that a long walk before the day began would be her only source of release, she dressed as quickly as she could. She was determined not to leave the house at all after breakfast, since she wanted to be there when William arrived… *if* William arrived.

Dressed for the outdoors, Elizabeth made her way through the kitchen to tell Mrs. Hill where she was going, and to pilfer a muffin and some fruit to eat while on her walk, as was her habit for morning rambles, though she was not certain she would be able to eat *this* morning. She made her way along a well-known path as the first rays of morning graced the land with their light, and many of the questions that had kept her awake during the night began to resurface.

Would her father give his consent? The last time they had spoken on the subject, he had said he would, but that conversation had taken place while her birthday was still a week away. She could not think of why he would not, other than that he might not want her to live so far away. William had followed her father's rules—they had parted, and he had made no attempt to contact her for eight months.

She had done all that her father had asked as well—attended all the assembly balls, parties, and teas, while trying her best to be lively company. She had even gone to London at Christmastide and attended the theater, two balls, as well as several parties and dinners that her Aunt and Uncle Gardiner had arranged for them to attend. She had lost count of how many young gentlemen she had met, conversed with, and danced with. A few were interesting enough to pass the time with in conversation, and several were entertained enough by her to call, but she was careful not to raise their expectations.

Meanwhile, her opinion that William was perfect *for her* in every way had never faltered. She knew she would never find a better man or a better match. His conversation was not merely interesting, it was captivating. William's moral standards were above any she had ever met with in another. Their tastes in many areas of interest were similar, and where they disagreed, he did not criticize; he respected her ideas even as they debated opposite point of views. William loved to add to her knowledge, and he was happy to share with her everything that he knew—and he accepted it if she was knowledgeable about something that he was not and even enjoyed learning *from* her. If neither of them understood a subject, he wanted to learn about it *with* her. He valued her opinion and wished her to be his *partner* in life, not just his wife. He was not entertained or frightened by her talents as so many others had been; he was mesmerized by them. William treasured that she was different from other women instead of ridiculing that fact.

But most important of all, he loved her as she loved him.

None of the seemingly endless line of gentlemen who had been paraded before her could even begin to compare to her William. Meeting these men had only made her appreciation of him grow stronger! She had told all of this to her father when they had spoken a few days ago, assuring him that William was indeed her choice, and she could not be happy without him.

What she had *not* told her father, but often thought, was that physically she was equally impressed by him. William was not merely attractive, he was absolutely exquisite. He set her heart racing and made her breath quicken with just a look or the slightest touch of his hand. His scent was calming yet exciting. Allowing her mind to dwell on his kisses and caresses caused her to think highly improper, but pleasant, thoughts—she knew she could never get her fill of him in *that* way, and William had implied that he felt the same about her.

Elizabeth sighed deeply and looked around, realizing she had walked farther than she had intended. As she turned back toward Longbourn, she quickened her pace.

She had experienced a terrible feeling of dread regarding William a few days ago. Her own screams had awoken her from a dream, and it had taken Jane a long time to quiet her. Elizabeth had begun to get dressed in a frenzy, asking Jane to lend her any pin money she might have saved—insisting that she *had* to go to Pemberley—but Jane had finally convinced her that it was just a dream. Though the memory of the dream faded immediately upon waking, the horrible fear that something terrible had happened to William and an ensuing violent sense of restlessness had stayed with her for almost three days. Over the next two nights, what little sleep she was able to manage was filled with nightmares which were equally elusive, and then, just as suddenly, a sense of relief filled her, and she began looking forward to seeing William again.

William would come today!

Elizabeth forced herself to think of the one and only walk they had taken together thus far, just before she had left Pemberley. She blushed as she remembered the passionate kisses they had stolen as they passed behind the yew hedge.

Upon her arrival at home, Elizabeth took great care with her toilette. When she finally made her way down to the breakfast room where most of her family was already gathered, Mrs. Bennet scolded her for sleeping late this morning.

"My dear, you forget that Lydia also is not present at the moment and is most likely still abed," Mr. Bennet pointed out with amusement.

"Oh…" Mrs. Bennet answered in an annoyed tone of voice, "Lydia *always* sleeps this late. Lizzy was late purposefully, hoping she would not have to accompany me into Meryton to visit her Aunt Phillips."

Panic filled Elizabeth's eyes and voice as she said, "Mama! I thought I had made it clear that I could not go with you this morning. I *must* remain at Longbourn today!"

Seeing Elizabeth's distress, Jane declared, "Mama! Mary, Kitty, Lydia, and I will accompany you. Lizzy has something else she must do today."

"No! You all have been to see my sister recently; Lizzy has not been there in this past week, and I will not allow her to avoid her duty any longer! What could Lizzy possibly have to do at home?"

Watching Elizabeth's alarm increase by the moment, Mr. Bennet intervened, "Mrs. Bennet, I have need for Lizzy to be at home all day today. She will not be accompanying you anywhere—tomorrow or the following day, *perhaps*, but not today. You may take the other girls to the village and stay as long as you would like."

Mrs. Bennet glared at him, but answered, "Very well, Mr. Bennet."

Elizabeth thanked him silently with her eyes and returned to moving the food around on her plate until her father left for his study, whereupon she followed him from the room.

Knowing that Elizabeth would not be very good company today, Mr. Bennet barely glanced at his daughter after he closed the door to his study. Instead he sat at his desk and began to work on his ledgers. Relieved that her father understood her so well, Elizabeth chose a book and sat in a different chair than usual—one from which she clearly could see the approach to Longbourn's drive from the window.

When the other ladies of the house left for Meryton, it was a little before eleven o'clock. At that time, she moved to the drawing room to sit by a window where the prospect of the drive was better. While in her father's study, she had made an attempt to distract herself with her book for his sake, but now that she was alone, she was unable to keep her eyes from the view.

~%~

Jane tried to keep her mother and sisters in Meryton as long as possible after their visit with her Aunt Phillips ended, but even *they* had their limits when it came to shopping at the shops they had frequented at least once a week for their entire lives. She attempted to convince them to have tea at the Inn, but Mrs. Bennet, usually not one to criticize her eldest daughter, felt that was a silly idea, and they all returned to Longbourn.

Upon hearing the ruckus of their return in the hallway, Mr. Bennet came out of his study. Jane caught his eye, questioning—and he shook his head in reply. William had not yet come.

Elizabeth, warned of her family's return when seeing them from the window, took up some embroidery, returned to her seat, and began to work on it diligently, angling her body so that she could see any movement in the drive out of the corner of her eye.

It was tea time once the family was settled, and Mrs. Bennet asked Elizabeth to serve tea. Jane saw her sister hesitate. It seemed she did not wish to leave the window seat, and so Jane stepped in once again. Mrs. Bennet screeched, "Jane! I have never witnessed such behavior from you! You are usually such a *good* girl, but today you are defying me at every turn! You are spending too much time with Lizzy!"

Jane paled, torn between behaving in her usual obedient manner and her concern for her sister. What could she say to her mother?

No one had noticed that Mr. Bennet had paused just inside the door to study Elizabeth's countenance before entering the room, but upon hearing the conversation, he could not allow his wife to further inflame Elizabeth's tender state of mind. "If Jane wishes to serve tea, my dear, then allow her to do so. Lizzy will do so tomorrow."

"It makes no difference to me, but I do not understand why Lizzy is being coddled so!" Mrs. Bennet said, and then turned to Elizabeth. Shaking her finger at her daughter she continued, "*You* had better not become accustomed to this treatment, Miss Lizzy, as I will not stand for it much longer!"

Mr. Bennet firmly replied, "Mrs. Bennet! You *will* do as I say without questioning my judgment."

Mrs. Bennet made what sounded like a grunt in answer to her husband, and then turned to Lydia and Kitty to discuss the purchases they had made in the village.

Mr. Bennet walked to where Elizabeth was seated and said quietly, "Lizzy? Will you take some tea? You have not eaten today."

"I will have some tea, Papa, but I do not believe my stomach would do well with food just now. I…" She could not say more in the present company and glanced about the room to convey this to her father.

"I understand, child. I only wanted to make you aware that I am paying attention. I will *not* allow you to make yourself ill."

~%~

As the hours passed, Elizabeth became more anxious. Though it was well past the usual visiting hours, Mr. Bennet could see that she had not given up the hope of hearing a knock on the door. Every time a servant entered the room from the hallway, Elizabeth's head would turn so quickly that her father thought it might snap off. Again she had not eaten a bite of food, and her agitation was so extreme that she could no longer be engaged in any conversation. He decided he must do something about this behavior lest she begin having fits of nerves like her mother—he had to tell her all. "Lizzy, come to my study after dinner. I have something I would discuss with you."

"Yes, Papa."

After the meal was done, Elizabeth followed her father into his study and sat in her usual chair in front of his desk. A look of confusion was on her face as he sat across from her instead of behind his desk as was his custom. He took her hand in his and began, "Lizzy, my dearest child, there are some things I have not told you about my letters to Mr. Darcy, and about Mr. Darcy himself. I need you to listen carefully to all that I have to say before asking any questions. I feel now that William has not come, I must disclose the painful truth to you so that you do not spend your life pining for a man you cannot have." He winced at the look of pain on Lizzy's face and sighed. "Perhaps I should have told you sooner so that you would have been more prepared for the lack of attention you have received, but I had hoped for your sake—and honestly, for William's sake as well—that I was wrong. Today's events prove that my initial reaction to the lack of communication was not a mistake.

"While on our way home from Pemberley you may remember that we talked quite a bit about your feelings for William. After hearing what you had to say and reviewing similar disclosures that William had made before we left, I decided that I was being selfish—I wanted to keep you home a little longer as my daughter, as if nothing had changed. It was wrong, I know, and by the time we arrived home I was glad that I had realized it in such a timely manner. Upon our arrival at Longbourn, I wrote to Mr. Darcy saying that I would give my consent to your engagement as long as the marriage itself did not take place until your birthday. I did not wish to tell you about this until I had heard from Mr. Darcy because I wanted to see what his response would be.

"You see, you and I did not go to Pemberley only for reasons of pleasure, my dear. Mr. Darcy is not in good health; he has a condition that will eventually lead to his death. The doctors are not certain how long it will take, but he will slowly lose his abilities. Since Mr. Darcy had no close relatives within the Darcy family, and he and his wife had never got along with the Fitzwilliams, he did not wish to entrust his legacy to those families. Mr. Darcy and I had been close friends since boyhood, closer than most brothers in fact, and since I have had experience in running an estate, he asked to have me along with him for a time as he ran Pemberley—to see the differences in running estates of such different sizes, and to witness his personal style—so that if the time came that he could no longer help William run the estate *before* William was fully prepared to do it alone, I could be there to support him.

"When Mr. Darcy initially brought up the possibility of you and William as a couple, my first reaction was one of surprise. Let me say that he had never held a very high opinion of the habits of most of the people at his level in society, but still, I had thought he would wish his son to choose a marriage partner from the first circle of the *ton*.

"Though we Bennets can trace our family ancestry back almost as far as the Darcys can and have always been a part of the gentry, we have never been connected to titled families and have always chosen a more quiet life than that of the *ton*. Perhaps if our ancestors had chosen to participate in London society we would be, but the fact is, we are *not* of the first circle. Yes, I am a gentleman, but I am considered nothing more than a country squire in the eyes of society.

"It pains me to say this, Lizzy, more than you could ever possibly understand—but in the eyes of the *ton*, the daughter of a country squire who married the daughter of a tradesman is *not* an acceptable marriage partner for a man of William's stature.

"All this I brought to Mr. Darcy's attention, and he shooed it away without a second thought. He felt that you would be the perfect wife for his William no matter what society would say, and he promised to help both of you navigate the shark-infested waters of the *ton*.

"We spoke at length about your being too young to marry, and he agreed to stand by my choice of having you wait for your engagement. That is where all stood when we departed Pemberley.

"I am afraid that the only reason I can fathom for Mr. Darcy's lack of response to my consent and the number of letters that followed it, and for his forbidding his daughter to write to you, is that he has thought over the differences in your stations and has rescinded his blessing for the union, Lizzy. He has effectively cut off all connection between our families.

"I had hoped that William was so much in love with you that he would come to see you today—even if for no other reason than to explain in person why he could not marry you—but he has not.

"I am sorry, my Lizzy, but this is what I am certain has happened. I know it may seem cruel to lay it all out in this manner, but I fear you must give up on the hope of ever seeing William again; the sooner you accept this, the better it will be for you. You must reconcile yourself to a life without him."

Elizabeth had listened to her father in silence. Outwardly, she had appeared quite calm though her skin had paled considerably during his speech. Inwardly, her anxiety had greatly multiplied. "But Papa, William and I had spoken of this as well, and he assured me that I need not worry about any of this. He loves me, Papa, I know he does!"

"Lizzy, I can only imagine that his Fitzwilliams relations have finally convinced Mr. Darcy that they have been right all these years, and that by now, he has threatened to disinherit William if he does marry you. You well know that you would not have been able to live without an income my dear. If this be the case—especially if William loves you as you both have assured me he does—he is an intelligent man, and he knows that he would have absolutely nothing to offer you and *could not* marry you."

Elizabeth rose from her chair and walked over to the window, standing silently for several minutes. When she turned around again to face her father, to Mr. Bennet's eyes she looked as if she had aged ten years. "I appreciate your honesty, Papa. I am sure you are correct that it is better that I know these things—whether or not it feels 'better' just now." She closed her eyes for a few moments and continued, "I find I have a sudden headache, sir, and with your permission I would like to retire for the night."

Mr. Bennet moved toward Elizabeth, pulling her into an embrace and kissing her forehead. "Yes, my Lizzy, I understand. I will make your excuses to the rest of the family. You are welcome here any time to discuss this further if you have need, my dear. I wish I could have done something to make the realities of life easier for you."

"Thank you, Papa. Good night."

~%~

Later that night, Jane went to Elizabeth's room to check on her. When she did not receive an answer to her knock, Jane entered anyway. Though Elizabeth appeared to be asleep, her elder sister sat on the edge of the bed. "I know you are not sleeping, Lizzy; I can tell. Will you not speak to me about it?"

Elizabeth answered while continuing to face away from her. "Oh, Jane, I do not know why I expected him to come."

"But why would you not, Lizzy?"

"We have spent time in London with Aunt and Uncle Gardiner, Jane. You cannot tell me that you have not seen the ladies that belong to the first circle... the ones who look down on us from their boxes when we attend the theater and opera. We have commented many times about how they are so elegant, sophisticated, and beautiful! William is destined to marry one of *them*—*not* someone like me."

"I do not believe that William would have given you the ring if he had not meant what he said, Lizzy."

Elizabeth turned onto her back, and in the candlelight, Jane could see her face was streaked with tears and her eyes were swollen. "William did mean it, Jane, of that I am certain... but Papa feels that his father has forbidden the match. It is true that Mr. Darcy did not know that William had given me the ring—*nobody* did, save you. Papa still does not know it. If it were not a family heirloom, I would hold it as a keepsake; but Jane, knowing that it has been meant as a gift to generations of Mrs. Darcys, I cannot. I do not know how to return it, though, so I will cherish it until I find a way."

"Lizzy, this may sound presumptuous and even disobedient, but no matter what Papa has told you he *thinks* might have happened, it may not be so! Why do *you* believe William has stayed away?"

"I do not know! I am too disappointed and confused tonight, Jane. I hope to take a very long walk tomorrow and sort things out; you know that I think best when outdoors. Ask me again tomorrow night. I might need your help hindering Mama's plans for me again tomorrow. Perhaps I should go out before dawn and not return all day." Elizabeth tried to quip, but it came out seriously.

"Of course, Lizzy, I will do what I can, but it seems Mama is not very receptive to my interference! After I tried to confound her plans several times today, she thought I was ill and tried to send me to bed!" Both girls laughed, but Elizabeth's was missing the bell-like quality that Jane had always associated with her Lizzy.

"You always know how to cheer me, Jane. Thank you, I feel much better now. Sleep well, and we will talk on the morrow."

~%~

The following day, Elizabeth did go out for her walk before dawn and walked for hours. When she returned, her eyes had a light in them that Jane did not expect to see this day, and so she followed her to her room.

"Lizzy? What is it?"

"Jane, William *does* love me, I am absolutely certain of it; I can *feel* it!" She put her hands to her chest over her heart. "I am also certain that he has a very good reason not to have come. Once he has overcome whatever obstacle has blocked his path, he will. As for the lack of correspondence… well that is a bit trickier to explain away logically, so I have decided to take on *your* usual attitude. There has been some sort of misunderstanding, and it will all work itself out. I need only to be patient, Jane, and not to allow doubt to poison my mind or enter into my heart. All will be righted in time."

Chapter 11

January 1810

One year and eight months later

Elizabeth was invited to return to London with her Aunt and Uncle Gardiner at the conclusion of their visit to Longbourn for the Christmas of her eighteenth year. In their opinion, Elizabeth had been in a state of melancholy for far too long, and they hoped the change would help. Though she attempted to conceal it, their niece's smile did not reach her eyes; her laughter did not ring out with the same enthusiasm that had been present in the past, and when she thought she was not being observed, her countenance betrayed all of her sorrow and disappointment.

During their visit to Longbourn, they discussed with Mr. Bennet and Jane their shared worry for Elizabeth, and all hoped that the trip to town, along with seeing a few plays, attending a concert or two, and accomplishing several shopping trips for her mother and sisters, would at the very least distract her, if not help to cheer her.

At the conclusion of her first week in town, when her beloved aunt and uncle had suggested attending a play, Elizabeth had not bothered to ask what it would be. Knowing they would not go without her, she did not wish to suspend any pleasure of theirs, and so she agreed with feigned enthusiasm. The moment she saw the playbill, she was sorry she had not inquired—if for no other reason than to have had some time to prepare herself. In the end, her relations' attempt at cheering her accomplished quite the opposite.

It was *Twelfth Night*, which had been her long-time favorite, and while she appreciated the sentiment, because of the memories associated with the play since she and Georgiana had performed it for William, she wished her relations had not extended themselves on her account. As she sat waiting for the first act to begin, she felt an odd sensation that caused her to look up at the boxes to her left, and her heart stopped beating momentarily. "**He** *is here*!"

William was entering a box with an older couple and a sophisticated lady, clearly of the *ton*. Elizabeth's heart wrenched in her chest, and for a long time she could not tear her eyes away from the exquisite torture of looking upon him once again. He was a bit thinner than when she had seen him last, but he was just as handsome as ever.

When the lady sitting next to him reached over to caress William's arm, Elizabeth moved her eyes to examine her. She was about the same age as herself, tall with golden hair—an absolute beauty in the classic sense of the word—and after watching her for a while it could be seen that she was graceful beyond measure. In Elizabeth's opinion, the lady was the exact opposite of herself in every way. Elizabeth was glad that she could not see his eyes well from this distance, remembering the love that shone from them when he used to look upon her, and convinced that if she witnessed the same love now as he looked upon this lady, she would surely shrivel up and die.

Though she turned her head slightly toward the stage, Elizabeth could not watch the play; her eyes were turned constantly on William. She remained in her seat during intermissions, avoiding an incidental meeting with him that would force an introduction to his lady. Toward the end of the last act, Elizabeth no longer tried to hide the direction of her attention and could not hold back the tears as she watched him turn to this woman, leaning closer to hear her speak, and then smiling at something the lady had said— no doubt something witty and clever.

Mrs. Gardiner noticed the silent tears running down her niece's cheeks and alerted her husband that they needed to leave the moment the play was over. The last thing Elizabeth needed at that moment was to be caught in the crowd by someone they knew.

~%~

William had spent the past year and a half working very hard. Between his rehabilitative exercises, the reconstruction of Pemberley, and the usual work of running the estate, William had been unable to make more than a few short trips to London to see a doctor, a specialist in his type of injury, who also kept regular correspondence with Mr. Smythe in order to monitor William's progress.

His Aunt and Uncle Fitzwilliam badgered him into attending several events whenever he was in London. Though he enjoyed an occasional visit to the theater or the opera, William found that he despised the social scene and the *ton* even more now than he had before he had fallen in love with Elizabeth. His aunt and uncle were constantly playing matchmakers, and they could not understand his reluctance to settle down.

William's tailor in Lambton had produced some fashionable-looking, useful coats for him that included a different type of pocket than was in style— but he *did* notice that upon his second trip to London, many of the other men were wearing similar coats! He had to laugh because his only reason for adding the pockets was to accommodate his useless arm; after all he needed to *put* it somewhere and not leave it hanging down at his side!

When in his presence, the ladies of the *ton* all pretended not to care about his injuries. Though they were unsure of what exactly had happened to him, there was no question that his arm was idle. They tried not to stare, but at one party when he had retreated from the insanity of the season by taking a breath of fresh air on the terrace, he had overheard a group of ladies talking about him—laughing about how they did not care about his arm as long as he retained his ability to sign cheques!

After not progressing very far with restoring the usefulness of his arm, William was beginning to lose hope that he would ever be well enough to approach Elizabeth. If he did not regain the use of his arm and hand, William had decided that after Georgiana married, he would be done with the *ton* and would retire to Pemberley for the remainder of his life—alone.

Elizabeth. Georgiana and he had ceased to discuss her about a year ago, but he had never stopped thinking about her, dreaming about her, or sketching her. Would this be how he would live the rest of his life? Daily, sometimes hourly, William wondered what she thought of him.

William's mind was brought back to the present by a clawing feeling on his left arm. *"Stop touching me! You have absolutely no right! Does she think I find this behavior attractive?"* William thought as the lady that his aunt and uncle had invited to join them in their box touched his arm once more.

Not only did he not think to ask what play was being performed tonight in advance, for if he had, he never would have accepted the invitation, but he also should have known that his aunt and uncle would try to match him with another beauty of their acquaintance. Why did the play have to be Elizabeth's favorite—the one that she had acted out with Georgiana during the happiest time in his life?

"I would much rather see Elizabeth and Georgiana's portrayal than to see this play beautifully performed on stage," he thought as he ground his teeth in an effort to hold back the tears that pricked at his eyes.

His nostrils flared as the vapid lady on his left said something that she thought was humorous. He tried to smile politely.

*"This is torturous! Why does she think she could say anything that would interest me? Humph! She dares to touch me yet again after the look I gave her the last time she did so? If she drops something onto the floor once more, she can pick it up herself! I absolutely refuse to look at her décolletage as she obviously wants me to. I will not go to dinner at Matlock House as originally planned. It will **not** be a lie to say that I am feeling ill!"*

Colonel Richard Fitzwilliam was attending the same play, seated with friends in the box directly across from the Matlock's. He had been trying to attract Darcy's attention since the last intermission because as he had been surveying the assembly to see if there were any interesting-looking ladies in the general admission section, he thought he had seen the lady that Darcy was always drawing—the one whose name he had heard Darcy screaming at the top of his lungs for hours on end after he was burned in the fire at Pemberley and so ill with fever, the one who held Darcy's broken heart in her hands, and the only person who could ever help him to heal—Miss Elizabeth Bennet. He could not be certain because he had never seen the lady in person, but Darcy's renderings of Georgiana's and William's parents were so well done that Richard felt his drawings of this lady would look very much like the original as well, except that even from this distance, she was even more beautiful than the image on paper.

Richard had been watching her since the last act had begun. He could swear that she was not looking at the stage at all, but at William! The silly woman that his parents had brought along to meet his cousin was fawning all over him, and Richard could only imagine that the scene in the box opposite him was not doing William any good when it came to his lady love's opinion of him.

Richard was tempted to throw something at his cousin in order to gain his attention, but with his luck he would probably miss and hit his father or mother instead! Richard wished the play was over so he could rush over to the Matlock box and point her out to his cousin, but he could not. *"It is just not done, Richard!"* he knew his mother would say, just as she had done many times in the past. His parents would never forgive him for making a spectacle of himself in front of the entire *ton*, and he was in no mood to risk it.

Finally the play was almost finished and, excusing himself from his party, he rushed around the outside landing, dodging those who had no real interest in the play and had already accomplished their goal—being seen— and were leaving early to avoid the crush. The moment the play ended, he pushed through the door and into the box, greeting his parents quickly, then said quietly, "I need to speak to my cousin privately for a moment if you will excuse us," while pulling Darcy through the door.

"Thank you, Richard; I needed to escape from that *lady's* claws!"

"William! I think *she* is *here!*" Richard exclaimed while pulling him toward the lobby in an attempt to gain a good point from which to view the general seating exits.

"I have never seen you so agitated, cousin. What lady has put you in such a state?"

"Your Elizabeth! She is here! I *saw* her."

The crowd of exiting patrons thickened around them as Darcy stopped suddenly, his eyes widening, and he stood in stunned silence for a few moments. Elizabeth was here, in the same building? Was it his imagination that there was suddenly a trace of lavender in the air? His eyes searched the crowd wildly for her face.

What could he say to her if they met? Was it truly her father's doing that she had never written, or was it in fact her own? How would she respond to his presence if her father had kept their letters from her and convinced her that he had never cared for her? Did she despise him for not coming to her and taking her away to Scotland as he had promised? *"What I would not do just to see her for a moment! But, my arm!"*

Darcy leaned toward his cousin, his mask in place but with panic in his eyes, and said quietly, "I cannot, Richard! Not until I am healed. I *cannot* see her!"

"William, if she still loves you as you said she did, she will not care about your arm."

His eyes hardened and he answered, "Do you not understand, Richard? I *never* want to see pity in her eyes. I must go! Make my excuses to your parents."

He turned with every intention of walking briskly to the theater's exit, but then—it all happened so quickly. He collided with a body that was blocking his path; his left arm instinctively came up to steady the other person, and all at once he was overwhelmed by the scent of *her*.

William looked down into the eyes he had been dreaming of for years. Someone moved through the crowd past Elizabeth, pushing her closer to him—almost crushing her against him. Her hands, which were pressed against his chest, moved up slightly, sending a shiver down his spine. Every inch of his body fortunate enough to be touching hers was tingling with a sense of life that had been felt only when he had held her so long ago. The last time they had been together had been in the garden at Pemberley, and his entire being screamed out for what they had shared then; his arm ached to wind around her back and pull her closer, and he had to fight the impulse to lean down and touch his lips to hers.

William took a deep breath and filled himself once more with the scent of heaven that he had yearned for so long to experience again. Elizabeth's face was pale and tear-stained—and even more beautiful than he had remembered. As if by instinct, his hand moved to wipe her tears away, but he stopped himself and placed it again on her arm. *"Why are you crying, my Elizabeth?"* he thought, but could not utter a sound.

William heard a lady call her name and ask her to follow. Fear gripped him—Elizabeth would be taken from him! He had to *do* something, say *something*! He only had enough presence of mind to say, "Miss Bennet."

A deep sadness filled her eyes as she answered, "Good evening, Mr. Darcy." Elizabeth pressed her hands against his chest and pushed away from him. She took the lady's hand and followed her—leaving him—again.

As she moved away, his hand slid down the creamy skin of her bare arm. Why had he worn gloves? Worried that he would never experience her scent again, he took a deep breath and held it purposely as he stood watching her until she disappeared into the crowd.

"*Elizabeth!*" William's thoughts shouted out to her, but he clenched his jaw and lips together so tightly that no sound could escape. When he could no longer hold it in, he exhaled with a long, trembling sigh, savoring every last bit of the breath that had held her scent.

Richard's hand came down on his shoulder, and William turned toward him, barely voicing, "Take me home, Richard."

Richard knew this was not the time to discuss this, but he had to ask, "It was she, then?"

William looked in the direction Elizabeth had gone and answered, "Yes."

Richard nodded and said forcefully, "Come! I will make a path; follow me."

William followed closely behind as his cousin made his way through the crowd and out to the Darcy coach which was already waiting not too far from the door. Richard pushed him towards the coach, and then got in himself before signaling the driver that they were ready to proceed.

William leaned his elbow on the door and covered his face with his hand. "In the past two and one half years, *every day* I have imagined meeting her again, Richard. I have composed a thousand different speeches that I had hoped to say to her. And when I did, all I could say was her name… and let her go."

"You did not have to let her go, William."

William quickly moved his hand away from his face, and his eyes flashed in anger as he shouted, "Yes, I did have to let her go! *Look* at this, Richard!" With his left, he pulled his right hand out of the pocket of his coat and let the arm drop down onto the seat, lifeless. "I cannot *do* anything with it! I am just beginning to feel something other than excruciating pain and—oh yes, I have made such *wonderful* progress that I can finally flex my fingers a miniscule amount," he said, his words dripping with bitter sarcasm as he demonstrated, his fingers twitching a little. "When I am able to take her into *both* arms, only then I will seek her out—but *not* before!"

"And what if by then it is too late?"

"Then it was not meant to be," he snapped as he turned to stare out the window, not really seeing the scene passing outside it.

"Cousin, I think you are being foolish! You should know that she spent at least the entire last act of the play staring at you and *that woman*."

William's eyes darted to Richard's. "Do you think she misinterpreted Lady Alyssa's presence?"

"William, *everyone* in the theater misinterpreted Lady Alyssa's presence, including Lady Alyssa. She was practically sitting in your lap, and I do believe that had you given her the slightest bit of encouragement, she would have done so! She was parading her décolletage so blatantly before you that even from across the theater I got quite the show! If your 'relationship' with Lady Alyssa is not in the society page tomorrow, I would be very surprised!"

"Good G-d, Richard! Elizabeth had been crying…"

The two were quiet for a few moments before Richard said, "Well, you could look at it as a good sign, William. She must still have feelings for you if your behavior can hurt her that much."

His chest and throat tightened, but somehow he forced out, "I do not *wish* to hurt her. I only want to love her."

"Then *find* her, William! Do you know who she was with?"

"I can only imagine it was the aunt and uncle whom she once told me she visits in London," he said thoughtfully, then he closed his eyes and said with a trembling voice, "But I cannot. She deserves a *whole* man."

"William… I have seen men come home from war with far worse injuries than you have, and their wives are only too happy to have them home *alive!*"

"Richard, I understand what you are saying, but it is not the same. Those men were injured defending the motherland, defending their families and friends—they are war heroes. Elizabeth and I are *not* married; she is *not* depending on me to provide for her, and unlike married ladies who have vowed to love, honor and keep their husbands in sickness till death parts them, Elizabeth has a *choice!*" William was silent for a few seconds and then whispered, "I would not blame her if she did not choose me as I am now."

"William, the woman you and Georgiana, and even your father, told me about would *not* decide against you because of this injury! Even *I* could see that she still cares for *you*, William Darcy—the man! If she did not, if she was just another mercenary lady interested in your material assets, she would have taken every advantage of the situation in which she found herself when the crowd pushed her against you. You must know how rare that is, especially for a man in your position—for a woman to look beyond the money and status is almost unheard of!"

"*Enough*, Richard!" William's shout seemed louder than it had been in the small space of the carriage. He took a few moments to check his temper and sighed. "Enough. I will work twice as hard on the exercises that Mr. Smythe and Mr. Miller have given me, no matter the pain involved. I *will* recover the use of my arm, and only *then* will I find Elizabeth again."

Silence prevailed for several minutes before William whispered, "I would not have thought it could be possible, but she has grown even more beautiful than she was the last time I saw her."

Richard kept his thoughts to himself. *"Well, if nothing else, perhaps this meeting will give him a new sense of purpose. Lately he has been acting as if he had given up. Saying he **will** recover is a great improvement! Georgiana will be relieved."*

~%~

When at home, Elizabeth normally read her father's newspaper every day, and when staying in London, she was permitted to read her uncle's. Though she had never read the society columns until the past year, now she did so every day—in search of *his* name. She had been proud of her restraint; usually she would wait until she had finished with the news, at least, but lately she found herself turning directly to the society column when opening a newspaper. In the past she had been relieved that there were not many mentions of William, but for the last month "FD of Derbyshire" had been seen in London society much more often.

Today she wanted to see what was written about the woman William accompanied last night to the theater; after she read it, she wished she had not. It was devastating. It seemed that all of London was expecting that since he had been seen in the company of this lady *and* his aunt and uncle, an engagement would soon be announced. Elizabeth needed time to think, and so requested that a maid accompany her on a walk.

"Papa was right all along." Elizabeth walked for quite some time with only that thought repeating in her mind.

"I must accept that he no longer loves me. I saw the look in his eyes; he seemed angry when he first looked at me...and then mortified to see me. And now the newspaper—his family obviously approves of this lady. She was so beautiful and sophisticated; she is everything I am not. I wish I had thought to give him his mother's ring, but I do not think I could have done so discreetly in such a public place. It is just as well; I do not know if I could part from it just yet."

Her hand moved to the chain that held his ring, pulling it from the bodice of her gown to touch it.

"I must let go of all my preconceived notions. I must find a way to return this. He should give it to his wife..."

Elizabeth stopped walking and closed her eyes for a few moments until she heard footsteps approaching.

Opening her eyes she saw a soldier coming her way on the path. Realizing that she was standing in his way, Elizabeth tried to move, but her knees would not cooperate and gave way. The man moved forward quickly and caught her by the arms, asking, "Madam, may I escort you to that bench?" The maid that was accompanying Elizabeth came scurrying over to offer her assistance as well.

"Yes, please. I am sorry to be such a bother; I do not know what is wrong with me."

The gentleman offered her his arm and steered her to the bench. "It is no trouble at all. Do you live nearby? Perhaps I can get some help for you?"

"I thank you, but I usually am not the type to swoon, sir. I was thinking of something, and it seems to have upset me more than I had anticipated. I shall be fine after resting a moment or two, I am sure. Truly, this has never happened before."

"Mayhap it is not something you have had need to think of before?" He helped her to sit, and then took a step back.

Noticing the insignia on his uniform Elizabeth asked, "Are you in the habit of asking such personal questions of young ladies to whom you have not been properly introduced, Colonel?"

She was smiling so he did not think he had insulted the lady, but the smile did not reach her eyes. Could she be teasing him? Well, then, that gave him every right to tease back! "Only when I think the lady will grace me with a smile as beautiful as the one before me, madam."

"My goodness, Colonel, you certainly are forward. May I ask if you are a rake, sir? Should I be alarmed that you have not yet continued on your way?"

"It so happens I am a gentleman, madam, the son of an Earl to be exact. Whether or not I am a rake would have to be reported to you by others to be a trustworthy account, I am certain, but I must ease your mind by saying that I promise you are in no danger from me."

They were quiet while Elizabeth narrowed her eyes and examined him for a minute or two.

The gentleman spent that time thinking.

*"William would kill me if he even knew I was here, let alone here **talking** to you! Though it is tempting to test your devotion to my cousin, I think I would rather be tortured by Attila the Hun than to face William if he ever found out that I had done so!*

*"He would also be very angry at Georgiana for telling me your uncle's name and the direction of his bookshop so that I could find you. I only rode here to see if I could contrive a way of just **happening** to drive past with William in the coach at a later date. When I saw you leave the house, I could not resist following to see what you were about. Unfortunate you are staying on this section of the road—I cannot think of a way to get William to drive past here 'by mistake.'*

*"What is this in your hand? Aunt Anne's ring?! William, you dog, you never told me you gave her **that**! Was it thinking of my cousin that made you so upset that a sturdy soul such as you swooned? Probably saw that damned column in the newspaper!"*

Elizabeth's brow smoothed, and she said, "I have decided to trust you for the moment, Colonel, not because I am so impressed with your rank and assurances, but because we are in a public place with a maid present, and you did not approach me with anything but the best intentions when I was not well. There is also something about you that is… familiar. I cannot quite place it. Have we met before, sir?"

"I thank you, Miss, but I know I have never met you before this day. Miss…?"

"Ah, and now you ruin all my trust by wishing me to introduce myself! Do you not know that it is most unladylike to do so?" Elizabeth's expression changed from one of teasing to one filled with such sadness that his heart wrenched in his chest.

Richard searched his own memory to see if there was anything his cousins or uncle had mentioned while speaking of her that might have caused this change. Remembering the account he had heard of her first meeting with William made him think that she had been reminded of the same. "May I escort you home if you are feeling well enough? I do not feel comfortable leaving you here on a bench in the park when you are unwell, but I must soon be on my way."

Elizabeth examined him once again and decided to take him up on his kind offer. "I think I am well enough to attempt it. It is through the park and across the street from the far entrance." She clasped her hands behind her back as they began to walk, and Richard took this as a signal that she would not be willing to take his arm—very unlike any of the usual women of the *ton* who would jump at the chance to flirt with even the second son of an earl!

"What division are you with, Colonel?"

Richard told her and was impressed when her eyes lit up as she asked if he had been with them at a certain battle in which his division had been involved while on the Continent. "You are interested in military history?"

Elizabeth laughed a little then said, "I must admit, sir, to being more interested in military strategy as a child than the more acceptable pastimes for little girls, and my interest has never faded. About that battle, I understand that what has been told afterward on paper must be very different than how events actually unfold in the field, and have often wondered…" she asked a specific question about the strategy his commanding officer had employed in the battle.

Richard explained it in more technical terms than he normally would to a person not in the military to glean whether or not she really understood it. He was only a little surprised when this amazing young lady displayed her superior knowledge by asking appropriate questions and using appropriate terms, even debating the general's choice in one matter. He had the impression that if they had been indoors with paper and pen available, she would be in the process of drawing out the entire battle as *she* would have planned it—and he could not deny that her design might have worked better! *"Miss Bennet really **is** as intelligent as William claims!"*

He accompanied her to her door while the maid hurried up the stairs and inside. Just as Elizabeth began to thank him again and bid him goodbye, Mrs. Gardiner came rushing out the door. "Lizzy! Mary has told me you fell ill while walking in the park?"

"Yes, Aunt, but I am well now. This gentleman came to my rescue and escorted me home. I was just thanking him again for his kindness *and* for a lesson in military strategy."

Mrs. Gardiner said, "May I thank you as well, Colonel…?"

"Colonel Richard…" he hesitated, thinking, *"Good G-d! Miss Bennet would undoubtedly know Darcy's first name!"*

"I am Mrs. Gardiner, and this is my niece, Miss Elizabeth Bennet. Will you join us for tea, Colonel Richards?" Mrs. Gardiner asked.

"No, thank you, ma'am. I was in the area on an errand and could not resist a walk in your lovely park, but now I must be on my way. I was only too glad to be of service to such an interesting young lady. Good day, Mrs. Gardiner. Good day, Miss Bennet." He bowed to the ladies and then walked away in the direction that he had left his horse.

"That was a lucky misunderstanding! Though I do wonder what Miss Bennet's reaction would have been if she had heard my surname." Richard chuckled.

*"I do hope she is not angry with me when we finally **do** meet properly!*

*"So, **that** was Miss Elizabeth Bennet, the famous lady who has charmed every Darcy she has ever known, all their servants, their doctor, and even the merchants in the village*

of Lambton—not one negative word against her from anyone—and after this meeting, I cannot disagree with any of what I have heard.

*"William, you **are** a fool!"*

Chapter 12

September 1810

Nine months later

When William was told by his friend Charles Bingley that he had found an estate to lease at last, it had been perfect timing for William. He had his business ventures well managed enough to be away from Pemberley and London for a time and had worked quite diligently at rehabilitating his arm and hand. Though they were still a little weak and painful during rainy weather, both were able to function almost normally as long as he did not over exert himself. The scarring had not faded much at all, but wearing gloves concealed it well, and the remainder was hidden under his clothing.

He did not think to ask the location before Bingley begged William to come and help him to learn how to manage the estate. Bingley had been such a support to him over the course of the past two years that William found he could not refuse the request.

When he learned that the house was located in Hertfordshire, William made up his mind that once there, he *would* inquire about Longbourn's location; he was absolutely determined to find out whether Elizabeth had married. If she was unmarried, he *would* go to see her and explain why he had not come sooner. He sincerely hoped Mr. Bennet would not be there at the time he chose to visit, since he was uncertain how he would manage to remain civil to the man!

William arrived approximately two weeks after Bingley had taken possession of Netherfield Park, and upon his arrival, he was informed that their party was scheduled to attend an assembly that very evening. Tired from travelling, but attempting to be a good guest, he agreed to attend.

William was the last of the party to enter the coach and, almost as an afterthought, he pulled James aside before stepping in. "James, while we are at the Assembly, would you speak to the other servants and ascertain where Longbourn is located in Hertfordshire?"

The usually stoic James started, and asked, "Longbourn, sir?"

"Yes... we were there once, do you remember? I know it is in Hertfordshire, and I would like to know how close we are to that estate."

"Yes, Mr. Darcy," James said. William entered the coach, and they were on their way.

James hopped down from the coach as it lined up behind others waiting to allow their passengers to descend in front of the assembly hall. He had a feeling he had been in this village before—and *that* could only mean one thing! Mr. Darcy must be warned if his intuition proved to be correct, so he set off quickly to inquire after Longbourn before his master disembarked. As the passengers stepped down from Mr. Darcy's coach, James approached and asked if he could speak to Mr. Darcy.

"What is it, James?"

"Sir? I think you should know... it seems Netherfield and Longbourn border each other. Longbourn is but one mile north of here." He nodded his head in the direction of a parked coach. "I am told *that* is the Bennet family's coach, Mr. Darcy." William's eyes widened and locked with James's. "I took the liberty of asking... Mrs. Bennet and the five *Miss* Bennets are in attendance."

William glanced up at the window to the Assembly hall, then back at James. James thought he looked very pale. "I see." He blinked a few times and continued, "I should have inquired sooner. Thank you, James; it is better to know before I enter." He hesitated before saying, "Can you please make certain the coach is not blocked behind others and is available to leave whenever necessary?"

"Yes, sir. I understand, sir." William did not walk away immediately as James had expected; he just stood there staring at the window, although he did not appear to be seeing it. His features were schooled as they were usually in public, but after so many years of being in service to the Darcys, James had recognized a bit of panic in his eyes when he had spoken. James knew he was the *only* one who had even the smallest idea of what his master was walking into, and took a chance, stepping beyond his station by saying, "Good luck, Mr. Darcy."

William closed his eyes and swallowed past the tightness in his throat before saying, "Thank you, James. I think I shall need it." When he re-joined his party, the group turned towards the door and entered the building, with William making himself last. He was relieved that Bingley had escorted his sister Caroline because he did not think he could manage being civil to her while warding off her advances in his present state of mind. He would have preferred to have had more time to prepare for this encounter but was also filled with pleasure at the thought of having the chance to glimpse Elizabeth again.

With each step he took as he climbed the stairs, his nervous anticipation grew. *"James implied that she is not married, but what if she is betrothed? Will I have to endure watching her look at another man with love in her eyes? I cannot explain all that I wish to at an assembly ball, but if I do not take the chance while I have it, the Bennets will know I am in the neighborhood, and perhaps her father will not allow me to visit her at Longbourn. Will she despise me for not coming for her on her seventeenth birthday and for treating her ill in London a few months ago? Would she understand all that I need to tell her and forgive me? Is it at all possible that she still cares for me?"* Taking a deep breath, he locked in place the mask of indifference that he always wore in public and entered the room.

His eyes searched the crowd; Elizabeth was dancing. *"She is even more beautiful than when I saw her in London—how does she manage it? So graceful! So elegant!"* The dance ended, and Elizabeth was talking to her partner whom he had barely noticed before. As his reason for existing laughed at what her dance partner said, William's chest tightened. Her partner was a tall, handsome man about his own age or maybe a year or two younger. William realized that most of the room had turned with curiosity to see the new arrivals to the neighborhood, but he could not tear his eyes from Elizabeth. Her partner walked toward her and leaned closely to her ear to say something privately to her. William had never felt such rage in his life as he did at seeing this. These feelings were unacceptable—but Elizabeth was supposed to be *his*! The man nodded in William's direction, and Elizabeth turned to look where the man had indicated.

William knew the moment she noticed him by the expressions on her lovely face. At first the way she lit up sent hope coursing through him, but then Elizabeth turned a ghastly shade of white and looked faint, and took hold of her partner's arm to steady her. Her dance partner turned to look at her, and his countenance reflected his concern. The man seemed to be insisting on escorting her to a chair at the side of the room.

Once Elizabeth was seated, her eyes met William's. Then her face turned to stone, her eyes cold and glaring.

Intense pain ripped through every fiber of William's body. *"Good G-d! She despises me!"* The thought repeated itself in his mind as he followed Bingley instinctively, moving the party away from the door.

Bingley was approached by a jovial gentleman whom Bingley introduced as Sir William Lucas. He heard Elizabeth's voice say, *"We must call him 'Sir William' now instead of 'Mr. Lucas,'"* as she had said years ago in the book shop where they first met. Sir William talked of introducing them to the other neighbors, and Bingley walked after him. William could not hear their conversation over the sound of his heart racing in his ears. He noticed Caroline Bingley staring at him and, knowing that he could *not* survive an attack by her just now, he followed Bingley as he walked away to meet his new neighbors.

~%~

The dance had just ended when Elizabeth's partner John Lucas mentioned that the highly anticipated new members of the neighborhood had arrived and motioned towards the entryway of the Assembly room. When she first turned to see the party from Netherfield, she did not notice anyone other than the tall man in the back—*William!*

Caught completely off guard that he was *here* in her own neighborhood, her first reaction was to think, *"He has come for me at last!"* and such joy spread through her entire being that it erased all the heartache that had become her constant companion for the past three years.

William was looking at her as well, but his countenance seemed so indifferent and severe, reminding her of all the time that had passed and of all the promises he had made—and had broken.

She felt the blood drain from her face and her knees go weak as they had done in London in the park, so she took hold of John Lucas's arm. He insisted on escorting her to a chair and she was grateful. Somewhere between the dance floor and the chair, deep within her mind a choice was made without her knowledge. She had been teetering on the brink of either collapsing into tears in front of the entire neighborhood or feeling intense rage toward William as a defense against her humiliation. Rage won out.

*"The look upon his face confirms it; I **was** correct in London! It is true—he does not love me. It was not his father's disapproval of me as Papa had assumed; it was **William** who did not want me! It was all lies—everything he said at Pemberley was lies! The ring was most likely not even his mother's! Why? Why would he have done this? I do not understand! I will **never** allow him to know that I have spent the last three years pining for him!"* she thought as she met his eyes once again.

Elizabeth watched William follow his friend down the room as Sir William introduced them to the entire neighborhood. They were moving toward— her mother! Elizabeth stood quickly and walked across the room to stand with her mother and Jane.

~%~

A concerned John Lucas was left standing next to the chair Elizabeth had abandoned, watching her go. Was one of these men the one who had been responsible for her heartache?

No one had ever had to tell him why she had changed over the past few years. When she returned from her holiday three years ago, he had known instantly that she had fallen in love, and he had been as happy for her as was possible, though it had dashed his plans completely. He had watched her slowly become more and more despondent and distracted over time until last January when she had returned home from London. It was as if someone had stolen any chance of happiness from her while she had been there, and yet, he could tell that she still loved this unnamed man. He had hated the man who had done this to her—the man without a face, without a name.

Just now, as he watched many emotions pass through his friend's eyes after seeing the newcomers, he saw her ire rise and knew she had made a choice. He had witnessed that look many times as they were growing up—it was the look that meant Elizabeth was enraged about a perceived injustice and was determined to defend herself.

Now, the man would have a face and a name, but John knew that *he* had no right to do anything about the pain this man had caused his friend. Besides, what could he do without hurting Elizabeth in the end? He could only watch and wait.

"Good luck, Lizzy," John Lucas whispered.

~%~

William was in a complete daze, but somehow he managed the bare civilities when being introduced to Bingley's new neighbors—until he looked up and saw that his friend was being introduced to Mrs. Bennet, Jane and Elizabeth.

His eyes locked instantly with Elizabeth's. He had not thought that the agony he had felt when he saw her from across the room could possibly get any worse, but he would soon learn that he had been mistaken. If, over the past three years someone had told William that he would *not* want to look into those eyes—the eyes that had been burned into his memory, the eyes that he had drawn and painted dozens of times, the eyes he had dreamt of every night and had seen every time he had closed his own—William would have scoffed at them and believed that they had gone mad. But he could bear no longer to look into those lovely eyes that were now filled with scorn. He wanted only to escape from the room and go back to the time when he had felt any measure of hope that on seeing her again, all would turn out right. Just now he felt as if *nothing* would ever be right again.

Should he allow her to see his pain? No! He could not. He had told Richard that if his next meeting with Elizabeth occurred too late, then it was never meant to be, and that everything that had happened to keep them apart would have happened for the best. Though he could not feel this sentiment to be true at the moment, William hoped that, with time, he could believe it.

Bingley's words were a jumbled noise to his ears, but when William saw Mrs. Bennet turn to look at him, his attention suddenly sharpened.

"And you, sir, do you like to dance as well?"

"Oh, I apologize," Bingley said, forced from his dreamlike admiration of Miss Jane Bennet by Mrs. Bennet's words. "I have forgotten my manners. May I introduce Mr. Fitzwilliam Darcy of Pemberley in Derbyshire? Darcy, this is Mrs. Bennet, Miss Bennet, and Miss Elizabeth Bennet."

William could see Jane start and glance at her sister. Elizabeth continued to glare at him. Remembering his manners at least, William bowed to the ladies as the daughters curtsied, but Mrs. Bennet stiffened and seemed to become lost in thought for a moment, not acknowledging the greetings. Then her expression changed dramatically.

~%~

Mrs. Bennet might not have been the most intelligent of ladies or the most perceptive of the moods of others, but the changes in Elizabeth over the past months had been so distinct that even *she* had noticed. She had brought up the subject with her husband after it seemed to be a lasting effect. It took several attempts, but Mrs. Bennet nagged persistently, and one day installed herself in her husband's study until she extracted at least part of the story from Mr. Bennet. She knew only that Elizabeth had been greatly disappointed by the son of his old friend, Mr. Darcy, and *his* opinion of the matter was that it had been because either Mr. Darcy or his son had deemed Elizabeth not good enough for him.

Nobody told Mrs. Bennet that one of her daughters was not good enough, even if that daughter was her least favorite and the gentleman had what she estimated as very likely more than ten thousand a year! She had been outraged, and on more than one occasion had written a letter to her husband's former friend to speak her mind on the subject, but Mr. Bennet would not allow them to be posted. Her husband had finally convinced her that it would do no one any good to insult a member of the first circle, and she had finally relented.

But, to have the gentleman who snubbed her own daughter here in the neighborhood was too much for her to resist, especially since Mr. Bennet had stayed at home!

Her countenance expressed clearly for anyone to see the disdain she felt toward the gentleman. "Darcy?" she almost screeched, "I had thought you looked familiar." Mrs. Bennet turned up her nose at him, and then moved her attention to a very confused Mr. Bingley, speaking to *him* about insignificant matters in a pleasant tone of voice.

~%~

The severe, stony expression that William had been wearing since Elizabeth first saw him standing by the entrance of the assembly room had been directed at her without deviation for several minutes while her mother, Jane, and Mr. Bingley conversed. Elizabeth surprised herself when her courage had endured through it well enough. In truth, her heart was beating so furiously that she thought all of Meryton might hear it and she felt such an overwhelming sorrow descend upon her so violently that the only thing she truly wished to do was to run from the building and weep until she could weep no more. Her mind filled with question after question and her head ached, but through it all she continued to glare at *him*.

William seemed to be challenging her—to what, she was not certain. Did he wish her to show that she still maintained tender feelings towards him after all this time, perhaps? What purpose would it serve other than to give him the opportunity to demonstrate before the entire neighborhood that he felt she was a fool, and he wanted nothing more to do with her? What else could this look mean after the encounter in London—after he had stayed away for so long? Perhaps he was attempting to tell her that he wished his ring to be returned?

She formerly was able to read his emotions and thoughts so easily, why could she not upon the last two meetings? Had he changed so drastically since they had been together at Pemberley that he was not the same man? Was he *ever* the man she had thought he was, or was it all an illusion? But what could he possibly have gained from all that had transpired if it had been false? Had it been a game, and had he felt pressed to go on because she did not agree to his proposal immediately, and once she did, the game was over? If he never made out a marriage contract, it would be her word against his that he had ever proposed. Nobody that could matter to someone of the first circle of the *ton* would ever believe that a man of his wealth and stature would offer for her, so there would have been no true risk to *his* reputation.

Since she could no longer read him, should she trust *any* impression she had of him since meeting him again, including their chance meeting in London? Was he challenging her at all or was this unreadable expression something else?

Or was her heart trying to make excuses for him to justify that she still loved him?

Just then, Mr. Bingley introduced her mother, Jane, and her to William. Two things happened simultaneously as her relations heard his name. Elizabeth felt Jane suddenly stiffen by her side, and she could see Jane glance at her from the corner of her eye. She saw her mother grow rigid as well, but her next action came as a complete surprise to both her daughters. After a few moments hesitation, her mother gave William the *cut direct*!

Jane and Elizabeth did not know what to do, and so they did nothing. William's mien did not change at all, nor did he move away or say a word. Mr. Bingley shot his friend an apologetic look which William did not seem to notice. He just stood there, staring at her with that emotionless countenance that was so confusing to her.

When her mother snubbed him, Elizabeth's expression faltered and softened with concern for his feelings for just a moment before she was able to reinstate her glare, but obviously a moment was long enough to convince him to act.

Surprising everyone who was within hearing distance—and quite a number of people were paying close attention after Mrs. Bennet's response to the introduction—William asked Elizabeth to dance!

~%~

When William had seen Elizabeth's continuous glare soften for a fleeting moment after her mother snubbed him, he was overwhelmed with a thought that had been lingering ever since he had heard at Pemberley that Mr. Bennet wanted Elizabeth to have a season *out* before marrying him— that she would be dancing with other men and yet *he* had never danced with her. Though he usually despised dancing, he had spent the past three years imagining sharing with her every possible dance he had ever learned from any of his masters—his favorite dance to dream about was the waltz. Since she seemed to dislike him so intensely now, he knew this might be his only opportunity to dance with her.

Before he knew what he was about, the request had already escaped William's lips. "Miss Elizabeth, will you do me the honor of dancing the next with me?"

Recognizing the look in her eyes after the surprise left them, as if he had challenged her, she could not refuse or else she would consider herself to be weak; he now felt confident that Elizabeth would accept him.

Accept him, she did.

~%~

To say that Elizabeth was surprised when William asked her to dance would be a severe understatement. *"Why would he do such a thing?"* she wondered. The skin around William's eyes creased just a bit, and she realized that she had let her "severe" countenance slip once again. *"He is attempting to unnerve me! I will not allow it. My courage rises with every attempt he makes to intimidate me!"*

Elizabeth arched her brow and said with strength in her voice, "Yes, Mr. Darcy, I will."

While Elizabeth and William were caught in a contest of who would look away first for very different reasons—on her side to prove that she would not be frightened off by him, on his because he had decided that even seeing anger in her eyes was better than not seeing her at all—neither had any idea of what had been happening around them. Mr. Bingley, Mrs. Bennet, and even Jane were at first all standing with their mouths slightly ajar, blinking, and staring at them with shocked expressions.

Mr. Bingley's thoughts were consumed with several things at once. The elegant and angelic beauty he had just met, the novelty of being witness to a matron with daughters of marriageable age actually *insulting* his friend, who just happened to be one of the wealthiest men in all of England, and his friend actually *requesting* the hand of *any* lady to dance—a pastime he absolutely despised—without feeling obligated by duty or having to be talked into it, let alone its being the hand of a lady whose mother gave him the *cut direct* just moments ago, was nearly more than he could bear with equanimity!

Mrs. Bennet was speechless, an event her husband surely would regret missing if it ever came to his attention. Why on earth would Lizzy, of all people, be willing to dance with the same man that Mr. Bennet had told her had insulted their entire family and had broken her heart?

Jane's shock turned into a brilliant smile as her mind was more agreeably engaged. *"**Here** is my Lizzy! **Here** is the spark in her eyes and fire in her soul that has been missing all this time! Just being in Mr. Darcy's company has brought her back to us. The misunderstanding will be cleared away soon, and all will be well!"*

~%~

When the musicians signaled that the next set was about to begin, Bingley was quick to claim his partner and lead Jane to the dance floor. William had been so distracted by the light dancing in Elizabeth's eyes that he missed the cue, but was awakened from his distraction as Bingley purposely brushed past him while he moved toward the dance floor.

William could tell that Elizabeth was confused by the triumphant gleam he expected was shining from his eyes when he was able to hold out his right hand, and she willingly took it. *This* is exactly what he had worked so intensely to achieve!

All at once he was thankful for while simultaneously cursing inwardly society's demands for gloves to be worn on such occasions. He was indeed thankful that the gloves covered any chance of his scars being exposed. But oh, how he wished to be able to touch Elizabeth's skin! Even through their gloves he could feel the warmth of her hand upon his, and it sent a thrill down his spine.

He did not remember doing it, but he had somehow managed to lead her to the dance floor. As they stood across from one another waiting for the sequence of the dance to require them to move, she held his eyes in an iron grip; it felt physically impossible for him to break the gaze even had he wished to, though he could not bear to look away from the magnificent vision before him.

When it was their turn to move, William breathed in deeply as she passed him, her scent a balm to him, rejuvenating his very soul, stripping him of his stony façade. He turned toward her as the dance required, and her glare turned to a look of utter confusion before he could again retreat behind his mask.

Both acknowledged to themselves that they could not manage to hold their protective countenances if required to speak as well, and consequently they proceeded through the set in silence. If only each of them had known that the other was struggling with the same dilemma, perhaps the evening would have proceeded much differently, but as it was, when the second dance of the set was done, William was obliged by the rules of propriety to return Elizabeth to her chaperone. He bowed over her hand, reluctantly released it, and whispered, "Thank you," while meeting her gaze one more time before somehow finding the strength to walk away from her.

Though he knew it was only right that he dance with his host's sisters, William would not sully his memories with a dance with any other woman, and so ignored his sense of duty for the first time in his life.

~%~

~Netherfield, the afternoon after the Assembly

As they gathered for luncheon, anyone in the hallway outside the dining room could have heard the complaints of Miss Bingley and Mrs. Hurst to their brother that the previous night William had danced with a "country nobody" and not with them. As fortune would have it, it was William's lot to be in the hallway at that moment. He held his hand up to the footman who was about to open the door, signaling him to wait. William took a moment to straighten his shoulders and take a deep breath to steady his demeanor. Looking at the footman and rolling his eyes, he nodded to signal him to open the door. The footman bowed his head in sympathy for the gentleman before straightening up and doing his duty.

The moment the door opened, the interior scene changed to one of feigned delight in the addition of William's company. For the hundredth time, or more, William thought that it was obvious that Caroline Bingley had painstakingly moulded her behaviour to duplicate that of the ladies of the *ton*. As much as she had succeeded at this task, Caroline would never realize that as she was the daughter of a tradesman, she would never be *accepted* by most within the higher circles of the *ton,* no matter what her accomplishments.

Why Miss Bingley continued to flirt with him, William could not understand. He knew that her brother had spoken to her many times informing her that William was not interested, and that if he had wanted a lady of the *ton*, he had almost the entire unmarried population of the first circle from which to choose. For some reason, every time he spoke to her about it, her enthusiasm for "catching" him re-doubled!

Before coming to Netherfield, he had asked Bingley *not* to speak to her about it again because if she got any worse, he would not be able to stay with them. Of course, at that time he did not know that Elizabeth lived in this area. Now that he *did* know, he would put up with almost anything to have an opportunity to win her again, especially since he also knew that he could always use the excuse of needing exercise or feeling fatigued to escape Caroline's attentions. The Hursts and Miss Bingley had been told he had been injured in the fire, and though they were not informed of the details of his injuries, they did seem to understand his need for rest and rehabilitative exercise.

At luncheon, between Mrs. Hurst's and Miss Bingley's criticisms of the neighborhood and Miss Bingley's fawning and simpering toward him, the two ladies drove William to leave the house for a ride.

He rode Poseidon in the direction he thought Longbourn would lie. Just the thought of being closer to Elizabeth helped to make him feel more comfortable. Coming upon an area that looked familiar, William dismounted. Realizing the tree directly in front of him was the one where the Dreaded Pirate Lizzy had first been spotted, he smiled. Lost in a whirlwind of memories, he did not notice Baron Leisenheimer's approach.

"That has always been her favorite tree to climb."

William spun around and, seeing who had spoken, relaxed and held out his hand. The Baron shook it.

"It is a pleasure to see you, Baron Leisenheimer." William smiled slightly. "Are you lately returned to the neighborhood? I was told that you were staying in London."

"Good afternoon, Mr. Darcy. Yes, my wife and I returned to Purvis Lodge only yesterday. We had been visiting our daughter and her new son."

"Congratulations, Baron. I remember that you had been expecting a grandchild soon after my last visit here as well."

"Ah, yes! This is the second grandchild since! You have a very good memory, Mr. Darcy."

"Thank you, sir." There was silence for a moment as the Baron seemed to be waiting for him to speak again. William obliged him by asking, "May I ask a question that has often been in my thoughts these years since we last saw each other? I remember that you had been whistling a tune when I first met you in these woods, and it has stayed with me all this time. I have often wondered what the piece is called. I would like to acquire the sheet music for my sister to play on the pianoforte. I know that there is little chance of it, but do you happen to remember what it was?"

"Well, this is a surprise. I always whistle the same song when I am walking through these woods, since I think of this as Miss Lizzy's woods. The song was *inspired* by our mutual friend, Mr. Darcy. I do have the sheet music—the one and only copy since it is one of my own compositions. If you like it that much I will make a copy for you to give to your sister." He looked at William with a quizzical eye.

"If that is the case, you are a better composer than you think, sir. I had always associated that song with Eliz… Miss Elizabeth." William blushed at the slip of his tongue and looked off into the woods towards Longbourn with a wistful expression. "I am afraid Miss Elizabeth would not agree with your calling her my friend, Baron."

"Ahhh—and what are your feelings on the matter?"

William's countenance betrayed his sorrow. "I would *like* to be considered a friend by Miss Elizabeth, sir."

Baron Leisenheimer clapped William on the shoulder, "I think I understand better than you realize, Mr. Darcy. My wife and I are very close to Miss Lizzy, and though she has not spoken to us of particulars, we have been able to deduce much from what she *has* said over the past three years… *and* from what she has only communicated with those expressive eyes of hers. I do not know what has recently occurred, but when she came to see us this morning, it was as if your coming to the neighborhood has disturbed a hornet's nest! I will not tell you what Miss Lizzy said—but would you like to hear my wife's observation just after Miss Lizzy took her leave, Mr. Darcy?"

"Yes, sir, I would."

"She was reminded of a line from Shakespeare's *Hamlet*, 'The lady doth protest too much, methinks.'"

William held his breath for a moment staring at the Baron before answering. "I wish, more than believe, that to be true, Baron."

"Having two daughters and Miss Lizzy about the house much of the time, I have learned to trust my wife's instincts about the feminine mind, Mr. Darcy. Think upon it… just why does the lady act as if she despises you so completely? Whom is she attempting to convince?" The Baron hesitated for a few moments and then continued with a smile at William's confused and wounded expression at what he had revealed, "I see I have given you much to think about. I must be off now, Mr. Darcy. Will we be seeing you at Lucas Lodge?"

"Hmm? Oh, yes, Baron. Shall I have the pleasure of meeting the Baroness?" William asked distractedly.

"Yes, you shall. Until then, Mr. Darcy."

The Baron bowed and began to walk away but had not advanced more than a few steps before he stopped, turned toward his companion, and asked, "Mr. Darcy? Perhaps this is impertinent of me, but may I offer a bit of advice?" At William's nod he continued, "We have only just returned to the neighborhood for a few hours and have already had several callers trying to be the first to tell us the latest news before the gathering at Lucas Lodge. I am not sure how to say this without insulting you, but we have heard much about your 'arrogance and conceit.' I do not see it here in our meeting, nor do I remember it from the past; I suggest you make a conscious effort to remain *this* way!"

William closed his eyes for a moment and then nodded. "Thank you, Baron Leisenheimer. I will make an attempt to follow your advice."

As he watched the Baron walk away down the path on which he had accompanied him the last time William had been at this location six years prior, William found he could not be offended by his counsel. Bingley and his cousin Richard had often teased him about the effect on others of the cold shroud he pulled up around him in public, and Baron Leisenheimer was only trying to tell him the same—to advise him that it was working against any suit he could possibly make to win Elizabeth's heart. The Baron could have no idea that he was asking William to overcome what he had struggled against his entire life—his very nature of being extremely apprehensive among strangers.

When he had met the Baron six years ago, William had been with two people he knew and was meeting only one stranger. He took strength from his father—and from Elizabeth—and had actually felt comfortable with the gentleman. The obviously close relationship Elizabeth had with the Baron and her sister Jane, and the way the Baron and Elizabeth had protected him from Mrs. Bennet's machinations, had made him feel safe enough in the Bennet drawing room not to raise his mask. Even though there had been so many strangers present, they had made him feel comfortable. Even after all this time, he still felt at ease with the gentleman, which had facilitated their chance meeting just now.

But to be expected to keep his mask from locking into place at Lucas Lodge, among so many strangers, with Elizabeth having such hostile feelings towards him? He was even uncomfortable with more than half of his own party! And who knew how Mr. Bennet would react toward him when they met again? Under such conditions, he knew it would be impossible!

Chapter 13

Bingley sat quietly sipping on brandy and watching William pace the drawing room at Netherfield, frantically twisting his signet ring and checking his pocket watch against the mantle clock every few minutes. His friend's agitation had begun upon their arrival at the assembly and had grown more intense with each subsequent day. Since William had acted so far out of character at the assembly by asking a lady to dance, he had a good idea of what—or who—was causing his perturbation.

Over the past few days Bingley had also noticed how William's muscles stiffened every time Miss Elizabeth Bennet was mentioned, and how he tried to control his reaction to Caroline's and Louisa's criticisms of the lady by grinding his teeth and clenching his fists. From what Bingley could discern, William was more than simply attracted to Miss Elizabeth. After taking into account what Mrs. Bennet had said at the assembly when she snubbed William, he suspected there was a much longer and more intimate acquaintance between the two than either had allowed to be generally known.

Bingley was certain that this dinner party would be an interesting event in regards to observing William's behavior—*if* he could find the strength within him to tear his attention away from the angelic Miss Jane Bennet, who had been occupying his mind in ways that no other lady ever had before now.

~%~

Caroline Bingley insisted on arriving late for everything. Recently when her brother had pressed her for an explanation as to why it took her so long to ready herself when she had retired hours earlier to begin the process, her excuse was that it was fashionable to be late. William knew it was done in an effort to set herself apart from the crowd so that she would be noticed, especially in a setting such as was expected tonight, which she considered to be "backwards"; therefore, she was dressed in a much finer material and more fashionable cut of clothing than would be expected of the locals. William personally did not think anyone *could* miss noticing her while she appeared in the bright orange shades that she preferred, even if she had been *first* to arrive and was buried behind a crowd of people.

If Caroline knew how much William despised having to wait or arriving late for any occasion, she might have changed her ways, but he had striven to keep any of his personal preferences from her notice since he did not want for her to do anything for *his* sake!

Having to wait for Caroline tonight was of no assistance in calming William's already frayed nerves. He had spent the days between the assembly and today alternating between a desperate hunger to lay eyes upon Elizabeth (even if her own countenance *would* be filled with animosity toward him), complete confusion when trying to puzzle out how he could achieve what Baron Leisenheimer had advised, and a deep sense of dread at the prospect of seeing Mr. Bennet for the first time after what he assumed the man had done to Georgiana and himself by his blatant disregard for his promise to his father.

As the clock ran further past the time they had been scheduled to arrive at Lucas Lodge, William's annoyance with Miss Bingley rose and so did his anger at Mr. Bennet. But by the time the Netherfield party arrived at Lucas Lodge, all of William's anxiety had focused itself into anger at one Mr. Thomas Bennet.

~%~

The Netherfield party's arrival at Lucas Lodge was as close to a repeat of their arrival at the assembly as could be in company of a smaller number. All conversation ended, and all eyes turned toward their group—except for the dark eyes flecked with gold that William longed to see again. Elizabeth continued speaking to John Lucas for several moments, and at the end of her discourse when Mr. Lucas replied, William heard her laughter ring out. It was missing a certain quality that he remembered hearing so often at Pemberley, but it was obvious that she was enjoying what another man had to say, and that knowledge caused William's stomach to coil into a painful knot and his blood to begin to boil with jealousy. Without realizing what he was about, he began to fidget once again with his ring, and then froze when Elizabeth turned her gaze in his direction.

Elizabeth's countenance quickly changed from the warm camaraderie she had displayed while conversing with Mr. Lucas to an icy glare upon meeting his own eyes.

The only obvious change in William's façade was the barely discernable tightening of the muscles in his jaw and neck—and if one knew him *very* well, one might have been able to detect a deep sorrow enter his eyes.

~%~

The subtle change in William's countenance had *not* gone unnoticed by one who may not have known *this* man well, but certainly had known his father very well indeed. In his younger days, he had been naturally attuned to watch for certain signals of George Darcy's discomfort so that he would know when it was time to tease him out of his reticence. Mr. Bennet saw it all and began to wonder—George Darcy had said that his son was even less comfortable in society than *he* had been when he was younger, and William had "had no Thomas Bennet to help him through it." The stony expression William was wearing *was* very much like what Mr. Bennet used to tease George about as being his "mask." Could William have taken after his father in the defenses he used while in society?

As he watched him, Mr. Bennet detected a certain *something* enter William's eyes and followed his gaze to Elizabeth's icy stare. Did he regret what he had done to Elizabeth, or did he regret that he did not have her heart as a plaything any longer? Would William make a try for her affections again, crushing her spirit even further when he left the area, as he surely would do judging by his behavior thus far? Mr. Bennet could not allow that to happen! He would watch William Darcy very closely from now on and warn him away from her if that seemed to be his intention… unless he proved himself worthy in some way.

"Oh, I apologize, Bennet. I only now recall that you have not met Mr. Darcy." Sir William Lucas interrupted his thoughts, noticing the way in which he was staring at William. "I will introduce you. You have met Mr. Bingley, yes?"

"Yes, I have had that pleasure, Lucas." Should he mention that he already knew William? No, it would be interesting to see how William handled the introduction. "Lead on!"

Mr. Bennet followed Sir William to where the Netherfield party stood. "Mr. Bingley, I believe you remember Mr. Thomas Bennet of Longbourn. I would like to introduce Mr. Fitzwilliam Darcy of Pemberley, Mr. Victor Hurst, Mrs. Louisa Hurst, and Miss Caroline Bingley." Everyone bowed and curtsied when appropriate.

When William straightened, he locked eyes in contest with Mr. Bennet. The younger man had a defiant look in his eyes that raised the elder's ire, but neither said a word to the other. Bingley went on with some social chatter to which Mr. Bennet paid the proper attention, but William's eyes never left the man who, in his opinion, had dishonored his father and had ruined his beloved's opinion of him, stealing any chance at his having a happy life.

When an opportunity arose for the two gentlemen to speak alone, William had to ask, "Why, sir?"

"I understand you not, Mr. Darcy," Mr. Bennet answered.

"How could you pretend not to understand, Mr. Bennet?" Mr. Bennet's ignoring his promise to his father had been difficult, but he must know that his interference in William's relationship with Elizabeth had been the single most devastating thing that could have happened to him. How could the man *not* discern his meaning?

"Mr. Darcy, you must speak more clearly if you wish others to comprehend what you say." Mr. Bennet was becoming quite annoyed.

"What did I do to deserve such treatment?" William said with a commanding air.

The pain in William's eyes confused Mr. Bennet, though his ire at the younger man remained strong. How could William not *expect* that he would be treated with disdain by the father of the woman he had disappointed so cruelly? Did he think all would be forgotten due to his rank and wealth?

"Where do you find the courage to ask me such a question as that? You know perfectly well what you have done. I do not wish to embarrass any of those present by airing our disagreement in company," Mr. Bennet replied, with a stern look.

"I had thought you understood my reasons for what had been done," William said with anger, though, within, his heart was aching for having gone to Elizabeth's rooms at Pemberley that night. If he had only *trusted* that Mr. Bennet would give him time alone with Elizabeth before they left, would Mr. Bennet have kept Georgiana's letters from her, cut off relations between the families, and turned Elizabeth against him? Was it all truly William's own doing—or had Mr. Bennet already planned it before he had gone to her rooms and had he been upset that William had found an opportunity to explain himself to her, making Mr. Bennet's job of convincing her that he had abandoned her all the more difficult?

"Yes, I understand your reasons perfectly… which answers your question exactly!" Mr. Bennet said a little too loudly, attracting the attention of those surrounding them. Of course, her father would resent the man who would think his daughter worthy of dallying with in the country, but unworthy of marrying and presenting to the *ton* as his wife. He had abandoned his favorite! What was William thinking by confronting him on this subject?

Mr. Bennet's reply made it clear to William that he had been correct! Mr. Bennet never had approved of him for his daughter. William had made it perfectly clear that he went to see Elizabeth in her rooms in order to make certain she knew of his regard for her! Or was it simply the fact that William had not trusted Mr. Bennet that bothered him? He could not ask Mr. Bennet here, but he was becoming so angry that he did straighten his back further and take a step closer to Mr. Bennet to take up a more intimidating stance.

A movement in the periphery caught his eye, and William turned to see Elizabeth with a look of panic on her face. Realizing it was *he* causing her such discomfort convinced him to back down from this confrontation. No matter how much agony her behavior was causing him, it was not *her* fault the situation existed, and he did not wish to be the author of any further pain of hers. He bowed slightly to Mr. Bennet and walked away.

William had spent a good portion of the first part of the evening after the encounter with Mr. Bennet attempting to calm himself while observing his favorite person in the world, Elizabeth. Feeling more comfortable when able to hear her voice, he followed her wherever she moved within the room.

After a while, William was surprised to find himself the subject of her discourse with Miss Charlotte Lucas. Elizabeth asked Miss Lucas if she could account for William's listening to her conversations and the scowl on his face. Had she said or done anything worthy of such harsh criticism?

William reluctantly moved further away from Elizabeth after hearing this comment. Baron Leisenheimer had been correct about his mask—she thought he looked at her to find fault! He wished he could discard it, but realized the effort it would have taken to even *attempt* to remove it was not at all possible in this hostile environment.

Later, as William was lost in reviewing in his mind Elizabeth's song that had just ended, Sir William approached and began to speak of dancing. William knew his responses to Sir William were rude, but he wished to be left alone with his fantasy that Elizabeth had been singing *to him* and hoped that Sir William would just leave him be.

Sir William took hold of a passerby's hand—Elizabeth!—and offered her as a dance partner. Every fiber of his being desired to have her accept his offer to dance willingly, but she said that she had not the least intention of dancing, and so continued on her way across the room without another look at the man whose cold expression broke her heart every time she saw it.

William returned to the pastime of watching Elizabeth from afar, and Elizabeth continued to attempt to pretend that she did not notice his icy stare.

~%~

~The Phillipses' Home, Meryton

Since the militia had been quartered at Meryton, many of the houses in the neighborhood had hosted teas and dinners with the officers as guests. Today it was Elizabeth's Aunt and Uncle Phillips who were hosting a dinner party, and among the officers was a new recruit, a Lieutenant Wickham. Having spent time with the Darcy's steward during her stay at their estate, Elizabeth's curiosity got the better of her, and she inquired as to his place of birth.

"Derbyshire, ma'am," said he. "My father was the steward on one of the largest estates in all of England—Pemberley." Wickham could tell her curiosity had been piqued; could *this* be the Miss Elizabeth Bennet that he had heard so much about from his father and Georgiana Darcy? If so, he had a debt to settle with her! The only reason he had not succeeded with his *seduction* of Georgiana Darcy was due to *this* woman's prior influence on the young girl! He intended to speak of the Darcys at length to see if she betrayed any acquaintance with them.

"Well, then, you might be pleased to know that Mr. Fitzwilliam Darcy is in the neighborhood, staying at Netherfield with his friend, Mr. Bingley."

Elizabeth was startled to see that Mr. Wickham did not look very pleased at all. "Ah… I see." He cleared his throat, and then said, "Well, I am glad that I did not know of it *before* accepting this post for I might have requested an assignment to a different area of England and missed meeting all of the fine people of Meryton. I suppose now that I am here, I will not be driven away by Mr. Darcy. If he wishes to avoid seeing me, *he* must go."

Elizabeth raised her brows quickly at this statement. She had never heard anything, good or bad, about Mr. Wickham's son, but something about this man's practiced charm did not sit right with her. She waited silently to see if he would continue, and that he did.

"We are not on friendly terms, you see, and it always gives me pain to meet him. I have no reason for avoiding him but what I might proclaim to the entire world — a sense of very great ill-usage and most painful regrets at his being what he is. His father, Miss Bennet, the late Mr. Darcy, was one of the best men that ever breathed and the truest friend I ever had. I can never be in company with *this* Mr. Darcy without being grieved to the soul by a thousand tender recollections. Fitzwilliam Darcy's behavior to me has been scandalous and an act of disrespect to his father's memory, but I do believe I would forgive him everything rather than publicly disgrace the memory of his father by revealing the truth about his heir."

Elizabeth's stomach had dropped halfway through his speech, and it took a few moments for her mind to clear enough to be able to speak. "Excuse me, Mr. Wickham… did you say 'the *late* Mr. Darcy'? Are you saying that Mr. George Darcy is dead?"

"Yes, Miss Elizabeth; Fitzwilliam Darcy is now master of Pemberley."

Elizabeth paled at this, confirming Wickham's suspicions that she was the lady he sought.

"Miss Elizabeth, may I get you some wine, perhaps? You do not look well."

"No… I thank you, Mr. Wickham, no. I will be well. It was just a bit of a shock." They sat in silence for a minute before Elizabeth said, "Pray, continue, sir. You were saying that Mr. Fitzwilliam Darcy's behavior has disrespected his father's memory?"

"I have been a disappointed man, Miss Elizabeth. A military life is not what I was intended for, but circumstances have now made it eligible. The church ought to have been my profession. I should at this time have been in possession of a most valuable living, had it pleased the gentleman we were speaking of just now."

"Indeed!"

"Yes, the late Mr. Darcy bequeathed me the next presentation of the best living in his gift. He was my godfather and excessively attached to me. I cannot do justice to his kindness. He meant to provide for me amply, and thought he had done it, but when the living fell vacant, it was given elsewhere."

"Good heavens!" cried Elizabeth. "But how could his will be disregarded? Did not you seek legal redress?"

"There was just such informality in the terms of the bequest as to give me no hope. A man of *honor* could not have doubted the intention, but Mr. Darcy chose to doubt it—or to treat it as a merely conditional recommendation. The living became vacant two years ago, exactly as I was of an age to hold it, and it was given to another man. I cannot accuse myself of having done anything to deserve to lose it. I have a warm, unguarded temper, and I may perhaps have sometimes spoken my opinion of him, and to him, too freely. I can recall nothing worse. But the fact is that we are very different sorts of men, and that he hates me for it."

"This is quite shocking! Perhaps he deserves to be publicly disgraced." It seemed to Elizabeth that William had changed greatly and needed to be put in his place.

"Some time or other he *will* be—but it shall not be by me. 'Til I can forget his father, I can never expose his son."

Elizabeth searched Mr. Wickham's face. What he had said so far validated how William had obviously not followed his father's wishes in contacting her own father upon his death—*if*, of course, that *was* still his wish upon his death, and it might not have been, but she would have to think upon that subject later. Of immediate import was the question of how Lieutenant Wickham could say he would *not* expose William's alleged misdeeds when he was, at that very moment, doing exactly that by speaking of it to *her*? How much else of what Mr. Wickham was saying was only partially true, or a contradiction she had not yet discerned? She spoke again, "But what could have been his motive? What could have induced him to behave so cruelly?"

"A thorough, determined dislike of me—a dislike which I cannot but attribute in some measure to jealousy. Had the late Mr. Darcy liked me less, his son might have borne with me better, but his father's uncommon attachment and favoritism toward me irritated him throughout his life. He had not a temper to bear the sort of competition in which we stood—the sort of preference which was often given me."

Elizabeth had *seen* William's father interact with William on many occasions, and she could not believe what Lieutenant Wickham was saying at present. Through all the years she had known them, the late Mr. Darcy had loved his son very well indeed, and she had no doubt that William was sure of it. Lieutenant Wickham's credibility was quickly wearing thin.

Lieutenant Wickham continued, "We were born in the same parish, within the same park, and the greatest part of our youth was passed together; inmates of the same house, sharing the same amusements, objects of the same parental care since his father treated me as if I were his own son. My father devoted all his time to the care of the Pemberley property. He was most highly esteemed by Mr. Darcy, a most intimate, confidential friend. Mr. Darcy often acknowledged himself to be under the greatest obligations to my father's active superintendence, and when Mr. Darcy gave him a voluntary promise of providing for me in his will, I am convinced that he felt it to be as much a debt of gratitude to him, as of affection to myself."

Half truths again, Elizabeth thought, but they were said with such conviction that she could not help but wonder if Lieutenant Wickham actually believed what he was saying. She knew that the elder Mr. Wickham had been greatly valued, but "objects of the same parental care?" He said it as if Mr. Darcy treated him as another son. If that were true, where was Lieutenant Wickham when she had met with the Darcys at Longbourn, those many times in London and at Pemberley, and why had not Mr. Darcy *ever* spoken of him in any of their meetings?

"Do you know Mr. Bingley?"

"Not at all."

"He is a sweet tempered, amiable, charming man. He is a great friend of Mr.   Darcy's."

"Ah, and you wonder how Mr. Bingley, being such a man, could be friends with him and not know what Mr. Darcy is? Mr. Darcy can please where he chooses. He does not want for abilities. He can be a convivial companion if he thinks it worth his while. Among those he wishes to please, he is a very different man from what he is to those he does not care for. His pride never deserts him, but with friends, he is liberal-minded, just, sincere, rational, honorable, and perhaps agreeable—allowing something for fortune and… figure." Lieutenant Wickham's eyes wandered down to *her* figure.

This last speech hit too close to Elizabeth's heart for her tastes, and so she changed the direction in which their discussion was headed, gauging the man on other subjects. She found him to talk smoothly around any issue— saying much of nothing in most cases—interspersing enough truths to convince most people who had general knowledge of the subject that he knew of what he was speaking, but there were too many half-truths, distortions, and conjecture which he attempted to pass off as fact, to fool someone as well educated and as intelligent as Elizabeth.

All this was analyzed thoroughly to keep her mind off the thing she did not wish to think of lest she become upset. Mr. George Darcy was dead—and William had not the decency to inform her or her father of that fact, not by letter and not even after being in the same neighborhood all this time.

~%~

Elizabeth knew that she must tell her father of the passing of his old friend. As with many things she did not like to do, she wished to be done with it as soon as possible; so after breakfast the following morning, Elizabeth knocked on her father's study door, and he bid her to enter.

"Papa… I must speak to you about a serious subject." Her father motioned to the chair in front of his desk and she sat fidgeting for several moments before taking a breath to speak, but then closed her mouth again.

"What is it, Lizzy? I have rarely seen you so disturbed."

Elizabeth's eyes filled with tears as her mind began to do what she had somehow prevented it from doing since she had discovered this information the previous evening—all of her own interactions with Mr. George Darcy played out in her mind unbidden, and after they were done, tears escaped her eyes as she said, "We met Lieutenant George Wickham last night at Aunt Phillips's home. He is the son of Mr. Wickham, the former steward at Pemberley."

Mr. Bennet's concern for his daughter was clearly displayed as he answered, "I heard the name come up several times this morning at breakfast and was wondering if he was somehow related. But why does this information have you so out of sorts, Lizzy?"

"Lieutenant Wickham informed me... Oh papa!" more tears escaped her eyes, "Mr. George Darcy has passed away."

Mr. Bennet closed his eyes and sat unmoving for several minutes before he spoke, "When?"

"I do not know exactly, Papa, but from what Lieutenant Wickham said, I could discern it was at least two years ago."

"Two years?" Mr. Bennet's face began to redden. "Two years!" He stood and began to pace the room. "William never informed me!"

"Yes... I know."

"Even if George did have a change of heart about the suitability of our friendship after our last visit, which he obviously did, still I deserved to be notified of his passing at the very least. We grew up together at school! We did everything together! We were closer than most brothers for many years!" Mr. Bennet's voice rose louder with every exclamation, and his color was rising so quickly that Elizabeth was becoming frightened.

"Papa, you must calm yourself. It will do nobody good if you make yourself ill!"

He sat down heavily in the chair across from Elizabeth's. "How could I have been discarded in such a fashion as this, Lizzy? George and I—we had always had the ability to work through our differences, no matter how angry we were at each other. We could have talked... why did he never answer my letters?"

Elizabeth sobbed. "Papa, I apologize for getting in the way of your valued friendship. If only I had not gone to Pemberley with you..."

Mr. Bennet's eyes opened wide and he leaned across the space between their chairs and took her hand in his. "No! Oh, Lizzy! My dear girl! Do not take the blame on yourself. You are the least culpable of anyone, and you are the person most injured by the actions of all.

"As I have said before, George and I had talked about the differences in your stations, and he had no qualms. He urged me not to wait too long to give consent because he was ill and wished to live long enough to see William happy, and he even spoke of meeting his first grandchild!

"I *cannot* understand what happened, unless perhaps his illness affected his way of thinking. But he had his senses when we left; how could it have happened so quickly? It still makes no sense to me; now I will never have the chance to find out the truth, since William is not the least bit inclined to speak to me in anything but cryptic phrases."

Mr. Bennet dropped Elizabeth's hand and sat back suddenly exclaiming as if hearing it for the first time, "George is dead!" His fingers gripped the arms of the chair so firmly that his knuckles turned white.

Her father was quiet for a minute while Elizabeth watched all the color drain from his face and his breathing quicken. Her concern for his health was increasing.

"Papa? Are you well?" she asked, feeling panic, but trying to keep her tone even.

"Lizzy? I fear you must call Mr. Jones." He was breathing so quickly now that he had to stop speaking between every word or two to take a breath, and his voice came out as a whisper.

"Papa?" Elizabeth said as she rushed to ring the bell for Mrs. Hill, and then kneeled at her father's side.

"I am feeling very unwell, Lizzy. I have a pain here," he said, placing a hand upon his chest, "and it is becoming very difficult to breathe."

Elizabeth knew this was not good news, but needed to keep him as calm as possible. "Just sit back and rest, Papa. All will be well."

Mrs. Hill knocked and entered when Elizabeth called out. "Close the door, Mrs. Hill." Elizabeth waited until she did so before approaching and whispering with a pointed look at her father, "Mr. Jones must be fetched at once, but do not alert the family that it is for my father's sake, Mrs. Hill. Mama would be in here in a moment if she knew, and he does not need *that* just now! If my mother asks, Mr. Jones has been called for my sake—she will not enter the study for *my* being ill. Bring in a pot of Mama's calming tea, please, as soon as you can. Tell Joseph to hurry, though, in case my guess about what is occurring here is wrong!"

Mrs. Hill's eyes had been wide since entering and seeing the master, understanding immediately the gravity of the situation. She rushed out of the room to do her duty.

Luckily, Mrs. Hill's nephew Joseph was a very fast runner, and Mr. Jones was in his curricle just returning to his office when Joseph got there.

When Mr. Jones entered the study, Mr. Bennet had already taken a cup of the tea at Elizabeth's insistence, and his breathing and color were a little better. Elizabeth explained what had happened, and Mr. Jones examined Mr. Bennet thoroughly. "Well, Bennet... I think it was *your* turn to have a bout of nerves instead of your wife!"

Mr. Bennet's eyes widened. "*That* was nerves?"

"Yes, thankfully, I do believe it was. Your heart sounds fine, and Miss Lizzy did say you had just received some disturbing news..." Mr. Jones turned to Elizabeth and said, "The tea was good thinking on your part Miss Lizzy."

Mr. Bennet's mouth was hanging open. "My wife has fits like *this*?"

"Most of them have not been quite as severe as the one Miss Lizzy described to me, but yes it is similar to what your wife experiences."

"My G-d! I had no idea! I had no control over it at all. And I have treated the idea of her nerves as a *joke* all this time!" Mr. Bennet's brow furrowed, and he shook his head. "Thank you, Jones. I will admit that if *this* is what she has been experiencing all these years—even a less severe version of it— I now cannot help but have a new sense of respect and sympathy for Mrs. Bennet!"

Chapter 14

Several days later while at breakfast, Jane received a note from Caroline Bingley requesting her presence at Netherfield to dine with the ladies, as the gentlemen would be dining with Colonel Forster and the officers.

"It is unfortunate that Mr. Bingley will not be present, Jane, but take advantage of this opportunity to display your good nature to his sisters! They could not be but impressed with you, my dear! You will go on Nellie."

"But Mama! It looks like rain! If Jane travels by horseback, she will be soaked through!" Elizabeth exclaimed.

"Oh Lizzy, your father is always speaking of how intelligent you are; how do you not understand something so simple? If it rains, she will have to stay the night and *will* see Mr. Bingley after all!"

Jane blushed, Lydia and Kitty giggled, Mary scowled and shook her head, and Mr. Bennet continued eating his breakfast as if he had heard nothing of what had just passed. Only Lizzy was upset that Mrs. Bennet would expose her daughter to the foul weather all in the name of "catching a husband," but since Jane expressed no opposition to the idea, she made no further comment.

Elizabeth regretted that decision when later that day, Mrs. Bennet received a note from Miss Bingley saying that Jane was ill and would be staying the night.

The following morning, Elizabeth received a note from Jane asking for some clothing to be sent. "Do not be alarmed, dearest Lizzy, if you should hear that Mr. Jones has been sent for. I am very unwell and will need some droughts." Elizabeth packed a trunk for Jane and had it sent to Netherfield with Joseph before going downstairs to break her fast.

After reading that Jane, who never complained, actually *stated* in her note that she was unwell, Elizabeth had decided that she would set off for Netherfield herself to see how Jane fared. She mentioned her plans at breakfast.

Mrs. Bennet reproached Elizabeth. "What nonsense, Lizzy! The horses are being used on the farm today. If you walk, you will be covered in mud and not fit to be seen! Besides, there is no sense in *your* going to Netherfield; there is *nothing* for *you* there. It would be a wiser course for you to leave any nursing to Mr. Bingley's sisters—it will create a bond between them and Jane. *You* would be better off going into Meryton with Kitty and Lydia to your Aunt Phillips's in order to be seen by the officers."

"I will be fit to be seen by Jane, which is my only purpose in going to Netherfield, Mama. Do you not believe Jane would be more comfortable with me there?"

"Oh, you are too stubborn to convince otherwise, and I will not hear the end of it until I agree. Go if you feel you must."

Mr. Bennet spoke quietly to Elizabeth after the others were busy discussing red coats, "I do not like this plan, Lizzy. I do not like your being in the same house as *he*."

"Papa, I have no intention of seeing Mr. Darcy while I am there. It is not as if he is a dangerous man who hides behind doors and will spring out at me; he is only offensive. You *know* very well I can defend myself from anything he might say if we do happen to meet. I will visit with Jane and see how she is feeling. Someone needs to wait on her, and I do not wish to leave it to a maid whom Jane has never met before. I am absolutely *certain* Mr. Bingley's sisters have no patience for a sick room," Elizabeth said in a teasing tone of voice.

Mr. Bennet sighed, "I suppose you are right, and you may go—but still, I do not like it."

Elizabeth set off soon after breakfast, walked with her sisters as far as Meryton, and then took a little-travelled path to Netherfield after passing through the village. As soon as she was able to see the manor house through the trees, she stopped to examine her attire. Her mother had been right—her skirts *were* muddied, but the walk had done her good in clearing the cobwebs from her mind, making her better prepared to encounter William if he dared to approach her.

As she was nearing the house, she came around a hedge and stopped short, almost walking into somebody who had turned the corner from the opposite direction. Hands reached out quickly and took hold of her arms to steady her.

"OH!" Elizabeth exclaimed, and she looked up to find herself being held by William. She deeply inhaled his scent, exactly as she had remembered it to be, and old memories of being close to him flooded her mind. For a few moments the two of them stood there in the same position staring at each other. The look in William's eyes shocked her, for it was anything *but* the cold exterior he had been displaying since she had met him again—it was the old William that she had known and loved at Pemberley—and her heart began to beat so frantically that she was certain he could hear it. He leaned down toward her just a little while tilting his head to the side, and for a moment she thought he was going to kiss her. Her intake of breath was barely audible, but enough for him to remember himself. He schooled his features and stepped back, dropping his arms to his sides.

"Excuse me, Miss Elizabeth. I did not know you were coming to Netherfield today." He continued in his thoughts, *"Though I should have expected you to; with your kind and generous heart, you* **would** *come all this way to nurse your sister, even though you had to walk! I wonder… if Georgiana had sent someone for you instead of relying on a letter that your father did not allow you to know of…"*

Blushing, Elizabeth blinked a few times before saying absent-mindedly, "I have come to see my sister, Jane."

"Yes, of course," William breathed as he motioned toward the house. He waited for her to begin to walk before he followed and caught up to her.

William decided he should *not* be thinking of what he wished would have happened if he *had* kissed her, lest he pull her to a stop and follow through on those thoughts. Elizabeth began walking very quickly, as if she had read his mind and could not wait to be away from him.

He fell into step beside and one pace behind her, hoping that being farther apart would make her feel more comfortable in his presence. This position also conveniently provided him with the perfect view of her profile.

The lock of hair he had cut off had grown back, and it was teasing him as it had done years earlier. William touched his ring, where this curl's predecessor now resided. He then became entranced by a little scar on her jaw line just below her right ear that he had not noticed before, and he was suddenly almost overwhelmed with the desire to caress it. William sensed an interesting story could be told about how it came to be and wondered if he should ask her to share it with him. But, no—that was a conversation one would have with a *friend,* and Elizabeth seemed to wish that he was not even among her acquaintances.

They continued on to the house in silence, where he showed her to her sister's room, and left her with a bow.

~%~

Elizabeth stood and admired the exquisiteness of his form as William walked away from her and down the stairs. She hesitated a moment as she blushed at the impropriety of her thoughts and leaned her forehead against the cool wood of Jane's bedchamber door—her mind was in a muddle, and she needed to compose herself before seeing Jane.

Had he *really* almost kissed her when they met a few minutes ago? Why? Did he expect that she was a wanton woman since she had kissed him in the past? She chastised herself; with the way she *had* behaved that night he had come to her chamber, it really would be a wonder if he did not! But then why did he look at her in that way before he stopped himself? If he thought her immoral, why would he have stopped at all? From where they had been standing, nobody would have been able to see them from the house, and they encountered no one on their approach to the house, so he could not have been afraid of witnesses.

She could not help but focus on his expression *before* he had raised his cold, stern countenance with which she was becoming quite familiar. That was *her* William! He was still inside that frigid shell somewhere. With a little encouragement from her, could the old William be summoned forward? If he did appear again, did she *wish* to encourage him after all that had happened—and had not happened—between them?

She could not help but wonder how things would have proceeded if he *had* kissed her. Would it have been as wonderful as it had been long ago, or would it have left her feeling sullied?

What would it have meant to *him* if they had kissed? Would it have been all part of a game to him, to see if he could deceive her into loving him again? Or was it as she had always hoped—that he had loved her all this time, but something had prevented him from coming to her before now?

But that made no sense at all! Even if his father *had* changed his mind and had begun to object to her as his heir's wife just after they had left Pemberley, Mr. Darcy had been dead for more than two years according to Lieutenant Wickham. Surely William would have been able to come before now if he truly loved her! If something had prevented him, surely he could have written to her father to explain why he could not come for her at that time! And why would he be acting the way he had most of the time since he had come to Hertfordshire if that were true?

The hope that he loved her was a foolish, childish dream, and she had to bury it deep inside and never let it come to the surface again!

Elizabeth's mind was distracted by so many questions to which she did not have answers that she forgot she was standing in the corridor at Netherfield with her forehead pressed against Jane's bedchamber door. The door to Jane's room flew open and Elizabeth fell forward, bumping into Caroline Bingley, who about to leave the room. It was obvious by Caroline's scream that Elizabeth had frightened her quite thoroughly. Elizabeth apologized—twice—and then began to laugh at the ridiculousness of the situation, but Miss Bingley was not amused in the least!

"Miss Eliza! Why are you here? What are on earth were you doing leaning on the door? Should we soon expect to find you listening at keyholes as well?"

"Again, I *am* sorry for frightening you, Miss Bingley! I have just walked here from Longbourn to see Jane, and I felt a little flushed, so I placed my forehead upon the cool wood of the door before entering to see how my sister fares. I should have realized that there was a possibility of the door's being opened, but clearly that thought had never entered my mind." She thought, *"I was too distracted by thoughts of William!"*

"With the redness of the mark on your forehead I would think you were there leaning against the door for quite a while. Are you certain you did not mean to overhear our conversation instead of the explanation you have given?"

"I assure you, Miss Bingley! I would never eavesdrop on a private conversation!" Elizabeth arched her brow, wondering if Caroline had a habit of listening to other's conversations and if *that* was why she was insisting that Elizabeth had been doing so.

Caroline caught her accusing look and sneered at her. It made no difference to Caroline that Elizabeth *was* correct; it was simply rude to accuse her *betters* of such things! Caroline said, "I was just leaving, Miss Eliza. You will excuse me."

"Of course." Elizabeth curtsied, but Caroline did not return it, walked through the doorway, and continued down the hall. Elizabeth closed the door and approached Jane, chuckling.

"Lizzy, it is so good to see you."

Concern for her sister became foremost in her mind when Elizabeth saw that Jane was flushed with fever and seemed very weak. She rushed forward the remaining steps to her sister's bedside. "Dearest Jane, you are very ill indeed! Has no one been bathing you to bring down your fever?"

Jane shook her head.

"Well, then, I will stay right here and do so, and I will tell you stories of the adventures of the Dreaded Pirate Lizzy until you fall asleep," Elizabeth said with a tender smile.

Once Jane began to slumber, Elizabeth refreshed the cloth only every few minutes for she knew, since Mr. Jones had told Jane she had a bad cold, that she needed rest most of all. With little to keep her occupied, her mind wandered back to her questions about William, and she became lost in thoughts of him once again.

A knock upon the door startled Elizabeth back to the present and she answered it. A maid had been sent by Mr. Bingley to ask if she would like a luncheon tray sent up for herself and some soup for Miss Bennet. Elizabeth thought that was a wonderful idea, and asked for a fresh pitcher of water as well, since the one that had been there was now empty.

When the maid returned, Jane was awakened and drank a little of the broth with a pained expression. "Jane, I know it hurts to swallow, but you must take some nourishment. If you are a good little girl and drink *all* of your soup, I will tell you another story!" Elizabeth teased a weak smile from her sister as she tenderly wiped Jane's brow again. A while later, after Jane had taken another short nap, Caroline and Mrs. Hurst came to visit.

"Oh, you do look *ill*, Miss Bennet," Mrs. Hurst said with such an expression of concern that at first Elizabeth thought better of her—until she continued, "Perhaps we should not be here, Caroline! We will both become as ill as Miss Bennet!"

"We will only stay a short while, Louisa—long enough to say goodbye to Miss Eliza and show her out," Caroline answered with a satisfied smile.

Jane became visibly upset, "Must you go, Lizzy?"

"I am afraid I must, or I will have to walk home in the dark."

Seeing Jane become even more agitated, Caroline realized that if Elizabeth stayed, *she* would not be inconvenienced by having to supervise a servant attending to her ill guest, and she did not have to visit or sit with Jane as often... *and* it would show off her excellent skills as a hostess to her *other* guest.

"Miss Eliza, it is plain to see that dearest Jane would be easier if you stayed until she is well enough to return home. Will you?"

Elizabeth's eyes widened. *"Stay in the same house with William? This **cannot** be happening!"* The memory of her own voice telling her father that someone needed to tend to Jane came back to her. Without further hesitation she agreed and walked over to the writing desk to send a note to her father, requesting that some clothing be sent as soon as possible. Elizabeth added:

Papa, please do not worry; I am fine. I will remain with Jane in her room as much as is possible without appearing rude to Mr. Bingley. The moment Jane is well enough to take the carriage ride home, you may be certain that we will return to Longbourn. All will be well.

After assisting Jane in taking some more broth, Elizabeth changed for dinner. Rejoining her sister, Elizabeth asked Jane once again if she was absolutely certain that she was well enough to leave her with the maid. Jane assured her that she wished to sleep for a while and would do fine with the maid that had been sent to attend her while Elizabeth dined.

Elizabeth smiled at the maid and stressed, "If Miss Bennet needs me, Helen, please do not hesitate to send for me immediately. I will check on her as soon as dinner is done. Will you please refresh the cloth on her forehead every few minutes?"

Helen agreed and curtsied, and Elizabeth looked back at Jane one last time before leaving the room. In the hallway, she stopped with a hand on the wall to steady herself and closed her eyes for a moment. Elizabeth felt guilty—while the main reason she did not wish to leave Jane was because she was ill, there was also a portion of it that was pure selfishness. William would be at dinner. It took an *enormous* effort not to display her tender feelings for him whenever he was simply mentioned, let alone when he was in the same room as she. But it must be done, and so she had better get to it! She took a long, deep breath and let it out slowly, straightened her back, and descended the stairs.

~%~

All day, William had been so distracted by knowing that Elizabeth was in the house that he was halfway into the hallway before he realized he had forgotten his gloves. Turning back to retrieve them, he left the door to his chamber open slightly—as a result, when he exited his room the door made no noise. He saw Elizabeth exit her sister's room at the same moment and turn right toward the stairs. The young gentleman paused, thinking he should allow her to get ahead of him lest she feel uncomfortable. Then she stopped suddenly, holding on to the wall as if to steady herself, and he watched her shoulders droop. Being behind her, he could not see her face, but for a short period of time, she had the posture of a person who felt completely defeated.

He was shocked, and realized he had seen Elizabeth in a vulnerable state of mind only once before, when she thought he had rejected her. His instinct was to gather her in his arms, offer her his strength, and make everything right again just as he had done years ago—and if she had remained in that position any longer than she had, he most likely would have given in to the impulse—but just as suddenly as it had come over her, it was gone. After sighing deeply, she straightened her form and walked on.

Though his intuition told him it was futile, he hoped that whatever had conquered her strong spirit in that way was not in any way related to him. Perhaps it was Caroline that caused her discomfort? Or worry for her sister? Just in case, he returned to his room for a few minutes.

After closing the door, William found he was not able to move any further into the room, and he leaned his back against the wall just inside, waiting to hear another's footsteps on the stairs. He did not wish to make Elizabeth uneasy by forcing her to be alone with him if none of the others had yet gone down to dinner.

"I should leave if my presence causes her to become so disturbed. I should return to London or Pemberley and not annoy her any longer. But I cannot—I am too selfish—I will not leave until all hope is gone. If this is a completely useless endeavor, I suppose the only time I waste is my own. But no time spent in her presence is wasted."

Hearing Bingley's distinctive footfalls on the stairs, he waited a few more minutes before he straightened his own form and followed. He was resolved to make an attempt to take the Baron's advice while Elizabeth was staying at Netherfield and do away with the mask he usually wore. It was probably his only hope!

~%~

Elizabeth was embarrassed. Apparently having dinner set for a certain time at Netherfield meant that one should not come down until much later than the appointed time. The cook must have been very annoyed with them all when they had first moved in!

During her wait, Elizabeth busied her mind contemplating her temporary housemates, attempting to keep herself from thinking about one person in particular.

Whether Jane admitted it or not, Elizabeth knew her sister was well on her way to falling in love, and it seemed to her that Bingley's feelings were even further along than Jane's.

Being a classic beauty, Jane had always had many admirers, but this was the first time that Elizabeth had ever seen Jane take such an interest in a man. It was also the first time she had seen a man take a *genuine* interest in Jane— the person—and not treat her like a china-doll that was useful only enough to be put on display. The two had spent their time in each other's company involved in earnest discussions, touching on many subjects.

At first Elizabeth had been surprised at the depth of some of their conversations, but no longer. She knew how intelligent Jane really was, but, unlike her own case, their mother had been successful in convincing Jane to conceal it. Elizabeth was pleased to see that Jane was hiding this aspect of her personality no longer! Most people assumed Bingley was not very bright, and Elizabeth wondered why. Yes, he smiled often, was extremely amiable, knew how please others, and liked having a good laugh, but judging from the conversations he held with Jane and her, he was quite intelligent.

Why William had sought out Bingley's friendship became clearer every time Elizabeth spoke to Bingley—but she could not understand why Bingley tolerated William! Bingley did not seem the type to *use* anybody for his own gain, as his sisters did. Caroline Bingley's and Louisa Hurst's only interest in William was obviously mercenary—of the material and social variety! But Elizabeth could not see that trait evident in Bingley's character.

Perhaps Lieutenant Wickham was right and when the two gentlemen were alone, William was more amiable. After all, she had seen it herself; when William wished to please, as he did with her at Pemberley, he could be truly pleasant.

Elizabeth caught herself—she was *not* supposed to be thinking of William—and so she changed the direction of her thoughts again.

Caroline Bingley was a nasty shrew, plain and simple, who thought herself far above her station in life and treated people who were *above* her in the social order as if they were far below her. Not that Elizabeth usually paid much attention to such things, but in this case she did because it was the basis of all of the complaints that she had overheard the lady voice about the neighborhood. No matter how diligently Elizabeth tried not to listen, it was very difficult *not* to overhear a woman who shrieked as loudly as did Caroline whenever she complained, and she complained most of the time! If it were not so hurtful to her friends, it would be amusing to watch the lady treat the local gentry as if they were trash. Caroline seemed to forget that she was the daughter of a tradesman, even if her brother *was* now a gentleman who was leasing an estate and even if her sister *had* married a gentleman. Neither of the men *owned* any land; therefore, the Bingleys were below the residents of the neighborhood with whom Caroline unwillingly socialized.

Elizabeth was shocked when she realized that if people were not useful to Caroline's social-climbing endeavors, they were obviously not worth even her effort of being completely civil to them. The only two people that the young lady treated with any respect were the Baron and Baroness Leisenheimer. Elizabeth did wonder why she was being so nice to Jane, and she had the feeling it was simply boredom—but then again, who could *not* be nice to Jane? Caroline did make comments to Jane that were mocking, but Jane's gentle heart was too good to understand them as they were meant.

How the lady treated the servants was absolutely horrid! Elizabeth took even greater care than usual to be especially kind to them all since they had to deal with *Caroline* on a daily basis!

Louisa Hurst was not much better, though she seemed to be the less strong-minded of the sisters and followed wherever Caroline led. Sometimes Mrs. Hurst reminded Elizabeth of a puppet.

Mr. Hurst—well there was a man she could not puzzle out at all! He did not seem of use to anyone other than having given his name to Louisa! He had spoken rarely, eaten too much, and drunk himself into a stupor every time she had seen him. Perhaps living in the same household with him for a few days would give her insight into his character, but for now he seemed not to have any character at all!

Elizabeth heard the door to the dining room open, and her heart skipped a beat in nervous anticipation. She turned to see who would be her first conversation partner for the evening. She was thankful that it was Bingley and not William, as she could not imagine being alone with him just now. Bingley was as pleasant as always and seemed truly concerned about Jane. Elizabeth smiled inwardly at the thought of how Jane's countenance would brighten when she gave her Bingley's messages.

Before long, William entered, and the others followed shortly thereafter. Perhaps Elizabeth would be better off being a full thirty minutes late to dinner the following evening! She was sure that if the others were on time, Caroline would not hesitate to start without her.

Elizabeth was more concerned with knowing when it would no longer be rude to go above stairs to check on Jane's health rather than remain to converse this evening. Keeping in mind her promise to her father, Elizabeth remained quiet, and instead of joining the conversation, she observed her companions to further her character study of the members of the household.

Conversation was centered on the subject of how the two ladies were looking forward to the Season in London. The schedule of operas and plays that would be performed was discussed as well. Elizabeth was amused that the ladies seemed interested only in "being seen" at these events and had no true interest in discussing the operas or plays themselves. While William and Bingley were debating a certain part of the text of one of the plays, Caroline attempted to join in, putting the character names with the wrong characterizations and revealing that her understanding of the plot was superficial at best.

During the dessert course, Caroline said with a smirk, "I apologize, Miss Eliza, for speaking on subjects that you know nothing of. Perhaps we should speak of pigs and sheep, so that you might feel more at home."

While Elizabeth had been amused with the comment and was too busy hiding her smile behind her napkin to reply at that moment, she glanced at William to see his reaction to Caroline's insult. It took her completely by surprise when she saw signs indicating that William was incensed and attempting to control his temper!

"It just so happens, Miss Bingley, that Miss Elizabeth not only has read and completely *understood* all of the plays that will be performed this season, but also she can discuss them intelligently in six languages," William said in a strained voice.

Elizabeth tried not to gape at William's defense of her abilities.

Caroline made no attempt to hide that she did *not* believe his statement. "Is that so?"

"No, it is not," Elizabeth stated seriously. William could see by the light dancing in her eyes that something she had found amusing would follow the pause. "Actually, Mr. Darcy, I read and speak *seven* languages at present."

His demeanor softened a little when his eyes met hers. "I do remember your mentioning that you wished to learn Spanish."

The intensity of William's gaze held her own eyes captive for a few moments before she could take a breath and respond with only a simple,

"Yes." Becoming very aware of the circumstances surrounding the conversation to which he referred, she felt her face beginning to flush. "I do need to check on my sister... if you will excuse me."

Only Bingley caught the brief expression of pain displayed in William's eyes as Elizabeth rose, and the appearance of utter confusion on Elizabeth's face as she left the room.

~%~

Jane was resting comfortably, and so Elizabeth made her way to the library to find a book to read during the short time she would stay in the drawing room and in case she was up during the night with Jane. Upon entering, she stood with her mouth open in amazement—she had never seen a library with so many empty shelves! There were only three in use. One shelf contained a few of the classics, which she had already read and memorized, of course. The shelf just above it held books on farming and animal husbandry, which she knew to be quite out of date. The one next to it was graced with a much more interesting selection. There were several that she had not already read, which could only delight her! Not mindful as to what the books were about—after all, beggars cannot be choosers—she chose the one with the title that was the most unique and removed herself to the drawing room.

When she entered she saw the remainder of the party was playing at loo. Elizabeth declined to join them since she would soon be retiring for the evening. Noticing that William's eyes were on the book in her hands, she held it out for him to see the title.

The corners of his lips turned up just a little before he said, "Thank you, Miss Elizabeth."

She blinked a couple of times before looking away from him, saying, "Mr. Bingley, I hope you do not mind that I took advantage of your kind offer to lend me a book from your library."

Bingley's glance at William was barely noticeable. "You were able to find something of interest within the few that were there, Miss Elizabeth?"

"Yes, I did, thank you."

Caroline pushed in to the conversation. "I am shocked that our father did not leave you a collection of books, Charles. You should begin a family library to be passed down through the generations using the delightful library at Pemberley as a model."

"Caroline! Pemberley's library is the work of many generations; I could not hope to accumulate so many books in my lifetime, even if I spent my entire income on the endeavor! Pemberley's library is not 'delightful,' it is magnificent and could never be reproduced by me alone. No, it will be up to my children and grandchildren to continue the tradition that I will begin—with Darcy's assistance in choosing the books, of course!"

Elizabeth held back a smile. After a few minutes passed, a maid came in to summon Miss Elizabeth saying that Jane's fever had risen, and she was needed above stairs. Bingley's anxiety was plain enough for anyone to see, and he asked if Mr. Jones should be sent for.

"Perhaps in the morning if she is not better, sir. For now, I have the droughts that Mr. Jones has left for her. I thank you."

Everyone bid Elizabeth a good night and sent their wishes for Miss Bennet's quick recovery before Elizabeth returned to her sister's bedside.

It was not until the middle of the night that she saw the elaborate bookplate which she recognized as identical to one in a book that had been in her bedside drawer at Longbourn for the past three years. Both books were from the library at Pemberley, added to the collection by Fitzwilliam Darcy. What this one was doing in Netherfield's library was beyond her willingness to hazard a guess, but there was a small part of her mind that could not help but wish that it had been placed there for her sake.

The following morning Elizabeth was able to report to the maid sent by Bingley that Jane's fever was lower and that she was resting comfortably; however, when Caroline and Mrs. Hurst came to visit a little while later, Elizabeth requested to send a note to her mother to ask if she could come to see Jane herself and form her own opinion. Caroline's look told Elizabeth everything she needed to know—Caroline despised the idea of having Mrs. Bennet in her house but would do whatever was necessary to be considered a good hostess.

Mrs. Bennet arrived in good time with her two youngest daughters in tow. It seemed that Bingley had been so worried about Jane that he had sent for Mr. Jones earlier that morning without checking with Elizabeth first, and the apothecary arrived at approximately the same time as the Bennet ladies. His examination complete, Mr. Jones announced to the ladies that Jane, although doing better than the previous day, was not to be moved as of yet. Mrs. Bennet met this news with a smile. As Mr. Jones was taking his leave, Elizabeth suggested they allow Jane to rest while they returned downstairs to call upon the ladies of the house.

The visit went as Elizabeth had expected. Her mother was overly warm and enthusiastic with her thanks and praise of her daughters' hosts, and sharp and cold with William—even ignoring him altogether at times. Kitty and Lydia whispered and giggled throughout and then pressed Bingley to have a ball.

Bingley thought it a wonderful idea. "I would enjoy a ball very much and will set the date as soon as Miss Bennet is feeling better!"

After her mother and sisters had gone home, Elizabeth escaped to Jane's bedside as soon as possible in order to avoid hearing the criticism of her family that she knew would follow, but found Jane sound asleep. Elizabeth inquired whether the maid could stay a little longer, and since she could, Elizabeth decided to go for a walk to clear her head of all the unwelcome thoughts following her family's visit.

Elizabeth walked toward the stables, and as she approached, she saw a familiar-looking horse in the meadow next to the structure. "Poseidon?" she asked aloud.

A stable hand who had been nearby answered, "Yes'm, 'tis Mr. Darcy's horse. We be comin' to get 'im to try groomin' 'im. 'e's a tough one, 'e is! Takes three of us to 'andle 'im!"

"Oh! That is nonsense. I will bring him into the stable for grooming myself!" Elizabeth said as she opened the gate and walked towards the horse. The stable hand yelled after her, but the lady would not return without Poseidon, so he ran to get help. When they heard what was occurring outside, most of the staff came running, expecting to have to rescue the foolish lady, but what the men found when they arrived astounded them all. Poseidon was nuzzling Elizabeth's neck and then lowered his head to her, laying it against her chest as she scratched his neck.

"Look at that! Ol' Lucifer is partial to the lady!" the head groom said.

"Lucifer? His name is Poseidon," she said as she led the horse over to the gate.

"Beggin' your pardon, ma'am, but we call 'im Lucifer 'cause 'e is always so downright nasty; 'e's like tha devil 'imself sometimes!"

"Really! Why does everyone insist this horse is nasty? He is sweet and spirited!" she laughed as Poseidon nudged her with his nose. "If you can proceed quickly, I will hold him while you groom him, but I must return to my sister soon. Do you have some carrots to keep him occupied?"

The head groom's face brightened. "Yes'm, that would be a great 'elp! We'll both work on 'im at once to make tha task go quickly," he said, pointing to the stable hand who had first come across Elizabeth.

~%~

William escaped the room shortly after Elizabeth's mother and sisters had gone. He had no intention of listening to Bingley's sisters make insulting remarks about his beloved's family and decided the best course would be to leave the house. He changed into his riding attire and headed for the stables.

As he rounded a corner entering the stables, William stopped short. The scene of Elizabeth holding Poseidon's head and whispering into his ear while two men groomed him was heartwarming, and he did not wish to interrupt. William slowly backed up so that he could watch but not be seen.

Elizabeth was such an amazing person! What other woman would do such a thing? Though many gentlemen had a special bond with their horses, most of *them* would not help the grooms do their work.

She laughed as Poseidon nudged the pocket where she must have been hiding extra carrots. William had not seen her look this happy since he had entered the neighborhood.

The last thought caused a mixture of emotions to swell within his breast. It was wonderful that his horse could make her happy, but that *he* could not elicit the same emotion from her was disheartening.

No, he would not think upon this now; he wished only to enjoy watching her amusement while it lasted.

~%~

Elizabeth arrived at the doors to the dining room a full thirty minutes after the appointed time for dinner. As she had descended the stairs a few moments prior, she had seen Mr. and Mrs. Hurst enter the dining room. She was still smiling at the ingenuity of her timing. The footman reached for the door to open it for her and cringed slightly as Caroline's voice could be heard screeching, "When Miss Eliza returned from her walk today she smelled as if she had been cavorting with a barn-full of animals!" The footman's eyes shifted to see if Miss Elizabeth still wished to enter.

With a smile Elizabeth said, "Open the door, Sam." He opened the door without further hesitation, and she walked across the room to her seat. As another footman held her chair, she said, "As a matter of fact, Miss Bingley, I was."

"You were what, Miss Eliza?"

"Cavorting with barn animals, Miss Bingley. It seems that your staff was having trouble with Mr. Darcy's horse, and I was pleased to be of assistance to them."

Bingley laughed, "Even the finest of stables have trouble with Poseidon! He is the devil incarnate, I think! Darcy usually has to groom him himself whenever he is not at Pemberley, but I know my staff was hoping to succeed where all others have failed. You must have a death wish to offer to assist my staff with him, Miss Elizabeth."

Elizabeth's eyes flashed, but she worked to calm herself. If it had been anybody other than Mr. Bingley to say such a thing, she would have been incensed, but as it was she answered civilly, "It just so happens that Poseidon is one of the gentlest creatures I have ever come across, Mr. Bingley."

Laughing, Mr. Hurst surprised Elizabeth by speaking. "Poseidon? Gentle? Are you certain we are speaking of the same horse?"

"Miss Elizabeth has a special relationship with Poseidon," William said simply, his eyes on the soup bowl which had just been placed before him.

Bingley's eyes brightened, and a slight smile pulled at his lips. Perhaps he would finally learn more about their shared past? "Do you really, Miss Elizabeth?"

"I have heard it mentioned, but honestly—I have never witnessed Poseidon act in any way other than spirited but gentle."

"How extraordinary! Well, Miss Elizabeth, I *have*. What exactly were you doing to help the stable hands?" Bingley said.

"I distracted him as they groomed him. I fed him carrots, stroked his neck and head, and spoke to him."

"He allowed you close enough to *touch* him? He ate from your hand without *biting* it off?" Mr. Hurst said with his eyes wide. Bingley's mouth was gaping open.

"Yes, but I do not understand your surprise, gentlemen! Poseidon has always allowed me to do so."

"Perhaps I can help you to understand, gentlemen. Poseidon behaves the same way with Miss Elizabeth as he does with me."

Mr. Hurst looked upon Elizabeth with a look of respect. *"It seems one must speak of horses to catch his attention,"* Elizabeth thought.

Bingley's eyebrows rose almost up to his hairline. "Well! That *is* interesting! How long have you known Poseidon, Miss Elizabeth?"

Elizabeth flinched and hesitated, but then said quietly, "A little more than three years, sir."

"May I ask how many times have you seen him in that time?"

"Four times, Mr. Bingley."

"Only four times? And he behaves with you the same way as with a man that has known him his whole life, while wishing to maim everyone else? Amazing!" Mr. Hurst said.

"Four?" William asked.

Elizabeth colored, took a deep breath and looked him in the eye. "I could not stand being indoors for one minute longer and sneaked out of the house. It seems Hanna applied to James to find me, and he did—at the stables. I did not do so again after Hanna and James threatened to tell Mrs. Reynolds if I went there again."

William laughed heartily, surprising everyone at the table. Elizabeth's breath caught when she saw his dimples and heard his deep laughter.

"How did you find your way out without your sojourn coming to Mrs. Reynolds's attention?" William asked.

Not looking away from William's gaze, the corners of Elizabeth's lips turned up slightly, and a hint of mischief twinkled in her eyes as she said, "I noticed an unexplained draft causing a candle in my room to flicker, and when I investigated, I found a hidden passageway in the wall. I followed it outdoors."

William smiled. "I should have guessed you would find the passageways."

"And just where was this, Miss Eliza?" Caroline asked.

Surprised that after Caroline had spoken so *many* times about staying at Pemberley that she did not at least recognize the housekeeper's name, Elizabeth hesitated—but then realized that Caroline Bingley gave so little attention to servants that she would probably not even recognize her *own* housekeeper if she saw her outside the house. "Pemberley, Miss Bingley."

"*You* have been to Pemberley? As what? A guest of one of the servants, perhaps? Why did you need to sneak out?"

Elizabeth's eyes flashed again, but this time she allowed her anger to take hold. "Miss…"

William interrupted—his face red with obvious rage, "Miss Bingley! I will have you know that Mr. Bennet and my father were the best of friends throughout childhood and into their adulthood. Miss Elizabeth was at Pemberley as an *honored guest* of my father and my sister. She stayed for more than two months, during which time she injured her ankle—an injury which was caused by over-exerting herself *to save my life*. The doctor had confined her to the house while her injury healed. Mrs. Reynolds was instructed by my father to make certain that *both* Miss Elizabeth and I strictly adhered to the doctor's orders."

His speech left everyone staring at William in shock, including Elizabeth.

"I did not save your life..." Elizabeth whispered.

William's tone was much softer when he interrupted again, "Yes, you did. More than once."

Elizabeth peered at him for a few moments longer, and then her attention was diverted by Miss Bingley's saying to William, "I apologize for making assumptions."

Elizabeth returned her gaze to her plate. Why had William defended her again? Why had he told everyone she had saved his life when she had not? Did *he* really believe that she had?

After several minutes of silence, Bingley cleared his throat and began speaking of another subject. The remainder of dinner was much the same as the night before, except that the Bingley sisters ignored Elizabeth's presence completely—much to Elizabeth's satisfaction—and William was as silent as she was.

~%~

After seeing that Jane was as well as could be expected, Elizabeth felt that if she did not join the others in the drawing room it would be understood somehow as admitting she was weak, especially after being ignored at dinner, and so she did join them.

When she entered, Bingley and Mr. Hurst were at piquet, and Mrs. Hurst was alternating between amusing herself with her jewelry and observing the game. William was attempting to write a letter while Caroline hovered nearby making so many comments about his superior letter-writing skills that Elizabeth wondered how he was able to concentrate well enough to write anything at all. Elizabeth sat down to begin her book, but could not avoid hearing their conversation.

When the person to whom the letter had been addressed was mentioned, Elizabeth stiffened. She wondered what William was telling Georgiana about her. Perhaps he did not feel her worth mentioning at all. Caroline finally ceased her ranting, and Elizabeth attempted *not* to think of Georgiana by distracting herself with her reading, but found that, for the first time in her life, she could not remember one word from any of the pages she had turned.

"Miss Elizabeth? Are you well?" Bingley's voice interrupted her thoughts.

"Yes, Mr. Bingley; I am well. Why do you ask, sir?"

"Your expression seemed so... forlorn."

"I am sorry, sir, I am not very good company this evening. Perhaps I should retire."

"I do hope you are not becoming ill as well!" Bingley said.

"No, no, Mr. Bingley; do not concern yourself, sir. I promise that I am not ill—only a little tired."

While taking her leave, Elizabeth saw such concern in William's eyes that she almost began to say something directly to him in order to quiet his anxiety. But no, that was silly! Of course he must be thinking of something else; that expression could not be for *her*!

After seeing that Jane's fever was almost gone, she retreated to her own room to change. Elizabeth could no longer delay thinking of William's reactions when Caroline had insulted her and when Bingley had voiced his fears that she was ill. It was hours before she finally fell asleep.

Chapter 15

The next day, Jane was feeling well enough to come down to the drawing room after dinner. While Elizabeth was assisting Jane in covering herself with blankets to protect her from any drafts, William approached to enquire after her health.

Uncomfortable with her feelings whenever she was physically near him, especially now that his defending her was causing her so much more confusion, Elizabeth began to move away. Not fully attending, she tripped over the edge of a rug.

His focus *always* being on Elizabeth, William reacted quickly, extending his right arm to steady her. So caught up was he in the sensations of being close to Elizabeth and actually touching his beloved's skin, he did not realize that while reaching out for her, his sleeve had risen high enough to expose the scar on his right hand. When William *did* notice that Elizabeth's gaze was *not* directed at the floor as he first thought, a sense of alarm came over him—she was looking at his *hand*. Quickly pulling his hand away, he looked at her. Elizabeth met his gaze, and seeing his eyes full of panic, her expression changed to one of concern, her eyes full of questions.

William was torn—on one side he longed to be on the receiving end of any sort of caring look from her and ached to answer any question she might have, but on the other, he refused to be questioned on *this* subject! He had gone to so much trouble to hide this from her! He chose to tear his eyes away from Elizabeth's and step away, though every fiber of his being was still focused on her.

Bingley had also noticed the scar and was reminded of the fire. He asked, "Has the damage from the fire been completely repaired yet, Darcy?"

Since William had not thought it possible to become more anxious than he already had been, it surprised him when his muscles stiffened further.

When he did not answer, Bingley probed further, "Was not the guest wing still being reconstructed when we last spoke of it?"

Realizing that Bingley was speaking of the damage to *Pemberley*, not to himself, William forced himself to relax a little. "Yes…" he spoke huskily, before clearing his throat and continuing. "Yes. It should be complete before the winter snows descend upon Pemberley."

Caroline interjected from across the room in an attempt to convey her superior knowledge of and acquaintance with the Darcys, "The fire happened two years ago, did it not, Mr. Darcy?"

"I believe it is now closer to two and one half years," Bingley replied when William did not.

"I wonder if you are being cheated, Mr. Darcy. Why should it take such a long time to complete the repairs?" Caroline asked.

"Rebuilding the servants' quarters was the primary concern and thus was reconstructed first, Miss Bingley. The guest wing was secondary. It was required that the entire wing be leveled and the grounds cleared before any new construction began. As much of the original stone as possible was cleaned and used in the new construction and matching stone needed to be found—it all took time."

"What month?" Elizabeth whispered.

William flinched and closed his eyes for a moment before looking up to meet her steady gaze. He was shocked to find her complexion pale and her lips trembling. He looked away before answering, "May… the end of May."

Jane gasped loudly. William's eyes darted to Jane's as she whispered, "I thought it was just a dream! I should not have stopped her!"

Attuned to Elizabeth's every movement, William *felt* more than saw that she had lost consciousness and was falling. He reached out to catch her in his arms in the same moment that Jane screamed, "Lizzy!"

William's right arm was supporting the entirety of Elizabeth's weight, and he was very well aware that he could not continue to hold her in this fashion for any extended length of time. He leaned down and slipped his left arm under her knees, maneuvering her so that most of the weight of his beloved's body was supported by it instead. His right arm pressed her upper body into his so that his chest bore her weight. "Elizabeth?" he whispered, but received no answer.

As he stood there, William was vaguely aware of the screeching of Bingley's sisters, the soft crying of Miss Bennet, and the attempts being made by Bingley to calm her. But he could only think of Elizabeth. What had caused her to faint? Had Bingley been correct; had Elizabeth caught Miss Bennet's illness? He placed his cheek on her forehead and was relieved to find that she had no fever.

William looked up and saw that Miss Bingley and Mrs. Hurst had left the room. "Bingley, open the door. I will carry her to her room. Is Miss Bingley sending for Mr. Jones?"

"Yes, Caroline and Louisa are sending for him. But Darcy, do you not think it would be prudent for *me* to carry Miss Elizabeth?" Bingley asked quietly while approaching his friend, thinking only of his weakened arm and Elizabeth's safety, but when he saw the look in William's eyes, he backed a step away from him in shock.

"I have had quite enough of seeing Elizabeth in the arms of other men!" William almost growled. "No one but *I* will carry her, Bingley!" He looked down at her lovely face and his countenance softened into an expression that left Bingley with absolutely no doubt of William's feelings for her. "I assure you I would endure *anything* rather than allow her to fall."

Neither of the gentlemen realized that Jane was close enough to witness their exchange. She took a step closer to make it seem as though she had only just approached and stated, "If you will lend me your arm, Mr. Bingley, I think I can manage the stairs. We must take Lizzy to her room. Mrs. Hurst has gone to fetch some salts and will bring them there."

William followed Miss Bennet and Bingley from the room. Bingley allowed him to pass them—William knew that he wanted to follow him up the stairs so that he could be of assistance in case he did falter.

He had meant it when he said he would *never* allow Elizabeth to fall, no matter what he had to endure. Yes, this was painful to his injured muscles. Yes, he was straining his arm past anything he had done since the fire. But—this was *Elizabeth*! He wished she had not fainted, but if it must occur, William was honored to be able to come to her aid. Perhaps there was even a slight chance that her opinion would soften just a little when she found out that he had?

When William reached the first landing, he felt Elizabeth shift and looked down. Her eyes were still closed, but her color was returning, and she no longer looked as though she was unconscious; she seemed to be asleep now. She would be well.

So beautiful! He felt his heart accelerate further when she turned her head towards him and nuzzled his chest, inhaling deeply through her nose as if she was taking in his scent, her hand sliding between his waistcoat and shirt and pressing against his heart. He remembered very well when she had done something similar at Pemberley—that night in her bedchamber....

Bingley cleared his throat, and William realized that he had stopped on the landing. "Oh! Excuse me," he said and continued up the stairs, hugging Elizabeth a little closer to his chest. One more flight of stairs, and he would have to let her go.

~%~

Though she had never seen Elizabeth swoon before, Jane knew exactly what had caused it, and so she was not *very* alarmed now that the initial shock had passed. She knew Elizabeth would come around soon, and all would be well—or as well as it had been before. She sighed as she thought, *"The dreams! Oh, Lizzy! I am so sorry that I did not let you go to Pemberley after the dreams! How did you know?"*

Jane saw that while carrying Elizabeth, William's sleeve had been pushed up well beyond where it had been while they were in the drawing room, and she could see that the scar continued up his arm. At first she thought he was trembling, but it was only his right arm; it was as if it had been weakened, and he was taxing its strength. She could only imagine the effort he was exerting to continue holding Elizabeth, but she could see he had a firm grip and would make certain he was true to his word to Bingley. If she had to venture a guess, she would say that William did not to want to let her go at all—ever; in fact, he had already stopped twice along the way to

Elizabeth's bedchamber without seeming to notice, with Bingley having to remind him of his errand.

Elizabeth did not seem to be in a swoon any longer. Did she think she was dreaming? She was almost snuggling herself to William's chest, and when Elizabeth slid her hand under his coat, Jane had to blush! If not for the look of bliss on Elizabeth's face—Jane had not seen Elizabeth truly happy for years—and the look of contentment on William's, she would have awakened her instead of pretending that she did not see it. As it was, Jane decided that she would not criticize Elizabeth for what she did in her sleep and thus, allowed this behavior to continue.

When Caroline Bingley and Louisa Hurst were heard on the staircase at least a floor below them, William stopped walking once more and closed his eyes. Leaning in towards Elizabeth he took a deep breath and gazed down at her lovingly for a few moments before he said huskily, "Miss Bennet, before they catch up to us... will you remove Miss Elizabeth's hand, please? Miss Bingley would become even more cruel towards her if she saw this." He swallowed hard, and she could see the muscles working in his jaw as she moved Elizabeth's hand.

Jane realized that, in the drawing room, William had been quite embarrassed when his injury was exposed. In the present situation, seeing it exposed even further had been accidental and unavoidable, but Jane assumed William would not wish the other ladies to see it. While she was close, Jane pulled several pins from Elizabeth's hair until enough of her locks were cascading down over William's arm to conceal the exposed portion. Both gentlemen looked at her curiously. She whispered as she glanced at the staircase, "Your sleeve has moved up quite high, sir."

Bingley smiled lovingly at Jane, and William just stood there blinking at her for a moment before he looked down at Elizabeth again.

It seemed that William needed another reminder of their mission, so Jane said, "We should continue to Lizzy's room... we *are* standing in the hall, Mr. Darcy."

Jane understood his hesitation; once they reached her room, he would no longer have any excuse to hold Elizabeth.

Bingley walked on ahead and opened the door just as Miss Bingley and Mrs. Hurst caught up to them. Jane gave Bingley a pointed look which Bingley understood immediately. He kept his sisters busy at the door to allow William a last moment with Elizabeth, with Jane alone in attendance.

Jane pulled back the bed covers, and William laid Elizabeth upon the bed. Elizabeth opened her eyes just at the moment that he was removing his arm from beneath her shoulders, and he froze. Elizabeth whispered something that Jane could not hear, and then closed her eyes again. William hesitated a moment, and then stood and moved back a step or two.

At this moment it was very obvious to anyone who cared to look, that William loved Elizabeth with all his heart—as much as Jane knew Elizabeth loved him. Oh, why had he been trying so hard to hide it? Why had he been acting so severely toward her since he came into the neighborhood? Was his injury the reason he had stayed away? Why had none of his family ever contacted them? Did his family disprove of Elizabeth so much that he would not be able to marry her even if they *were* so much in love? It was too cruel! Jane's gaze shifted again to her sister, and the scene blurred as her eyes filled with tears.

She heard Miss Bingley and Mrs. Hurst's voices as the women approached.

Miss Bingley said, "I have sent a boy for the apothecary."

Mrs. Hurst stepped around Jane and William to get close to the bed with the jar of salts in her hands. Moving her own face away from it as she opened the jar, she placed it near Elizabeth's face. Elizabeth winced and pulled her face away from the salts, mumbling, "Go away, Lydia!"

Jane blushed; Lydia often played tricks on her sisters while they were sleeping, and one she most often engaged in was the use of their mother's salts to awaken them.

Mrs. Hurst put it close to her nose again, and Elizabeth did the same as before but said loudly, "Lydia! Please stop! I was having such a lovely dream…" As she said the last, she had opened her eyes and had seen Mrs. Hurst with the bottle of salts and an annoyed Miss Bingley standing next to her. Looking around she saw that behind Miss Bingley was a group of concerned looking people—Mr. Bingley was moving a chair closer to the bed, and just behind Jane was William! *"Oh no! Was it not a dream?"* Elizabeth's countenance turned crimson, and she whispered, "Jane? What has happened?"

Jane moved between the Bingley sisters and sat in the chair newly placed next to the bed, taking Elizabeth's hand. "You swooned, Lizzy. How are you feeling now?"

"I am... better?"

"That does not sound very convincing, Miss Elizabeth. Caroline has sent for Mr. Jones; he should be here shortly," Bingley said as he moved to take an extra blanket off the chest at the foot of the bed and placed it around Jane's shoulders, gaining him a look of thanks from Jane.

"Oh, that is not necessary, Mr. Bingley. Please..."

"Miss Elizabeth, Miss Bennet says this has never happened before. Perhaps you have come down with the same illness?" William surprised her with the amount of concern in his voice.

"It *has* happened once before, when I was in London last January." She did not wish to mention that it had happened at the assembly as well since they might then suspect that all three times it had occurred were related to William. She glanced at the gentleman in question and turned a brighter shade of crimson. Her gaze then rested on Jane, and she continued, "I have not mentioned it to you, Jane, because I was soon well again after resting for a few minutes. I even walked across the park opposite Uncle Gardiner's house to return home afterwards, though I did accept a gentleman's assistance, but only because he would not leave until he saw me home. I am certain I will be well; there is no need to bother Mr. Jones." Elizabeth noticed William stiffen a bit when she mentioned that a gentleman helped her, and she wished that she might ask why.

"I do believe we would all feel easier if you see the apothecary, Miss Elizabeth. When one's determined intentions interfere with one's health, it is best to defer to someone else's stubborn ideas of what is the correct thing to do in that circumstance." William ended this speech with a mischievous look in his eye that melted her heart.

Elizabeth blinked a few times—how did William remember her exact words from three years ago? "But..."

Jane interrupted, "Lizzy, Mr. Jones is already on his way here. You would not wish him to make the trip to Netherfield only to be turned away, would you?"

Elizabeth crossed her arms over her chest. "Very well; you will get your way." She glanced at William with an amused sparkle in her eyes as she said, "If only so that you will see that *I* am correct in *this* circumstance as well!"

She could not know what her look did to the rhythm of William's heart.

A knock on the door announced the arrival of Mr. Jones, and he was bid to enter. "Mr. Jones! You certainly came quickly!" Jane exclaimed.

"Good evening ladies, gentlemen. Miss Bennet, I was not far; your messenger found me on the road just leaving Lucas Lodge, and I was very concerned when I heard Miss Lizzy was ill! Being called to treat *her* for something that did not result from a fall from a tree is unheard of! It is usually *she* who sends the messenger and begins treatment on my patient before I can arrive," Mr. Jones replied with a small smile directed toward Elizabeth. But the smile could not hide the fact that he was watching her very carefully.

Elizabeth laughed, "Mr. Jones, I do hope you did not put off another call to see me first. You will soon see that this was a wasted trip for you. Is all well at Lucas Lodge, sir?"

Mr. Jones's expression was much less concerned than it was before she spoke. "I was there only to see how Lady Lucas was faring, as she was afflicted some days ago with a terrible cold. She is much better now—as I can see you are as well, Miss Bennet, but you should still rest a few days longer. Now, what seems to be the trouble, Miss Lizzy? Have you caught your sister's cold?"

William, who had been fidgeting through this discourse, was becoming very impatient with the idle talk and said firmly, "Mr. Jones, Miss Elizabeth collapsed and was not conscious for several minutes."

Mr. Jones's countenance turned quite serious. "Well! Are there any injuries from the fall?"

"Lizzy did not fall, sir. Mr. Darcy caught her," Jane said, and it was William's turn to color slightly.

Mr. Jones looked back and forth between Elizabeth and William, and caught William's gaze for several moments before saying, "Will you all excuse us please? Miss Bennet will remain for the examination."

William was the last to leave the room.

Once the door was closed, Elizabeth said, "Really, Mr. Jones, I am well…"

"*I* will be the judge of that, young lady! Now, tell me exactly what happened."

"Sir, it was the same as had happened in London last January. I heard some very disturbing news and then felt weak. The last time was not so very bad; I did not lose consciousness, only my balance. This time everything turned black. The next thing I remember is awaking here."

"She was very limp at first, but then after a few minutes, it seemed more as if she were asleep than unconscious—she had shifted herself while Mr. Darcy was carrying her. You did also mention a dream, Lizzy, just after Mrs. Hurst had you breathe in the smelling salts."

Elizabeth blushed again, and mumbled, "Yes, and I wish I had not!"

After his examination, Mr. Jones said, "Well, my dear, it seems that you are in perfect health and were only in shock temporarily from the news you had received. No walks tomorrow, Miss Lizzy, as I do not want a chance of this happening when you are out alone. Other than that, I see no reason to restrict your activities beginning the following day as long as this does not recur and you are feeling well. If you feel weak again, I suggest you sit down immediately so you do not fall, even if it means sitting on the ground." As he returned his equipment to his bag, Mr. Jones seemed to be struggling with a wish to ask something else but was not certain that he should. He finally said, "Miss Bennet, will you leave us for a few moments?"

Jane was surprised by the unusual request but agreed when she saw Elizabeth nod.

After the door had closed, he turned back to a very curious Elizabeth and said, "Lizzy, I know this is a delicate matter, and you might not wish to discuss it with me, but you know very well that I will keep your answer in the strictest confidence. Is there any chance you might be… in a family way?"

Elizabeth's eyes widened, and her mouth hung open until she regained her senses. "No, sir! That would be quite impossible!"

"Er… are you aware of what is involved… that is to say, what would need to occur for that to happen?"

Now both Mr. Jones and Elizabeth had colored. "Well… I *do* live on a farm, sir! The animals…"

"Yes. Quite." He cleared his throat and said, "Some ladies are not aware until it is too late and so I had to ask. And you *are* certain…"

"Very certain, Mr. Jones! And… well…"

"Yes?"

"Do you remember that Papa has a shelf in his study that I was not supposed to investigate?" Knowing exactly what was on that shelf, Mr. Jones nodded, a little amused. "A year or two ago, Papa's book order had not yet arrived, and I already had read everything else in the library and… you know," she tapped her head indicating that she remembered everything she had read, "and I had been curious for such a *long time*, Mr. Jones! So, I read one of the books. It was very… informative. I also looked at some prints." Elizabeth blushed and continued, "The human body is quite a good deal more flexible than I had realized, sir."

Mr. Jones laughed in spite of himself. "Ah, yes. I think you are more informed than most maidens—which is nothing new, of course."

"So you can see I am quite certain that I have not done anything that would end in…" Elizabeth said with force, and then asked, "Why do you continue with this line of questioning, sir?"

"Oh… fainting is a common symptom… and you have never had these symptoms before… and the way you both were acting…"

"Sir, you will *not* leave this room until you have explained that *last* comment!"

"Very well!" he sighed, "It was the way you and the taller gentlemen looked at each other, Lizzy, and also how you both were trying so very hard *not* to look at each other. The gentleman was attempting to conceal it, but he was extremely worried about you. I have not seen such a terrified look as was in his eyes unless it was a man desperately worried about a wife whom he loves very dearly!"

Elizabeth blinked back some tears and said in a voice full of grief, "Mr. Jones, I assure you that you are imagining things. Mr. Darcy does not care for me in that way."

He smiled and placed his hand on hers. "Oh no, Lizzy, I am *not* mistaken about his feelings for you... no more than I am wrong about your feelings for him." Mr. Jones's smile faded, and he said, "I will miss you, but this is the way of things. You deserve to be happy, my dear. I do hope you will come to see me when you visit your parents." Patting her hand, he continued, "I will come around to check on you tomorrow."

Elizabeth blushed, but saw it was pointless to argue for she could see that Mr. Jones would not be convinced otherwise. If only he were correct. "Oh! But Jane is feeling so much better we thought of going home tomorrow. She is able to travel the short distance to Longbourn, is she not?"

"Yes, she is at that. If you have no further symptoms, you will be able to as well. I will come to Longbourn close to dinnertime then... by design, of course; perhaps I will be invited to stay and dine with my favorite family in the neighborhood?" he asked with a smile.

"Perhaps!" Elizabeth answered as Mr. Jones walked toward the door. Relief was evident on his face that she had forgiven his false assumption so readily.

~%~

When Jane had come out into the hall, she was not very surprised to find the gentlemen waiting there. Bingley was standing against the wall examining his friend's behavior with amused interest. William was pacing and turning the ring on his left hand, worry clearly expressed upon his features. Taking a few hurried steps toward Jane, he asked, "How is Miss Elizabeth? What says Mr. Jones?"

"He says Lizzy is healthy, and this should not happen again, but she should not go for a walk tomorrow. If by chance this does recur, he does not wish her to be out alone."

"Mr. Jones is certain she is not ill? Perhaps I should send to London for my physician?"

Jane's eyes danced with pleasure at William's conduct and what she knew that it meant, but she said in a serious tone, "Mr. Darcy, my family is quite confident in Mr. Jones's opinion. He has taken care of Lizzy since she was born—in fact he delivered her! I do believe he is correct, sir. Please trust him; Lizzy does."

William closed his eyes, took a deep breath, and nodded, but then returned to the behavior she had witnessed as she came through the doorway.

~%~

Mr. Jones opened the door to the hallway very quietly, with every intention of observing what was occurring there before being noticed. He was a bit nervous about what he had said to Elizabeth… perhaps he should not have mentioned Mr. Darcy's feelings for her, but they had been so obvious to him that he felt certain she already knew. Her reaction was quite a surprise—his most honest friend did not deny her feelings for the gentleman, but she did deny his. Mr. Darcy's behavior was discreet, but after so many years in the sick room he had come to recognize patterns of behavior.

The apothecary truly cared about the people in the neighborhood and always felt better when his patients would be taken care of properly by people who loved them. Whenever he saw that love was lacking, Mr. Jones would make certain they had either a caring servant to tend to them, or he would send someone he knew he could trust to sit with the patient.

Elizabeth might not be very ill, but he still saw the evidence that she was well loved by this man, and judging by what he had heard about Mr. Bingley's guest, she would be taken care of financially as well. He was relieved that his favorite patient of all, who was also usually quite misunderstood in general, would have a happy life.

What he found when he stole into the hallway was even more convincing than what he had seen earlier. "*Yes, Lizzy, he loves you—most definitely!*"

Chapter 16

William had been pacing his room for hours, as he had done every night since Elizabeth had come to stay at Netherfield. To have her in the same house, with her bedchamber just two doors down—it was too much. He wanted what they had had at Pemberley; he wanted to go to her room, hold her all night, and be assured that she was well—and this consuming urge to be near her was twice as strong now that she had swooned!

He was so worried that the apothecary might have missed something, and she might be ill; what if it had been a disease such as had afflicted his father? His father had seemed well but had said he would slowly lose his abilities. Bingley, Jane, *and* Mr. Jones had spent quite a long time dissuading him from sending to London immediately for his physician to attend Elizabeth.

He had seen the looks the three of them had exchanged—they had practically laughed out loud at him—and for the first time in his life, he honestly *did not care* that he had made a fool of himself! He had always trusted Bingley and, well, Elizabeth trusted Mr. Jones, so he was trying his best to trust him as well.

Jane had earned his trust by acting to save his dignity, covering his scars so that Bingley's sisters did not see them. Elizabeth and Bingley were right—Jane Bennet was an angel. Bingley and Jane would do well together; he was certain of it.

Mr. Jones—yes, he would trust what he had said to be true. William had finally been convinced when he calmed down enough to remember all the things Elizabeth had said about him after he had been injured… when they had been in the woods and they had spent hours talking… before they had shared their first kiss…

The events that occurred when he had placed her in her bed tonight kept replaying in his mind: the way she felt in his arms, her breath caressing his hair, her cheek as it grazed his own, her voice whispering in his ear, "Stay with me, William…."

Good G-d, if he were to stay here so close to her, he knew that he would end up rushing down the hall and dismissing Jane—by physical force if necessary—and taking her place in Elizabeth's bed! He needed to get farther away from her to protect her from his terrible longing!

William took hold of the portable drawing desk that the carpenter at Pemberley had made when his arm was at its worst and headed to the library. He did not wish to be seen; his arm was not working correctly due to overuse, but nobody else in residence used the library—except Elizabeth—and he doubted she would leave her room tonight, so he did not expect to be disturbed.

As he entered the room, he took a moment to look around the neglected space. It was so poorly stocked, that should Elizabeth have wished to have something interesting to read while staying here nursing her sister, there would have been nothing available to her. The day she had arrived at Netherfield, he had instructed Hughes to relocate all the books he had brought with him to an empty shelf in the library, hoping there was at least one amongst them that she had not already read. His heart had swelled earlier in the day when he had seen her selecting one of them. To have been able to provide her with any amount of pleasure was immensely satisfying! He would gladly spend his entire income on books just to see the corners of her lips turn up the way they had when she had spied a title she had never read!

He removed his coat and waistcoat, rolled up his sleeves, and reclined in a comfortable chair. Opening the travelling desk on his lap, he took out a clean sheet of paper and pencils and began to sketch that smile. After a while, his eyelids became very heavy, and William fell asleep—dreaming pleasantly of Elizabeth, as usual. So when he became aware of her scent while in that place halfway between sleep and wakefulness, it did not seem odd.

~%~

Jane was sleeping soundly, but Elizabeth's mind was too actively engaged. Why had she agreed to Mr. Jones's examination? Had he not come, he never could have said those things about William, and she would not have that sense of hope she now had growing inside her. Jane was no help; her accounting of William's behavior, while displaying that knowing smile of hers, only added kindling to the fire that Mr. Jones had begun.

No, she had to be honest with herself; Mr. Jones had not begun the warmth of hope that had slowly spread within her. The first spark was lit by her own heart the first moment she saw him at the assembly hall. She had seen small glimpses of "her William," the man she had remembered, at each encounter since. Tonight—goodness, they were right! Tonight he was much more like the old William, the one who had looked at her with love shining from his eyes.

But she feared what tomorrow might bring. In the light of day, when there was no chance that her life was at risk, would he revert to the "other William," the one that he had been since coming back to Hertfordshire— the cold, severe-looking William who looked at her only to find fault? She shivered as a tear fell from her eye, and she brushed it away with the back of her hand.

No! She would not lie here and ruminate on this all night! But unfortunately, she had finished her book and had nothing else to distract her mind from these musings. Surely nobody else was still awake; she would put on her robe and go to the library to get another book—and she would *not* look at the bookplate this time in case *his* name was there again! He put the books there for his *own* benefit and not for hers; *that* was another very silly idea that this infernal hope had put into her mind. She should read of war perhaps, as that should help get these romantic visions of the future out of her mind.

Elizabeth could not find her slippers, and the floor was very cold, but she was determined to complete her mission, so she padded barefoot down the hall then down the stairway, making no noise.

She slipped into the library and was surprised to find a fire blazing. Her eyes were drawn to a number of lit candles standing on the tables near the fire. Her first thought was that someone had been careless, but then she noticed a slight movement in the chair. It was William, and he was asleep!

She moved closer to him, taking advantage of his slumber to study him intently and unobserved. He truly was the handsomest man she had ever seen, and in sleep, he was handsomer still. He looked happy, and she wondered what was occurring in his dream to provoke such a pleasant response.

After she had made a thorough visual examination of what she could see of his form, she looked at his right arm which was lying across his stomach. Tears pricked at her eyes. The scars looked painful; she hoped that they pained him no longer. She wanted to reach out, caress his arm, and take all his pain away.

She pondered the unusual box that rested on his lap. It looked to be a sort of portable writing desk, but bigger. His left hand rested on the picture he had been sketching, blocking her view. Some sort of latches held the paper in place, and another larger latch, seemingly designed to keep the side closed, was currently open. Inside were several compartments. One held writing and drawing supplies, and two were for paper. One of the sections was holding what looked to be used paper, and it seemed he had been busy. She loved to see his drawings and wondered what all those sketches depicted.

Elizabeth froze as William shifted in his seat, but he did not awaken. With the way he was sitting now, though, the box was on such an angle that the open side of the compartment was facing downward. Before she could even think about what to do to prevent it from happening, what looked almost like a waterfall began. She held her breath as page after page slid out of the box and fanned out across the floor of the library.

As he became more and more aware that he was waking from a dream, William noticed he could still detect her scent. Shifting in his seat, he began to hear paper sliding across the floor, and he knew what had happened, but at the same time he heard a soft gasp, and his breath caught in his chest. Her scent was *not* in the dream! Elizabeth was here, in this room, and all of his sketches had just fallen onto the floor!

Terrified of her reaction if she saw all those drawings *of her*, he opened his eyes just barely enough to see where she was and what she was doing. He was thankful that all the drawings seemed to be facing the floor so she could not see them. But then a spark from the fire landed on one of the sheets of paper close to the fire, and it began to smolder. Elizabeth walked over to it—he nearly exclaimed aloud, her feet were bare—and she stamped on the paper to put the fire out. William began to tremble as she picked it up and turned it over. She gasped again, louder this time. He could not see her face, for she was facing away from him, but she looked at the sketch a long time and then reached for another, and then another, and then she began to turn them all over. Elizabeth lowered herself to the floor and just sat and stared at them all. *"What should I do?"* He found he could not move, could not utter a sound, and he just watched her.

Elizabeth stood again and moved from one part of the room to another, stopping where most of the drawings had settled—directly between his chair and the fire. He struggled to keep his breathing even. She was clad only in a thin nightgown and robe. With the light of the fire behind her, William was spellbound by the silhouette of her form showing through the thin cloth. Though as a gentleman he knew he should have looked away, instead he was committing to memory the vision of splendid beauty before him. He would not draw *this* sight—it was for him alone. When she turned slightly to the side so that his view was now of her partial profile, he could not stifle his gasp. The guilt of violating her privacy in this manner was too much for him to continue admiring her without her permission, and he reluctantly closed his eyes.

He knew Elizabeth had discovered that he was awake when he heard her ask, "Why?"

William's eyes flew open, and he noticed her gaze was still upon the drawings. "I – I was afraid I would forget," he said huskily as he pulled his sleeve down over his scars.

"But since you have arrived, you have acted as if you *had* forgotten… or wished you would."

"No."

She turned around, an angry fire in her eyes boring into him, seeming to burn him as if he were still in the fire at Pemberley. "What does 'no' mean? You come here after all this time… after all of our letters, and we have heard not a word from any of your family… after the way you behaved in London, you come here and act this way, and then you tell me you do not want to forget? I do not understand!"

William spoke calmly, "It is just as I suspected. Your father must have kept our letters from you, and he must have taken anything that you wrote before it was posted. *We* received no letters from you or your father, Elizabeth."

"How can you *lie* this way? *I* am the one who walked to Meryton with all the letters—mine *and* my father's. I posted the letters directly at the postal office with my own hands! *I* am the one who made certain I was home at the time the post was delivered twice a day for so many months that the delivery boys sought me out to hand the post directly to me since they could tell I was so anxious for it. *I* went through the letters before my father even had a chance to see them! And never—*not once*—was there a letter from your father, nor Georgiana, nor you."

William sat in shocked silence, which slowly turned to anguish as she continued on.

"You dare to accuse *my father*, who has been almost as pained by your family's lack of consideration as I have been? And then, we find out that your father has passed, not through *you*—who had already been in the neighborhood for a fortnight—but through Lieutenant Wickham, the son of your father's steward, who has been ignored by your family as well. Imagine my shock when Lieutenant Wickham told me of your father's death while we are at a dinner party!

"Even after all this, after he and his daughter had been snubbed by your family for *three years*, I have never seen my father more affected than when I had to tell him that your father had died! I was so frightened for his life that I called Mr. Jones to attend him!"

Elizabeth's anger had slowly turned to pain and sorrow, her eyes were filled with tears, but she refused to blink lest they fall. "Until London, I tried to blame your father... thinking that *he* did not approve of me... but *never* you.

"Even my father did not blame you. The day I turned seventeen, and you did not come, he tried to blame himself—saying that *he* was not good enough, not highly placed enough, that he had married a tradesman's daughter, and so it was *his* fault that I had been rejected.

"But after seeing you last January, after witnessing the lack of emotion in your eyes when you looked at me, I *knew* what a complete fool I was—and still, I could not stop loving you!

"Then you come here to Hertfordshire, and you display a horribly stern countenance, staring coldly at me whenever we are in company. Do you know I have been listening to the entire neighborhood whispering—I cannot get away from it no matter where I go! They are wondering what I ever did to cause you to despise me so greatly! Yes, they are gossiping of it, and from what I have overheard, they have practically decided that I am a tainted woman—that you know of something terrible that I must have done in London since they have not heard of any wrongdoing here! This afternoon my old friend Mr. Jones even sent Jane from the room to ask me if I am with child, suggesting perhaps *that* is why I fainted! You know as well as I do that once the gossips have decided what it is that I have done to cause you to hate being in the same room as I am, they will soon shun my entire family.

"The only person who does not agree with the opinion that you abhor me is Jane—who in her infinite goodness and naiveté has spent the past few hours unwittingly torturing me, trying to convince me that you *love* me, of all the ridiculous notions!"

Elizabeth's tears spilled over as the anguish in her voice and countenance increased during her speech. William felt as if he were dying, but he had to let her purge herself of this before he spoke again. He continued to sit in the chair in which she had found him and covered his eyes with his left hand, for his right arm was not responding at all to his will now that the exertion of carrying her was coupled with the emotional stress her words were causing.

"I need to know *why*; you owe me that much! Was everything that occurred at Pemberley some sort of game to you? Is this something that the rich play at? Did you perfect the persona of 'William at Pemberley' just for me, or has he been used on other women as well? Did you and your friends have a good laugh at my expense? Did you come here to store up some new stories to tell them? What have I ever done to deserve such treatment other than to commit the *great crime* of loving you?

"Oh! I am so completely disgusted with myself! I *swore* I would never give you the satisfaction of knowing *any* of this... and here I am, so weak that I could not even get through a few weeks in your presence before confessing it all! Now you will be able to tell your friends that your little game was a complete success since I am about to be ruined by conjecture! At least I will be of some use for *something*, since I am certain that I will never be of interest to anyone again!

"I told you once that this detailed memory of mine can be a curse—a curse it is when it comes to you! I *want* to forget that you ever existed, but I cannot! G-d help me, what I would not do to forget! Perhaps your disclosure will at least help to counteract the rest and dull this ache of loss within me—if I must continue to remember and dream of what we shared at Pemberley, then at least the remembrances can end with that! Please reveal to me the horrible truth of why you did this, and then go back to London and the *ton* and leave me be!"

William wiped at his red-rimmed eyes with the heel of his left hand, and then said, "I will..." his breath caught as if he were choking on the words that were about to be said, "I will go and leave you be if you wish it after you have heard what I have to say. I beg of you to give me the courtesy of listening all the way through as I did for you.

"I believe you when you say that you had posted letters to us, for I know you too well to doubt it, but I swear it, Elizabeth, on all that is holy—we received *not one* letter from you or your father. I sent the first letter the day of my father's accident... which was the day you left—my father even asked me to include a few lines from him. My sister wrote almost daily for quite some time. I wrote to your father several times asking for his help, and then as the weeks passed, I was *begging* him to come and to bring you. Georgiana needed you; *I* needed you!

"I made many excuses but, after two weeks had passed, I finally gave in to the worry about your safety and sent an investigator to see if you were at least unharmed. When I heard that you both were at home, I had to come to *some* sort of conclusion as to why all of our letters went unanswered. I could not believe that *you* were receiving the letters and not responding and so, yes, I blamed your father... but really deep down inside, I blamed myself for my disregard of propriety which I thought had caused him to withdraw from us and from his promises to my father.

"I kept my promise, and I stayed away for eight months, but I had every intention of coming here and explaining to you, and taking you away if necessary. I even told Georgiana of my plans and my suspicions... she was so happy that you were to be her sister..."

William closed his eyes and continued, "Here I must ask, Elizabeth, why you swooned today? Why did Miss Bennet say she should not have stopped you? What did she mean?"

"A fire at Pemberley was mentioned... I had many nightmares about a fire at Pemberley. You were trapped and burning. I would awake screaming, and Jane would have to restrain me from leaving Longbourn to somehow make my way to Pemberley."

William closed his eyes again and took some time to compose himself. Nodding, he continued, "It happened just a few days before your seventeenth birthday. *This* was the only thing that could have kept me away." William looked down at his arm that bore the scars of his suffering.

"My cousin Richard came in response to Georgiana's express to him, and he told me later that I had acted very much like he was told I had behaved when the fever was at its worst the previous September; I was hallucinating and calling for you, and nobody could quiet me. Mr. Smythe told Georgiana that if I did not calm and rest, I would die. Georgiana had written an express to your father imploring him to send you to Pemberley; she even sent horses to all the post stations so that your driver could change horses quickly. Obviously, you did not come, but Richard was able to communicate with me somehow, telling me that Georgiana and you were depending upon me to live. Even Mr. Smythe does not understand how I survived... but I did."

William stopped speaking for several minutes, but Elizabeth remained quiet. "My arm and side were badly burned, and I had completely lost the use of my right arm and hand. I could *not* seek you out until I had overcome the injuries. I did *not* want you to accept me out of *pity*.

"I spent most of my time at Pemberley, but I had been visiting a special doctor in London occasionally. When in London, my relatives hounded me to attend them, and I found it easier to do so once or twice during each visit if only to quiet them. When you saw me that night in London, they had tricked me into meeting a lady—I did not know she would be there, Elizabeth! I had absolutely no interest in anyone else! She was vulgar, but I did not know how to fend her off without making a scene. I did my best— though Richard told me later it had been quite a show, and he was not speaking of the play. G-d knows I should have gone home claiming illness, but hindsight is always much clearer.

"Richard was in another box across the theater, but he had seen my drawings and recognized you as he was examining the general seating area during an intermission. When the play ended, Richard pulled me from my uncle's box and down to the lobby whilst explaining. He was insistent that I was a fool for not seeking you out, and I had just finished arguing that I could not expect you to love half a man—I was so angry at myself for not healing as quickly as I had hoped... no matter how hard I worked at it. I was angry at fate for putting me in that position, angry at Richard for tempting me to find you and put the decision to you instead of taking it on myself, angry at myself for wanting to beg you to come back to me, and so incredibly frightened that if I did, you would reject me… and just then, I turned around, and you were there."

William's eyes filled with tears. "I…" he stopped and took a deep, trembling breath, "You were pressed against me, and I ached to take hold of you and escape from that place. But you were so beautiful and *whole*… and I was not! I could not be as selfish as that. I continued to have no use of my arm; I had just begun to be able to move my fingers a little." He saw her eyes close. William continued, "It took an immense effort not to follow when you walked away, not to beg your forgiveness and…"

His emotions tightened his throat so badly that he had to stop speaking for a minute or two. "Richard said I was hurting you, but I insisted that I could not saddle you with *this*." He put his left hand on his right arm.

"I saw what I was putting Georgiana through—I sent her away last summer to give her a respite from *me*. What a disaster that was!" His eyes opened wide as he remembered some of what Georgiana had said to him after Ramsgate. "Do not trust Wickham, Elizabeth—he knows of you and will attempt to take revenge upon me through you. Georgiana's new companion had deceived me; she was not what she seemed to be. I was not careful enough when I researched her references. She was actually a friend of Wickham's.

"Wickham followed them to Ramsgate and attempted to persuade Georgiana to elope with him… he was angry that when his four thousand pounds from my father's bequest ran out after only a little more than two years, that I would not simply give him more, and he wanted her thirty thousand pound dowry. But she had been forced to mature when I was injured; she knew it was wrong and suspected him. When she refused him, he tried to force himself on her…" Elizabeth gasped.

"She was very grateful, as was I, for your having taught her how to protect herself. Georgiana escaped him safely and went to James, who brought my sister and her lady's maid back to London immediately.

"Her early maturation would seem to have been for the best. Had she not been forced to think more as an adult than would be normal for the usual young girl, what would have happened when Wickham tried to convince her to elope with him? Would he have succeeded in persuading her to go with him? With her companion a party to his plan, how would I have discovered it? Would Georgiana have written to me once she was in Scotland, signing the letter 'Mrs. Wickham'? Or would she have written only after he had stolen all of her dowry and left her with child in a worm-ridden room somewhere? And even *had* she seen through his plan from the beginning as she did, what would have happened had she *not* known how to protect herself as you taught her? I shudder to think of all the possibilities!

"She would not be well now had it not been for you, Elizabeth. Georgiana has recovered nicely, though I have worried about leaving her to come to Hertfordshire. But she has a stronger sense of confidence than she had before the encounter, and her new companion, Mrs. Annesley, is truly wonderful."

He spent a few moments gathering his thoughts before saying, "Elizabeth, about my behavior since coming to Hertfordshire... I must remind you of a conversation we had, in which you had inquired about whether I had met anyone of interest on my voyage home from Italy. I had told you that I do not do well with strangers. You had never seen me in public before.

"On the day of the assembly, you must understand... I had been Master of Pemberley for three years and, though I had spent very little time in London during that time, I was weary of being pursued by ladies of the *ton* who were interested in me only for mercenary reasons. I had already perfected what Bingley and Richard have for years jestingly called my 'Mask of Indifference.' The moment I walk into a room of any social occasion, the mask is firmly in place... but in that particular instance..."

He closed his eyes and shook his head. "When I came to Bingley's estate, I had no idea that Longbourn was close by; I knew only that you were in Hertfordshire. When we arrived at the Assembly, I had sent your old friend James to inquire from the other servants outside if anyone knew the location of Longbourn so that I could visit—*after* fully preparing myself for the encounter, of course. James returned immediately and told me you were in attendance, and then I followed Bingley into the building directly after gaining this knowledge... into a room full of strangers who instantly began whispering estimates of my income.

"What I am attempting to convey is that when I first saw you, I was terrified! It was *not* disapproval that you saw at all. I was inwardly rejoicing in the fact that I would be in your presence, but at the same time I was worried that you might never forgive me for not coming to you sooner and for what had happened in London. When I found you among the crowd, for a brief moment, you seemed happy to see me and I was filled with hope, but then your countenance changed to one so harsh... I did not know what to do! I could not explain anything to you in a crowded assembly room, and then when I walked over, your mother snubbed me, and your expression was severe. I decided to retreat and seek out a better time to explain. But I could not resist what I thought might be the only time I would ever have to dance with you, not after I had been dreaming of doing so for years.

"The look that everyone is gossiping about is the damn mask mixed with despair, Elizabeth! I had little hope of your ever caring for me again, but I was desperate to be near you. I did not know whether to speak to you of this or not—which would make it worse? I made many excuses for not speaking, but I can see now that the truth is that *had* I explained, and had you responded by telling me that there was no hope, I would have had to leave Hertfordshire. Even the fleeting thought of a life without the remote possibility of *seeing* you again filled me with such anguish that I found that I could not speak of any of this at all.

"The man I am when I am alone with you is the only true William. I have never hidden myself from *you*, only from others!

"You said you still love me, Elizabeth..." he said her name as if it were a caress. "Please, I beg of you, forgive me? I do not wish to leave you again, ever. You are my life, my soul. While we were apart, my heart was dying a little each day. I was numb inside... I do not believe I could have gone on that way much longer. No matter how my mind doubted since coming to Hertfordshire—I do not think I would have survived this long if some part of my being was not convinced that you truly do love me. Thoughts of you are the only thing that has helped me through every hardship that has befallen me since we parted."

Elizabeth moved closer and knelt before him. She tentatively reached out, took his right hand in both of hers, and touched the edge of his sleeve with her fingers. He tried to pull away; if ever he had the good fortune of winning her love again, he had every intention of keeping *all* of his scars covered! She held tightly to his hand and moved closer to him, not allowing him to pull away, but instead gently pushing his sleeve up his arm, exposing that portion of the scar.

"Does it hurt now?"

"My arm aches when the weather changes, but not otherwise. It is weakened now. I had thought I was healed enough to safely come into Hertfordshire—I had sworn to myself that I would not come until I could hold you in both my arms. But I overused my arm today, and now it will be useless until I sufficiently rest it. I cannot even carry the woman I love to safety without consequences!" he whispered, and then shuddered as she grazed her fingertips across the blemish, gently stroking it, causing a tingling sensation to spread throughout his body.

She looked up into his eyes, and his breath caught. There was nothing in her eyes but affection—no disgust, no revulsion—only a deep love that filled every corner of his being with hope and relief. He watched, mesmerized as she returned her gaze to his hand. Raising his hand, she pressed her lips to the scarred portion of his skin again and again, covering it with gentle kisses.

With tears streaming down his face, he said in bewilderment, "How... how are you not sickened by the sight of it?"

Elizabeth looked up at him and shook her head, and then reached up and caressed the tears from his cheeks, whispering, "If it is you... then it is me." Moving closer, she accepted his hand pulling her up and into his lap, laid her head upon his chest, and wrapped her arms around his waist as she said, "I wish I had been there for you, my love."

William's left arm pulled her even closer to him. Burying his face in her hair—in her scent—he released all the tears that he had forced himself to hold back all night... no, for the past three years, as did she. As they both calmed, they clung to each other, marveling at the feeling.

He knew not how, but her hands found their way around his neck, her fingers laced through his hair. She pulled his face toward hers, pressing gentle kisses to his forehead, his cheeks. When he could not wait another moment, his lips sought out hers, and their breaths mingled as she whispered his name. The first gentle kiss slowly intensified as more followed, the years of longing could no longer be repressed. He repeated his actions from that night in her room at Pemberley—he had dreamt of doing so every night that they had been apart—and he groaned when that same soft moan escaped from deep within her. She turned her lips to his ear, and when she nibbled on his earlobe, he was almost undone.

William began to pull away when she said between quick breaths into his ear, "Please do not stop, William!"

His answering moan made her think he would do as she asked, so she was surprised when he said huskily, "My Elizabeth... we *must* stop!" He leaned his forehead against hers and once his passion had cooled sufficiently, he said in explanation, "Years ago, I swore to your father that I was *not* that kind of man—that I respect you too much—and I must keep my word."

Elizabeth said, "The first letter Papa sent to Pemberley contained his consent to our engagement, William."

He closed his eyes and said, "If only I had I received that letter!"

Opening his eyes again, he saw hers were filled with curiosity. "What do you suppose could have happened to all those letters? I sent so many!"

William shook his head and said, "I cannot even begin to think of how they disappeared. We received many others with no problem."

He watched as his favorite of Elizabeth's many smiles slowly dawned across her face. "You must ask Papa again for his consent, and then I can finally wear my ring on my finger for *all* to see it!"

Shaking his head as if to clear it, he took a deep breath and said, "When you were not wearing the chain I thought..."

"I have been wearing your ring in a little pocket that I had sewn into all of my corsets. It took a bit of work to find a place to wear it that was not uncomfortable!" She laughed.

He had seen a corset once when he had visited a tenant's house unannounced and the laundry had been hanging out to dry. It had taken him a few minutes to figure out what it was, and then, and even though no one had *seen* him staring at it, he had been mortified at his behavior. Without conscious thought, his eyes had been drawn to the neckline of Elizabeth's nightdress as he was imagining what she had meant by her statement since he had never actually seen a corset *on* a lady. He blushed when she placed her finger on his chin and lifted his face to meet her twinkling eyes.

"The laundry maid and the lady's maid that I share with my sisters were a bit confused about the pockets, but they have become so used to my odd habits that they did not question me about it after I confirmed that I wanted it there." She hesitated, her countenance turned thoughtful, and then she continued, "The reason you have not seen me wearing the chain is simple. I told you that Mama would not allow me to wear my chain when at a more formal event; the assembly was a perfect example.

"When I saw you in London, your looks were so severe, and even more so when we met again at the assembly. I was certain you had lost all tender feelings for me, and I did not wish to wear the chain in your presence. I had decided, after the way you were looking at me across the assembly room, that you would *never* know that I had spent the past three years pining for you.

"I did not think you would wish for me to have it any longer; in fact, I was shocked that you had not demanded that it be returned. Knowing the history of the ring, and that you would want to give it to your future wife—at the time it was quite evident to me that that lady was *not* going to be me—I felt it was only right that I should return it to you. I told myself that I *would* return it if I had the opportunity to do so without any witnesses. But even though I was very angry at you and thought you despised me, I could not force myself to part with it…"

William caressed her cheek. "I must say that if you *had* returned the ring, it would have been proof enough to convince me that you no longer cared, and I would have had to admit defeat. It would have been yet another misunderstanding, and the worst of it all is that the truth would never have been discovered! My dearest, loveliest Elizabeth, I am very glad you selfishly held the ring from me because, had you not, I would not now be the happiest of men, nor would I now have the prospect of remaining so for the rest of my life."

Her arms wound around his neck once again, and he kissed her gently. Elizabeth pulled away slightly and said between a series of additional delicate kisses, "You do… know that you… have not… asked… me to… marry you… for… more than… three years. I *should* demand… another… proposal."

He pulled his face away and, with mock insult, said, "Madam, I seem to remember asking for your hand *six times!*"

She laughed. "Well then, it falls to me, I suppose." Elizabeth became very serious. "Three years, one month, one week and two days ago you asked me to spend my life by your side. Today I ask the same of you, sir… Fitzwilliam Darcy, I love you with all of my heart and all of my soul. Will you be my friend, my partner, my lover, and my husband?"

He kissed her again. "Shall I say 'no' five times before finally accepting?"

"Actually, I *never* said 'no'; I simply told you to ask me again when you were recovered, *and* if I remember correctly—and you know very well that I *do*— I did say 'yes' twice."

"You might not have said 'no' those first four times, but you did *not* say 'yes'... and I did have to ask six times. So, I now choose to answer... mayhap." He kissed her again.

In an attempt to persuade him, she initiated a deeper kiss and pulled away. "Marry me, William?"

"I need more convincing..."

More kisses. "Marry me?"

"Perhaps," he said breathlessly.

She feathered kisses along his jaw line and asked again.

"Maybe," he whispered huskily.

She nuzzled his neck and worked her way up to his ear and whispered the question again, causing him to shiver.

He barely forced out a hoarse, "It is *most* probable."

She asked once more.

He turned the tables and began to kiss her neck as if it were air to a drowning man. When finally he elicited the breathlessness he was striving to produce, he whispered into her ear, "Yes! I will marry you, my Elizabeth." He moved to touch her face and looked deeply into her eyes.

Elizabeth pulled his head down and laid it on her chest. She said, "I told you years ago that my heart belonged to you and always would. I meant it, William. It has always been yours and will beat only for you for the rest of my life. I have never stopped loving you."

William listened to her heart for several minutes, with his hand over his own heart. "Our hearts are beating as one, Elizabeth!"

When she did not answer, he moved to look at her face. Elizabeth's eyes told him more than words ever could, and he lay his head down again. After a time, he straightened, kissed her, and said, "The servants will be waking soon, my love. We really should return to our rooms, or there will be more gossip spreading about Meryton."

She pulled herself against his chest again, saying, "Yes, I know, but I do not wish to leave you."

"When shall I go to your father, Elizabeth? I must explain everything to him."

Elizabeth was thoughtful for a few minutes before saying, "We will explain together, William. Oh! I cannot wait until our betrothal is public!"

"You will find me hard-pressed not to shout it out to everyone I meet. When I leave Longbourn, I may go to a rooftop in the center of the village of Meryton and do just that," he said with as serious a demeanor as he could manage, causing Elizabeth's laughter to echo throughout the library, inciting his own to join hers.

"*That* would be a sight to see, especially after the impression you have made here. Oh, please do tell me if you plan to do it, for I would dearly love to see the faces of my neighbors!"

There was no doubt that his countenance did turn serious after her statement, and she regretted teasing him. "William, you may have made the wrong first impression, but after they hear of your accomplishing the impossible, they will think better of you."

His eyebrows rose. "The impossible?"

She turned toward him. "Yes! First, you have won the heart of the *only* lady in Hertfordshire who has never been impressed by *any* man—as far as they are aware… you must have heard some of the gossip about me?" William shook his head.

"Well… before this newest round began, I was deemed a hoyden or bluestocking—take your pick between the two, for I will not repeat the others—who would never marry due either to my refusal to even look at a man or my never having met a man intelligent enough who could best me… at *anything*.

"Additionally, my love, being a wealthy landowner of the first circle, it is in your favor to value one of their own enough to condescend to choose to marry her over all of the ladies in the *ton*. And, rest assured, you will be loved by one and all in a matter of days once Mama begins to sing your praises!"

He chuckled. "I do hope so, but after what happened at the Assembly…"

"William—my mother will forgive you anything after she knows we are betrothed!"

The clock chimed, and Elizabeth looked at the window. There was a hint of light in the sky, which meant she must leave, and soon! "Would you mind if I tell Jane? She will be so pleased to know that she was right!"

"I do not mind at all. I am looking forward to having her as a sister. She quite impressed me last night."

Elizabeth delicately arched an eyebrow. "Oh, should I be jealous of that sentiment, sir?" she teased, but his look became serious.

"Elizabeth! Promise me that you will never again doubt my love for you, no matter what happens between us, no matter what you think you see or hear. I love you more than my own life. I will never betray you, and I will never stop loving you."

She nodded and said, "And you must promise me the same. If nothing else, being apart these three years has guaranteed that we will never take each other for granted." She sighed. "I must go, my sweet William."

He helped her off his lap and stood in front of her, his hand caressing her cheek. She reached up and kissed him gently, and then said, "I will see you at breakfast?"

"Yes, but I do think we should both get some sleep first. I will worry if you do not rest, Elizabeth… You have no idea what it was like for me after you fainted!"

"I will try my best to sleep a few hours, William. You will do the same?"

"Yes, I will." He captured her lips once more before walking her to the door. With a last long look back at him, she left the room.

William stared at the door for a time before turning around and surveying the room. So much had happened since he had entered just a few hours ago; even with her scent and the warmth where her body had pressed against his still lingering in his senses, it was difficult to believe it was real. He walked over to the sketches still scattered on the floor and began to gather them and put them away into the case. Enough time had passed... he left for his own bedchamber in a much different state of mind than when he had fled it the night before.

Chapter 17

Although Caroline Bingley was not usually the early riser that most of the others of the party were, she insisted on being present whenever one or both of the Bennet ladies would be at table. She was overjoyed at the prospect of having the Bennets leave her house! Her brother had been much too attentive to Jane, and his friend behaved so strangely that Caroline thought for certain he was having a difficult time where Elizabeth was concerned. Of course, Charles would forget all about Jane within a few days and move on, as usual, and Mr. Darcy could *never* offer for Elizabeth since she was too unfashionable, unlike herself, so she had not been overly concerned during their stay. The only worry she did have was that Elizabeth might use her arts and allurements to trap him; Mr. Darcy was such an honorable gentleman, he would feel obligated to offer for her. He was too intelligent to fall for any such maneuvers as to be placed in a compromising position—a fact that she had learned first-hand—but since he seemed to be unusually attracted to Elizabeth, she worried that he would be carried away by his manly urges if Elizabeth made an improper advance upon his person. And so, it was for the best to have Elizabeth Bennet out of the house as soon as was possible.

Bingley's thoughts were quite different from those of his sister. Though he was very glad that she was feeling well enough to do so, Bingley was extremely disappointed that Jane would soon be leaving his house. He had been of the opinion that the Bennet sisters should stay another few days, but they had both stated that they felt well enough for the journey of three miles and did not wish to impose on his hospitality any longer. He did not want Jane to feel uncomfortable by his urging her to stay, and so he agreed.

Jane's countenance was even more serene than usual, but gave some tell-tale signals to Elizabeth's experienced eye that she was very sad to be leaving Bingley's company and protection—and would be very happy if she never had to leave his side again.

Mr. and Mrs. Hurst were still above stairs sleeping.

Elizabeth was feeling quite out of sorts and had spent the whole of the meal thus far simply staring at her plate. Though through the years she had learned to hide her emotions to some degree, as was expected by society, her natural tendency toward jesting when unsure of what to say had been quelled during the extenuating circumstance of having William in the neighborhood. Instead, she had turned to anger to hide the passionate torrent of emotions she had been feeling since his arrival.

After the previous night's disclosures and reconciliation, Elizabeth wished to admit to the entire room that she and William were in love and to be married, but she knew she should not until they had gained her father's consent. Though so far this morning, she had managed to school her features and check the silly grin that she had felt free to display while alone in her chamber, she was absolutely certain that the moment her eyes met William's, any pretense she had already achieved would melt away. Therefore, Elizabeth was determined *not* to look at William while they were at the table with the others—and she hoped that he would understand the reason behind her behavior.

When the door to the breakfast room opened once again and William entered, Elizabeth followed his progress through the room from the corner of her eye. William moved to the side table and filled his plate without looking at any of the room's occupants. It seemed to Elizabeth that he had the same idea as she!

As he approached the table, Bingley laughed and said, "Good morning, Darcy! I am happy to see that at least *one* of my guests is hungry today! Are you making up for the past few days when you have barely eaten?"

Looking down at his plate as if it were the first time he had seen it this morning, William realized that while he had not been attending, he had filled it with more food than two people could possibly eat at one sitting. He colored and bowed slightly, ignoring his friend's question. "Good morning, ladies. Good morning, Bingley."

Finding the only unoccupied chair being the one across from Elizabeth, William seated himself there to avoid the appearance of obviously dividing himself from the rest of the party. It took a great deal of restraint to keep his eyes directed *away* from his beloved Elizabeth, and soon he could control the urge no longer. When she did not return his gaze, he at first was afraid that she had changed her mind with the sobering light of day, and he could not tear his eyes away from her—desperately seeking some sort of reassurance.

Elizabeth could feel William's stare upon her and, after maintaining her control for several minutes, she could no longer resist. When their eyes finally met, her heart skipped a beat. Their eyes engaged for several moments while questions were silently asked and answered, and their feelings from the previous night were confirmed. So much was communicated between them in that short time that it was overwhelming her ability to control her countenance, and so, sooner than either of them would have liked, Elizabeth broke the spell created by their mutual gaze and returned her eyes to her plate.

The meal continued on with very little in the way of the consumption of food having been accomplished by anyone but Caroline.

Though much of Jane's attention was focused on Bingley, she could not help noticing that her sister and William were behaving quite differently than usual. Unaware as she was of the events that had passed the previous night after she had fallen asleep, she pondered the couple for a few moments.

Deciding that she would wait to enquire about Elizabeth's change in manner until the privacy of their carriage ride home to Longbourn, Jane considered the alterations in the gentleman's demeanor. While William's usual countenance was steady and stern, and last night he displayed his heart on his sleeve, this morning she could not describe him as anything but nervous. What could account for this change? Was he upset that he had exposed his feelings for Elizabeth, even if it had only been to herself and Bingley? Was he still concerned for her sister's health after her swoon? Or... there was *something* about him that made her think he had decided to seek out Elizabeth's good opinion after all.

Jane smiled as she thought how interesting it might be for Elizabeth to stay another few days in the same house with William, but at this time she could think of no way to accomplish that, short of deceit.

"Miss Bennet, it seems we all need a bit of cheering up and since you have found something to make you smile, will you share with us the subject?" Bingley asked.

Jane's smile widened as it always did whenever Bingley spoke to her, and though she hated to lie, she quickly recognized that a small fib was necessary, "I was just thinking of what an enjoyable evening we will have at the ball you have promised us, Mr. Bingley."

"I quite agree, Miss Bennet, but I am afraid that subject will serve only to put some of the occupants of the table into a deeper state of gloom. Darcy is not fond of dancing, and usually can never be found on the dance floor."

"Do you prefer cards to dancing, then, Mr. Darcy?" Jane asked.

"No, he does not." Bingley, not willing to give up Jane's attention, answered for him, "He usually stands around stalking the crowd, giving anyone who dares to approach him a stern look in order to frighten them off. You saw it, I believe, at the assembly."

Jane was feeling quite mischievous. "I did notice that Mr. Darcy did not dance much at the assembly ball... but he did dance with *one* partner."

William hesitated, struggling to form an answer. "I do not dance unless I am particularly familiar with my partner."

"And so does this mean, now that you are familiar with me, that I should expect an invitation to dance, sir?" Jane was beginning to feel rather wicked, but she wished to give him an opportunity to ask Elizabeth to dance without having to introduce the subject himself.

William stared at her for a moment, stunned that she would be soliciting a dance with him... but then noticed her eyes move slightly toward Elizabeth. *"Matchmaking, Miss Bennet? You approve of me for your favorite sister and best friend? I suppose Elizabeth has not told you that we are engaged?"* He could not help but feel a surge of confidence at the thought that Jane would approve. "Yes, Miss Bennet, you should..."

Bingley interrupted, "May I take this opportunity to ask for your hand for the first two dances, Miss Bennet?"

Jane smiled sweetly and colored, embarrassed that her idea had worked in her own favor instead of Elizabeth's. "I thank you, Mr. Bingley, I would be happy to dance the first set with you."

William chimed in immediately, "Miss Elizabeth, would you honor me with the first set as well?"

Elizabeth held her betrothed's gaze as she said, "Yes, Mr. Darcy, I will be pleased to do so," and watched the joy enter his eyes before he looked away again.

Elizabeth had been listening to the conversation in awe, wondering from whence her sister's boldness had suddenly appeared. She had never acted thus in the past and Elizabeth did not know she possessed the will within herself to do so at all. She saw Jane's intent, and if she had been any closer to her, she would have kicked her under the table to tell her to stop since Jane was avoiding her eyes. But the chances were that at this distance she would kick either Miss Bingley or William instead. Though she had little doubt that he would have asked her, she would have preferred it to be *William's* idea to ask her to dance instead of his feeling obligated by Jane's maneuvering... but Jane had planned it well. Jane knew that William would never ask *her* for the first set, and so she left open the opportunity for William to ask herself. Elizabeth could not be angry with her sister since her scheme had worked so perfectly in both their favors.

Caroline Bingley stood quickly, almost knocking over her chair. Huffing loudly, she turned up her nose and promptly exited the room.

~%~

As the Bennet ladies were returning upstairs to prepare to leave Netherfield, Jane remembered that she had been unable to find her shawl earlier that morning and told Elizabeth that she was going to check the drawing room to see if she had left it there during last night's confusion. Bingley was there and was not surprised to see her. Jane blushed, assuming correctly that he had been waiting for her, hoping for a few moments alone, though the subject he wished to discuss was *not* what she had originally hoped for.

Not knowing anything of what had occurred the previous night between his friend and Elizabeth, Bingley had devised a plan. "I am sorry, Miss Bennet, but I found your shawl and decided to wait for you here. We need to speak... I can see what you are about, and I would like to help if I can."

Jane's eyes opened wide in surprise. "Whatever do you mean, Mr. Bingley?"

"Why, Darcy and Miss Elizabeth, of course! You obviously know more than I about their history; Darcy can be quite tight-lipped about personal matters. I only know what his cousin, Colonel Fitzwilliam, told me years ago but I did not know the name of the lady. From what I have observed since Darcy has come to Hertfordshire, I suspect that the lady was in fact Miss Elizabeth. I know not what occurred to separate them, but I must say that I have known Darcy for years, and I have never seen him act thusly toward any other lady. I have even seen my friend when distressed about his sister's being ill, but never have I seen him behave as he did last night! After what you saw as well, I do not think I am betraying any secrets when I say that he is thoroughly enamored with Miss Elizabeth. By your actions this morning, I can also see you are trying to forward his suit. I do not wish you to break any confidences, Miss Bennet, but I think the reason for it is that Miss Elizabeth feels the same way about my friend and is hesitant about giving her heart to him again.

"I can vouch for Darcy, Miss Bennet; he is the best man I have ever met in every aspect of his character and is *not* the type to dally with a lady's heart. In fact, I have never seen him interested in any lady before Miss Elizabeth. Since I also have the greatest respect for her, I am certain that whatever *did* occur to divide them in the past was based upon misunderstanding. I promise that you will not be sorry for helping him win your sister.

"Darcy has had a difficult life and because I would do almost anything to see my friend happy, I offer my services in this most worthy endeavor."

Jane smiled brightly and said, "You are a very good friend, sir. I think we have already begun to work together nicely, Mr. Bingley, as I observed your actions this morning as well—giving Mr. Darcy the hint to ask my sister for the first two dances."

Bingley colored. "I did at that, but I assure you that I was in earnest about wishing to secure the first with you, Miss Bennet! It was only a very convenient way of accomplishing both of my heart's desires in the same moment."

Jane extended her hand and said, "Mr. Bingley, I gratefully accept your offer of assistance."

Without looking away from her eyes, he bowed over her hand, hesitating a moment before brushing a gentle kiss across her knuckles. "It is a pleasure to be of service, Miss Bennet."

Little did the couple realize that their plan's happy conclusion had already been achieved!

~%~

After retreating to his room previous night, William had found it difficult to sleep, and so he did the same as he usually did whenever this occurred—he took out his journal to write to Elizabeth. He wished to tell her that she had made him the happiest of men. After staring at the blank page for a while, the solution of how to put into words the entirety of his feelings presented itself. He would give her the journal! If he handed it to her as she left Netherfield in the morning, Elizabeth would know for certain everything that had been in his heart these past three years.

After breakfast, William returned to his chamber to retrieve the journal. Any last-minute doubts about giving it to Elizabeth were pushed aside, and he brought it with him when he heard the ladies upon the stairs as they were descending to leave.

As Jane was being helped into her coat by Bingley, William approached Elizabeth and stood with his back to them, blocking Elizabeth from their view. "Miss Elizabeth, I hope you will read this book as I am certain it will answer any questions that might remain on the subject of which we last spoke. It will also provide you with much more information on similar subjects."

Elizabeth's eyes twinkled with mischief as she made certain that her hand caught his under the thick volume though she made it appear as if she reached to take it from him. William intertwined their fingers as he asked so quietly that only she could understand him, "May I speak to your father tomorrow, Elizabeth?"

She whispered, "Yes! I will make certain I am at home. I would not like to allow even one day to pass without seeing you, my love."

A warm glow shone from William's eyes as he stared lovingly into hers for a few moments. If he did not look away soon, he knew he would take her into his arms. Glancing down to the book they held between them, William asked, "You will read this?"

"If you wish it, I will. What is it?"

"I began a new journal the day you left Pemberley..."

Elizabeth interrupted, "Are you certain, William? A journal is usually full of such private thoughts..."

"Every word was *meant* for you to read. You will understand what I mean when you begin. Please, will you do this for me, Elizabeth?"

"I am honored that you wish to share it with me. Though, I cannot help but ask once more—are you perfectly sure that you will not regret allowing me to read it?"

"Yes. But... please keep in mind that I did not know your father had not kept our letters from you..."

Elizabeth arched her brow. "Ah! I can only imagine what you mean by *that*! I promise to remember and will not take offense."

"Thank you. Until tomorrow, then." William kissed her hand without releasing her eyes from his intense gaze. Their eyes remained locked until the carriage could be heard approaching. Bowing, he stepped back and waited for her to don her gloves before he escorted his beloved to the coach.

Both ladies peered out the window of the carriage to see the gentlemen as they stood in the drive watching the retreating carriage.

~%~

Once Netherfield was out of their view, Elizabeth noticed that Jane was still quite distracted, most likely with thoughts of Mr. Bingley's kindness—or other amiable attributes—and so she opened William's journal. Turning to the first entry, she saw it was written just after she had departed Pemberley. It was written as if he were writing a letter to her! Knowing that she could not read it now, she quickly turned the pages—enough to see that *every* entry was written as if it were a letter to her, and that the book was almost filled with his handwriting. She closed it quickly with a resounding snap, which attracted Jane's attention.

"What is it, Lizzy? You seem out of sorts today, and you are quite flushed just now. Perhaps Mr. Jones was mistaken? Do you feel ill? Mayhap we should not have left Netherfield today after all!"

Elizabeth wished for a reason to stay in her room for a while so that she could read William's journal, and therefore, she took advantage of her flustered state. "Jane, it is not so very far to Longbourn! I do believe I will survive a coach ride of twenty minutes in duration. You are partially correct, though; I did not sleep well last night, and I am very tired. I believe I will stay in my room and rest today."

Jane removed her glove and pressed her hand to Elizabeth's forehead. "You do not have a fever, but I agree that you should rest, dearest Lizzy. If you begin to feel ill, Papa will send for Mr. Jones, I am sure."

"Jane! Truly, there is no need! I shall be well."

~%~

When Elizabeth reached her room, she immediately settled in at the window seat and began reading. At first, she read it from the beginning, but then began flipping through William's journal, searching for certain dates that she felt were important. Elizabeth found it difficult to put it down— she had an urgent need to know all of what had occurred in William's life for the three years they had been parted.

Much of what she read caused her tears to fall upon the pages, in some cases adding to the stains that had been left there by *his* tears. She read of William's grief over his father's death, his confusion over the absence of communication from her father and herself, his desperate yet unsatisfied need for her love and support, his dissatisfaction at his inability to manage the estate perfectly, his elation whenever something he tried worked out right, his rage at his relatives, his fear for Georgiana, and William's excitement as her birthday neared.

It was at this point in her reading the journal the day following her return to Longbourn that Elizabeth heard the telltale sound of horses approaching the house. Glancing out the window, she saw that William and Bingley had arrived. She said a little prayer of thanks that her mother and youngest sisters were at Lucas Lodge, and only Jane and Mary would be present in the parlor for at least the first portion of the visit.

Elizabeth descended the stairs at the moment the gentlemen were handing over their coats and hats to Mrs. Hill. She stopped a few steps from the bottom of the staircase when William's eyes met hers, and she was treated to the sight of a wide smile spreading across his handsome face, causing sudden warmth to settle into her soul. She found that she could not move, afraid that she would rush into his embrace if she did. Elizabeth loved how the dark colors William preferred to wear deepened the chocolate brown of his eyes, even at this distance, and how the fine cut of the cloth accented his perfect physique. She certainly hoped theirs would not be a long engagement for she was quite looking forward to peeling off those layers of fine cloth and discovering exactly what lay beneath. The thought made her shiver as she saw William move toward her.

She could have no idea how the manner of her gaze soothed the doubts William had entertained about having given her his journal. Relief spread through him at seeing her love for him reflected in her eyes.

William bowed before Elizabeth and said, "Good day, Miss Elizabeth. May I ask if you have recovered?"

It was several moments before she could recall to what he was referring. "Oh, yes! I am quite well. I thank you for your concern, Mr. Darcy."

"I believe we were about to be shown into the parlor. May I?" William held out his arm for Elizabeth, and she laid her hand upon it, immediately stepping down the remainder of the stairs and close to his side.

Hearing a chuckle from across the entryway, Elizabeth noticed for the first time a very amused-looking Bingley and a wide-eyed Mrs. Hill standing there. "Good day, Mr. Bingley. I hope your sisters and Mr. Hurst are well."

"It is good to see you, Miss Elizabeth. They are, thank you, and they send their regards."

Elizabeth turned towards Mrs. Hill so that the gentlemen could not see her face and answered her inquiring look with a bright smile, a wink and a glance towards William that made the housekeeper briefly raise her eyebrows almost to her hairline before she could school her features. "Mrs. Hill, will you send in a tea service, please?"

Mrs. Hill stole another look at William, who was gazing lovingly at Elizabeth, then returned her eyes to Elizabeth and answered while unsuccessfully attempting to hide a smile, "Yes, Miss Elizabeth."

Distracted by Elizabeth's presence as usual, William almost forgot the day's errand. "Mrs. Hill, I would like to speak to Mr. Bennet after greeting the ladies of the house."

"I will see if he's available, Mr. Darcy." Mrs. Hill curtsied and made her way down the hall to the kitchen to order tea before going to the master's study. Once out of the sight of the gentlefolk, Mrs. Hill smiled broadly, thinking that Miss Elizabeth deserved the happiness of a love match!

Mrs. Hill's return to the parlor did not come with the message she had originally thought it would. When Mr. Bennet heard that Mr. Darcy wished to speak to him alone, the master refused to see him! It was with great sadness that she had to inform the gentleman. "Beggin' your pardon, Miss Bennet," Mrs. Hill interrupted then turned to William, "Mr. Bennet isn't available to see you today, Mr. Darcy."

The pleasant look that had been directed at Elizabeth a moment before disappeared from his face as William briefly closed his eyes and then nodded. "Thank you, Mrs. Hill. Do you know if he would be free to meet with me tomorrow?"

"I don't believe so, sir." Mrs. Hill responded, remembering the master's angry words in a tone so harsh that she had startled, *"Not till Hades freezes over!"* She hoped that he had used it as a figure of speech.

Mrs. Hill saw the concern on William's face and noticed Elizabeth's hand move to William's arm. Their eyes met, and there was a silent form of communication shared between them that Mrs. Hill had previously noticed only in couples who had been married for a length of time. A little of William's concern left his countenance, and she heard Elizabeth suggest a walk in the garden.

As she helped the two couples with their coats and hats, Mrs. Hill pondered the situation. Having been a member of the household since before Elizabeth had been born, the Bennet girls were almost like daughters to her—especially the eldest two. She also knew many of the Bennet family's secrets and had been privy to much of what had occurred between William's family and the Bennets in the past. Any feelings of resentment she had held for the Darcy family were outweighed by seeing how deeply in love this couple was. They deserved happiness, no matter what had happened in the past! Unfortunately, being the housekeeper, Mrs. Hill knew there was nothing *she* could do to convince Mr. Bennet to speak to William.

Mary had declined walking out, but Jane and Bingley accompanied Elizabeth and William. The group naturally divided into couples and Jane and Bingley fell back, out of hearing range of the other two.

Elizabeth broke the uncomfortable tension that had come between them. "William, I will speak to my father. Perhaps it would be better if *I* explained what happened without your being there…"

"Though I would appreciate the support your presence would provide during the interview, *I* should be the one to explain to your father what has occurred, my love. I know it will not be an easy conversation, but I wish to have the chance to clear my family's name with Mr. Bennet—and to apologize for the way I acted toward him at Lucas Lodge."

"That would be ideal, but I cannot force him to see you, William. Maybe if I told him a *little* of the situation, he would agree to meet with you?"

They walked on in silence for a few minutes, William absent-mindedly tracing patterns with his fingers upon her gloved hand that rested on his arm as he thought. "That may be the only option. I will return tomorrow in the event that he chooses to see me." William abruptly stopped walking, and she looked up at his worried face. "Elizabeth… if your father should not approve…"

"I have every confidence that he *will* approve once he knows all. If he does not—after all avenues to convince him have been explored—shall *I* need to beg you to take me to Scotland, or is it *your* turn to beg, Mr. Darcy?" The corners of Elizabeth's lips twitched as she held back a smile, but her amusement was apparent in her eyes.

Elizabeth's attempt at teasing William out of his brooding state of mind was highly successful. "I think perhaps it would be *my* turn—though I do hope you would resist the idea a little, requiring my having to *convince* you the way you convinced me to marry you, my beautiful temptress. I do look forward to your having the need to convince me of many things once we are married, Elizabeth."

The couples took another turn around the garden before the gentlemen feared it might be too cold for the ladies, and they returned indoors briefly before the gentlemen took their leave.

After they left, Elizabeth attempted to gain access to Mr. Bennet's study, but was refused. That evening after their meal, Elizabeth followed him into the study when he left the table. "Papa, may I ask why you would not see Mr. Darcy this afternoon? He wished to speak to you about all that had occurred over the past three years, sir."

Mr. Bennet's countenance exhibited his ire, a side of her father that Elizabeth rarely saw, "It is all too late, Lizzy."

"But, Papa…"

"No, Elizabeth! *Nothing* can excuse the way he has treated us. I will not hear him. You are excused!"

Elizabeth was shocked and dismayed. Her father had never spoken to her in such a way in her life. She retreated to her room to think for a while before joining her mother and sisters in the drawing room. After a few minutes, she decided that she would try again in two days, hoping he would be willing to listen to what she had to say after having had some time to cool his temper.

~%~

Retiring early that evening, Elizabeth continued to read William's journal. After his excitement in looking forward to seeing her again on her birthday, there had been a long gap in time until he wrote about the fire. He told her of the pain of his injuries, his aversion to ever having her know of his state until he had healed, and of his frustration at his lack of progress in healing. She was shocked to learn that William had almost given up hope that he would ever heal, but then he saw her at the theater and it had given him a new sense of determination to work harder so that he could win her love again. Elizabeth felt all of the pain that he and Georgiana had felt at Lieutenant Wickham's actions. She read of his apprehension and anticipation at going into Hertfordshire, his surprise at seeing her at the assembly, and his feelings about her own reaction to seeing him. His reactions to what had happened since he had been in Hertfordshire were so different than what she had assumed they had been. William wrote quite a lot while *she* was staying at Netherfield.

Very late that night, Elizabeth turned the page to the final entry and read:

My dearest Elizabeth,

More than three years have passed since I first began writing this journal, but I am at the same cross-roads as I was at that time. Tonight, you have made me the happiest of men again by agreeing to marry me.

I wrote to you in this journal of all the things I would have liked to have discussed with you in person, or would have written had we been officially engaged. And so, I have decided to give this to you so that you may be acquainted with what was in my heart while we were apart.

As much as I have learned over the time covered within these pages, the most valuable lesson I have learned has occurred since meeting you again — tonight, in fact.

By not seeking you out after I had been injured, I thought I was being selfless, putting your comfort over my own — because I thought the only thing I wanted was you — I wanted to feel your touch, to hear your voice, to see your face once again; I wanted you to comfort me when I was in pain, and when I was discouraged, I wanted to hear you urge me to go on.

But as I reflect over what I have written in this book and all that we said to each other earlier this night, I realize that my reasons for staying away were quite selfish, indeed! I did not wish to burden you with my injuries; I did not wish to see your face when you witnessed the pain I was having; I did not want you to see how difficult the exercises were for me because I was afraid you would think me weak; I did not wish to see disgust or pity or regret in your eyes when you looked at me; I did not want to risk rejection; I wished to be able to use my arm when I next saw you so that I did not feel humiliation.

You should have been given the choice, Elizabeth, and yet I did not allow it. Instead of protecting you from information that would have been painful for you, I hurt you by leaving you with no information at all. What else could you do but guess at what might have happened? What more logical conclusion could you reach than that I no longer cared for you, or possibly never had?

I would not have blamed you if you had lost all the tender feelings you once had for me, and I cannot explain to you how ecstatic I am that you did not. I thank you for loving me even when you thought all hope was gone.

The remainder of my life will be spent attempting to make certain that you are never sorry for loving me, my heart!

I am forever yours,
William

~%~

The following day was much like the one previous to it, though Mrs. Bennet and all her daughters were present. When the gentlemen arrived at Longbourn, the couples were quite happy to see each other, but Mr. Bennet continued to refuse to see William. Mrs. Bennet acted quite rudely, speaking civilly to Bingley and either ignoring or sending bitter comments in William's direction. Following their mother's example, Kitty and Lydia ignored William as well. Elizabeth was mortified, and William stood by the window looking out to avoid causing Elizabeth any more discomfort. Jane suggested a short walk in the garden, and Elizabeth joined her and the gentlemen. Mrs. Bennet had the younger girls attend as well, but as soon as they were outdoors, Kitty and Lydia, not wishing to be near William, went off on their own. Again, those remaining paired off to stroll, and again Elizabeth and William remained silent until Jane and Bingley were well away and unable to hear them.

Elizabeth could not look at him as she said, "Oh, William! I must apologize for my mother's behavior! She knows not what she is about. If only my father would speak to you—she would truly be overjoyed at the news."

"My Elizabeth, I understand that Mrs. Bennet's behavior would be quite appropriate if what she *believes* I have done was actually true. That is why I forgive your father for refusing to see me as well, though doing so will not help to clear up this misunderstanding. I hold no ill will towards *anyone* for what they do in the name of protecting the most important person in my life—you." They shared a loving look in silence.

"My father would not speak to me on the subject, and so I could not give him any information about you. He practically threw me from the room when I brought up your name. I have never heard him speak so harshly."

With a pained expression, William replied, "Do not risk your relationship with your father, Elizabeth. Allow him another day or two to become accustomed to the idea that I wish to speak with him. I will make another attempt to speak to him before the ball, and I will be a little more insistent on seeing him next time. I hope to have this resolved before meeting any of your family in public again."

They walked on for another few minutes in silence before Elizabeth said, "If only we had a few minutes without being in full view of the house…"

His return look was warm before seeing the expression upon her face. Elizabeth was not looking at him, but beyond him toward the house, and her mien was one of fear. William turned to see Mr. Bennet walking towards them, looking quite furious.

"Lizzy, return to the house!"

"I will not, Papa. Mr. Darcy and I wish to speak to you…"

"That is quite enough, Elizabeth! Return to the house at once."

Elizabeth stood her ground, and when she did not move, Mr. Bennet took her hand off William's arm and gently pulled her away from William's side. "I will speak to Mr. Darcy right now, *after* you have returned to the house."

She looked to William who nodded, and then said, "Yes, Papa," and walked toward the house.

When Elizabeth was out of sight, Mr. Bennet turned to William and began to speak in a low, but threatening tone, "I know what you are about, Mr. Darcy, and I will not have it! I have seen the damage your game has wrought in the past, and I will not allow you to dally with my daughter's affections once again!" He began to walk away from William, but stopped when William spoke, though he did not turn to look at him.

"Mr. Bennet, I have always been honest about my feelings for Elizabeth, and I remain so now. You cannot understand unless you hear what I have to say, sir. Please allow me to explain..."

Mr. Bennet turned to face William, and took a step closer. "*That* conversation should have taken place on Elizabeth's seventeenth birthday, or when your father died. I find I no longer have the need to find out what happened. After all you have done to our family, I have no wish to hear what you condescend to tell me now, Mr. Darcy. Goodbye."

William watched Mr. Bennet walk briskly to the house.

~%~

Elizabeth was waiting just inside the door to her father's study, expecting both he and William to come to this room once William had convinced her father to listen. When her father entered alone, she asked, "You *still* will not listen to what he has to say? You have sent him away?"

"I will not listen, and yes, I have sent him away."

"Papa, I *have* listened, and I have *forgiven* William, completely. You will as well if you give him a chance to explain. Since we left Pemberley, too many false conclusions have been assumed on both sides; you owe it to William to listen to the truth. If you will not allow William to tell you, at least allow me..."

"I will not listen to his falsehoods!" Mr. Bennet interrupted, "And I certainly will *not* hear the lies with which he has poisoned your mind. You will not speak of this again!"

"I have not been poisoned by the *truth!* You disappoint me, Papa. You have always impressed me as a man who sought the truth in any situation. William is not to blame for what has happened any more than you or I. That *is* the truth. You do *need* to hear the remainder of the story, sir, and when you are ready to listen, I will tell it to you—but I will not speak to you before that time!" Elizabeth turned on her heel and left the room.

~%~

Due to heavy rains and unsafe travelling conditions, the following three days did *not* see a return visit from William to attempt to speak to Mr. Bennet.

With the exception of meals, Mr. Bennet remained in his study. These days were not spent idly; he was deep in thought. Several times he was very close to calling Elizabeth in to discuss the situation with William, especially after the two had spent their meals sitting next to each other in deafening silence. But he did not.

Elizabeth spent much of her time reading William's journal. She had decided that she would read no more of the hardships he had faced, for she had every intention to discuss those with him personally; instead she concentrated on reviewing the parts where he told her how much he loved her and missed her and how every night he would fall asleep thinking of her—especially the passages in which he would describe what he thought their life would be like once they married, the places he would like to take her to see, what they would do there, how he dreamed of just having her by his side while doing the simplest of things like reading in their library and sharing meals, and how he looked forward to the time that she would sleep in his arms every night.

She had never before felt the need to read the same page twice, but there were several portions of William's journal which she read several times over—even though she had them memorized the first time—finding great comfort in tracing his lettering of certain words with her fingertip.

Elizabeth had not told Jane about her engagement to William or of the continuing argument with Mr. Bennet. The latter would have upset her sister too much, and she could not divulge the former without exposing Jane to the gravity of the argument. Jane had inquired once about the lack of communication between Elizabeth and their father, but Elizabeth had avoided talking about the estrangement. Jane could see that she would not speak of it until she was ready, and she wisely refrained from questioning Elizabeth again.

Chapter 18

William had spent the days between the last time he had seen Elizabeth and the ball alternating between a state of extreme unease and pure joy. He barely knew what to do with himself. When he was not lost in thoughts about his future with Elizabeth, displaying a silly grin for all to see, he was brooding over not being able to speak to Mr. Bennet or make his future known to the world and wearing an accompanying scowl.

He also wondered what Georgiana was about. Though he had sent several letters since he had arrived at Netherfield, Georgiana had not written once. He chose to believe that she had been angry for his remaining in the area after he discovered that Elizabeth lived so close by. He had never known his sister to act in such a way, but, then, they had never been in such a situation before either. William's last letter was written the morning after Elizabeth left Netherfield explaining the strange circumstances of none of them having received posts from the others. He also shared a brief accounting of his new understanding with Elizabeth, telling her how happy he was and asking for her blessing upon their marriage, reminding her that at one time she had loved Elizabeth as a sister and telling her that he was confident she would feel that way again soon.

But first, Mr. Bennet had to agree to see him and grant his consent!

Bingley seemed to sense his distress and tried to distract him with games of backgammon, billiards, chess—but the most helpful activity proved to be a few heart-to-heart talks about their mutual interest in the eldest Bennet daughters. Bingley's hearty congratulations were accepted with an expression of joy upon William's face, the likes of which he had never before witnessed upon his friend's countenance. Secretly, Bingley applauded himself on working well with Jane to forward the match, and he was looking forward to discussing it with her!

As the day of the ball drew closer, William became even more anxious. Would Mr. Bennet allow him to dance with Elizabeth, or would he make a public statement against him without knowing all the facts? There was one thing of which he was certain, he would have to spend most of the evening watching Elizabeth dance with other men... and so the ugly head of jealousy was reared in addition to the turbulent mix of other emotions he was feeling.

William was in quite a state when the first carriage arrived at the door on the evening of the ball. He thought himself to be looking quite casual as he observed the arrivals from the second floor window just above the entrance to the house.

When Mr. Bennet disembarked, William's back stiffened. He had to prepare himself! Mrs. Bennet and Jane Bennet alighted... and then Elizabeth stepped down.

He could never understand how every time he saw her, she was more beautiful, even if it had only been a few hours since last they were together. The amount of time between sightings seemed to make a great deal of difference in this phenomenon—the greater the time, the more beautiful she became. But *this* was almost as great a change as it had been between the times he had seen her at Longbourn and Pemberley three years ago. Though not physically changed this time, there was an inner glow that radiated from her soul outward in every direction. He was completely entranced by her. His features displayed absolutely every emotion he was feeling. His right hand reached out towards her, only to be stopped by the glass of the window.

She looked up at him, their eyes met, and his heart swelled with love.

~%~

If Elizabeth thought her anticipation could not become more intense when the family entered the coach, she was greatly mistaken. By the time the coach had begun the approach along Netherfield's drive, she was grasping Jane's hand so firmly that Jane had to signal for her to loosen her hold a bit.

Mr. Bennet was watching Elizabeth carefully, but she had not noticed. Her eyes were sparkling, her smile was genuine, and he could not help but smile at her obvious happiness. He wondered at this change, and if her exceptional state of mind over the past few days could be credited to what had occurred between Elizabeth and William at Netherfield. If so, then it might have been for the best after all. Perhaps it had been wrong of him— perhaps he *should* listen to what William had to say? Was it all a misunderstanding as Elizabeth had implied?

Elizabeth was the most intelligent woman—person—he had ever known, and normally he would not doubt her judgment on any matter. Was it only bitterness that gave him doubts about her interpretation of William's reasons for abandoning them?

If Elizabeth could forgive William, it was time to consider it himself.

When he helped his second eldest daughter from the coach, Mr. Bennet noticed she was trembling, and then she froze, and the most brilliant smile that she had ever displayed spread slowly across her face. Elizabeth's eyes were filled with such love that Mr. Bennet's own eyes began to sting. Mr. Bennet followed her gaze up to the second floor to the window overlooking the front steps, and there he saw William, just in time to witness his features transform. It was as if dawn had broken after a wretched night.

There it was displayed for everyone to see plainly. Mr. Bennet fully realized just how wrong his accusations had been! There was no way even he could doubt the sincerity of the young man's look; William truly *did* love Elizabeth even more than he had when they had left Pemberley. William *had* been hiding behind a mask like his father used to do!

Mr. Bennet did not realize until a few moments later that he said aloud, "Thank G-d!"

Jane took his arm, and he looked down to find her eyes filled with tears as she said, "I am very thankful as well that the misunderstanding has finally been put to rights, Papa! It is wonderful to see Lizzy happy again!"

He squeezed Jane's hand and said, "I am certain that if Lizzy is satisfied with his explanation, I will be as well." He hesitated as they began to climb the steps. "I expect I will be giving my consent after hearing his account myself. Do you think that your mother could put a wedding together in the three weeks time that it takes to read the banns, my dear? I think they have waited long enough, do you not?"

Jane smiled as she said, "Yes, I do. And I believe my mother can manage anything if she puts her mind to it, sir."

~%~

As Elizabeth entered the house, William stood about half-way down the stairs watching her look around the chamber until she found him, and her smile widened again. He said a silent prayer begging that this was *not* another dream that he would awaken from in a few minutes, resulting in his plunging into utter despair when he found that it had not been real. As she was helped from her wrap, he made his way towards her. Having eyes only for Elizabeth, he was surprised when Mr. Bennet stepped in his way. "Good evening, William."

A touch of concern entered William's expression, though he did notice that Mr. Bennet called him "William" instead of "Mr. Darcy" as he had since meeting him again. "Good evening, Mr. Bennet. I have been granted the first set from Miss Elizabeth. May I, sir?"

"From the look on my daughter's face since we have arrived, I do not think she would ever forgive me if I did not agree to it. I suppose you and Lizzy have made amends, but you and I still have much to speak of, William. Will you join me tomorrow afternoon in my study for a discussion?"

William smiled slightly. "Yes, sir! I would be happy to clear up all the misunderstandings between us, Mr. Bennet, and I would like to apologize as well for any rude comments that I have made to you in the past. Miss Elizabeth has set me to rights about what has taken place at Longbourn, and I have been eager to enlighten you as to all that has occurred at Pemberley. I will be prepared for a long discussion, sir."

William held out his hand and Mr. Bennet shook it, and then Mr. Bennet stepped aside while saying, "Enjoy the ball, William. I will see you tomorrow."

"Thank you, sir!" William said with a smile as his eyes focused once again upon Elizabeth.

As William approached, he bowed and spoke, "Good evening, Miss Elizabeth. May I escort you into the ball?"

She gracefully curtsied, and her smile brightened once again. Placing her hand in the crook of his right arm as he offered it, she replied, "Good evening, Mr. Darcy. Yes, you may. I must congratulate Mr. and Miss Bingley. Netherfield has never looked so festive."

He did not take his eyes off her as he said, "I have never seen anything more splendid than the sight before me." He hesitated and then added, "You look quite lovely tonight, Elizabeth."

He pronounced her Christian name as if it were sacred, and it made her blush even more than she had at his compliment. Her throat was too tight to answer him. How often had she imagined similar scenes to the one playing out now?

William looked to the place where her hand rested on his arm and was delighted that she had not yet donned her gloves; the feel of her hand on his recovering arm was heavenly, and he pulled her a little closer to his side. Though he did not believe any touch of hers could have ever truly pained him, he knew that just a few months ago, even *her* touch would have been uncomfortable. As they neared the ball room, he placed his hand over hers; he had spent the past three years longing to touch her and was determined to take any opportunity to do so again. Tingling warmth began where their skin met and spread throughout his body. He felt her shiver and was thrilled to think that his touch might cause a similar sensation within her. She met his eyes again at last, and what he saw there made his heart sing.

From behind him, William heard Bingley clear his throat and startled… he had forgotten they were not alone. Bingley came closer and said loudly enough for them both to hear, "*You* may not wish to go further into the ballroom, Darcy, but the rest of us do. Move off to the side if you would rather stay in the hall; you are holding up the entire party!"

William looked around him and realized that he and Elizabeth had stopped at the door to the ballroom and that indeed there was a crowd behind them waiting to enter. He began to move forward once again as Elizabeth started to laugh—that wonderful, magical tinkling laugh that he had not heard since they had been together at Pemberley.

When Elizabeth's laughter rang out, it echoed about the ball room, and a number of people turned to look, recognizing the genuine happiness in it— a sound that they had not heard from her in years—causing several people to smile and a few to sigh in relief. One sigh had a hint of regret to it.

The sound of his beloved's laughter caused William to smile widely, displaying his dimples for the entire assembly to see. William answered his friend's comment while looking at Elizabeth, "Bingley, *tonight* I am actually looking forward to dancing—at least the first set."

"Well, well! What a memorable occasion this is; I must take note of the date! All of London will be jealous of those in attendance! We shall not only be witness to Fitzwilliam Darcy's dancing the first set, but we can also attest to Fitzwilliam Darcy's anticipating a dance with pleasure! I wonder what has changed his opinion so completely. Is the Hertfordshire air good for his disposition, do you think, Miss Bennet? Or perhaps, it is the pleasant company?"

Bingley had Jane on his arm and was gazing upon her with an expression similar to the looks William had been bestowing upon her sister. Jane smiled beautifully but did not comment.

William colored a little—why was Bingley speaking so loudly now? He never took his eyes off Elizabeth's, gauging her reaction to his friend's words. He saw understanding dawn within her—Bingley had confirmed what his usual habits were at a ball. William was glad that his friend did not announce to the entire neighborhood the usual jest that Bingley was so fond of—that William always had to be *dragged* onto the dance floor practically kicking and screaming.

Gazing into Elizabeth's eyes and seeing there all the love that he had seen long ago caused William to feel as if he was not just the master of Pemberley—weighted down by responsibilities and afraid of failure because so many people depended on his making the correct decisions. Suddenly, he was the same carefree young man who had seen that look in Elizabeth's eyes years ago while he was recovering from an accident in the woods, the man who was not embarrassed for anyone to know his feelings for her, and who was *so certain* that she would eventually agree to spend the rest of her life with him if he was honest about his feelings, that he had continued to ask her to do so no matter how many times she had put him off.

Pulling out all the stops, William answered, "Unquestionably, it is Miss Elizabeth's company that has inspired my welcoming *any* course of action in which she wishes to engage that, among *any* other company, I have striven to avoid... whether it be a simple diversion or a long term endeavor. It is as it has *always* been." William's hand was still covering

Elizabeth's, and he unconsciously caressed the back of her hand with his thumb.

~%~

This exchange attracted quite a bit of attention, to say the least. Bingley had purposely timed his own speech to coincide with their passing not only the most capable gossips of Meryton, but a few of Caroline's friends from London as well—well-placed friends who were also most effective at spreading the most recent gossip among the *ton*.

William's smile and the look he directed at Elizabeth were enough to convince the ladies of Meryton that he did *not* disapprove of her in the least, especially since he was engaging in this behavior before a number of guests from London—shocking them all into believing their previous suppositions had been incorrect. After much debate as the evening progressed, and knowing Elizabeth Bennet's temper when riled, it became the accepted opinion of the group that their earlier behavior was the result of a disagreement between a couple very much in love, a misunderstanding which was now obviously resolved to the complete satisfaction of both parties.

The ladies whom Caroline had invited tended to stand together unless dancing, and many of the local gentlemen stayed as far away from their glares as was possible, so they did not dance often this night. Much of their conversation centered on the behavior of one Fitzwilliam Darcy. The opportunity of spending time in his company happened to be the *only* reason they had travelled the three hours from town, and his current behavior was rather disappointing to them all. When William displayed his dimples, those among the ladies who did not practically swoon were wide-eyed in shock. Fitzwilliam Darcy smiled, and he smiled for a lady! All of the ladies agreed that this awe-inspiring sight had been absolutely unheard of previously! Though each was more than a little disappointed that this smile was not directed at them, the entire group knew what an excellent piece of gossip this was and paid very close attention to the Master of Pemberley and his mystery lady from that moment on. All were privately plotting as to how to manage an introduction to Miss Elizabeth Bennet to attain first-hand knowledge of her.

Caroline Bingley and Louisa Hurst were well sought after as conversation partners since they were the only people these ladies knew who would have information about the Miss Bennets. The Londoners admitted among themselves that they expected the opposite of what these two ladies said about her would be true. It was well known that Caroline had convinced herself long ago that *she* would be the next mistress of Pemberley, and though *everyone else* knew it was a lost cause, her sister seemed to support her in her delusion. This obvious turn in the status of Mr. Darcy's heart would not be well received by either of the sisters, though their brother seemed to approve whole-heartedly... and more than a few thoughts about *his* love interest were exchanged as well.

All of the gentlemen whom Bingley had invited from London had known William for years and were among the members of the *ton* that William *could* tolerate—and they had been invited by Bingley for the express purpose of helping his friend feel more comfortable with the crowd at the ball. Some had married worthy ladies of whose personalities even William could not disapprove. This group spent the evening commenting on the changes in their friend's behavior and the attractiveness of the lady who seemed to have brought them about.

Not wholly unexpected by some of those from London, their every word was devoured by the locals, who in most cases were anxious to learn how those of the *ton* behaved at events as grand as these. Once they heard what—or who—was the most frequent subject of conversation between the fashionably rich set, their only interest was in spreading about what the Londoners were saying: Fitzwilliam Darcy, one of the most honorable men and eligible catches in England, had finally been *caught*.

~%~

William and Bingley were on an errand to fetch their ladies glasses of punch while said ladies stood watching their progress. Elizabeth was amazed that William had made such a statement to his friend in full hearing of so many people, even before speaking to her father!

A few minutes after the gentlemen had returned, Bingley gave a signal to the musicians who in turn played a few notes to alert the crowd that the dancing would soon begin. The gentlemen disposed of the ladies' cups and led their partners to the dance floor. Bingley was opening with Jane; second in the set were William and Elizabeth, and the others lined up beside them. There were many gasps from those who had not already seen the changes in William's demeanor... including a loud exclamation which few could mistake as coming from anyone other than Mrs. Bennet.

"What could Lizzy mean by dancing with that... that *man*?" Mrs. Bennet was heard to say.

Mr. Bennet answered, "Be careful what you say here tonight, Mrs. Bennet. You may soon regret it. It would not do to insult the good friend of Mr. Bingley, would it?"

"Oh well... when you put it like *that*, I suppose it would not. But I still do not understand what Lizzy could be thinking!"

"*Look* at Lizzy, Mrs. Bennet."

"I *am* looking at her, Mr. Bennet. How else do you think I know with whom she is dancing?"

"Mrs. Bennet, you are looking in her direction, but you are not really looking *at* Lizzy. Watch her for a few moments."

Mrs. Bennet did, and when she turned to speak to her husband she did so with tears in her eyes. "She looks happy, Mr. Bennet. Happier than I have seen her in several years."

"Yes, she does at that." He gave her a pointed look and continued, "We do not wish to do anything to ruin her happiness, do we?"

Mrs. Bennet shook her head. "Did he give any explanation as to why his family has done what they have to her and to you?"

"Not as of yet, but we will meet tomorrow afternoon to discuss it. If Lizzy can forgive him, I will do my best to do the same depending on whether his excuse is reasonable enough. Though I may not be able to forget... we shall see what he says."

She choked on her breath. "He has ten thousand a year and very likely more!"

Mr. Bennet laughed loudly.

Kitty and Lydia were moving down the set towards where the couple was standing. At first, Mrs. Bennet watched her youngest daughters with a small smile, but then as she looked at the other ladies dancing near them, realizing they were from the London group, she noticed the looks of disgust on their faces as they glared at her youngest daughters in obvious disapproval of their behavior. Looking down the set and seeing the great difference between the behavior of these two and *all* of the other ladies,

Mrs. Bennet said, "Mr. Bennet, I believe I should speak with Kitty and Lydia when this dance is done. They will need to tame their behavior or else one of us shall need to take them home."

Mr. Bennet's eyes widened, "Excuse me, madam; have we been introduced?"

"Mr. Bennet! And you call *me* silly!"

"It is just that, for a moment, I thought I must have mistaken someone else for my wife. Are you feeling quite well, my dear?"

"Yes, I am, Mr. Bennet. I do not know why you would think otherwise."

"This is the first time I have ever heard you criticize Lydia's behavior, or for that matter, Kitty's when she was following Lydia's lead."

"Oh, Mr. Bennet! How you tease me! Just look at the way they are behaving compared to the other ladies. They are making quite a spectacle of themselves, are they not?"

"Do not misunderstand me; I agree with you completely. It is only that I am surprised to hear *you* say these words, even though everybody else has been saying them for years."

"Everybody else? Do you mean gossip? That is impossible—I would have heard it before now if that were so."

"Do you think anyone would have repeated gossip about your own daughters within your hearing? You tend to… make your presence known whenever *you* are in a room, my dear, while I am usually quietly in the background, and many do not notice I am there before they speak. I am certain I have heard much that you have *not*."

"Are you saying that our daughters have been the subject of gossip for years, and you have not told me?" Mrs. Bennet was horrified.

"I have attempted to, Mrs. Bennet, but you would not listen. You told me it was all nonsense, that they were just spirited girls, and others were jealous of them."

Mrs. Bennet watched the dance as she thought back over quite a few occasions that she had used those exact words. "I do remember now, Mr.

Bennet. I apologize; I thought you were only teasing me—*as usual.* But why have you not corrected their behavior if you have often found fault with it?"

Mr. Bennet's eyebrows shot up as he stared at her in surprise. "I have—many times in fact—but as soon as I did, *you* told them not to pay me any mind and encouraged them to do the opposite. After a while they both stopped listening to me at all and acted any way they pleased. I often retreated to my bookroom only to escape *them.*" He gestured toward the girls in question, who were becoming quite rowdy. "It seems that even after all these years of marriage, you and I have not found an effective way of communicating with each other, Mrs. Bennet. Perhaps we should discuss this subject at length tomorrow?"

She looked at him with surprise as well—was her husband actually taking something she had to say seriously? "I agree that we should, Mr. Bennet."

Just then the music ended, and Mrs. Bennet scurried away to intercept her youngest daughters before they could do any more damage. Mr. Bennet noticed how she had them sit out one dance to watch the other ladies' behavior and then moved closer in time to hear his wife say, "You will behave as if you are *ladies,* or you will be taken home immediately and not permitted into society until you can. Is that clear?"

Both girls were staring at their mother with wide eyes, nodding in agreement. They knew once their mother had her mind made up there would be no convincing her otherwise.

~%~

Elizabeth and William's dance was much different than the one they had shared at the assembly ball. There were no uncomfortable moments, no glares, no stern looks, and no stone mask pushing them apart this time. Every move was synchronized as if they had danced together their entire lives, and it was often noted by those watching that they were the most graceful couple they had ever seen. Their eyes never appeared to leave each other's, and more than one person commented upon the fact that they seemed to move a bit too closely, brushing arms and shoulders as they passed each other. Not many words were exchanged; their eyes spoke a language all their own, rendering conversation unnecessary. Whispers moved through the crowd like a wave—the gist being, "It seems they were created for one another!"

After the first set, William requested the second, but Elizabeth only smiled. When he asked again she responded, "I heard you the first time, sir... I was only trying to puzzle out how to answer you. You could not possibly have meant to ask me to dance again immediately following our last. What would everyone think?"

"I have no interest in what anyone will think. *You* seem to enjoy dancing, and *I* have no wish to see you dance with anyone else!" William said with a smile.

"You will insist on every dance this evening?" Elizabeth laughed.

How he had missed that teasing sparkle in her eyes. "It may be selfish of me, but yes—absolutely; I insist upon it."

"I will grant you the supper dance, sir, but I will not insult my neighbors by ignoring them. I *will* dance with my friends, if they ask me. I always dance the second set with John Lucas—it is a tradition—and I see him coming this way right now."

William felt the need to speak quickly before her old friend encroached, "If you will not oblige me for them all, will you at least agree to grant me the last set of the evening?"

Elizabeth hesitated before saying, "The opening set, the supper set, *and* the closing set? You do know you will be as good as declaring your *intentions* to the entire neighborhood?"

"I have no fear of laying out my intentions for all to see, Elizabeth," he whispered close to her ear as John Lucas was almost within hearing range.

William glared at John over Elizabeth's shoulder as she took a step backwards to see his eyes. "I am thoroughly disappointed to see a scowl upon your face after saying such a thing, Mr. Darcy."

His eyes darted to hers and saw the smile playing with the edges of her lips, and relief flooded him.

With one brow arched, Elizabeth warned, "You will *not* chase away my friends to prevent me from dancing with anyone else. They are only friends, and *they* are all certain of it. *All* of them."

Though he did not look very pleased at the moment, William nodded in reply. Elizabeth turned to make the introductions between her beloved and her oldest friend. When William saw the look in John Lucas's eyes as he looked from Elizabeth to himself and back again, William actually felt sympathy for the gentleman. He had never seen such defeated anguish in another man's eyes—up 'til that moment, he had only seen it in his own reflection when he had thought all hope to win Elizabeth's good opinion had been lost. But sympathy was not enough for William to actually *like* the fact that John Lucas was dancing with the woman who had only just begun to look upon him again with favor.

William could not have known that John Lucas had lost all hope of winning Elizabeth's heart the moment she had returned from Pemberley three years prior. John had tried to be the man to put the sparkle back into her eyes and return the happiness to her laughter, but had failed in the attempt. Here stood the man who had taken those qualities away from her, but he was also the man who was able to return them simply by directing a smile at Elizabeth. John resented William for it all, but above all else, he wanted Elizabeth to be happy; consequently, he was making a valiant attempt to accept the gentleman. He could not help but feel a slight victory as he walked away with Elizabeth on his arm, and he made certain to meet William's gaze whenever their hands touched during the dance.

While William was keeping a very close watch on their set, he heard a familiar voice say, "I see you *have* finally taken my advice, Mr. Darcy, discarding that stern manner of yours earlier this evening."

Turning to see Baron Leisenheimer, he smiled. "Good evening, Baron. I am trying, sir."

"Do not allow it to return the moment Miss Lizzy walks away from you, or else you will lose all the ground you have gained tonight."

"Have I done that, Baron?"

"Well, actually, it is more of a glare this time. I am not sure which *I* prefer, but I think Mr. Lucas would certainly prefer the former! Miss Lizzy *will* be angry at you if you scare away all her dance partners, son."

"I suppose I require practice with showing a *limited* amount of emotions without hiding it *all*. I will attempt to control myself, sir. I thank you for the warning—I did not realize—I just do not like seeing Miss Elizabeth dance with other men."

"Ah, yes, I do understand that—you see my wife dancing just now." He nodded his head in her direction, "I have always felt the same way. But *I* am the only man she looks at in that special way… and I am the man she goes home with at night. I have been watching Miss Lizzy tonight, and she has been looking upon you in much the same manner that Lilias looks upon me. It seems my wife's intuition was correct again, eh, Mr. Darcy?"

William smiled briefly, but then it faded as he said, "Until I am the man Miss Elizabeth goes home with, I will not feel comfortable watching her being led away from me by another."

~%~

Most of the single ladies from London were envious of Elizabeth, but they held no ill will against her. They could not blame the lady for taking advantage of the situation in which she found herself with Mr. Darcy!

The only person in the room truly put out by the occurrences of the evening thus far was Caroline Bingley, who had spoken poorly of the Bennet family at every opportunity to the other ladies of the *ton*.

Louisa Hurst was also slightly upset, but only because she knew she would *never* hear the end of this when in the company of her sister. She spent most of the evening lost in thoughts of planning a long trip with her husband to see his family in the very near future—*without* Caroline.

Caroline was more than a little disappointed when the supper set began, and she saw William claim Elizabeth for another dance, feeling it was *her* right to dance this set and sit with him at dinner since he had been their house guest for such a length of time. *"He is making a fool of himself! It would not matter if it was only the locals, but in front of his peers from the* **ton***, it does! He could never marry Eliza Bennet, so why he wastes his time on that little chit is beyond my comprehension!"*

~%~

Upon walking into the dining hall, Bingley waved Elizabeth and William over and had them sit across from Jane and him. He had arranged around them some friends that he had invited himself. William's good friend Lord Luke Hamilton, who was two years William's senior, was sitting on the opposite side of Elizabeth. William knew they would get along pleasantly, and he had no worries about the man vying for her attention since he was happily married to the lady seated next to him. Lady Augusta Hamilton was a friend to one of the daughters of the Leisenheimers and was occupied in conversation with the Baron and Baroness seated next to her.

Across from the Hamiltons was Peter Barnes. "New money" like Bingley, his family had made their fortune in supplying ammunition to the Army. Barnes had been in Hamilton's year at Cambridge, and the two had become close friends. Barnes had partnered with Charlotte Lucas for supper, and the two seemed to be getting along splendidly.

Next to William were the Reverend James Owen and his wife, Mrs. Elise Owen. Mr. Owen was the fifth son of the Earl of ---, and had been in Bingley's year at Cambridge.

Across from the Owens and next to Bingley was Mr. Christopher Warren. Though Warren's father had been partners with Bingley's family in business, his family's investments were not as large; therefore, he remained in trade, mostly supplying much called for items to the Royal Army and Navy. His supper partner was a friend of Caroline's who, having mistaken Mr. Warren for a gentleman, was highly displeased to discover that he was in trade, and as a result, was engaged in the act of ignoring him.

Caroline and the remainder of the guests that *she* had invited from London were sitting next to this lady and across from them. William felt grateful they were too far from him and Elizabeth to engage them in conversation.

William gave Bingley a slight nod, thanking him for surrounding them with such well-informed, open-minded people. William had only the expectation of entertaining conversation, but he received so much more. As supper progressed, he watched in awe as Elizabeth was able to engage in discourse on any subject. Topics ranged from politics with the Viscount, arms with Barnes, some recent legal issues concerning trade with Warren, and sermon-writing with Owens. With the ladies she was equally at ease, discussing music, literature, housekeeping, servants, and fashion—even the dreaded subject of embroidery came up, which made William chuckle and Elizabeth to look at him conspiratorially.

Lady Augusta Hamilton discovered through the Baroness that she had met Elizabeth several years earlier while visiting at Purvis Lodge during a summer break from the school she had attended with their daughter. "Miss Elizabeth is little Lizzy? No... it cannot be!" She turned to Elizabeth and said, "Miss Elizabeth, I am sorry I did not recognize you sooner!"

"Perhaps you would have, Lady Hamilton, had I been wearing a torn dress, no shoes, some mud smeared on my face, and carrying a snake in my hands!" Elizabeth said with a serious demeanor and a teasing sparkle in her eye.

Lady Augusta laughed. "Yes, I do think that would have helped a little! Was it a snake? I seem to remember a frog!"

"Originally I had brought you a frog, but you were afraid it might really be a toad and that it would give you warts, so I brought you a snake in its stead."

Leaning forward to see William, Lady Hamilton said, "Oh, what a dear child Liz... Miss Elizabeth was, Mr. Darcy! She overheard me say that I missed my pet cat who had passed on while I was away at school that year. One of Miss Elizabeth's cats had recently given birth to kittens, but until one of them was ready to leave its mother, Miss Elizabeth decided that, in order to cheer me, I should have a temporary pet. She worked diligently to find the right match for me, but I was afraid of snakes as well as frogs!" She smiled widely at Elizabeth and said, "I still have Duchess, you know."

Lord Hamilton's eyebrows raised in surprise, "Duchess? She was a gift from Miss Elizabeth?"

His wife answered, "She was indeed. Miss Elizabeth, I must thank you again for helping me with my Italian while I was visiting. My tutor was most impressed when I returned to school. I do not think I ever would have learned the language if not for you."

Elizabeth blushed and was about to answer, but William replied before she could begin speaking, "I know exactly what a 'dear child' Miss Elizabeth was, Lady Hamilton; I have known her since she was nine-years-old and I was fifteen-years-old. Did she try to catch you a badger for a pet?" He said with a mischievous smile... He had spent years wondering about the badger and was hoping to hear more now.

"Actually, I did make an attempt, but I could not manage it. You, sir, know of my stubborn nature—I had to continue to try. It took me about a year to finally catch one." Elizabeth blushed when she noticed everyone within hearing distance was waiting for more. Looking at William she asked, "Did James not tell you?"

William feigned an insulted air. "James is a trusted Darcy footman, trained in the utmost of discretion..." his featured softened, "and a devoted fan of *yours*, Miss Elizabeth. He would never have divulged your secret... no matter *what* Georgiana or I offered or threatened him with! The only hint we ever had of the event was of your own doing." William laughed, attracting the attention of many ladies who had been eager to see his smile again.

Elizabeth matched his dazzling smile with one of her own, but then her features schooled into a very serious expression. "Well... when I *did* catch one it was a good thing James was nearby trying to puzzle out what I was about. The reason this one had been easier to apprehend was that it was a cub. James was very useful when its mother returned to the burrow." Those who were listening could be discerned by whose eyes had widened at this time—since badgers were known to be vicious when their young were threatened, and there were tales of people seeing them kill animals much larger than themselves, including humans. "I had observed quite a few badger clans and mothers with their young from afar, but never had I witnessed one who was protecting her cub before that day. I do believe James saved my life."

William was obviously stunned, and turned to look at James where he was stationed, on loan to Bingley for the ball. James happened to be looking in that direction and met William's gaze—James's face showed a hint of concern, but William waved his question off. He heard Bingley say, "I would wager that James is about to get a raise in pay!"

Barnes replied, "After Darcy's behavior tonight, I do not think anyone would bet against you, Bingley."

William turned to Elizabeth and said, "When I joined you in the garden before dinner that evening, I wondered what you had been doing while I was preparing for dinner. The state of your clothing..."

"Yes, well, I had gone there to calm down before sneaking into the house to change for dinner."

"Reading Plato in Latin and instantaneously translating it into English aloud calms you?" he teased, trying to lighten both their moods.

Elizabeth raised one eyebrow. "Only when being sketched at the same time." She answered, and then looked away blushing and taking a great interest in her wine glass as she remembered seeing that sketch on the floor of the library a few nights earlier.

Several others at the table noticed William's color change as well, but none could suspect the true reason for it.

The topic of conversation moved on to less serious matters until the supper break was at an end and the dancing was to begin again.

~%~

After observing Mr. Darcy's behavior towards Miss Elizabeth Bennet, and knowing that her sister Caroline was beginning to feel quite desperate at the perceived favoritism, Mrs. Hurst had been watching her sister closely all evening. During the interval between dances before the last set of the ball, Mrs. Hurst noticed that Caroline had disappeared from the ballroom. When she saw Caroline return sporting a self-satisfied expression, her sister felt an icy shiver of fear run down her spine. Mrs. Hurst *knew* that look and approached Caroline without delay. In the event that her interference was necessary to save her family's reputation, she knew she must attempt to learn the reason behind such a dramatic change in her sister's countenance from the sneer she had been wearing all evening to the smirk she now sported.

"Caroline?"

"Louisa! You will never guess what I have arranged!" Caroline took her sister's hand and led her to a corner where she was certain they would not be overheard. "I have had such a clever idea! I will prevent Mr. Darcy from dancing again with that *chit* while in the same moment I have practically guaranteed that he will close the ball with *me*! My name will be mentioned in every drawing room in London for weeks to come!"

Mrs. Hurst gave her sister a sympathetic look, thinking that with the news of Mr. Darcy's heart being lost to Miss Elizabeth—which she was certain would be broadcast all over London before the week was out—Caroline's name most likely *would* be mentioned, but not in a way that her sister would enjoy! The *ton* would find it very amusing that, after Caroline had made a fool of herself chasing after the gentleman for years, Mr. Darcy's attachment had been made public at a ball at which Caroline had actually been *hostess*! "If you do not suppose that I can guess what you have done, then I shall not attempt to guess. You had better tell me at once, Caro."

"It is now absolutely impossible for any of these country bumpkins to participate in the final dance of the ball. I have spoken to the musicians—the final dance will be a *waltz*! I am quite certain that none of the locals in attendance would have learnt it since even something as simple as their taste in clothing is so completely out-of-fashion. Once he sees that Eliza is so backward and countrified, Mr. Darcy will realize that an alliance with Eliza would dishonor his good name, and he will finally understand the terrible error he has made *before* it is too late. Only those who have frequented London will know how to dance the waltz, and since *I* am the most eligible lady of fashion here, he will dance the last with *me*!" Caroline ended her speech with a smirk.

"Oh, Caroline! Half of the *most* fashionable set in London either have not yet learnt the waltz or think it is too scandalous a dance to participate in! For all you know, Mr. Darcy is one of the latter! Do you not see, sister? It is more likely that if Miss Elizabeth does not know how to dance the waltz, Mr. Darcy will not blame her. He will refrain from dancing altogether and spend that time with her!"

At her sister's words of disapproval, Caroline shot Mrs. Hurst a sharp look. "Why can you not be happy for me, Louisa? Are you jealous?"

"No, Caroline, at the moment my feelings could be considered *far* from being jealous of you! Up until this night I have supported you in this endeavor, but honestly now I am beginning to pity you! Tonight Mr. Darcy has openly displayed his feelings for Miss Elizabeth before the entire neighborhood and all of the people that we have invited from London. With so much proof before you, how can you continue to delude yourself by believing that you still have even the smallest chance to win Mr. Darcy's affections?

"You must face the facts, sister—you will *never* be Mistress of Pemberley. You will gain more favor among the *ton* if you abandon this useless quest and display no scorn whatsoever towards Miss Elizabeth! It would be better to be among those in good standing with the future Mrs. Darcy than to be named among her enemies if you ever wish to be invited to Darcy House or Pemberley again!"

Caroline cast an ice stare upon her sister, "Then *you* should attempt to stay in *my* good graces, Louisa, instead of throwing insults my way. Pity, indeed! Before long it will be *proven* that *I* will be the next Mrs. Darcy!"

Mrs. Hurst shook her head as she watched Caroline stomp off towards Mr. Darcy who was deep in conversation with Miss Elizabeth Bennet. Yes, a visit to see Mr. Hurst's family seemed more attractive every moment! Perhaps they would depart on the morrow!

~%~

When the first dance of the last set of the evening ended and the music for the second dance began, William's heart accelerated even more than it already had from having had the honor of the previous dance with his beloved. He had dreamed of dancing the waltz with Elizabeth so many times over the past three years that he thought he was imagining the music at first, but then when he noticed that many of the dancers were leaving the floor and those who remained paired off, he realized that this was no dream, and he smiled widely. Too affected to speak, he simply stared into Elizabeth's eyes, which were already dancing—with amusement.

"Can you not dance the waltz, Mr. Darcy?"

"Georgiana's dance master insisted she learn it, and *I* insisted on being her partner when she practiced. I…" William swallowed hard, afraid that even *suggesting* they waltz might offend her.

"Sir? Do you fear that Mrs. Bennet of Longbourn, who, as you well know, has spent almost every waking moment of every day since her fifth daughter was born teaching her daughters how to *catch a husband*, would *not* have had them learn the latest fashions in dancing?" Elizabeth took a step closer to him, her eyes twinkling with a teasing light and something deeper—was it longing?

"I have often hoped you would favor me with a waltz someday, my love," William almost whispered.

"And I have often wondered what it would be like to dance the waltz with someone other than my sisters!" she laughed, hoping the statement served to convey to him that she had never danced a waltz with any man.

Elizabeth waited patiently for several moments as William continued to gaze at her lovingly. "Since you felt it was my task to propose, must I ask you to dance as well, William?"

He smiled and then replied without hesitation, "I accept!"

William took Elizabeth into his arms, leaving the proper distance between them. The very air between their bodies seemed to be tingling with life—both were very conscious of the points where their bodies met and of a pulling sensation emanating from the other. His eyes never leaving hers, William's arm twitched with the need to draw Elizabeth closer to him.

Without either being aware of it, the couple slowly drifted closer to each other as they twirled about the dance floor. When the music came to an end, they stopped dancing but continued standing in the same position, so close that their bodies were almost touching. William almost moved the additional few inches that would have been necessary to pull her against his frame, but the sound of the crowd applauding the musicians' efforts brought him back to the present.

In his dreams, the waltz with Elizabeth had *never* ended on the dance floor—the couple always quickly reconvened in his bed chamber! Even if William had not blushed at the direction his thoughts had turned, the smoldering look in his eyes would have given him away. Elizabeth could do nothing but return the gaze at the same level of intensity, causing his heart to skip a beat and a pleasant shiver to run through him.

He closed his eyes for a moment or two to break this intoxicating exchange, and then took a step backward, away from his enchantress.

"One day soon, I will count on the *gentleman's* complete retreat, my love. I would like to meet the man." Elizabeth gifted him with a look that he hoped to see again on their wedding night.

William sharply caught his breath. "I look forward to his introduction, Elizabeth!" he answered while placing her hand in the crook of his arm and covering it possessively with his own.

He had to look away from her! If she continued to look at him in that beguiling manner, he would not be able to prevent himself from whisking her away to his chamber after all. Mr. Bennet would have to break down his bedchamber door to retrieve his daughter this night!

As William looked about the room for something to cool this almost overwhelming desire for Elizabeth, his eyes met with the perfect sight—Caroline Bingley. William could not help but notice that she seemed to be in a complete rage; the crimson coloring of her skin had heightened to the point where its tone clashed quite horribly with her gown of bright orange silk. He saw that Mr. and Mrs. Hurst were attempting to physically remove her from the ballroom.

William wondered what could have happened to arouse her to such a state, but since he saw Bingley was still accompanying Miss Bennet, William was certain that he would be summoned if needed. As it was, he felt it could wait until he could inquire from Bingley *after* the guests had departed. He refused to miss one moment he could spend with Elizabeth this night!

~%~

After the waltz, those gathered began to call for their carriages to leave the ball. William held Elizabeth back for a moment to avoid the crush of the crowd. When she was sure nobody was within hearing distance, she looked up into his eyes and said low enough for only William to hear, "Your father was correct."

"He often was… but do you refer to something in particular?"

"I have been thinking… my stubbornness is not always a gift."

William chuckled, "And what makes you change your mind about that subject just now?"

She was thoughtful for a minute or two before asking, "Had I not been so afraid to show my feelings to you when you first came into Hertfordshire, would you have behaved more like *this* rather than the way that you did?"

His smile faded, but due to the implications of her statement—that she had loved him all along—the light did not fade from his eyes. He took her hand and led her outside to a terrace where they could have a few words in privacy. "Not exactly. I needed to learn a few lessons first… which I might not have learned if you had been more transparent. *I* am still of the opinion that a stubborn streak is a gift. Look at where I am right now, Elizabeth. I have spent the evening at a ball, in a house full of people, and I was not afraid to let every single person in attendance know my feelings for you.

"As I have told you, somehow your presence—even at our first meeting— has always prevented me from needing it, but all my life I have hidden behind a stone façade when in public. When I came to Hertfordshire, the fear that I had lost your good opinion forever had only made it more unyielding, but over the past few days I put my *own* stubborn will into motion after deciding that the only way I could ever expect to reverse the widely held poor opinion of me was to rid myself of what Bingley and Richard refer to as my 'mask' once and for all.

"However grateful I am for your most recent behavior," he smiled, "it was not the reason for the change in mine… though it *was* the goal. I wish only to make you happy, my Elizabeth, and improving the opinion of me held by the people that you love will help to do that, I am certain.

"Perhaps if you had smiled instead of glared at me at all this while, I would not have learned that I should never be ashamed to be myself. You tried to teach me this lesson years ago by setting an example, and your father also tried by pointing out that I found this quality admirable in you, but it took me all this time to actually learn it, and only at the risk of losing the only thing that mattered to me.

"The only thing that truly matters to me is your caring for me, Elizabeth. If I lost all else, I would survive, but I have long known that I could not go on without you. I have lived these last few years with the hope of being with you someday, and that hope was the only thing that gave me the motivation to get up every morning and do what needed to be done—so I that could be the man you wanted and needed, and could be proud of, and so that I would be able to provide for you the best that I could.

"My feelings for you have never changed, not in all the time we were apart nor since I have been staying at Netherfield, no matter what I seemed overtly to have been feeling. In fact, they are stronger than ever. Every time I think I could not possibly love you more, you do something to bring about just that.

"I was able to make an appointment with your father for tomorrow afternoon, and I will ask for his consent. I am certain we will speak of all that has occurred to keep me away for so long. I would very much like for you to be present at our meeting."

Elizabeth was looking at him with such love shining from her eyes that he could not help but to wish for a more intimate setting. As William's hand reached out to caress her cheek, the sound of the door to the terrace opening startled him back to reality, and he pulled it back. Mr. Bennet stepped out and sent a warning glance to William while saying, "Lizzy, it is time to go home."

William watched as she took her father's arm and walked away from him. At the doorway, she paused and looked back over her shoulder at him, a smile gracing her beautiful face. *"Soon **I** will be the man who carries her home—to* **our** *home."*

Chapter 19

The following day… somewhere along the coast of England

"It is all so strange!" Colonel Richard Fitzwilliam thought as he prepared his mount to ride to London. There was a mystery afoot, and now that his latest mission was completed, he was eager to solve it.

Richard's cousin William Darcy had written to him several times since he had joined his friend Bingley at an estate in Hertfordshire, begging Richard's advice on what to do about his sister Georgiana and keeping him abreast of the situation with Miss Elizabeth Bennet. Since William's arrival in Hertfordshire, he had not heard from Georgiana at all, and William assumed that the reason his sister had not written was that she must be angry at him for remaining in the neighborhood in which Miss Bennet lived.

Richard had originally thought that it would be very odd indeed if William's reasoning had been true. Though William had no knowledge of it, a few months ago when William and Richard had seen Miss Bennet in London, Georgiana was only too happy to provide Richard with the information necessary to locate Miss Bennet.

Richard had heard from Georgiana several times during that time period as well, and she had not said a word about her brother's news beyond informing him that William had gone to Hertfordshire. She *had* mentioned that she was hopeful that William would seek out Miss Bennet while he resided in the same county!

So then, why in the deuce had Georgiana not been writing to William?

The nature of Richard's assignment had kept him from being able to write letters to his cousins, but he could always find time to read theirs. The only letter he had managed to write, with great difficulty, had been a short, extremely sloppy note to William stating that Richard *had* heard from Georgiana several times and that she was well.

Fortunately, Richard was waiting for some urgent papers that he would deliver to his general in London, and he had not yet left for London when a letter from a panicked Georgiana arrived. In the letter Georgiana declared that she had not heard a word from William since he had left Pemberley for his friend's estate! She had attempted to remain calm about the situation, but suddenly found that she could no longer do so, and was writing to Richard to inquire as to what she should do next.

Richard answered Georgiana's letter immediately, sending his response by express. His letter stated that *he* had heard from William several times while he had been staying at Netherfield Park, and that William's letters were full of concern for Georgiana because he had not heard from her! Richard also told Georgiana that because he was now between assignments, he had some leave time available, and he would make haste to Hertfordshire to discover the problem with the post service after a short stop in London to see his parents. Unless she heard differently from him, she should not worry—William was well.

After sending the express, the urgent military correspondence arrived and Richard departed for London. Richard arrived at the home of his parents when both were out, so he bathed and then headed for his father's study. While in the army, he had learned to take advantage of any opportunity to rest since one never knew when the next chance to do so would come about, and so he lay down for a nap on his favorite comfortable sofa while he waited for his father to return. Being a light sleeper he thought he would awake when his father entered the room. The sofa was turned away from his father's desk, facing the fire.

Soon after Richard had fallen asleep, the Earl of Matlock entered his study so quietly that Richard did not hear him, but he did, however, hear the knock of the footman several minutes later.

Exhausted, Richard did not react right away; instead, he continued to lie on the sofa. He had to smile as he remembered the times in his childhood when he, his brother and his sister used to hide on the overstuffed sofa and spy on their father as he worked. He doubted his father had ever discovered their trick as the boys had never been on the receiving end of the strap because of it. Richard held back a chuckle.

The footman entered and told the earl, "M'lord, I received a letter from Mr. Booth, the post worker in Lambton. Your nephew Mr. Darcy is sending letters from Hertfordshire, and since his instructions have always been to stop *all* letters between Hertfordshire and Pemberley, he wishes to know whether he should let Mr. and Miss Darcy's letters through or not. He has not burned them as he has all the others."

The earl answered, "What is Fitzwilliam doing in Hertfordshire?" He hesitated for a few moments while deciding what the next course of action should be, and then said, "Inform him that he should forward by express to *you* all of Fitzwilliam's and Georgiana's letters to each other, but continue to burn any letters between them and the Bennets! When their letters arrive, bring them to me immediately. I must discern exactly why Fitzwilliam is there, and who he is spending his time with. If he has seen the Bennets, all of my plans may be ruined!"

Richard became livid while listening to this exchange, his exhaustion forgotten. When the footman left the room, Richard stood from the sofa and boomed in his best commanding-officer voice, "Father! How *could* you? Good G-d! If I had not heard it with my own ears, I would never have believed you capable of such a thing! Do you have any *notion* or *understanding* of the pain you have caused with this scheme? Do you have no remorse for the suffering you have brought, not only to the Bennets, but to your own flesh and blood, William and Georgiana—and to anyone who cares about them, including *me?*"

The earl, startled at first at his younger son's presence, became almost frightened by Richard's tone of voice. He had never seen his son in all his military glory! Having learned throughout the years that the best defense is a good offense, the earl attempted to take control of the situation by speaking forcefully. "How *dare* you to speak to me in that manner and tone of voice? You *will* speak to me with the respect owed to me as both your father and as the Earl of Matlock!"

"Respect?! How dare *you* speak of respect! Respect is *earned*, not *owed*, and after *this* any shred of respect for you that had been remaining is gone forever."

"You condemn me for protecting my family from the Bennets—a pair of mercenary, social climbing nobodies with no fortune and no connections? Thomas Bennet always had his eye on gaining control of Pemberley, and George Darcy had *always* trusted him. Can you imagine that George snubbed *my* friendship while welcoming Bennet's? He would have simply handed the estate over to Bennet when he died if not for the actions of Catherine and me. I was kept up to date during the whole of their visit by a servant at Pemberley—you know not what went on there! Bennet's machinations included using his *harlot* of a daughter's arts and allurements to trap William! The nerve of that girl and her father for thinking *she* could ever become mistress of Pemberley!

"Catherine and I conferred and agreed that the best solution was to keep the Bennets from contacting William and Georgiana—having it *appear* that they had been abandoned by the mercenary leeches. For the past three years, the Darcys have been released from the Bennets' unexplained hold on them! I am certain this has brought William closer to the realization that he should rely *only* on family. Eventually he will learn to appreciate his duty and, for the good of the entire family, he *will* marry his cousin Anne!"

Richard's rage only grew with every word his father uttered. "You will *not* speak of the Bennets in such a way! The Darcys trusted and cared for the Bennets, and I will not allow you to insult them any further in my presence. I happened to have met Miss Elizabeth Bennet, and I know she does *not* resemble in the slightest way the woman you have painted her as today. The Darcys are intelligent people and have a much better sense than you of the characteristics that are truly worthy in others.

"It astonishes me that you have resorted to blackmail and trickery in an attempt to gain favor with William and Georgiana. Did you really think that by taking the Bennets out of their lives that William and Georgiana would suddenly trust *you*? They have good reason *not* to trust you, sir!

"I have never been more *ashamed* of anything in my life than I am at this moment… ashamed to be *your* son! Good bye, sir; I do not know when— or *if*—I will see you again." Richard left the house without heeding his father's shouted demands to return.

~%~

Richard rode directly to Darcy House to speak to the housekeeper and gain knowledge of the directions to Netherfield. After the housekeeper had instructed the kitchen workers to pack saddlebags for him, he asked to see her in Darcy's library. "Mrs. Martin, I am acting as Miss Darcy's guardian in this matter. I know very well how valued you are by the Darcys and how much affection you hold for them personally. I implore you not to give any information on your master's whereabouts to anyone else at this time, especially not my father nor our Aunt de Bourgh. They are not to be trusted!"

Mrs. Martin allowed a shocked look to pass across her face before schooling her features. She had known Richard Fitzwilliam for most of his life and knew what kind of man he was, and had always found that she could trust his word over that of his father any day. "Yes, Colonel Fitzwilliam. I understand completely, sir."

"I am sending an express to Mrs. Reynolds. I will need you to address it and be sure that it leaves here immediately. You are also to remain vigilant—especially when Miss Darcy returns to town. Under *no* circumstances, whatsoever, are my father or Lady Catherine de Bourgh to be allowed entrance to this house, or indeed any of the Darcy properties. The results if they get close to Miss Darcy would be disastrous. In the absence of Mr. Darcy to give these instructions, I take the liberty of doing so on his behalf—you must be scrupulous until you hear directly from Mr. Darcy or myself.

"As soon as I can be ready I will be travelling to Netherfield to speak to Mr. Darcy and then straight on to Pemberley. I trust that you understand my instructions completely."

~%~

As soon as Richard rode into Netherfield's stables, he dismounted, ordered his horse to be fed and watered, and asked that the Darcy carriage be readied to leave as soon as possible. When he encountered Bingley's butler, he asked that he not be announced to the family, but only to Mr. Darcy. Mr. Robinson, being a soldier himself in the past, and acquainted with Colonel Fitzwilliam, knew that the man would not be visibly upset without good reason. Mr. Robinson asked the Colonel to follow him, and led him to the library where Mr. Darcy was alone.

William looked up when the door opened, and his eyes widened in astonishment. He launched himself out of his seat at seeing Richard's agitated countenance, assuming something was wrong with Georgiana. As soon as the door closed, Richard said, "I can see what you are thinking. Do not worry; Georgiana is fine... for the moment anyway. We must away to the Bennet's estate immediately! I must speak to you, Mr. Bennet, and Miss Elizabeth Bennet all together directly and for as short a duration as possible!

"I know that the Bennets are of the opinion that you abandoned *them* and that *you* think Mr. Bennet abandoned you... but none of it is so! It was intended to seem that way *by design*, Darcy!

"I wish that Georgiana were here to hear this as well. I plan to leave here and ride for Pemberley as soon as we are finished with our conference, William. You will need to stay here and clean up the mess on this end!"

"Richard, what do you mean by saying that Georgiana is well *for the moment*? You cannot say that and expect not to explain further!"

"I know your curiosity is piqued, but please be patient, Cousin... Georgiana is safe for now, and I do not wish to tell this tale more times than is absolutely necessary; it is far too humiliating! Come, I have ordered your carriage; I will tell all of you together."

William nodded and followed Richard from the room and out the door to the waiting carriage, hesitating for just a moment at the door to tell the butler where they were headed.

After the gentlemen entered the carriage, William asked, "Do you have word about when Wickham will be transferred?"

"It is certain he *will* be transferred, but these things take time. I hope it will be within the next few days." Richard raised his eyebrows and asked, "Have there been any improvements in your situation since your last letter?"

A slow smile spread across William's features and shone from his eyes... a smile brighter than any Richard had ever seen grace his cousin's face. "The situation is greatly improved indeed, Richard! Elizabeth and I have come to an understanding! Though I have not had a chance to speak to Mr. Bennet as of yet, I have an appointment scheduled with him for this afternoon. I was just about to order the carriage when you came in."

Richard could not help but smile as a sense of relief filled him, and he wished Georgiana could be here to see her brother's joy at this moment.

~%~

Elizabeth was reading in her father's study, when Mrs. Hill announced that two gentlemen would like to see Mr. Bennet. Mr. Bennet glanced at his daughter, then back to Mrs. Hill, "And just who are these gentlemen?"

"Mr. Darcy and Colonel Fitzwilliam, sir."

Elizabeth seemed surprised that Colonel Fitzwilliam had accompanied William to this meeting. "Show them in, Hill," said Mr. Bennet.

Elizabeth stood, smoothing the wrinkles from her skirts to hide her nervousness at meeting a member of William's extended family, and after William made the introductions, she finally looked up. When she saw Richard, she arched her eyebrow and crossed her arms over her chest.

"Ah! I forgot about this part!" Richard said while taking a step away from William.

"You forgot about greetings and introductions?" William asked.

"No, Mr. Darcy, he means he forgot about being *caught out*, did you not Colonel *Richards*?" Elizabeth said, with more curiosity in her voice than anger.

Richard took another step away from his cousin and blushed. "Well... hmmm... yes. That misunderstanding was not entirely my fault, Miss Bennet. I hesitated in the middle of introducing myself, and your aunt took my first name as my last."

"And it would have been so very difficult to correct her, would it not?"

"Yes, well... but you would have recognized 'Fitzwilliam.' That would have been..."

Elizabeth interrupted, "Perhaps the word you are searching for is 'honest,' sir?"

William, fuming by this time, took a step closer to Richard.

Refusing to look at William, Richard replied, "Er... counterproductive!" Richard moved a step further away from William once again.

Mr. Bennet was losing all patience by this time. "*What* is going on here?"

"Well, Papa, last year I came across Colonel *Fitzwilliam* in the park across from Aunt and Uncle Gardiner's house in London."

"And a good thing that was, too. I seem to remember that you were in the process of fainting at the time, Miss Bennet."

Elizabeth blushed. She glanced at William, and, noting that his expression was a mixture of anger and confusion, she hoped those feelings were directed at his cousin rather than at her. "Yes, that is true. Colonel Fitzwilliam did render me a service that day and escorted me home; he then introduced himself to Aunt Gardiner. But just *what* were you doing there, sir?"

"Well, to be *honest*, Miss Bennet, I wanted to meet you... a lady that I had heard much about."

"And just how did you find out where I was staying, Colonel?"

"Georgiana knew your uncle's name and the name of his shop. The rest was... well, I am very good at interrogation. Most people do not even realize that I have obtained the information for which I was seeking."

"Georgiana was a party to this scheme?" William spoke, confusion coloring his voice.

"Yes," Richard said as silence descended over the room for a few moments.

"Since you had 'forgotten about this part,' Richard, then I assume you had another reason for insisting that you come along with me to visit Longbourn today?" William asked.

At first relieved to change the subject, Richard now realized the next piece of information would be even more of a shock to everyone in the room. "Yes! I think you should all sit down since *this* part is a bit more involved. I came from London after a very short visit at my father's house, where I accidentally overheard a conversation and then gleaned information that you all need to know."

"And just who is your father, Colonel?" Mr. Bennet asked.

"My father is Lord Robert Fitzwilliam, Earl of Matlock."

Mr. Bennet's look darkened, and he sat up straighter. "Go on."

Richard stood with both hands behind his back pacing the length of the room, speaking as if he were giving a military report. "One of my father's servants has been blackmailing a postal employee, but in truth the earl and his sister Lady Catherine de Bourgh are responsible. The postal employee's assignment was to confiscate and destroy all correspondence between anyone by the name of Bennet and Darcy, and between any location in Hertfordshire and the estate of Pemberley. For approximately two and one half years, all correspondence that any of the people in this room, as well as my cousin Georgiana, have sent to any of the others was *not* received by the intended addressee. I do not know for certain but can guess that similar steps were taken for Darcy House in London."

Everyone in the room was stunned for several minutes as the meaning of what had been revealed took shape. Elizabeth whispered, "What does the earl say were his reasons for this interference?"

"I refuse to insult any of the good people present by repeating his ridiculous excuses. Suffice it to say that they did *not* succeed in their ultimate goals of gaining control over Pemberley and having Darcy marry our cousin Anne de Bourgh. I am thoroughly ashamed of my father's actions, and those of our aunt as well. I will have to apologize for them, for *they* will never recognize the wrongs they have committed nor apologize themselves. I have left my father's house." He hesitated a few moments before continuing, "It seems that your letters, William, from Hertfordshire to Georgiana at Pemberley, and her letters to you, had confused the postal employee. When he saw *your* name on letters coming from Hertfordshire and letters from Georgiana going to you *in* Hertfordshire, he held them all and wrote to his contact—the earl's footman—to request further instructions. I originally overheard the footman informing my father of this development. I then confronted my father."

Elizabeth gasped, "Do you mean to say that Mr. Darcy has been here for weeks and Georgiana does not even know that he arrived here safely? She must be panicked!"

William, dazed by all the implications of what had been revealed, had jumped from his seat and began pacing upon Elizabeth's exclamation.

"Yes, it would seem so, Miss Bennet. I received a letter from Georgiana just this morning in which she voiced her concerns for her brother. Since *I* had received letters from William, I sent a letter by express from my location this morning after completing my mission, minutes before I was about to leave for London. It was pure luck that I stopped at Matlock House in time for that conversation, eh? We might never have known…"

"I should—" William began.

Richard interrupted with, "*I* will go to Pemberley, cousin. There is much that needs to be sorted out *here*. Since I have the name of the postal worker, I will take care of *him* as well. William, it seems there was a servant who had informed the earl of certain…" he glanced at Elizabeth, "*developments* in the weeks leading up to your father's death, which led them to these despicable actions. As far as I know, the flow of information stopped at about the same time that your father died, which makes me think that either it was one of the staff members who also died in the carriage accident or it was a servant who was let go about the same time."

Mr. Bennet finally found his voice. "Carriage accident? But I thought his condition…"

William swallowed hard. "No, his condition never had a chance to take hold, sir. The accident was the same day that you left Pemberley. Mr. Wickham and a stable boy died that same day. My father died from his injuries the following day, Mr. Bennet."

"The timing of it explains why we never saw an obituary. With the heavy rains, it took longer to travel home than it should have since we were detoured off the main roads. We stayed at rustic, out of the way inns… Lizzy and I had not seen a newspaper for some time…" Mr. Bennet's face drained of all color as all that had been said caught up to his awareness. "Wickham, too?"

William nodded.

Richard cleared his throat. "I am sorry, but I must interrupt. I need to know if anyone has any further questions for me. The reason I am going in my cousin's stead is so that you all can discuss these matters while I am on my way to Georgiana."

Richard looked at each one of them in turn, and they all shook their heads to indicate they had no further questions for him. He saw that Elizabeth's eyes were filled to the rim with tears, and he walked over to her, bowed deeply over her hand, and whispered, "Years ago, my uncle wrote to me saying that you would make a wonderful mistress of Pemberley, Miss Bennet."

"Safe journey, Colonel Richards," she said softly, the corners of her lips slightly upturned.

"Ah, good. She forgives me."

Turning to the gentlemen, Richard again bowed, saying, "I will send a messenger directly from Pemberley's staff to bring you news of my arrival. I suggest you wait for him to arrive and send any return letters back with him. Do *not* send anything to Pemberley through the post until all this is straightened out. Good day to you all."

As the door closed behind Richard, William took a step closer to Elizabeth and handed her his handkerchief, which she took with a trembling hand. She was unable to meet his eyes just yet.

Mr. Bennet voice was rough when he said, "George never had a chance to show you anything. Wickham was gone, and I was unreachable. I know how that is, on quite a lesser scale—my elder brother died, and I inherited Longbourn, a much smaller estate, without being prepared. As difficult as it was for me, *I* had an experienced steward to assist me. Whatever did you do?"

William pried his eyes from Elizabeth and looked at Mr. Bennet. "I did what I had to do, sir; I learned by trial and error... mostly *errors* at first. My father had told me that no matter what happened, I should not take advice from my uncle, and so I did not, but the earl descended on Pemberley the day my father died and Lady Catherine arrived two days later. It was not easy, sir; they stayed for months, ordering the staff around and attempting to disrupt the routines at Pemberley. My uncle even rode out to the tenants and changed my father's orders; I did not discover *that* until later. While under my own roof, Lady Catherine spent every available moment trying to convince me to allow her to have Georgiana return with her to Rosings Park so she could rear her there, terrifying my sister into believing she would be taken from her home. What I did *not* know until months later was that she also had a lawyer in London attempting to legally change Georgiana's guardianship to include her daughter, Anne de Bourgh, so that they would have the right to take her from me if I did not marry Anne. When I could not stand any more, my staff physically removed both my aunt and uncle from the property, and they were told in no uncertain terms not to allow them to return.

"My solicitor assisted me in finding both a steward and a secretary, and the three of us eventually muddled through it all. I was just beginning to feel comfortable leaving Pemberley for a short time when..." he stopped, trying to decide whether to speak about the fire and his injuries, but he realized he had gone too far to conceal it... "there was a fire at Pemberley in mid-May of the following year. The servant's quarters and guest wing were destroyed, and both have since been rebuilt. I could not leave." He paused again, looking down at the floor, trying to swallow past the tightness in his throat so he could continue.

Mr. Bennet asked, "Was anyone lost?"

William's voice was just above a whisper as he said, "No, sir. There were several minor injuries that have since healed. There was one person with a significant injury..." hesitating, he looked to Elizabeth for strength and he continued, "...it has taken all this time to recover the use of my arm and hand." Seeing Mr. Bennet start and wishing to change the subject before he asked any more questions about his injuries, William said more forcefully, "I have to admit that when we received no answers to our letters to Longbourn, I had some very uncharitable thoughts about you, Mr. Bennet. I should have known better.

"After a few weeks without your arrival at Pemberley as promised, I had an investigator come here to Longbourn to make certain that you had arrived home safely at least. Knowing the damage to some of the roads and bridges from the rains and that you had left the same day as my father's accident... when we received no letter stating that you had arrived at home, Georgiana and I were more than a little concerned that a fate similar to my father's had befallen you both." He visibly shuddered and then said, "But I told him not to contact you. If you both *were* safe then the only logical conclusion I could come to was that you must have been angry at *me* because of..." he glanced at Elizabeth, and then back to Mr. Bennet and continued, "Well, I thought you wanted nothing further to do with me, Mr. Bennet. I became quite bitter and resentful toward you... blaming you for not honoring any of your promises. I apologize for thinking such things. If I had only sent a letter with the investigator..."

Mr. Bennet interrupted, "I do not blame you in the least, William. I must say that I was not holding you or your father in very high esteem after our letters went unanswered. In hindsight, it seems that I should have traveled the distance to Pemberley to see for myself whether all was well, but at the time that did not seem to be a wise course of action. The letter I had written to your father when we arrived home... well, I took the lack of an answer as if it *were* your father's answer to a very important question, and I assumed that he wished to cut off all contact between our families. I felt insulted personally and assumed that my daughter had been misused and discarded. If that had been the case, it would have explained the reason for Elizabeth's letters to Georgiana going unanswered as well. But, I am still confused about one point. You say you wrote upon your father's death?"

"Yes, sir. Actually, I wrote while Father was still alive…he asked me to pass on messages to you both. He knew he would not survive long."

"But then, why did we not receive *that* letter if your uncle did not arrive until the next day?"

Elizabeth's face lit up and she exclaimed, "The fire at the postal sorting station! Remember, Papa? We heard of poor Mr. Jaresberry's death a few days after we arrived home and that many of the letters that were at the sorting station were lost. We sent another set of letters just in case ours were among them. The news of a fire at a *local* sorting station would not have reached as far as Derbyshire. If the letter from Pemberley had been lost in the fire…" Elizabeth's throat tightened with emotion, and she knew that she could not discuss any more of this without breaking down into sobs. She got up and rushed from the room and from the house. William left his seat and moved toward the door, but stopped and looked at Mr. Bennet, desperately seeking permission to go after her.

"Just a moment, William. The letter I had sent to your father upon our return to Longbourn included my consent to an immediate engagement. I had recognized my error in insisting that you wait." He pointed out the window and said, "There she goes… go after her. If you still wish to gain it, you have my consent."

"Did Elizabeth know what was in the letter, sir?"

"Lizzy did not know at first. After months of increasing melancholy which she failed to hide for long from those who love her best, I told her. When you did not come to see her on her birthday, Lizzy's state of mind became much worse, and I thought perhaps it would be helpful if I told her in no uncertain terms that she had been rejected. It did not help, not in the least—another of my mistakes. The only event that breathed a spark of life back into her was *your* entry in the neighborhood," Mr. Bennet smiled a little, "and Lizzy became quite ornery!"

"Mr. Bennet, even after *everything* that had happened between us, the hope that somehow some day Elizabeth would become my wife was the *only* thing that got me through all that has occurred. I have never stopped loving her, sir." William said.

"Then go, son! Do not waste any more of your time with me. I suggest that you head toward Oakham Mount since that is most likely Lizzy's destination."

William rushed out the door of the study, leaving the door open in his haste. Mr. Bennet crossed the room to close it and saw Jane and William collide in the hall. "Excuse me, Miss Bennet," William said while executing a sloppy bow; then he turned and hurried out the front door, leaving that open as well.

Jane had a concerned look on her face when she moved to close it and noticed her father in the hall. Approaching him she asked, "Father, whatever is the matter with Mr. Darcy?" But Mr. Bennet only waved Jane into the study. He pulled her to the window, and Jane inhaled sharply, surprised to see William *running* in the direction that Elizabeth had gone.

"My dear Jane, mark my words, Lizzy finally will be publicly engaged before the day is out."

"Papa! Mr. Darcy has explained? You would consent?"

Mr. Bennet chuckled. "Jane, *you* were the only one who was correct in your estimation of the situation. No matter what Lizzy or I said, *you* had always believed it to be a terrible misunderstanding—and though the circumstances were initiated and maintained by those who were set against us all, it truly *was* only a terrible misunderstanding between the Bennet and the Darcy families! After all has been explained, there is no ill will left between us… only the guilt of having entertained thoughts that such deplorable behavior had been possible coming from the other."

William stopped to catch his breath, frantically trying to detect some indication of which way Elizabeth had gone. Through some trees he saw a flash of color and hurried off in that direction. Moving through a gap between some bushes, he saw her sitting on a fallen log, her face buried in her hands. He said a silent prayer of thanks—the log was so well hidden from the public path that if he had not seen her walking toward it, he never would have found her there. It was a chilly autumn afternoon, and in her haste, Elizabeth had not thought to take a wrap, so he took off his own coat and placed it around her shoulders.

Elizabeth, not have heard his approach, startled momentarily, but he saw her take a deep breath as she moved her hands from her face to the lapels of the coat, pulling it closer around her and burying her face in the cloth. She breathed deeply, as if taking in his scent, which made his heart skip a beat. Elizabeth opened her eyes and looked intensely into his.

"Elizabeth..." he said, still breathing heavily from his run... or was it something else now? "What is it? I..." he hesitated when she moved to stand and then began to pace in front of him.

"Your family disapproves of me so much that they would stoop to blackmail and deception to keep us apart. They will surely break with you if you marry me. How can I do this to you, William? If I am that much of an embarrassment, with what will you have to contend from the remainder of society?"

Panicked, William answered, "Elizabeth, do not let their despicable actions sway you! Only out of respect for my mother's memory have I ever had anything to do with her family. Even *she* did not enjoy spending time with them, and my father certainly did not. They did not approve even of *him* at first; though he was of the first circle, he had no title, and he was not the man they had chosen for my mother to marry.

"My uncle, who was already the head of the family at that time, had agreed to the marriage only after my mother told him she would elope to Scotland with my father if he would not consent, and the Fitzwilliams could not risk a scandal after the whispers of my Aunt Catherine's son, Anne's older brother who had died a few years after he was born. It was said that he was not Sir Lewis de Bough's child. There was also some rather disgusting gossip about my Uncle Robert circulating, which I refuse to repeat to a lady.

"Their reason for not approving of *you* is because you are not Anne de Bourgh, who they had always intended for me to marry. Anne and I agreed years ago, long before I ever thought of marrying you, that we would not marry each other—but no matter how many times Anne and I have told Aunt Catherine and Uncle Robert, they would not give the plan up. You heard what I said in your father's study relating to what they were trying to do to Georgiana after my father died? They are so arrogant that they thought they could just order Anne to take Georgiana from me if they were successful. Even though Anne would not have followed their wishes, I still could not allow them to take Georgiana's guardianship from me, and so I hired the best lawyers to have the suit dismissed.

"Does that sound like a family that I will *regret* breaking with, Elizabeth, especially after hearing what they have done to *us*? Even if you refuse to marry me—and I beg that you do not refuse—I would no longer consider myself part of their family for what they have done.

"As for the rest of society—Elizabeth! I have told you how much I despise them! The good people whom I respect will welcome you; the others—I could not care less about their opinions of us. Georgiana feels the same... we were reared to be true to our own morals and instincts and not to follow the *ton* blindly. If I spent the rest of my life avoiding most of the society of the first circle, I would consider myself lucky! As for Georgiana, I do not wish her to marry anyone who would snub her because I had married a woman as magnificent as you are, and I know she felt the same way the last time we spoke of it."

His tone of voice turned desperate as he said, "Elizabeth, my love... do *not* allow these people to take you from me yet again. I honestly do not believe I could survive it!"

She stepped into his arms and whispered, "I do not believe I could either, William. I love you too much."

After a few minutes of reveling in the feel of his beloved in his arms, William said, "Your father has consented to our marriage, and I do not think he will force us to wait any longer than it takes for the banns to be read."

Elizabeth pulled back far enough to look into his eyes and smiled so brightly he thought his heart would burst. "Papa has consented? Truly?"

"He did... as I left the room to follow you." His smile widened. "I did not even ask for his consent! Then again, I did not ask for it when he refused his consent at Pemberley, either."

"I do not understand."

"At Pemberley, after witnessing my proposal during the fever weeks earlier, he had guessed that you had finally accepted me by our behavior at dinner that night. I never had an opportunity to request his consent; he refused it immediately upon my entering the study after we separated. Just now, after you ran out of the room, he told me that the first letter he wrote to my father upon your return to Longbourn had contained his consent... and that if we both continued to wish for it, we had it."

Her eyes widened and she joyfully exclaimed, "Ohhh!"

His breathing quickened again as he watched her with intense fascination— Elizabeth reached down inside the neckline of her dress with one hand while the other was fidgeting with her dress on the outside. She was doing... something. A little part of him knew as a gentleman he should turn his back, but after all, he was also a man, and she had not requested that he do so. What could it be that she was working at so diligently? He had not a clue, but William was quite enthralled. After a minute or so, she pulled his mother's ring out of the neckline of her gown and smiled brilliantly. "Undoing the button is a bit difficult while I am actually *wearing* the corset! *Now* I can finally wear it on my *finger*! I would *very* much like to make our betrothal publicly known at last!"

William took the ring from her and placed it on her finger, kissing it once it was in place.

"We should return to Longbourn. Your father and Miss Bennet will be wondering what happened."

Elizabeth agreed, and they walked in silence for a while.

Elizabeth asked if he would send for Georgiana and Colonel *Richards* so they could attend the wedding. "OH! I had every intention on doing so, but I had not thought it through... how can I? I cannot be certain the post from Hertfordshire will be received at Pemberley."

Elizabeth thought for a moment and then said, "Perhaps you can send a letter enclosed within one addressed to your housekeeper in London, and then she can forward it on to Pemberley as if it were from that address?"

"Yes... I will send it express to Darcy House, and then ask Mrs. Martin to send it express to Georgiana. Thank you, my love; that is a wonderful idea. Would you like to enclose a letter of your own?"

"To Mrs. Martin? Certainly, though I am not sure what I should say to her." He looked to her with a confused air, which changed the moment he recognized the teasing light in her eyes, and she laughed, "But, I *can* think of a thousand things to say to Georgiana if you would allow."

"I most certainly would allow it... both in fact!" he chuckled, "After what Richard said, it seems that Georgiana was only avoiding speaking of you in hopes that it would ease my mind. Little did she realize that you were never far from my thoughts! I do hope she and Richard will receive our letters and join us here."

"As do I, William. I have missed her terribly, though not as much as I had missed her brother." She hugged his arm to her, and they shared a tender kiss.

They were approaching Longbourn when Elizabeth broke their comfortable silence by saying, "Are you prepared for what you will most likely experience upon entering my mother's presence, especially *after* the announcement is made?"

"Though I would rather not, I am quite willing to suffer through any amount of attention... as long as it is in regards to the subject of our engagement, Elizabeth."

"That is very good—for I am afraid you shall suffer, willing or not!" she said as they entered the house, both smiling.

Chapter 20

When Mr. Bennet made the announcement of the betrothal of William and Elizabeth, Mrs. Bennet's demeanor was the opposite of what had been expected. Clasping her hands in front of her, Mrs. Bennet stood and drew herself up to her full height—which was not truly impressive as her stature was not much more than Elizabeth's height. Taking on a haughty expression, she asked that Jane, Mary, Kitty, and Lydia leave the room, instructing her girls quite adamantly *not* to repeat their father's announcement to anyone at this time.

While completely ignoring the presence of William as she had done before, after the others had departed, Mrs. Bennet first took in the confused countenance of Elizabeth. She then turned to face her husband, who stared at her in obvious astonishment. Mrs. Bennet began to speak in a quiet voice, but as she continued, anger and resentment seeped into her tone, "You might think it impertinent and disrespectful of your authority that I should question your decision, Mr. Bennet, but I have been witness to the consequences resulting from Mr. Darcy's transgressions against my family, and I will *not* permit it to happen again when it is in my power to prevent it. Before I accept this man into my family, I would like to be told just what explanation he has given for all that he has done to injure you and, more especially, our Lizzy. I am concerned that tender remembrances of what once had been may have influenced your decision to accept Mr. Darcy's excuses when the correct course would be to send him away from this house and inform him that he is never to return. Perhaps you have been taken in by him once again! If this is so, *I* will not allow it!"

William was not very surprised at her reaction as it was much in keeping with the way she had been behaving toward him since he came into Hertfordshire. He watched as Elizabeth's bewildered expression morphed into one of warm affection for her mother. His gaze shifted to Mr. Bennet, who gaped at his wife in amazement.

After several moments of silence while he gathered his wits, Mr. Bennet cleared his throat and answered, "Mrs. Bennet, I am certainly enjoying the improvements in your character of late! I shall be happy to share with you all that William has told us. Have a seat, my dear, and make yourself comfortable. It is a lengthy tale that I must tell."

Mr. Bennet proceeded to summarize what he had learned from William and Colonel Fitzwilliam earlier in the day while Elizabeth and William sat quietly. Elizabeth, assuming William would need support while hearing the entire history once again, took his hand and did not release it throughout the communication, even after being on the receiving end of a stern look from her mother as a result of doing so. Throughout her husband's speech, Mrs. Bennet's expression slowly changed from one of cold dissent to one that Elizabeth had rarely seen upon her mother's face during her entire lifetime—contemplation.

At the end of her husband's tale, Mrs. Bennet stared at William for a few moments before her expression softened and she said, "Mr. Darcy, please forgive my false assumptions and my ill-mannered behavior toward you since we have been in company again."

Relieved, William answered, "Mrs. Bennet, I believe *everyone* in this room is guilty of drawing false conclusions of the others' intent. I understand and appreciate your sense of loyalty to your family. I am especially grateful that you would protect Elizabeth from a man you thought might harm her. Please be assured that Elizabeth's happiness and protection is of the highest priority to me as well. I hold no ill will against you, and I hope that you feel the same. I believe it would be best if we begin anew."

Mrs. Bennet held out her hand to William. William rose and bowed over her hand as she said, "I agree to begin again, Mr. Darcy. But I do have one further question."

"I will answer if I can, Mrs. Bennet."

Mrs. Bennet's mien transformed into one closer to her old self as she asked, "Do you *really* have ten thousand a year?"

"Actually, Mrs. Bennet, my income is slightly higher than rumored."

Eyes widening, she reacted in the manner she had been expected to when first told of the engagement. "*More* than ten thousand a year! My dear Lizzy, such a good match you have made! An estate and a house in town! The gowns, the jewels, the carriages—OH! The *pin money* you will receive! Lady Lucas and Mrs. Long will turn green with envy!" Mrs. Bennet fairly waved the handkerchief in her hand.

Happy that the tension in the room had been broken, William, Elizabeth and Mr. Bennet attempted to disguise their amusement at her antics. Mr. Bennet suggested that the other girls be allowed to return to the room, and Mrs. Bennet was only too pleased to invite them in again and tell them the news, forgetting that they had been told once before.

William was asked to stay for dinner so that Mrs. Bennet would have some time to plan the wedding with the happy couple. Though at first the mother of the bride had complained about the short period of time she would have to plan the wedding festivities, even *she* was able to recognize that after *three years* of waiting, the couple had little patience of opposition to their being wed immediately after the banns had been published. It was trouble enough to have Elizabeth and William agree to compromise and hold the ceremony on the Wednesday instead of the Monday morning immediately following the last reading of the banns, and her instincts told her that they would deprive her of planning a wedding and celebration at all and *elope* if she attempted to push the date any later!

Mrs. Bennet had thought of insisting that William apply for a special license, but that idea was quickly discarded, for she suspected if William *could* manage it, she would have even *less* time to arrange the wedding festivities, and *that* certainly would not do!

Instead, she decided to look upon it all as a challenge, one at which her success would prove her superior hostess skills to the entire neighborhood and her future son-in-law. The couple was of little assistance as neither of them wished for anything nearly as elaborate as she envisioned and attempted to convince her to have a more modest affair. The words "modest" and "simple" were not in Mrs. Bennet's vocabulary when it came to a subject so highly anticipated as a daughter's wedding, and so, happy it was for Elizabeth and William that she discontinued asking them for their preferences only to immediately dismiss them. Her manner changed to one reminiscent of Napoleon himself, reminding William a little of his Aunt Catherine, though she was certainly more pleasant than *that* lady could have managed.

~%~

After dinner, Mr. Bennet guessed that William would appreciate a respite from the talk of menus, flowers, lace, and silk, and asked the young man to join him in his study for a glass of port. The moment his future father-in-law seemed comfortably settled into his chair behind the desk, William could not wait one minute longer—he placed some papers before him.

Mr. Bennet could not help but laugh. "William! Marriage contracts? You certainly came to Longbourn prepared today!" Noticing the date that the contract had been drafted, Mr. Bennet raised his eyebrows and said, "This was written and signed by you more than three years ago!"

"Yes, sir. In the months leading up to Elizabeth's seventeenth birthday, I had my solicitor make out this marriage contract with every intention of bringing it to Longbourn to present to you, Mr. Bennet, but my injuries resulting from the fire prevented this from being possible. It has been a comfort to me knowing that the document was always nearby, and so the contract had remained in the valise in which I keep important papers when I am travelling. I made certain these papers were with me when I journeyed into Hertfordshire. I have reviewed the terms and find nothing that I wish to change—pending your approval, of course. Now that we have your consent, after this is signed by you, if anything should happen to me, even before we are married, Elizabeth would be protected."

"And it would protect *you* as well. It would cause a great scandal if I changed my mind after signing the contract." The older gentleman smiled at William's blush.

"Sir, I cannot help but fear that something *else* might go wrong before..."

Mr. Bennet interrupted, "I understand, son—truly I do." Mr. Bennet began to read again. "This is more than generous, William. I cannot possibly imagine disapproving of your terms, though I would like some time to review the contract in more detail before signing it. Will you meet with me again tomorrow?"

"Yes, Mr. Bennet, I would be happy to. With your permission, I would like Elizabeth to be fully aware of and in agreement with the terms of the contract as well, sir."

"Would you like to be present when she reads it? I must say *I* would like to see the look on her face when she sees this!" Mr. Bennet laughed.

William became flustered. "Do you think she will not approve? I will increase her pin money if you think she needs more, sir. I…"

"No, no, William, you misunderstand me!" Mr. Bennet interrupted again. "But you *should* be prepared for an argument from Lizzy. She rarely spends the entire amount of the pin money she is allowed as it is, and she receives far less than this from me—she will protest the need for such a copious amount as you have spelled out in here *in addition* to the funds you have provided for housekeeping," He gestured to the contract. "You will get no argument from me, and certainly none from my wife if she was ever to find out—and I do *not* suggest that you ever tell her the amount. I just thought I should to warn you of what to expect during your discussion tomorrow."

"Thank you, Mr. Bennet. I shall formulate my argument so I will be prepared for Elizabeth's objections. You may not be aware that I rarely lost an argument on the debate team at Cambridge."

"Did you know that Lizzy has won several arguments against Henry Bickersteth*?" Mr. Bennet understood William's shocked expression, Mr. Bickersteth's being a well-known and highly accomplished debater. "Yes, *that* Henry Bickersteth."

"Ah… then I see I am in good company." William cleared his throat as Mr. Bennet stifled a laugh. "But in this case I *will* prevail since mine is the better position. I can think of many reasons that Elizabeth's pin money and settlement should be so high. My arguments shall be logical while hers can be based only on preference."

"Perhaps I was mistaken earlier in my advice—if Lizzy will not be convinced to accept the contract, you could always inform my wife of the amounts, and I am certain that she *will* influence her to alter her opinion. I

---

* Henry Bickersteth was one of the founding members of the Cambridge Union Society, a union between three debating societies at the university. He graduated from Cambridge in 1808 as Senior Wrangler and won the Smith's Prize.

have often witnessed how my Fanny's nagging wins out over many a logical argument. I would save it as a last resort, however."

The gentlemen both chuckled as they rose from their chairs. Mr. Bennet held out his hand and William shook it. They soon rejoined the ladies.

~%~

The following morning, Elizabeth walked out before sunrise as was her usual habit when the weather allowed. As she walked along the path to Oakham Mount just beyond the sight of Longbourn, the rustling of brush along the path caught her attention, and she hesitated. As she turned toward the noise, she felt hands upon her waist, pulling her back until she was fully enveloped by the arms attached to them. A spicy, male scent surrounded her and warm, sweet breath tickled her ear with a whispered, "Good morning, my love," followed by a number of light kisses along her neck trailing downward as far as the collar of her coat would allow.

Elizabeth smiled and closed her eyes, leaning her head to the side to allow him better access to her skin. "Promise me something, William?"

A return path of kisses, with his pausing to taste her exquisite skin along the way, delayed his answer. Once his lips reached the location that prompted his beloved to moan softly, he breathed, "Anything."

She hesitated a few moments, delighting in all the sensations of her William's ministrations and the wonder of being held in his arms—exactly where she belonged. "After we are wed, I wish to begin *every* day with waking in your arms."

William took a deep breath, indulging in the aroma belonging only to Elizabeth. "Your wishes match mine exactly, Elizabeth. Though many couples do, I have often hoped that you would *not* prefer to sleep in separate bedchambers."

Elizabeth shivered with pleasure and angled her head to catch his eyes with hers. Turning in his arms, she caressed his cheek, her eyes darting to his lips time and time again. When she moistened her lips with her tongue, William could no longer resist her silent request for him to taste her lips. Her fingers lacing through his hair was encouragement enough to deepen the kiss. William's arms wrapped more tightly around her, pulling her as close to him as possible.

After a few minutes engaged in similar undertakings, William loosened his hold on Elizabeth, pulling away to see her face. His breath caught at the expression of love that he found in her eyes. Burying his face in her silky curls to avoid the temptation that she offered, he said huskily, "We should begin our walk, my heart, for I do not believe I will be able to behave myself if we continue in this manner."

She moved away slightly, giving him a look that communicated all the gratification that she felt in being able to induce the same passion within him that he always seemed to be able to achieve in her. He took her hand and together they began the trek to Oakham Mount.

After a few minutes, Elizabeth spoke, "Not that I mind seeing you, but in your meeting me this morning, my intuition tells me that you do not think I should walk alone. Why is that?"

William's expression hardened as he considered how to answer without frightening her. Knowing that only the truth would satisfy her, he stated, "I apologize that I did not explain it yesterday. Before I ever set out for Longbourn, I had every intention of discussing it upon my arrival, but once Richard appeared and his news had been revealed, it slipped my mind. By the time I thought of it again, it was late at night.

"I fear for your safety from Wickham, Elizabeth. After Ramsgate, I had thought to write to your father with a warning, but never did I truly believe that Wickham could have been able to find you." William sighed, shaking his head. "Not that Mr. Bennet would have *received* a letter had I written one!

"I knew not that Wickham was in the neighborhood until that night in the Netherfield library when you told me that you had spoken to him recently. I have not been able to speak to you or your father about him since then."

"I would see you safely to Longbourn after our walk, and wish to speak to you and your father on this subject. But at present I would much rather enjoy our walk together."

And that they did.

~%~

When Elizabeth entered the house with William, noticing the raised eyebrows on her father's face, she announced to the family gathered at the table, "Mr. Darcy and I met while taking our morning exercise, and since he was returning to Netherfield only to break his fast before meeting with Papa directly afterward, I invited him to share our meal with us."

After their appetites were satisfied, Mr. Bennet requested the company of William and Elizabeth in his study.

"Mr. Bennet," William began, "before we begin to speak of the contract, there is another matter that I wish to discuss. Elizabeth knows something of my dealings with Lieutenant George Wickham, whom I have been made to understand is in Meryton with the militia, but I wish to tell you of it in more detail—and to warn you about this man."

Knowing he could trust Mr. Bennet, William explained the particulars about Wickham's relationship with the Darcy family and Wickham's crimes against them and others. He went on to say, "Wickham is a jealous and vengeful man when he perceives he has been wronged—but what you must understand is that his *definition* of right and wrong are completely different than that of the remainder of society. To Wickham, what is 'right' consists of his receiving exactly what he wants whether he deserves it or not... I should say whether it is even legal or not. His being 'wronged' is defined by his not having all that he wants simply handed to him the moment he wants it. For example, in my refusing his request for more money after he quickly had wasted the four thousand pounds that he had earlier agreed was sufficient compensation for the living mentioned in my father's will, his opinion changed to my having committed a great wrong toward him.

"Previously, I mentioned to Elizabeth that Georgiana had only escaped from Wickham's ... *attentions* due to Elizabeth's teaching my sister how to defend herself from men like him. Unfortunately, during the time leading up to Wickham's advances—when she still thought him a friend—Georgiana spoke of Elizabeth. According to Georgiana, it seems that his father, our late steward, had written to his son of Elizabeth during her visit to Pemberley three years ago, stating that he expected we would marry soon after, and so Wickham inquired about Elizabeth and encouraged Georgiana to speak of her. After Georgiana's employing some of aforementioned defensive maneuvers during her escape from him, in my sister's anger she revealed to Wickham that 'Elizabeth had taught her well.'

"Sir, I fear it would be within Wickham's nature to conclude that Elizabeth *owes* him the thirty thousand pound dowry that, had his plan been successful, he most certainly would have gained by being forced to marry Georgiana.

"In addition, I cannot help but worry that he has a compulsion to revenge himself upon me by harming those whom I love. In a round-about way, Wickham did admit that this *was* one of his motives for his advances upon Georgiana.

"Respectfully, I must insist that Elizabeth does not walk out alone while Wickham is in the area and that you do not welcome this man into your home. This is the reason I made certain to escort her to Longbourn this morning, sir. I feel that *all* your daughters are at risk, Mr. Bennet."

For a moment Elizabeth felt her ire rising. She thought that William had understood how important her independence was to her, and she could not believe he would limit her in such a way. But then she thought back to earlier that morning. How easy it had been for William to creep up on her from behind and take her in his arms before she had time to react! What had been a pleasant memory was now weighed down by the thought of what *could* have happened had it *not* been William. If she had screamed, would anyone have heard her? She was certain that had she been further from the house, her distress would have gone undetected. Though she knew the area to be safe to walk out alone in general, with a man like Wickham nearby, she had to agree to restrict her rambles for a time.

William's attention was drawn by Elizabeth's sharp intake of breath, and he saw all the color drain from her face. He suddenly felt guilty for having spoken of this with her in the room as he did not want to frighten her, but at the same time he knew that she would want to understand the reason her walks would be curtailed—and he had promised to be honest with her in all matters. Wishing to be reassured that he had done right and that she was well, William willed her to look at him.

When Elizabeth finally did meet his eyes, she immediately comprehended his concerned expression and gave a small nod.

Mr. Bennet was unaware of this exchange, as he had been staring out the window, distracted by his thoughts. "What can be done to rid us of this man?"

"Soon after I became aware of Wickham's location, I contacted Colonel Fitzwilliam about this very subject. I have been assured that Wickham will be transferred to a different regiment. The commanding officer at his newly assigned regiment is a friend of my cousin. The gentleman is already aware of Wickham's character through his younger brother who had attended

Cambridge in the same year as Wickham and I." With a glance at Elizabeth all but stating that he could not give details with a lady in the room, William continued, "Let us just say that Wickham led this gentleman's brother into some less-than-proper circumstances that required his family to call in many favors in order to save their name from ruin as a result of these incidents. Wickham will be well watched once he arrives at his new assignment, and I pray it will do him some good. Yesterday Colonel Fitzwilliam informed me that the transfer will take a few days more. In the meantime, we must proceed carefully."

Mr. Bennet felt that the answers to the questions that he wished to ask would not be fit for his daughter's ears. "Lizzy, would you mind going to the kitchen to ask Hill for tea to be sent in?"

Elizabeth shot her father an accusing look. "Certainly, Papa... and just what length of time should this trip to the kitchen keep me away from this room?"

Mr. Bennet smiled slightly, but his brow was furrowed with worry. "Five minutes should do nicely, my dear."

After Elizabeth closed the door behind her, Mr. Bennet asked, "How could Wickham expect to extract thirty thousand pounds from Elizabeth? Even if all the girls' dowries were to be added together, I would not have it to give."

"If he truly expected money, I would think he would assume that *I* would pay, perhaps not all but at least part of the amount, to keep him quiet. Being paid Darcy money would mean a great deal more to him than money from the Bennet coffers. But... Mr. Bennet, I do not think he is beyond finding another way to satisfy what he feels is an obligation due him while at the same time taking his revenge upon me. Though to my knowledge, before Ramsgate it has always been with the lady's consent, he has tampered with many tradesmen's daughters and servant girls. After what he tried to do to Georgiana, I would not put it past him to arrange to be found in a compromising position with Elizabeth. Even if it were with one of her sisters, it would hurt Elizabeth, and by extension, me. Whether *she* was willing or not would not matter—your family would be ruined in the eyes of society, and Wickham would *expect* that I would not marry Elizabeth."

"Are you insinuating that you *would* marry her if that came to pass?"

"Sir, after all that occurred yesterday it was not until late in the evening that I realized I had not discussed this with you as I had originally planned. I spent the night awake, and I admit to thoroughly torturing myself with all the possible consequences of this oversight! Now that she has declared her wish to marry me, I find there is *nothing* that could prevent me from marrying Elizabeth. I cannot live without her, Mr. Bennet." William's tone was of passionate conviction. "Of course, we would have to stay away from the *ton* for a number of years, but to give up the society of people like my aunt and uncle would be no hardship on me. By the time Georgiana would be ready to come out, the worst of the gossip would have passed. Either way, I would not wish my sister to marry a man who would shun us without taking into account the truth behind a piece of gossip."

Mr. Bennet stared at William, thinking of how impressed he was with his friend's son, and how ashamed he was for the opinion he had held of him since Elizabeth's seventeenth birthday.

"I would like to visit Colonel Forster to warn him about Wickham's character and request notification of the receipt of transfer orders. I believe the meeting would have better results if you were present, sir, being one of the principal land owners in the area. If it is convenient for you, I would like to go into Meryton as soon as we are finished here."

Mr. Bennet nodded. "I must complete some business, but I shall be available after luncheon."

A knock interrupted the silence left in the last comment's wake. "That will be Lizzy," Mr. Bennet stated, and then called out, "Enter!"

William rose from his seat as Elizabeth peeked into the room, asking, "Shall I find something else to keep me occupied, or may I come in now?"

Mr. Bennet looked to William to inquire whether he had anything further to say on the subject that had required her absence, but the young man's eyes were firmly set upon his betrothed. At seeing William's expression, Mr. Bennet knew their previous discussion was at an end whether there was anything remaining to say or not. Mr. Bennet chuckled. "You may have a seat, Lizzy. I am certain you have surmised you will not be permitted your solitary walks until Wickham leaves the area. I think it would be safe enough for you to walk with William *and* one of your sisters." Mr. Bennet, who suspected the newly engaged couple had spent the entirety of Elizabeth's walk earlier this morning together and unchaperoned, gave them both a knowing look. "You may walk out with Mr. Bingley and Jane as well, of course. If your sisters are inclined to go visiting, you may only go out in groups of three or more. Meryton is off limits for now, my dear. Do I make myself clear?"

Elizabeth nodded. "Perfectly clear, Papa. How will you explain this to Mama and my sisters?"

"I am the master of the estate and the head of this family. I should not have to explain the reasons behind any restrictions I lay down." At Elizabeth's doubtful look he continued, "But, I will warn them discreetly against Lieutenant Wickham's character nonetheless."

"Papa, I have spent the past few minutes delaying Kitty and Lydia's departure. They were planning to walk into Meryton this morning…"

"In that case, I will return shortly." Mr. Bennet made a show of leaving the door open as he left the room.

"Perhaps I should begin to read the contract?" Elizabeth asked.

"Please wait, Elizabeth. Your father would never forgive me if I allowed you to begin reading it before his return. He has been looking forward to… being with you when you do."

Elizabeth seemed quite confused. "He has read it, I assume?" William nodded and she continued, "Then may I ask why he wishes to be present when *I* read it?"

William squirmed a little. "I beg that you simply wait for his return without any further questions."

An air of surprise mixed with chagrin fell across Elizabeth's features, a look identical to the one that she had displayed in William's dream the previous night. In the dream, this expression had come after she had begun to read the contract, and William had responded by explaining all his reasons for wishing to give her such a high amount in the settlement—while he distracted her with gentle kisses, caresses, and other such attentions. He had had no trouble at all convincing her that he was indeed correct. If only the door were closed and her father was not expected to return so soon, he could employ this method of persuasion in reality this time!

Elizabeth began to laugh. "Why are you grinning at me in that manner, William?"

William leaned forward in his chair and whispered huskily, "I promise I shall *explain* my grin quite thoroughly the next time we are alone."

Her eyes sparkled in response. "I believe your expression has inspired my anticipation for your fulfilling that promise, Mr. Darcy."

After several minutes, Mr. Bennet cleared his throat loudly before entering the room. His daughter and her fiancé noticed he was looking quite a bit more frazzled than when he left to speak to his wife and other daughters. "Lizzy, once you leave Longbourn, I doubt I will *ever* hear two words of sense spoken together again." Mr. Bennet shook his head as if to clear it, and then continued, "I am glad to see you waited to begin reading the contract. I find myself in need of some entertainment. Would you like to peruse it now, my dear?"

William closed his eyes for a moment and held back a sigh. Elizabeth arched a brow and responded, "Entertainment?" her eyes darted back and forth between William's slightly annoyed look and Mr. Bennet's amused one before she continued, "I shall attempt to live up to your expectations, Papa."

Elizabeth was more than a little curious to read the contract after her father's comments, but as she perused the document she soon realized that he was waiting to see her reaction when she saw the numbers. Though she was careful to maintain her features in a schooled expression of nonchalance, a feeling of shock spread through her. About to object to William's giving her too much money, Elizabeth discerned the better course of action would be to examine the reasons that William would have settled such large amounts on her.

As she feigned reading and began reviewing in her mind what she remembered of Pemberley and Darcy House, Elizabeth became aware that all she had known while growing up at Longbourn could not compare to the elegance and grandeur of William's homes. The standards of behavior she would have to accept would be set much higher than they had ever been in the past or else she would risk embarrassing William.

She imagined that her pin money had been set so high due to the anticipated requirements of dressing appropriately for her new station. Analyzing the apparel she had seen on the ladies of William's class in London's theaters, while shopping, or during visits to a tea shop, Elizabeth related it to her own attire. It quickly became apparent how inadequate her usual style of dress was for the wife of Mr. Darcy. As if to prove that point, several conversations that she had reluctantly overheard between Caroline Bingley and Louisa Hurst came to mind. When the ladies had remarked upon Hertfordshire's inadequacies, they always included the style, cut, and quality of material of those they criticized. In general, whenever a new person was introduced into their conversation, whether they considered the person to be fashionable or not, the two ladies would comment on the quality of their attire. From what William had written in his journal, it seemed that most ladies of the higher circles of the *ton* judged others similarly. Elizabeth would have to work hard to impress others so that William would not be ridiculed for his choice of a wife.

When she came to the amount of her settlement, she knew that William had been preparing for all possible futures. No matter how she despised thinking of it, he was determined to provide for her if he passed on before she did. Elizabeth had spent the past few years helping her mother with the housekeeping books for Longbourn and knew that the day-to-day expenses of William's homes must be much higher. If he passed on, William would wish for her to continue to live in the same style she had enjoyed while he was alive. If she met her demise before him, he would expect to provide for their younger children through her settlement. Keeping this in mind, she read the remainder of the document.

"I do not know what Father expected, but I fear my reaction will be a disappointment to him." Elizabeth thought, then said aloud, "I have one question, William. Am I permitted to do what I wish with pin money that I may not have spent at the end of the month? I would like to donate to charity if I may."

William hesitated. This was not a question he had prepared for. "Elizabeth, you need only to inform me of any worthwhile causes, and I would be happy to make donations from the both of us."

"Then may I invest anything I have not spent in order to provide for our younger children's futures?"

"Yes, of course. But Elizabeth, I do not wish for you to spend less on yourself so that you can save for our children. Do you not trust that I would provide for them in my will?" At Elizabeth's nod, he continued with part of what he had prepared, "I will *not* be convinced to lower the amounts set in the contract. Once we are married, you will have to embrace a new type of lifestyle." Stopping short, William glanced at Mr. Bennet. He had thought that Mr. Bennet would have left them alone for a few minutes to discuss the matter in private, but the older gentleman did not offer to do so. Thinking about what he had planned to say next he suddenly became aware that he might insult his future father-in-law's financial situation if he continued.

Elizabeth placed the contract on her father's desk and folded her hands in her lap. "I understand completely, William."

"You do?"

Not taking her eyes from her lap, Elizabeth said, "Do not worry, I will do whatever is expected of me. I do not wish to be an embarrassment or a disappointment to you, as I am certain your relatives have predicted I will be."

Surprised at the way she misunderstood his intentions, William moved forward in his seat, took her hands in his, and waited for her to look at him. Seeing Elizabeth's eyes shine with unshed tears, William was no longer concerned about what he said in front of her father. All that mattered to him was Elizabeth! The arguments he had prepared were forgotten as he tried to reassure her, "The only way that you could ever disappoint me is if you pretended to be something you are not in order to please others. I want *you*, Elizabeth, as you are. You could never embarrass me. There is not a woman in the *ton* who could match your intelligence, your wit, your vivacity, or the beauty that radiates from within you. I will always be proud to call you my wife.

"I only ask that you indulge me—as long as it is in my power, it would make me very happy if you would allow me to spoil you a little. What good does all my money do me if I am not permitted to spend some of it on you?"

Seeing Elizabeth's smile, Mr. Bennet felt there was no reason to delay any longer. He signed the contracts below William's signature, which had been placed there more than three years prior, and coughed to gain the young couple's attention. Passing the documents to William, he said with feeling, "I will be proud to call you 'son,' William."

Elizabeth watched as the two most important men in her life shook hands—the younger was almost giddy with joy, the elder displayed only a small smile.

William unfolded the contracts and looked at Mr. Bennet's signature in such a way that upon seeing his expression, Elizabeth felt he could not believe that this milestone had truly been reached unless he had actually *seen* her father's signature below his own. As William was busy making out an express to his solicitor to forward his copy of the document, father and daughter's eyes met for a moment. His eyes immediately darted away as if he were hiding something from her sharp gaze, but she had been too quick for him. Elizabeth could see that the smile reached his eyes only partially and that there was a touch of sorrow present as well. She sighed silently.

Elizabeth had expected that her father would regret losing her company. She also knew that she would miss her father very much and felt a little bit guilty about leaving him.

But she could not allow these feelings to outweigh her happiness at spending the rest of her life at William's side. This was the way of the world—daughters left the protection of their fathers and took their place with their husbands. *"No,"* she decided, *"I know Papa wishes me to be happy at last. I will feel guilt no longer!"*

Once the papers were safely stored away in his pocket, William's smile widened and Elizabeth could not help but match it with a brilliant one of her own.

Elizabeth said, "Shall we join the others?"

"Bingley was planning to meet me here. He should have arrived by now."

"Well then, you should rescue him from the gaggle of ladies in the parlor. Perhaps you all could go for a walk?" Mr. Bennet suggested, obviously looking forward to some time alone after such an emotional morning.

~%~

Bingley offered Elizabeth his congratulations on the news. When Elizabeth asked after his sisters and Mr. Hurst, Bingley replied, "They are well. I was just about to explain to your mother and sisters that I saw them off before coming to Longbourn."

"Oh? Have they returned to London, then?" Elizabeth inquired. "They spoke of looking forward to the season during our stay at Netherfield while Jane was ill."

Bingley looked a bit uncomfortable as he responded, "Caroline is headed for London, Miss Elizabeth. The Hursts will deliver her to a friend in

London—a Miss Walters—perhaps you met her during the ball? Louisa and Hurst are off on an extended visit to Hurst's family seat in Cornwall. I do not think they will return to London for quite some time." He and William exchanged a knowing look which piqued Elizabeth's curiosity.

"I do hope they have a pleasant journey, Mr. Bingley," Mrs. Bennet replied. "Since it is only the two of you gentlemen in such a large house, perhaps you would both dine with us this evening?"

There was nothing the two gentlemen would rather do than spend the day with their ladies, and so they quickly agreed to the scheme. Elizabeth caught another significant look pass between William and his friend after he suggested a walk.

Mary and Mrs. Bennet stayed behind, and the others naturally paired up, with Kitty and Lydia in the lead, and Jane and Bingley falling behind.

William adjusted their pace to stay out of hearing range of the younger girls, but kept them in view. "I saw the looks you exchanged with Mr. Bingley. What happened to make his sisters leave so suddenly?" Elizabeth asked.

"Miss Bingley has been… *unhappy* since the ball and wished to return to London."

Elizabeth's eyes danced with mischievousness. "Yes, I can imagine she would have been *unhappy* with the attention you paid me. She certainly did not do well upon seeing us dance the waltz!"

"Ah, I was hoping for Bingley's sake that nobody saw her behavior."

"I doubt anyone else noticed. I certainly have not heard gossip about Miss Bingley's behavior, and we both know that my mother would have repeated it if there had been any! Did the news of our engagement have anything to do with Miss Bingley's sudden removal?"

William seemed very uncomfortable, as he answered, "I believe it did." He began fidgeting with his cravat, refusing to meet Elizabeth's eyes.

Elizabeth tightened her grip on the arm she was holding. "I can see something is terribly wrong. Tell me, William!"

"Very well, my love, but before I begin, first I must say that she was not successful." He dared a glance at her and noted he had never seen

Elizabeth look so surprised. "I told you I could not sleep last night. As it turned out, it was a good thing I did not. She must have overheard me tell her brother that our marriage contract had not yet been signed and thought it was her last chance."

Elizabeth gasped. "What happened?"

"After everyone in the house had retired, I heard the knob on my chamber door being turned. Though my door was locked, I had my suspicions, and so I awoke my valet, Hughes, and had him come into the room so that he could be witness to what occurred. Miss Bingley returned a few minutes later with a key. Hughes hid behind the door with a sheet and threw it over her head as she came into the room. Having a good hold on her, he took her out into the hallway—all the while hollering that he had caught a robber breaking into my bedchamber. Hurst and Bingley came rushing out of their rooms just in time for Hughes to 'realize' that the screeches emanating from the *robber* sounded rather feminine. He pulled off the sheet to reveal a haggard-looking Miss Bingley."

Elizabeth could not help but laugh, startling William for several moments until he joined her. When she had quieted enough to speak, Elizabeth asked, "How perfect! What was Miss Bingley's reaction to all this?"

"Oh, she was livid! She screamed for quite a while at Hughes, 'How dare *you*, a *servant*, touch a *lady* in such a manner!' and other such nonsense—as if the entire thing were his fault. I finally tired of it and suggested that since she had been handled in such a way perhaps her brother should make Hughes marry her."

"You did not!"

"Yes, I certainly did! I felt rather guilty after I saw Hughes' reaction to the suggestion—I was afraid he would faint! You should have no worries for Hughes' sake, Elizabeth; Miss Bingley did not take kindly to that suggestion. She calmed herself only after she had extracted a promise from Bingley that she would not be made to marry my valet. Her brother asked just what she was doing trying to enter my bedchamber in the first place. After a while she said she must have been sleepwalking."

"I certainly hope Mr. Bingley did not believe her!"

"No, he did not. I will not go into details, but Miss Bingley then had the audacity to insult not only you but Miss Bennet as well. I have known

Bingley for years and never have I seen him so angry. He threatened to send her to some relatives in the north of York, but Mrs. Hurst had by then joined us, and she suggested that she and her husband take Miss Bingley to London to visit with her friend so that she could attend the season. Bingley *encouraged* Miss Bingley to accept any offer of marriage made to her this season for he would support her only until the season is over. After that she would have to live off her own inheritance."

"Oh dear. What of the Hursts?"

"I think they have had enough of Miss Bingley's antics. After this scene, they refused to take her in as well. I am certain that now that she has been put in her place, she can at last find a respectable gentleman of some status who would marry her for her twenty thousand pounds. It does not sound like the ideal life to you and me, but it is all *she* really wants—though she had set her sights on the wrong man up till now. For some reason she felt that since I was her brother's friend, that Pemberley would eventually be her home. She could never accept that I would not pay her any such attentions." He hesitated and then said, "The events of last night made me aware of what lengths desperate people will go in order get what they feel they are *owed*."

"Wickham . . ." Elizabeth breathed.

"Yes." They walked on in silence for a minute before William noticed Kitty and Lydia were almost out of sight. "We must catch up with your sisters for I fear Bingley will be too distracted today to keep watch on them." Elizabeth noticed William glancing back at Jane and Bingley.

As she arched an eyebrow, Elizabeth asked, "Does Mr. Bingley's distraction have to do with his sister or does it stem from another quarter?"

William attempted unsuccessfully to hide his smile. "There is another reason. You will find out soon enough, my love."

They walked on for a few minutes in companionable silence until, without warning, Elizabeth began to giggle. The sound of William's laughter drowned out hers after she explained, "You *do* realize that if Mr. Bingley *had* insisted that Caroline marry Hughes, she would have ended up calling Pemberley her home after all!"

Chapter 21

Elizabeth could barely contain her excitement as she stood examining Jane's dreamy expression in the reflection of the dressing table mirror. She took the brush from her elder sister's hand and began the nightly ritual of each smoothing the other's hair before retiring.

Earlier in the day, when Jane and Bingley had rejoined the group as they returned to Longbourn from their walk, their expressions had been radiating with joy. William had hinted that his friend and her sister would have some good news to announce after their ramble, but Jane had told her nothing about it, and Bingley had remained with the family instead of requesting an audience with Mr. Bennet as Elizabeth had expected. The gentlemen had remained at Longbourn to dine, and Jane and Bingley had been even more lost in each other's presence than was usual. Elizabeth was certain they had become engaged.

Since this had been the first opportunity for the sisters to be alone, Elizabeth had expected the news to come bursting from her elder sister's lips the moment they had closed the door behind them, but instead Jane remained silent. Elizabeth reminded herself that she should be patient. If Jane wished to keep her news to herself for the moment, then she should *not* press her, but Elizabeth herself was so happy for the obvious bliss emanating from her sister that she was having trouble containing her own emotions.

After Jane's hair had been plaited, they switched places. Forced to clear her throat several times to bring Jane's attention back to the task at hand from wherever it had wandered—Netherfield she imagined—Elizabeth found that she could wait no longer. "Jane, *please!*"

Jane's confusion was evident in her expression. "Lizzy?"

"*Tell* me!"

"Why do you believe there is anything to tell?"

Elizabeth giggled, "Jane! If you continue on in this distracted manner, we shall not get to bed until it is almost dawn! You have been positively glowing with happiness all evening, as was Mr. Bingley. You *must* tell me your news!"

Jane's troubled expression in response to her speech surprised her sister. "Oh, Lizzy, I am sorry. I did not mean to… we had decided to wait for…"

Understanding dawned upon Elizabeth, and she turned toward Jane. Taking the brush from her sister's hand and laying it on the table, she took Jane's hands in her own. "You thought to keep it a secret until after our wedding, afraid that your news would take attention away from William and me? Oh, Jane! My behavior must be faulty indeed if you believe me to be as selfish as Lydia!" The teasing sparkle in Elizabeth's eyes coupled with her amused smile took the sting from her words. Pulling Jane toward the bed, Elizabeth sat cross-legged upon the coverlet and, wearing a wide smile, she exclaimed, "Come now! You must tell me *everything* or I shall never forgive you!"

After many minutes of whispered conversation and delighted exclamations, it was decided between them that Bingley would ask for consent to marry Mr. Bennet's eldest daughter the following day; however, Jane emphatically would not allow the engagement to be announced before the wedding. "Charles agrees with me, Lizzy, and we will hold firm to this decision. You and I both know what Mama's reaction will be, and I will *not* have the news of my engagement distract her, or anyone else, from your wedding."

"I will respect your wishes, Jane, but you must respect mine as well. I will not be satisfied unless Papa announces your engagement at the wedding breakfast. I can think of no better wedding gift than to share my own happiness with you and Mr. Bingley!"

~%~

Though William loathed the thought of spending any more time than absolutely necessary away from Elizabeth, the letters from his solicitor and steward, forwarded from his house in London, had been piling up, and his attention *was* now absolutely necessary. William woke before dawn, abstained from his morning exercise, and took breakfast and luncheon on a tray at the desk in Bingley's study while he worked.

At the earliest possible moment, William emerged from the study. Bingley blushed at being caught pacing the hall outside the door, anxious for the excuse of accompanying him for a visit at Longbourn. His old friend smiled widely and clapped his shoulder. "I understand completely, Charles! Allow me a few minutes to refresh myself, and we shall be off."

When the gentlemen arrived at Longbourn, they were shown into a room they had never seen before. Jane was busy with sewing from the poor basket and Elizabeth was writing at a large desk. After the usual greetings, Jane motioned for Bingley to follow her to a sitting area near the window, eager to discuss what she and Lizzy had spoken of the previous night. The couple instantly became absorbed in conversation.

Elizabeth turned to her betrothed and asked about his morning.

"I have completed the most urgent of my business, but there are other concerns that shall require my attention within the next few days. I apologize, Elizabeth, but it seems I will need to spend the next few mornings in a similar manner."

"William, if any woman can understand, I can. In spending so much time in my father's study over the years and assisting him with business concerns on numerous occasions, I have been familiar with how much work is involved in managing a *small* estate. Any time that Papa was required to leave Longbourn for more than a day or two, it was left to me to do as much of his work as I could. Yet, I can probably only imagine a portion of the work involved with an estate the size of Pemberley, let alone any other business you might have. There is no need to apologize to me, of all people! I am thankful that you have had so much time to spend with me. But tell me, have you written to anyone of our impeding nuptials? Family or friends, perhaps?"

William smiled before saying, "Other than informing both Mrs. Reynolds and Mrs. Martin that they should ready the mistress's chambers at both Pemberley and Darcy House, the letters I have written were all business. I have not yet notified any of my family or friends. There are several Darcy relatives that I should inform. They will be very glad to hear that such a worthy woman will soon be mistress of their ancestral seat, especially when I inform them that my father himself had known and approved of you." William's eyes twinkled. "I should also write to a few friends—especially those you met at Netherfield at the ball. I must say they all adored you and will be very happy for us both. You made such a favorable impression on them that they teased me mercilessly with the fact that I am more than likely not good enough for you."

His smile faded as he voiced his next thought, "I cannot think of many within my mother's family whom I feel the need to inform personally at this time—or correspond with in any way. If they care to look, the announcement will be in all the usual papers within the next few days. I would like to write to the Lord Reginald and Lady Clara, Richard's brother and sister, but since at last report they were both due to be visiting their father's house in London, I will not do so at this time."

Elizabeth took William's hand and squeezed it gently. "When you came in, I had just begun to pen my missives. Are you too tired to write your letters now? If you have had enough letter-writing for one day, I shall put it off."

"*This* task is one that is not unwelcome, Elizabeth, and since I must write these letters at some time or another, I would much rather do so now, with you, than while sitting alone at Netherfield." William looked to the desk at which Elizabeth had been writing. "I *had* been wondering at the placement of this desk within the room since I had not noticed the second chair, but now I see it is a partners' desk. May we sit across from each other?"

"Yes, of course. When we were younger, we used this room as sort of a school room. It was while sitting here that Jane and I first learned our letters and numbers as well as many other subjects."

William held her chair as she sat and then walked around to the other side of the desk and sat opposite her. It was not an overly wide partners' desk so when Elizabeth moved her supplies toward the middle of the desk, everything was within reach of them both. "It seems that I have only one inkwell at this desk at present. Would you like to share it or shall I fetch another?"

It seemed silly but the thought of sharing an inkwell with Elizabeth seemed to make the act of letter writing a more intimate experience than if they each had their own, and judging by her question, William guessed that she felt the same way. There was a sudden shift in the expression of her eyes that told him that she was thinking about something mischievous, but since he could not imagine what it could be, he began the first of his letters.

After William had busied himself with his letter, Elizabeth glanced at Jane and Bingley, happily concluding that they could not see under the desk from where they sat engrossed in quiet conversation.

She and Jane had spent many an hour here at this desk as children. No matter what level of interest the subject held for her, it had always been a trial for Elizabeth to sit still for any length of time. Whenever they had been long at their studies, Elizabeth would slip off her shoes and move her legs about. The girls would inevitably find the need to suppress bouts of giggles whenever Elizabeth had mistakenly nudged Jane with her toes as she fidgeted, and Jane would turn the situation into a game and begin to nudge her in return.

Today, as soon as William had sat in Jane's place at the desk, Elizabeth had decided on repeating this game with him. Little did Elizabeth realize that engaging in this behavior with *William* would not elicit the feelings of amusement as it had with Jane, but ones of a very different nature!

William had just begun his letter to the eldest member of the Darcy clan when he felt a weight upon his boot. Assuming his long legs were taking up too much space under the desk, he excused himself and moved his leg to the side. Twice more did the same occur before he began to suspect that Elizabeth was up to something—not only due to the lack of response from her when he moved his foot away, but also the expression of exaggerated innocence that her glance held after the third time it happened. The fourth time, he left his foot in place to see what she would do next.

Before long he found himself thanking the heavens for placing the sharp stone in his way—the stone that had very recently pierced the sole of his high-topped Hessian boots, requiring him to wear the only other boots he had brought with him, a pair that were cut so low that they could only be worn under trousers. As Elizabeth's foot had moved upward from his boot, he realized that she must have removed her slipper. William closed his eyes, savoring the sensation of her stocking-clad foot slowly travelling up his calf muscle. He thought that it was probably a very good thing that there was a desk between them preventing him from taking her in his arms just now!

When her foot stopped moving upwards, his eyes snapped open and met Elizabeth's smoldering gaze, causing a pleasant shiver to run down his spine. William could not help but notice that her rate of breathing had quickened, which brought to mind that his own had increased as well, and he endeavored to regulate it lest they be found out.

Bingley's hearty laugh emanating from across the room caused them both to startle, bringing to the forefront of both of their minds the fact that they were not alone, but a quick look in that direction confirmed that they had not been discovered. William had expected Elizabeth to remove her foot at the reminder, but instead she began to write while repeating the same movement until his lower leg was being continually caressed by her nearly-bare foot. He noticed that his trousers suddenly seemed too tight.

Glancing at Jane and Bingley, Elizabeth pushed a piece of paper across the desk. There in her elegant hand, were the words:

Does this bother you?

William almost laughed out loud, and then wrote his reply:

That depends upon what definition you are using for the word bother, my heart.

After he returned the page, Elizabeth's back straightened, and her ministrations ended immediately. In a panic, he grabbed the nearest sheet of paper and wrote:

Do not misunderstand me, Elizabeth! I did not mean that you should stop!

Elizabeth bit her lip as she read the note and then looked up at him, her eyes sparkling with mirth. She began again, but this time giving his other leg its share of attention.

Eventually, Bingley announced that he was going to speak to Mr. Bennet, startling the pair and bringing them back to reality once more. Elizabeth wrote:

I believe we must attend our letters now that my sister will no longer be distracted.

Only in his thoughts did he reply, *"It is for the best, for if you do not cease, I will not be fit to be seen in company!"* He gathered the notes they had passed to each other and reluctantly threw them into the fire and then spent some time observing Elizabeth as she wrote a letter, admiring her many charms.

Bingley returned a short time later with a huge grin on his face. Elizabeth could see that Jane was overwhelmed with emotions that she did not wish to express within the house and suggested the foursome take a walk.

As soon as they were out of sight of the house, there were congratulations made to the now officially engaged couple. Bingley told them that Mr. Bennet had agreed to delay the announcement of their engagement. Though William enumerated all of the reasons that the engagement should be announced *now*, Jane and Bingley would not capitulate. It would be announced at the wedding breakfast and not before.

After several minutes in conversation, they began to walk again with Jane and Bingley lagging back behind. Before the couples had separated very far apart, Bingley called out, "Darcy, what happened to the legs of your trousers?"

The others' attention shifted to William's legs and saw that the bottom portions of his trousers were rather severely wrinkled.

Jane gasped, remembering the stray thought that had crossed her mind when she had seen William about to sit at the desk earlier in the day and now realizing what must have occurred to spoil his trousers. Before she knew what she was about, Jane had already exclaimed in a disapproving tone, "Lizzy!"

Elizabeth's eyes widened, and both she and William blushed deeply.

Though he did not understand what was happening, Bingley was very sorry he had brought attention to whatever it was that caused his companions to react so strongly.

Surprising everyone, Jane began to giggle, and then to laugh outright and before long her laughter proved to be contagious.

They all began to walk once again with Jane and Bingley now in the lead. When the other couple was well ahead of them, William turned his gaze to his betrothed. It seemed that Elizabeth was mortified and could not look at him. William placed a finger under her chin and lifted it so that she could not help but look into his eyes. "Elizabeth… you *will* remind me to acquire a similar desk for the studies in each of our houses, will you not?"

An expression of obvious relief was replaced by a slow smile spreading across her face, "I see I shall look forward to writing my letters as a married lady."

He laughed, "I am afraid that today I did not accomplish the writing of *any* of the letters that I had set out to complete. Do you think we should write them separately after all... or should we try again tomorrow?"

Elizabeth made a show of thinking the matter over before replying, "I, for one, would like to try again tomorrow. If we again accomplish nothing, then we will have to reconsider the matter."

William smiled, glad that she had agreed to repeat today's antics for he had every intention of travelling to Longbourn in his carriage on the morrow so that he could wear his evening shoes—ones that would easily slip off his feet when necessary.

~%~

2 December 1810

The next few days continued in a manner which had quickly become a routine at Longbourn. William and Bingley took care of their business in the mornings while the ladies paid special attention to the details of the upcoming nuptials, and in the very early afternoons the gentlemen would join the Bennets, usually to engage the eldest two ladies in a walk when the weather was good enough, which would follow with their staying until after dinner.

Three days had passed and on this day, the walking party's return to Longbourn was marked with the arrival of a carriage. Noticing William's smile, Elizabeth asked if he recognized it.

"Yes, it is one of mine. It must be Georgiana and Richard!"

As Richard assisted Georgiana from the carriage, Georgiana's attention was caught by the group's approach. William was only a little surprised that Georgiana set out in a run toward them crying out "Lizzy!" and rushing into Elizabeth's embrace, meeting with such force that, if not for William's quick thinking to support them, the two would have ended on the ground in a heap. The younger woman's words were strained with emotion, "Oh, Lizzy! How we have missed you! We are to be *sisters* at last!" Elizabeth voiced similar sentiments. She met William's gaze, and they exchanged a smile filled with all the joy of this reunion.

Richard clapped his cousin's shoulder in an attempt to distract William from the tears Richard could see were being choked back after witnessing the emotional greeting between the women who owned his heart. "Well, old boy! You seem to have been forgotten for the moment!" He chuckled. "When we arrived at Netherfield and found you missing, even the fatigue of travelling could not stop Georgie from seeking out Miss Elizabeth, knowing you would more than likely be here. I was barely able to convince her to allow us time to change out of our travel clothes before setting off!"

"I assume there is no need to ask if you received my letter, Richard! I apologize for not being present to greet you, but I had no way of knowing when you would arrive and had no intention of remaining alone at Netherfield all day every day waiting for you."

"You mean you had absolutely no intention of staying away from Miss Elizabeth and, since there were no ladies in residence at Netherfield, she could not visit you there! Do not worry; both Georgie and I understood completely. As to my failure to notify you of our coming, it seemed silly to send one of your servants galloping all the way from Pemberley with a message only to arrive a few hours ahead of us—especially since you stated in your letter that Bingley would be ready for us at any time. Your letter followed me by only a few hours. Georgie was so excited after learning that it was all a misunderstanding that with the news of your engagement, she began to pack immediately, insisting on beginning the journey the following morning. I hope you intend to stay put for a few days as I am very tired of all this travelling!"

As Richard had spoken, William motioned for Richard to walk, stopping outside of hearing of the rest of the party. "What news of the postal worker from Lambton?"

"As suspected, Mr. Booth was a naïve young man. Generally speaking, he has been another victim who made a terrible mistake and saw no way out of the situation in which he found himself without risking the welfare of his younger siblings whom he supports. He was quite remorseful and rather grateful for the opportunity to purge his conscience of his misdeeds. As a matter of fact, I have never heard a more willing confessor! I have taken the liberty of using *your* money to send him and his siblings to their relatives in Ireland where my father should never find them—if he should even care to look."

William nodded and then asked, "Have you heard anything from your father or Aunt Catherine?"

"No, I have not, but the staff at Darcy House and Pemberley have strict orders not to admit either of them or inform them where any of us have gone, though I do not think it would be difficult for them to find us since my father has your and Georgiana's letters in his possession by now. I brought extra footmen with us in the event there was a need for them along the road."

"We will not go into hiding, Richard. With the addition of my staff to Bingley's, I am certain that all will be well."

Noticing that their conversation seemed to be at an end, Elizabeth steered Georgiana toward the gentlemen to continue the greetings and receive congratulations from "Colonel Richards."

~%~

The next day, when Georgiana and the gentlemen came to visit in the afternoon, Georgiana was shown into the drawing room to visit with the ladies, but the gentlemen were informed that Mr. Bennet had asked Mrs. Hill to show them into his study.

"Gentlemen, I had a visitor early this morning—Colonel Forster. It seems that Wickham's transfer orders were finally received yesterday afternoon. However..." he looked directly at each of the gentlemen to insure that he had their full attention before continuing, "I must stress that what I am about to say should not leave this room. There seems to be a bit of a problem."

Richard responded first, "What has Wickham done *this* time? No, wait... let me guess. He has run up credit with all the shopkeepers and, of course, at the tavern. Once his gaming debts are considered as well, the total of what he owes is *not* covered by his salary."

"Very good, Colonel Fitzwilliam; you are correct on all counts, but the picture is not yet complete. His debts are not the problem as Wickham has recently acquired the ability to pay them. You see, there is the small matter of a *lady*..." Mr. Bennet's expectations were not disappointed. All three gentlemen sat up straighter and their color rose considerably, "...a Miss King, who has recently arrived in Meryton to visit relatives. It seems that

Wickham was none too pleased when he heard of the transfer—to be more precise, of whom his new commanding officer would soon be. He slipped away from his duties at camp and went directly to the tavern. Wickham was well in his cups by the time he was seen climbing into Miss King's bedchamber window. Unfortunately, the window is close to the street and the escapade was witnessed by a few of the townspeople. By the time her uncle had been notified and rushed home from his shop, Miss King and Wickham had been alone in her bedchamber for some time. From what Colonel Forster said, the lady was only too happy to accept the *charming* Lieutenant Wickham's offer of marriage, and her uncle had no choice but to give his immediate consent."

William made no attempt to hide the anger and disgust in his voice. "Wickham is usually not so indiscreet! Unless... what is Miss King's *dowry*?"

Mr. Bennet nodded, "Miss King has recently inherited ten thousand pounds."

Richard growled, "And with so many witnesses, there is nothing to be done! I am sure of one thing—the scoundrel made *certain* he was seen climbing into that window! Knowing him, he probably made a great deal of noise to attract attention to himself! Bah! 'Happy to accept Wickham'? That poor girl knows not what kind of life has been thrust upon her."

"Perhaps..." Bingley began, "though I cannot help but wonder... now that he will be married and have ample funds, might he settle down and behave?"

William opened his mouth to speak but Richard interrupted, "Bingley, you do not know the man like we do. There is little chance of that! He went through Darcy's four thousand in less than two years! With two of them to support I estimate it will it take him four years to go through ten thousand—less if there are children. Where will that leave Mrs. Wickham and the children when he has gone through all of her money? Abandoned in a one-room flat somewhere, penniless? I truly pity Miss King!"

Mr. Bennet decided to regain control of the discussion. "But, as you said, Colonel, there is nothing to be done. They *must* marry. There is one more piece of news—Wickham's transfer to your friend's regiment is void as he has resigned from His Majesty's service and sold his commission."

Richard suddenly stood and walked toward the door.

"Richard! Do not do anything rash!" William called out.

"Though I *would* like to beat the blackguard to a pulp, worry not, cousin! If Wickham does not marry Miss King, she is completely ruined, and *I* will not be the cause of the ruination of a young lady. I only wish you had not dissuaded me from calling him out after Ramsgate!"

Mr. Bennet spoke up, "William did right, Colonel. You would do no one any good dangling on the end of a rope."

"Excuse me, gentlemen. I find I am very angry and unfit to be in company, especially that of ladies. I will see you at some point later in the day when I can behave in a more genteel manner. Please make my excuses to Mrs. Bennet." Richard bowed and strode out the door.

The three remaining gentlemen startled when, before Richard closed the door behind him, they could hear Mrs. Bennet screaming for Mrs. Hill and her smelling salts.

Mr. Bennet cleared his throat. "It seems that Mrs. Bennet has just heard the news. I am certain we shall soon hear what exaggerated version of the truth is being spread about the neighborhood." He hesitated a few moments before continuing, "One of the reasons that Colonel Forster had come to see me was to inquire whether I knew of anyone who would buy Wickham's commission. *I* have purchased the commission with the condition that Wickham and Miss King leave the area immediately to prevent Miss King's being subjected to any more gossip than absolutely necessary. I would like to know if either of you, or if not perhaps Colonel Fitzwilliam, knows of a young man that could benefit from this situation. It would be a gift."

"Mr. Bennet, I cannot allow you to take this upon yourself. It was through my father's misguided generosity—thinking that he was assisting Wickham in preparing to succeed his father as steward of Pemberley by sending him to school—which gave him the idea that he was *owed* a life of leisure. Purchasing the commission is a small price to pay to get him far away from my family—*before* my wedding!"

"As you recently had mentioned, William, there is nothing that would please the miscreant more than to receive *more* money from the Darcy family. Even if he never knows where the money came from, I will *not* permit one more penny of Darcy money to be spent on that man! I would not have the money to do this is it were not for your father's urging me to invest my income instead of having it sit idle. I am ashamed to say that it is more likely I would have handed it all to my wife to spend recklessly if it had not been for George's influence. Allow *me* to remedy this situation and pass on a small piece of your father's generosity by gifting the commission to a *worthy* young man this time—one who would not otherwise be able to afford it. Do you know of anyone who has proven himself? A tenant's son, perhaps? I can think of no one in this area who could be spared by his family to leave home."

William's eyes lit up. "Actually, I have the perfect person in mind. My footman, James, has a grandson who fits this description—quite a respectable and able young man. James is here at Longbourn today, sir, if you would like to speak to him. Though he has never mentioned it, Elizabeth recently told me that years ago James had done her a great service. This would be a fitting reward."

Nodding, Mr. Bennet replied, "Send James in to see me, William."

Chapter 22

With so little time before the wedding, the days passed quickly. Georgiana often spent the entire day at Longbourn assisting with the wedding preparations. She and Elizabeth were as close as they had been in the past, and she also found something of common interest with Elizabeth's sisters—fashion with Lydia, drawing with Kitty, music with Mary, and conversations with Jane as their characters were very similar. Though she found the youngest two livelier than the company to which she was accustomed, all in all, Georgiana was very pleased with the prospect of having five sisters.

Several days after Wickham and Miss King had left the area, Georgiana was to stay with Elizabeth at Longbourn while William travelled to London to retrieve the wedding ring and personally see how the arrangements to welcome Elizabeth to Darcy House were proceeding.

The general atmosphere at Darcy House could not have been called anything but festive. A few of the servants remembered Elizabeth from her previous visits with Mr. Bennet years earlier and, after passing on their good information to the others, *all* at Darcy House were looking forward to having her as their mistress.

More than three and one half years ago, wishing to be prepared for the time when he would bring Elizabeth home with him, William had ordered the mistress's chambers at both Darcy House and Pemberley completely renovated, replacing everything other than a few furnishings that were heirlooms. He had painstakingly chosen paper for the walls and patterns for the coverings for the furnishings and upholstery that he thought Elizabeth would like, though he had had every intention of offering to change them if she did not. His belongings had been moved into the master's chambers in London, and the staff in Derbyshire had been scheduled to do the same when he was on his planned trip to Hertfordshire—but that journey did not occur.

Since the work had been completed, only once had he allowed himself to enter what he had thought of as Elizabeth's chambers at Pemberley, that visit being made to approve the alterations *before* the fire, but never after. Since the fire, William had absolutely refused to put himself through the torture of entering the mistress's chambers at either house—until today.

Upon William's arrival in London, it was all he could do not to dash up the stairs to Elizabeth's rooms. As he walked through the door that joined the two bedchambers he could see that he had chosen well; Elizabeth *belonged* in this room. He dared not spare more than a glance for the bed, and then only to check that the pattern of the coverings were appropriate, but he did allow himself to imagine her all around him elsewhere—brushing her hair at the dressing table, standing in front of the full-length mirror dressed for the theater, reading in the window seat, or sitting in one of the comfortable chairs by the fire.

Approaching the dressing table, he carefully unwrapped a package and laid the box upon the table. William traced his finger over the letters "*ED*" so beautifully engraved upon the silver brush set that he had purchased in Lambton as a wedding present for his Elizabeth... so long ago. Since then it had been tucked away in the safe in his study, along with all the other gifts he had purchased for her throughout the years, some for special occasions and others for no purpose at all other than that he had seen them by chance and knew that she would like them.

How many hours had he devoted towards selecting these gifts? How much time had he spent imagining Elizabeth's reaction when she would receive each of them? William shook his head to clear it.

"Elizabeth will be my **wife** *in nine days! I have dreamt of this for so long... will it truly become reality? If something else goes wrong..."* William's breath caught as a moment of panic seized him. He closed his eyes, took a deep breath and purposely remembered the look of pure love that he had seen in Elizabeth's eyes as they ended the kiss they had shared just before he had left her a few hours ago. A feeling of contentment filled him. *"Yes, it will happen. The dark time has ended... she loves me still!"*

When his eyes opened again, he realized he had unconsciously turned toward the bed. *"Only nine more nights!"* William smiled, and turned to leave through the door that led to his own chambers, knowing the next time he passed through this door, it would be to join Elizabeth there.

~%~

Georgiana awakened with the distinct feeling that something was not right. It took a moment for her to remember that she was in Elizabeth's room at Longbourn... but where was Elizabeth? A noise off to the side of the room caused her to turn her head in that direction, but she could see nothing in the low light from the dying fire. Slipping from the bed, she moved toward the source of the noise. *"There it is again! It sounds like..."*

Georgiana moved the curtains aside and saw Elizabeth sitting in the window seat, her knees bent, and her hands covering her face, sobbing quietly. Georgiana whispered, "Lizzy?"

Elizabeth quickly looked up, embarrassed, and wiped her face with her hands. After a few moments spent in an attempt to swallow past the emotion tightening her throat, she forced out in a hoarse voice, "Oh, I am so very sorry I woke you, Georgie!"

Georgiana placed her arm around Elizabeth's shoulders and pulled her into an embrace. "What is wrong, Lizzy?"

Several minutes passed while tears silently streamed down Elizabeth's face, soaking into the shoulder of the younger girl's night shift. "It is so silly, really! I – I cannot stop myself from feeling afraid that something unexpected will happen, and William will not come back again."

Georgiana felt her shudder and smoothed Elizabeth's hair while saying, "Lizzy, you did not see him when he had lost all hope—when he thought he would not see you again, or feared that you would marry someone else while he recovered—but I did. William loves you, and there is *nothing* that could keep him from you again, not even his own pride, for that is what it was, Lizzy. He did not want you to see him in such a vulnerable state because he did not wish for you to think him weak."

Elizabeth pulled away and looked her future sister in the eye. "I know... William gave me his journal to read." She smiled a little at Georgiana's expression. "You are surprised that he did?"

"No, not that he would share his thoughts with you. My surprise is that my brother realized this himself!"

Elizabeth laughed. "It was a recent discovery. I *told* you my fear was silly. Thank you, Georgie, I am certain that I am only tired and a bit spoiled by being able to see him every day. I missed your brother terribly today! I will feel better once I get some sleep. Come, let us try."

~%~

The following afternoon, Elizabeth and Georgiana were in the drawing room embroidering when a terrified Mrs. Hill appeared and announced, "The Earl of Matlock and Lady Catherine de Bourgh."

As the two young ladies stood, Georgiana, wide-eyed with fright, whispered, "Heaven help us, Lizzy!"

Elizabeth took Georgiana's hand and gave it a squeeze as they curtsied, inwardly wishing that she and Georgiana were not the only two at home just now.

"You are Elizabeth Bennet?" Lady Catherine asked in a haughty manner, completely ignoring her niece.

Elizabeth summoned courage from deep within. "I am," she answered in a strong voice, determined not to show any sign of weakness to the two people who had caused them all so much strife and heartache.

"Oh! Get on with it, Catherine! There is no reason for pleasantries with this charlatan; come right to the point, and let us get out of this... *place*. I do not wish for anyone to recognize my carriage sitting outside; it would be degrading," the earl sneered while looking around the room displaying a clear expression of disgust.

Lady Catherine spoke again, "Elizabeth Bennet, you *will* accept our offer of ten thousand pounds to break off the engagement with Fitzwilliam Darcy. Our nephew will marry *my* daughter."

At first, Elizabeth's mouth dropped open momentarily in shock, but this emotion was quickly replaced. Attempting to stifle her outrage at the offense that this offer represented, Elizabeth responded, "I will *not* accept *any* such offer."

"Foolish girl! You rely upon your negotiation skills? Do not waste our time—you will not receive a higher amount no matter what you say or do."

"For the final time, my answer is 'no,' Lady Catherine. I should like to know why anyone would attempt to force two people who do *not* wish to marry to do just that?"

"*That* is none of your business."

"It is my business when you are speaking of my fiancé, your ladyship."

The earl turned to his sister and spat out, "You waste your breath and my time speaking to her in this manner, Catherine. If the chit will not be persuaded, *take* Georgiana as we had discussed. Fitzwilliam *will* do what we say and marry Anne if we have his sister."

Eyes flashing, Elizabeth quickly stepped between the noble pair and Georgiana, clasping her hands in front of her. "You will not."

Lord Matlock stepped forward and boomed out, "How *dare* you tell us what we can and cannot do! You, a pretender of the highest order, the daughter of a tradesman's daughter and a man who is practiced in the art of deceit, who has drawn in the entire Darcy family and convinced them to trust you both—you have no right! Georgiana's father was gullible and weak, but we could do nothing for the girl at that time. We will not permit Georgiana's obviously incompetent brother to be of any further influence over the poor, simpleminded girl. Fitzwilliam has taken after his father and has allowed himself to be completely deluded by your machinations. Somehow you have even turned my own son against me! You and your father have taken advantage of them all, and we—Georgiana's *family*—will now take charge of her care."

Elizabeth heard a quiet whimper from behind her as Elizabeth stood in undisguised shock at the ridiculous statements she had just heard. Taking a steadying breath, she answered, "Lord Matlock, Lady Catherine… you will fool no one with these fabrications. Not only have you insulted my family, my home and myself, but you have also emphatically abused my fiancé, his father, *and* my invited guest, all in the space of less than one quarter of an hour. I shall have to ask you both to leave my home."

The distinct sound of a slap echoed throughout the room.

Unprepared for the attack, Elizabeth had been thrown off balance slightly. Recovering quickly, she stood up to her full height, eyes blazing with anger, and said in her most authoritative *Dreaded Pirate Lizzy* voice, "Lady Catherine, I care not what your relationship is with Georgiana, you will *not* touch her! Nor will you, Lord Matlock! Georgiana has been left in *my* care by her legal guardians, and I *will not* allow you to take her from here.

"I must ask you once more to leave my house. I am quite certain you do not wish to be *removed*!" Knowing the only other person in the house was Mrs. Hill, Elizabeth could only hope that her bluff was convincing enough to have them leave without causing any further problems.

The earl laughed. "If there were anyone else in this house, they would have come in by now—you are *alone*. Exactly what do you think you can do to stop us, *girl*? My sister's slap was nothing compared to what you will face if you force my hand. I will take care of you myself, and my niece *will* leave here with us. Besides, *you* may be an insolent, headstrong girl, but no one else would *dare* stand against the Earl of Matlock!"

Elizabeth stood her ground with both her foes towering above her. "You would have to get through me first. I have no other cheek to turn to you, sir; I have only two. If either of you strikes me again—I warn you now—I will not be held responsible for any of your injuries! I *will* protect my sister."

"I would see to it that you *hang* if you dare to strike an earl!"

"And I would take my chances with the law rather than allow Georgiana to be taken from here by either of *you*."

Elizabeth steeled herself as she saw the earl begin to move toward her.

~%~

James rushed through the servants' entrance at Netherfield and began to search the rooms, finding Bingley and Richard in the billiards room at last. "Colonel Fitzwilliam! I've just returned from Meryton. While there, I saw a coach bearing the crest of the Earl of Matlock pass through the village. Since he has not come here, sir…"

"Longbourn!" Richard barked as he threw on his coat, looking at Bingley. "They must have gone to speak to Georgiana and Miss Elizabeth! We must go at once!"

They determined crossing the fields as the quickest way to Longbourn. Along the way the three men saw the Darcy carriage on the road to Longbourn through the trees. James was sent to overtake the carriage, hand over his horse to his master, and follow with the carriage.

~%~

Elizabeth looked down at the floor where the Earl of Matlock lay writhing in pain and the great Lady Catherine de Bourgh crouched over him, ranting about the *nerve* of one so low doing such a thing to an earl.

It was probably one of the oldest tricks that a lady might use to protect herself, and Elizabeth was shocked to find that the earl had never taken the time to learn to expect, let alone protect himself from, a lady's knee. He had seemed so certain of himself when he moved to overpower her that she had thought he was experienced in the matter of using force on a woman. She expected to need to use several of the protective tactics in her arsenal before having the hope of being successful.

The look of shock on the man's face when she carried through with this simple maneuver had been priceless. Elizabeth had to assume that no one had ever had the *nerve* to employ such a primitive technique upon one so high in rank before... or at least not *this* earl.

"Georgiana, since his Lordship is in no condition to do so, I do believe it is time for *us* to leave," Elizabeth said with her head held high, as she nearly pulled the gaping young lady from the room. They left the house as quickly as they could though the kitchen, avoiding the earl's carriage out front. Elizabeth had no idea what orders the earl's men had, and she had no intention of finding out!

Elizabeth knew these woods better than anyone else, and her highest priority was to keep Georgiana safe, but adding to their dilemma was the temperature. Having stowed their coats upstairs in her bedchamber closet, in their haste they had left the house without any protection from the elements. It *had been* unseasonably warm of late, but the weather had turned very cold today. Setting a brisk pace to warm them a little, she decided to lead the way through the woods toward the tenant farm closest to Longbourn, knowing her father had planned to visit this afternoon to discuss the plans for renovations that would be taking place there.

When they came to a large meadow, Elizabeth knew they had no choice but to venture out into the open. "Georgie, we must run across the meadow. I do not know if the earl's men are looking for us, so if anyone comes, we must lay down in the long grass to hide ourselves as best we can."

Georgiana's teeth were clamped together to keep them from chattering, so she just nodded.

When they had walked about half-way across the field, the ladies heard horses, and Elizabeth pulled Georgiana to the ground. Both ladies peeked through the grass, and suddenly Georgiana began to squeal, "Will! Richard!" The ladies stood and began to run in the direction of the horses.

William was the first to reach them, and he began to dismount before his horse had fully stopped. "Elizabeth! Georgiana! Are you well? We were told that the Earl…"

Breathless, Elizabeth nodded and, not caring who witnessed it, she threw herself into the safety of his arms, inhaling his scent as deeply as she could. William *had* come! She felt Georgiana join her and wrapped one arm around her as well. William enveloped the ladies as best he could within his coat to warm them.

A few moments later, recovered a little, Elizabeth said, "We are well and glad to see you!"

"Where is Jane?" Bingley asked.

Elizabeth turned her head towards him, but would not release her hold of William. "Georgiana and I were home alone. Jane is with my mother and sisters in Meryton, and my father is at a tenant's farm. I was taking Georgiana there just now to seek help."

"We left Aunt Catherine and Uncle Robert at Longbourn, and I imagine they are still there. Oh William, Lizzy was *wonderful,* and so very brave!" Georgiana exclaimed while stepping away from her brother. Richard placed his coat around her. "You should have been there to see Uncle Robert's face! And Aunt Catherine's!"

"Will one of you tell us what happened? I need to be better prepared before stepping into the lion's den!" Richard insisted.

"To put it simply, when I would not accept their money to end the engagement, they demanded to take Georgiana with them so that they could use her to force William to marry Anne de Bourgh," Elizabeth explained. "Of course I could not allow them to take her..."

"They *what?*" William roared.

"They both said such horrible things to Lizzy!" Georgiana nodded. "When Aunt Catherine slapped her for asking them to leave, it made such a frightening sound. I did not know what to do! And then your father, Richard—I had never seen *anyone* so angry! I thought he would do Lizzy a great harm when he took hold of her, and then she... well... do you remember what I told you I had to do to escape from Wickham?"

Richard's face lit up, though he tried to hold back a smile. "You used your knee on the earl!"

Elizabeth nodded. "I *had* warned them that I would protect Georgiana, and that I *would* respond if either of them struck me again! He had taken hold of my arms so forcefully; I had little choice but to defend myself." Her brow furrowed. "Someone had best go to Longbourn. I fear my mother and sisters will return... or my father! I do not understand why the earl hates him so." As Georgiana and she had spoken, Elizabeth could feel the tension in William increase.

"Jealousy, Miss Elizabeth. My father had always wanted a true alliance with George Darcy, for his own selfish reasons, of course. My uncle was too intelligent to trust him. For some reason, my father always blamed yours for this—never himself.

"William, while I am certain you would like to confront them, judging by the look in your eyes, I do *not* trust you anywhere near my father or our aunt right now. I know very well that what they say would only make you angrier, and we do not want anyone calling the magistrate as a result of *your* behavior! *I* will go to Longbourn and deal with them. Your men will be there with the carriage by now, William, and they probably are wondering what to do next. We shall *escort* them away from Longbourn." Richard bowed to the ladies and mounted his horse.

Bingley bid them goodbye as well and followed.

They watched for several moments as the two gentlemen rode away, and then Georgiana glanced between her brother and Elizabeth, exclaiming,

"Oh! There is an interesting.... bush just over there! I must have a look at those ... green leaves." And she walked off a few feet in the direction she had been pointing, remaining in sight of the couple but facing away from them.

Elizabeth looked up at her betrothed and saw that he did look quite angry. Trying to distract him, she said with a laugh, "Though I do not mind, I fear your sister has never been the best chaperone." It had not worked. "William, we are fine—truly. I made certain they never got near enough to Georgiana to touch her."

"But at what cost?" William gently took her face between his hands; his thumb tenderly caressed the red mark on her face, obviously where Lady Catherine had slapped her, and searched her eyes. Satisfied with what he saw there, he continued, "Thank you, Elizabeth."

"For protecting our sister? There is no need to thank me. I would have done the same for any of my sisters."

William looked at her tenderly. "I know you would have... it is who you are. I love you, Elizabeth Bennet, and I will be so proud to have you as my wife."

"I love you, as well, William. I missed you terribly!" Her eyes began to fill with tears. "I – I have never been so afraid."

The muscles in William's jaw tensed, and his expression grew angry as he looked toward Longbourn. Elizabeth realized he had misunderstood her, and she shook her head. "I was not afraid today, William! You know that I had worried about your family's disapproval and the disapproval of the *ton*. This may be difficult to understand, but today's events belied those worries. Protecting Georgie and staving off their degrading assumptions and horrid accusations only proved to me that I have a strength within that I never knew existed before. Believe me, the *ton* cannot say much worse than what was said of all of us today, and I can honestly say that to have people like *that* say these things did not really matter—nor would anyone who was truly important to us ever believe any of it." Elizabeth placed her hand on the side of his face. "It was *last night* that I was afraid! Once the occupation of the day was no longer distracting me, and Georgie had fallen asleep, I was filled with an overwhelming fear that something would happen, and again, you would not come back to me."

"I am sorry – very sorry – that my relatives have abused you so, but even more so that my past misjudgments have instilled this fear within you, Elizabeth. Had I known then what I know now, how many things I would have done differently! I would hope that once we are married, I will always be able to take you with me, but the truth is that I know at one time or another during what I expect to be a *very* long life together, we will be parted. I promise you now that if ever I am injured or ill, I will somehow get word to you of where I am and send for you as soon as may be. I promise that if ever again we must spend time apart, I will always return to you, my Elizabeth."

Elizabeth reached up on her toes and kissed William gently, then whispered huskily, "If Georgiana were not here, I would welcome you properly."

The look in his eyes communicated much more than could words, and he once again pulled her into his embrace.

After listening to his heart beat for a few moments, Elizabeth judged a change of subject to be in order. "What shall *we* do? Georgie and I cannot walk far with men's coats on; they are too long for us."

"One horse cannot carry the three of us, and I will not let either of you out of my sight while my aunt and uncle are still in Hertfordshire. Where is the closest house?"

"Longbourn is the closest. Could you and I switch? I will wear your coat and you wear your greatcoat? Georgiana is taller, and I can help her hold Colonel Fitzwilliam's greatcoat so she can walk more easily... or..." she walked over to Georgiana and said, "Georgie, untie the belt." William helped her fold up the length that was too long and tied the belt around Georgiana's waist, with the belt holding up the length of the coat so she would not trip. "There!"

Georgiana laughed, "I wish I could see it. I doubt it will inspire a new fashion, but it *is* more serviceable this way!"

"I am certain that Richard's valet will not agree when he must work out all the creases. We will walk towards Longbourn. If Aunt Catherine and Uncle Robert are still there, I will drive us to Netherfield in our carriage," William said as he shrugged out of his coat and held it for Elizabeth, and then donned his greatcoat. "I will not allow them to approach either of you again."

Chapter 23

As Elizabeth, Georgiana, and William approached Longbourn, all was quiet, but they were disappointed to find that there were still two carriages and a number of horses in the drive in front of the house. William asked the ladies to wait where they were and indicated his intention to bring their carriage closer. Then they would all travel to Netherfield.

"Lord Matlock and Lady Catherine *must* be leaving soon, William. I have been thinking ... I will *avoid* them to prevent any further unpleasant scenes, but I refuse to *hide* from them. Georgiana is safe, as am I." Elizabeth's determination was reflected by the set of her jaw. "I will remain here for now, but when you return with the carriage, I *will* be going inside. For eight more days this is my home, and I will not be chased away from it again—not by the two of them, of all people!"

William closed his eyes and took a few deep breaths to calm his temper before speaking. "Elizabeth, you must see that I will not allow you to enter the house while two people who have assaulted you are within—and definitely not without me by your side. Please do not ask this of me. I cannot. It is unsafe."

"But I am not afraid. I promise to go upstairs to my room to pack Georgiana's things immediately upon entering the house. I shall have her bag sent to Netherfield as soon as they have departed and enclose a note so that you will know they have gone and all is well. Have faith that all will be well, especially since there are so many gentlemen about. Remember that Colonel Fitzwilliam and Mr. Bingley are also within, as is James and any other of your men who were on the carriage."

"No. Not without me, and I will not expose Georgiana to people who would kidnap her if they had the chance! Please be sensible about this, Elizabeth. My uncle's men must be within as well for there is nobody with the carriages other than your stable boy. I have no idea what the situation is inside the house. You will come with us."

"I will not be forced to scurry away from my own home as if I were afraid of them! They *wished* to frighten me, and if I do leave, it would be as if I were admitting that they had been successful. Do you not see that they will think they can continue to intimidate me and will come to me once again before the wedding? I will not go to Netherfield, William, and that is final."

He could see that Elizabeth was quite determined, and if he forced her to go, he would be no better than *they* had been. "I have often said that I love your stubborn nature, but at this moment, I wish that it was not being expressed against my own wishes. I understand your argument, and your point is well taken, but you must admit that *I* am right as well. If you will not come with us, then Georgiana and I have no choice but to stay here *with you* until they have gone."

"I did say I would stay here, but I only meant while you were gone to fetch the carriage, William."

"You *said* that you would stay here until I bring the carriage, Elizabeth! I choose not to bring the carriage at this time."

Georgiana began to laugh. "You have lost this debate, Lizzy. He is as stubborn as you are! Besides, if William does not stop you from going into the house, I will! By staying outside with us, it is as you said you wished; you are not hiding, only avoiding an unpleasant scene..." Georgiana looked up at a movement near the house, and she sighed. "Though it seems that we will not be able to avoid an unpleasant scene after all."

Both of her companions turned to follow Georgiana's gaze. Lady Catherine and Lord Matlock had been leaving, but apparently had noticed them standing nearby and so now were arguing with Richard, pointing and gesturing wildly in their direction. The lady was speaking so loudly that several derogatory phrases had already carried over the space between the two groups. William would avoid confronting them no longer.

As he rounded the front of the house, William could see James standing near the doorway. Hearing the ladies following closely behind him, he said,

"Go into the house with James." Georgiana did as she was told, but Elizabeth caught up to him, threaded her arm through William's as he came to a stop, and stood proudly beside her fiancé. Richard moved to stand beside Elizabeth.

Mr. Bennet rode up at that moment, quietly dismounted and joined them, glowering at Lord Matlock.

While maintaining his glare directed at his uncle, William covered Elizabeth's hand with his own, thinking, *"We face adversity together, as one."*

"Send your Jezebel and her puppet-master away, Fitzwilliam," Lord Matlock spit out.

William's eyes blazed with anger. "Elizabeth's place is by my side, *always*! You *will* cease speaking of my fiancée and her father in a disrespectful manner! As long as I can remember, your behavior has continually shamed the memory of every Fitzwilliam who has ever lived. Among your despicable acts, you have striven to keep Elizabeth and me apart by using blackmail and deception, only to be unsuccessful in the end. Today, you both have sunk to new lows! Not only have you made insulting offers to my fiancée, physically and verbally abusing probably the most honorable and respectable woman in all of England, but also you have threatened to remove a young girl from her home so that you can force others to bend to your will—I am ashamed to admit I am related to either of you!"

Lord Matlock was incensed. "I will speak of them any way I wish! *She* is vulgar, crude, impertinent and mercenary!" He gestured towards his sister. "Catherine and I are *both* certain that *girl* has used her arts and allurements quite *expertly* and effectually to have gained such power over you—and today she has physically attacked a member of the peerage! All of which has been directed by *him*!" he barked the last word, pointing at Mr. Bennet. "Before now, I could not believe that you would truly cast off duty and honor for this trollop, but now I see very clearly!"

The earl nodded, displaying an attitude of disgust. "Do you not recognize what she and her father have done to you, Nephew? What they had done to your father? Your sister, being a simpleton, we can excuse for being taken in by these opportunists. George Darcy proved that he was a weak-minded fool… but we had hoped that *you* would become a better man than he! Now *you* show your true mettle; your inability to see the power that this grasping woman holds over you is proved by the disrespectful way you speak to *us* today—your own flesh and blood!"

William moved a step closer to Lord Matlock. "I will say this once, and not again, so listen closely. I hereby denounce all connection to you both, familial or otherwise! If you say so much as one word more against my family or my future family, I *will* demand satisfaction. Up until now, your advanced age has been the only consideration that has kept me from calling you out, *Lord Matlock*, but know this—it will protect you no longer!"

Lady Catherine gasped, "You would not *dare* to make a public break with us! It would cause a scandal of unmatched proportions within the *ton*."

"Your concerns are very telling, madam." William glanced at Lord Matlock, wondering if he had realized that his sister was *not* concerned that her brother's life might be lost in a duel, and then returned his eyes to meet those of Lady Catherine. "Elizabeth, Georgiana, and I might be affected by gossip at first, but the *ton* is nothing if not curious. They will seek out the new Mrs. Darcy eventually, and when they do, I am quite confident that they will learn that Elizabeth is a *more than* valuable and worthy addition to their acquaintance. She will be highly sought after—and *not* only for her position as my wife, but on her own merits.

"It might actually work in our favor that you are no longer associated with us, since both of your *reputations* are well known." William glared meaningfully at both of them for a moment before continuing, "You also have made no secret of your wish to have me marry my cousin, and I have never hidden the fact that I refuse to do so. I am certain that the people who *matter* will immediately recognize any slander you may toss about for exactly what it is—a tantrum filled with jealousy and resentment—and those who do not come to that immediate conclusion *will* see it in time. Until their curiosity is piqued, I have no doubt that I shall enjoy every minute that I do not have to share Elizabeth's time with the *ton*!

"Neither of you are welcome into the presence of any of my *family* from this moment forward." William began to lead Elizabeth away toward the house.

Mr. Bennet stepped forward and stated forcefully, "Robert, you and your sister *will* leave my property—*now*—as you are not welcome *here* either."

Lord Matlock stood still for a few moments longer, then turned and limped to his carriage, screaming out abuses and orders to his men.

Lady Catherine ranted at her nephew until the carriage door closed on her reddened face, "You will be exceedingly sorry for what you have done today! You will see! There will come a day—and soon—that you will regret not marrying my Anne! I am seriously displeased, Fitzwilliam!"

Mr. Bennet caught up to Elizabeth and William, and clapped William's shoulder. "Your father would have been very proud of your actions today, son. If I remember correctly, some of what you said was very much like a speech of his own which I had the privilege of witnessing... directed towards the same parties."

"Thank you, sir." They stopped and watched the earl's carriage leave the grounds.

Mr. Bennet turned to Richard and said, "Colonel, I am very glad that you are nothing like your father! Come to my study—you owe me a game of chess. Mr. Bingley can continue to entertain the ladies." The two gentlemen went inside, both knowing very well that they would not be playing chess today.

Once they were alone, Elizabeth glanced at the drawing room windows and saw Georgiana, her mother, sisters—and even Bingley—all dash away from the glass. "I do believe we had an audience!" Elizabeth pulled on William's arm, "Let us seek a more private place."

"Are you not cold, Elizabeth? I do not wish you to become ill."

"Actually, my love, what I have in mind is more than talking, and I do believe it will warm us both."

William smiled, which brightened when he realized that she was leading him to the bench that they had sat upon together when he had first been at Longbourn years ago—where he had drawn her likeness while she read Plato aloud to him.

His smile faded as more recent events intruded upon his thoughts, and he stopped walking. She turned to look at him and he said, "Elizabeth, I must apologize for not insisting upon your removal to the house earlier. When you took my arm, I selfishly wished to have you by my side, but I should have realized... for you to have heard such insulting remarks..."

"William, truly—it was nothing I had not already heard from them earlier in the day." She blushed slightly before saying, "Well, perhaps it was a *little* more than what they had said to me before, but it was not wholly unexpected. And, it did my vanity some good to know just how highly you think of me," Elizabeth quipped in an attempt to put him at ease, but then her expression turned serious. "You know there is no place I would rather be than by your side, no matter what the task at hand, through pleasant encounters or otherwise, I shall *always* stand with you."

Elizabeth wrapped her arms around his waist and leaned into the warmth and strength of William's embrace. As he pulled her even closer to him, he bowed his head and breathed in the only scent that could relax and comfort, and at the same time, stimulate him in such a way... the very essence of all that was Elizabeth. His entire body tensed once more as he thought, *"How could anyone wish to harm this incredible woman?"*

Elizabeth pulled away and reached up to caress William's cheek. "Excuse me, Mr. Darcy, but I believe that I must use my *arts and allurements* to effectually change the direction of your thoughts." Her hand laced through his hair, and she pulled him down for a kiss.

After several minutes, he pulled away slightly and pressed his forehead against hers. "Eight more days."

"Actually," she glanced at the sun which was just beginning to set, "closer to seven."

He opened his eyes and gave her a look that left little doubt as to what he meant by the words he said next, "But there are eight more *nights*, my love."

On the evening following these events, after the men had finished their brandies, Mr. Bennet asked William to stay behind as the other gentlemen moved to rejoin the ladies in the drawing room. William assumed his future father-in-law wished to discuss with him privately all that had occurred the previous day and settled back into his seat for a long discussion. He was surprised, therefore, when Mr. Bennet moved to stand at the window. There was nothing to see out of doors since the twilight had long since faded into darkness. Having used this tactic himself many times in the past, William knew that Mr. Bennet was trying to avoid looking at him, causing him to become apprehensive about the conversation about to take place.

After several minutes of silence, Mr. Bennet began, "Your being the son of my closest friend, who is no longer with us, leaving you without any married male relatives with whom to speak, I feel it is my obligation to speak to you about a certain… subject."

William's eyes opened wider than they had ever been in his life. Was Elizabeth's *father* about to speak to him about what to expect on his wedding night—which would be with his own daughter?!

"I must admit that it is a relief to finally clear my conscience about something, William. I must confess to you that I had *overheard* a conversation that you had with your father years ago while we had stayed at Pemberley. So I do know that you have…" he cleared his throat, "*limited experience* with certain… *matters*… of no small importance… especially to a married man. Unless, of course, this has changed since then?"

William closed his mouth, which he had just realized had fallen open at some point during Mr. Bennet's speech. More than just a little uncomfortable with the turn of this conversation, but realizing that Mr. Bennet was probably feeling even more awkward than he at this moment, William took a deep breath and answered in a dispassionate tone. "That has not changed, sir."

"Ah ha…" Mr. Bennet nodded, taking hold of a book from a small table that he was standing near and fidgeting with it. "Well then, I suppose I *should* ask if you have any questions."

William was quiet for some time, not quite certain how he should answer. If he did not have any questions, would Mr. Bennet think that he had lied? But he could not possibly even begin to *think* of asking his fiancée's father… "No, sir, I do not."

"Good… good." The older gentleman now picked up a stack of books and shuffled through them, obviously not paying any mind to what was in his hands. "I should direct you to read two books in particular on this subject. You see, I believe my *very curious* daughter has read them and… well…" Mr. Bennet raised his hand to his face and rubbed his eyes. "…you see… I know for certain that these books have been disturbed—and since *she* is the only person who frequents this room, other than me—we must assume that she has read them." He seemed more than a little surprised to have communicated that thought successfully.

William squirmed as a forgotten memory from the bookshop when they had first met invaded his mind. Suddenly he could hear Elizabeth's young voice saying, "*I am glad that Papa allows me to read anything in his library, and he* *does not forbid me from studying any subject I wish. Well, except for the books on the uppermost shelf by the window on the left, at which I am **never** to look."*

William swallowed hard as he realized that indeed, she *would* more than likely expect him to be aware of all that was within these books! *"Good L-rd, I will have to study every page vigilantly to live up to her expectations!"* He was only vaguely aware of Mr. Bennet reaching up to the very shelf that Elizabeth had mentioned years ago and removing two books.

William stood automatically and accepted the offering as the older gentleman handed him the books.

After several moments where both men stared at the books in William's hands, the younger man spoke up hesitantly, "Sir? How shall I... er, transport them? I imagine it would not be proper to simply carry these into the drawing room with me?"

Mr. Bennet startled. "OH! Quite right! That would not do!" Taking the books from William, he moved to his desk, unwrapped brown paper from the book order he had received earlier that day, and then wrapped the older books with the paper he had just removed.

Taking the books once again, William said quietly, "Thank you, sir, for your time... and for the *warning*."

Removing a handkerchief from his pocket and wiping his brow, Mr. Bennet closed his eyes and said, "William, will you please do me a favor? Since Bingley is in a similar situation—with no living male relatives—I trust *you* will have the first part of that conversation with him when the time comes. I do *not* believe I would survive if I had to do this again!"

William could not help but burst out laughing at Mr. Bennet's tone while making the last remark, and the older gentleman joined in—relieving the tension that had grown between them.

~%~

Elizabeth watched in the mirror as the maid put the finishing touches on her hair, and nodded in approval. Glancing to her left, she smiled widely at Jane. "Do you think William will like it?"

Jane laughed. "William would be satisfied if it were in a simple bun tied with string, and you were wearing a sack, Lizzy, as long as you arrived on time! He made me promise to make certain you were not late and *suggested* the sack as an alternative if you have trouble with the dress that would cause a delay."

"At the very least that proves that he has not changed his mind about marrying me!"

"Of course, he has not!"

"Perhaps I shall be five minutes late on purpose!" Elizabeth declared, stifling a smile.

"Lizzy!"

Elizabeth laughed so hard at Jane's shocked expression that she had to wipe the tears from her cheeks. She caught her elder sister's hands in her own. "Oh, Jane, how I shall miss you!"

"You are still planning to return for Christmas, are you not?

"Yes, we will spend a few days in London and then rejoin Georgiana and Richard at Netherfield the day before Christmas Eve. After the new year, we will travel to Pemberley when the weather will allow our journey, and we will return in April for your wedding. This is the first Christmas that William and Georgiana will not be spending at Pemberley, though. I do hope they do not wish we had delayed the wedding until January."

"They will be happier at Netherfield with you than they would have been at Pemberley without you, Lizzy; you know it is true. And it is good that Charles will not be alone in the house for Christmas since his are sisters away."

"You *do* know what happened with Caroline, do you not, Jane?"

Jane nodded, her eyes focused on the floor.

"William and I have decided that next Christmas the entire family will be invited to Pemberley. I hope you and Charles will be able to join us."

"I am certain that we will not miss it!" Jane exclaimed. "But if you do not begin to dress this instant, you *will* miss your wedding. Please, Lizzy—I promised! I will help you."

After she stepped into the gown, Elizabeth looked at herself in the full-length mirror while Jane tied up the back. It had been made of the finest cream colored silk with gold threads throughout that made it shimmer when she moved, and the color set off her complexion perfectly. Roses of gold, which matched the flecks of color in her eyes, were embroidered along the empire neckline and at the ends of the long sleeves that were puffed at the shoulders. Elizabeth thought that her mother had made the perfect choice after all as cream and gold scalloped lace trimmed all the edges, matching that which marked the high waistline. It was the most beautiful gown that she had ever owned; so elegant that while wearing it, she could easily fit in at the opera or at a ball at Almack's. But *this* was her wedding gown!

A sharp intake of air denoted the moment that Jane had finished fastening the dress and looked up. She pressed her cheek against her younger sister's. "Oh, Lizzy; you are so beautiful! You are glowing with joy!"

"I *am* very happy, Jane! I do hope I will make William a good wife."

"You could not disappoint him, dear. He loves you so."

"To prove that I am determined to be the very best of wives, my first accomplishment shall be to arrive at the wedding *early* so that the groom's anxieties may lessen sooner and you may keep your promise. Let us go, Jane."

Elizabeth took one last look around the bedchamber in which she had grown up and sighed as a wave of melancholy swept over her. Nothing would ever be the same again... nothing. When she next came to Longbourn, even later today for the wedding breakfast, she would have the title of "guest." The feeling passed as quickly as it had come when familiar sounds floated in through the door as Jane opened it. She smiled when she heard her mother's admonishments, rushing the other girls into the Bennet carriage. Lydia was questioning why *she* did not get to ride in the more elegant Darcy carriage that William had been so thoughtful to send to convey Elizabeth to the church. Kitty echoed Lydia's expression of discontent while Mary lectured both of the younger girls about the sin of coveting. The house quieted as the ladies left the house. Jane preceded her sister down the stairs.

Mr. Bennet took Elizabeth's hand to help her down the last few steps. "There has never been a more beautiful bride, my Lizzy," he said with much feeling, his eyes suspiciously moist. "I will miss you very much, my dear, but I know you shall be happy with William."

"Thank you, Papa. I am quite certain I shall." They took a few steps, and then she hesitated just inside the door, looking around once more.

Smiling up at her father, she said, "I am ready!" and then stepped through the entryway of Longbourn for the last time as Elizabeth Bennet.

~%~

Georgiana made a valiant attempt to stifle the laughter that threatened to escape her lips every time she exchanged glances with Bingley. They were both finding amusement by the prospect of William's frequent habit of anxiously peeking out the door of the small room off to the side of the church, looking for the boy who would tell him that it was time to take his place before the altar. William had practically begged the pastor to be allowed to wait here until the bride arrived at the church so that his nerves would not be on display to the neighborhood, giving the wrong impression. After seeing the groom's countenance, the pastor agreed wholeheartedly.

She knew her brother was not nervous about the marriage itself—not at all. He was unable to prevent sharing his concerns with her this morning as he paced the breakfast room at Netherfield. His first worry had been that his aunt and uncle might return to Longbourn this morning and make another attempt at dissuading Elizabeth from marrying him. The second was that they would interrupt the wedding ceremony itself.

It was expected that William would calm a bit once Elizabeth arrived at the church but would continue to be highly uneasy until the ceremony was complete and the register was signed—especially at the moment when the pastor would ask "if any man can shew any just cause why they may not lawfully be joined together, let him now speak." He admittedly knew they *would* marry even if someone did cause a ruckus, for though his relatives believed to the contrary, there truly were *no* just causes that William and Elizabeth should not be married. Just the thought that they might cause a disruption of the holy ceremony that would join Elizabeth and him for life was his undoing.

Richard, too, was fearful that something would go awry this day. Though it was not obvious to anyone who did not know him well, he startled ever so slightly at sudden noises. Early this morning, Georgiana had also overheard part of the speech that Richard had given to the footmen and drivers for their carriage and the one which was sent to Longbourn soon after. She had guessed that the latter group had not as great a need for the instructions since she noticed they were the same men who had witnessed much of what had occurred there recently. The younger Darcy knew the staff that had been assigned to *protect* Elizabeth had not been randomly chosen.

Though Georgiana understood their concerns were based on real possibilities, *she* was not alarmed. Deep within her, she felt that all would be well, and so she had made it her task to do whatever she could to calm the gentlemen. Bingley, as best man, had done his best to distract the groom, but both he and Georgiana found that William was not at all receptive to their endeavors. Before long they had discovered that remaining silent was actually more helpful and concluded that containing their amusement at his behavior was paramount to the success of their cause.

Georgiana imagined that she and Bingley had already done all they could to calm her brother on the day of the incident with her mother's siblings, and the day following it when she explained to William what she and Bingley had done to contain the risk of Mrs. Bennet and the younger daughters gossiping about their aunt and uncle's *visit*. Worried about what she had overheard the youngest two Bennets discussing just after her uncle's carriage had departed, Georgiana had requested the company of Bingley and Jane to accompany her to the study so she could speak to Mr. Bennet.

She giggled a little as she thought of the result of that meeting. Mr. Bennet had taken the situation under control by declaring the subject off-limits to speak of anywhere, especially outside the house or within the hearing of the servants—threatening his wife's and youngest two daughters' pin money for an entire six months if even the slightest mention of the event was spread abroad.

Georgiana came to think that perhaps she had been too confident in thinking that this day would turn out well when she noticed a Darcy footman—who was *supposed* to be at Netherfield—had signaled Richard from the doors at the rear of the church. Richard quickly excused himself, stating a need to stretch his legs outside for a few moments, and then slipped out the side door of the church. She could only be glad that William had not noticed the reason for Richard's removal, but it was not long before he became suspicious of Richard's absence.

~%~

Elizabeth was quite proud of herself when, as the coach pulled up in front of the church, she asked her father the time and learned that she was ten minutes early! She turned to look out the window and saw a very grand-looking coach was standing in the courtyard. Her heart began to pound frantically when she noticed the coat of arms...

"The Earl of Matlock!" Elizabeth closed her eyes and whispered, "Please, not *today*?"

Mr. Bennet reached across and gave Elizabeth's hand a squeeze. "They will *not* disrupt the service, I promise you, my Lizzy!" Turning to Jane, he said, "Do not leave her side, Jane. Stay in the coach." He disembarked, closing the door firmly behind him, and went to speak to James who was standing nearby.

"What is happening, James? Have you seen the earl?"

"No, sir, I have not. They had arrived only just before we did. One of Mr. Darcy's staff was on the coach and went to the door of the church. He then returned to the coach to speak to someone inside. I should tell you that we have strict orders to take Miss Elizabeth away from here if there is any disruption, Mr. Bennet. We will not allow her to alight from the carriage if the earl is on the church grounds."

Mr. Bennet nodded and just then they saw Richard emerge from the side door of the church and walk towards the coach. Mr. Bennet waited a minute and then approached to offer support, but when he came within view, he saw Richard displaying a wide smile while looking at a gentleman who looked very much like the earl from behind. For the briefest of moments, Mr. Bennet thought that they had been fooled as to where Richard's allegiances lay—but then decided not to jump to conclusions.

"What exactly is going on here?" Mr. Bennet barked, prepared to do battle.

Richard looked toward Mr. Bennet and exclaimed with a pointed look, "A *pleasant* surprise for William, Mr. Bennet! May I introduce the Viscount Bainbridge, Lord Reginald Fitzwilliam, and Lady Clara Fitzwilliam. This is the father of the bride, Mr. Thomas Bennet, of Longbourn. My brother and sister have come to attend the wedding, Mr. Bennet, and to show their *support* for the happy couple."

Mr. Bennet's eyebrows shot up almost to his hairline. Bowing, he said, "Ah, yes. A pleasure to meet you, I am sure. Will you be staying for the wedding breakfast?"

"Thank you, Mr. Bennet, but since we were not expected, we could not think to impose," responded Lady Clara.

"It would be no trouble, I assure you. My wife would never forgive me if I did not convince you to attend, and I am certain that Elizabeth would like to meet you."

At a nod from Lord Reginald, his sister accepted the invitation.

"Reginald and Clara; you had best be seated as soon as possible. Mr. Bennet, please do not delay very long. Our cousin is inside in a state of nerves such as I have never witnessed before! Every moment increases his worry that our father or Aunt Catherine will arrive and make a mockery of the wedding ceremony. I fear that if Miss Elizabeth does not enter the church soon, he will run mad!"

Lady Clara smiled widely, "Well, then, you may remove William's worries, brother! Aunt Catherine was staying in town with us. Anne wished to come as well, but she knew she could not get away from her mother, so instead she promised to keep her mother occupied today."

"Clara and I took separate carriages so that Father would not have one left for his own use and my carriage is in the process of having the wheels replaced." Lord Reginald stated. "I made certain that Aunt Catherine's coach was undergoing some conveniently urgent maintenance and was in such a condition as it would take hours to reassemble. You know that that neither of them would ever travel in an *inferior* hired coach or by horseback. William's wedding is safe!"

Richard and Mr. Bennet laughed at their scheme. The latter felt a degree relief, though he would not express it aloud, that Elizabeth and William would have the support of two members of the peerage at the very least, including William's friend Lord Hamilton.

"We shall enter the church directly after I have relieved the bride's curiosity and concern about who belongs to this carriage. Prepare the groom, Colonel!"

"With pleasure, sir!"

"Just one moment—Lord Reginald... are you married?"

Lord Reginald was quite surprised at the question, but replied, "No, I am not, sir."

Mr. Bennet shot a look at Richard. "Well then, Colonel, you should warn your brother about my wife!" Turning back to the viscount, he continued, "After today, I will still have *four* unmarried daughters, and a wife who has just had a taste of arranging a wedding." Mr. Bennet wiggled his eyebrows and walked away towards the carriage in which he arrived.

"Do not fret, Reginald, Mrs. Bennet has no hidden agendas; she is quite obvious in her machinations. I must say it is refreshing. A hint, though—I have reason to believe that the heart of the eldest Bennet daughter is already spoken for, whether her mother knows of it or not." Richard guffawed at the look of shock on his elder brother's face. As he walked around the side of the church to enter through the same door he had left, his siblings entered through the front with just enough time to find a seat before William stepped up to his place before the altar.

Richard entered the room that housed his cousins and Bingley still smiling. He found their state exactly as he supposed they would be; all three now had worried looks upon their faces. Richard chuckled. "All is very well indeed! My brother and sister have sent word to you that there will be *no* disruptions today."

A smile spread slowly across William's face and he sighed in relief. "Thank you, Richard, and thank Reginald and Clara for me."

"You may thank them yourself. They arrived a few moments ago to show their support of your marriage. It seems the current generation of Fitzwilliams is much more sensible than the previous, with the exception of your mother of course." Richard walked over to William and shook his hand. "For any other couple, at this time I would wish the groom luck, but I know in *this* case there is no need for *luck*. I expect you to be very happy." He clapped William's shoulder. "It is time, cousin! Your bride has arrived." Turning he said, "Georgie, we must take our seats."

Now that the time had come, Georgiana was so choked up with emotion she could not speak. Her smile was wide, and her eyes were filled with tears as she kissed her brother's cheek before taking Richard's arm.

Bingley said, "Are you ready, Darcy?"

"I have been *more* than ready for this moment for years, Bingley!" William walked into the church and stood in the place the pastor had shown him earlier in the day. His gaze was fixed on the doors at the back of the church with joyful anticipation.

~%~

Squeezing her father's hand, Elizabeth sighed. "It makes me happy to know that not all of William's family is against us, Papa! Their coming relieves my mind a great deal."

"I knew it would, my dear. Come, let us not keep William waiting. Colonel Fitzwilliam tells me he has been quite nervous."

Elizabeth's smile widened, and her eyes sparkled mischievously. "Nervous? About marrying me?"

Mr. Bennet's heart jumped. "No, no, Lizzy!" About to explain, he stopped as he realized she was teasing.

"Do not worry, Papa, I have every faith in William's love for me." She patted her father's arm, and then turned to her sister. "Jane, lead the way."

Mr. Bennet nodded to James and another Darcy footman, and they opened the doors. As Jane began to walk through, Elizabeth turned to James—the man who had saved both William's life and her own—and said, "Thank you, James… for everything. If you had not…" Emotion welled up within her, and she could not continue.

James broke his usual stoic demeanor and smiled down at her. "It is always my pleasure, Mistress."

Looking down the aisle towards the altar, her eyes met his… and all was right in the world. Elizabeth walked towards her beloved William.

~%~

The wedding breakfast was all that it should have been, and Mrs. Bennet was highly praised by all, though it was plain to see that *she* was most impressed with the compliments paid her by the Viscount and his sister and Lord and Lady Hamilton. Elizabeth and William spent their time mingling among the guests who had come to wish them well, Elizabeth conversing smoothly with all, and William following along behind her, adding a sentence or two when necessary—as always in awe of her skills in social settings. The newlyweds were always touching in some way whether it was his hand placed gently on the small of her back or her hand wrapped about his arm, their contact broken only during a brief show of emotion when the Baron and Baroness Leisenheimer embraced Elizabeth.

The couple spent a longer time speaking to William's cousins than with anyone else thus far; after all they *had* defied the older members of the family by coming to show their approval of their marriage, and they had been the only guests that Elizabeth did not know. During a break in their conversation when Richard came to tease his siblings about the stealth of their escape from their parents and aunt, Elizabeth saw a chance to have a few minutes alone with her husband—her husband!—and pulled William into the hall. The look in her eyes betrayed her thoughts, and William eagerly followed her up the stairs and through a doorway, which she immediately locked behind them.

Turning to William, she reached up to caress his cheek and stepped closer as she said, "Though it seems that my mother had planned the remainder well, the open carriage was badly done indeed! I have been wishing for a few moments alone…"

Her speech was silenced by William's gentle kiss before taking her face between his hands. Smoothing her silky skin, he swallowed hard past the tightness in his throat and whispered, "Elizabeth! My wife!"

Elizabeth's eyes sparkled with all the love she felt for him. "After so long… I can hardly believe it is true that we are finally married."

William leaned down and kissed her gently once again. Cognizant of the need to return to the party, he had every intention of moving away until she responded by winding her hands around his neck and pulling him down to her lips, pressing herself as close to him as she possibly could. After several minutes, both breathless, they parted, and William placed his forehead gently against hers for a few moments, saying huskily, "Must we stay much longer? I would like to leave for London very soon, Mrs. Darcy."

Elizabeth smiled widely at hearing him use her new appellation. "I will call for Hannah to assist me in changing immediately." William's disappointed expression confused her. "Would you like to stay longer?"

"No, no." His panicked look at her misunderstanding his intentions changed to one of desire. "I - I was hoping... could you not wear this gown?" His hand brushed up and down the criss-cross design of ribbons down her back, which happened to be what was keeping the gown closed. His fingers played with the ribbon, and his gaze moved to her neckline. Perhaps in a few days he could tell her exactly what he had been imagining since he had first seen her in this gown, but at the moment he was afraid his ardor would frighten her. "You have always been the most beautiful woman I have ever seen, but I have never seen you in a more becoming gown than this, my love."

Elizabeth blushed and replied, "Normally, I would not wish to wear such a fine gown to travel, but in this case, I do believe I will make an exception. There are a few things I need to put away before we leave..." she kissed him lightly and moved away towards the dressing table.

For the first time since entering, William looked around the room. His eyes widened as he found he could not remove his gaze from the bed. "What is this room?"

"This is – *was* my bedchamber." Elizabeth began to place a few items into the case she would bring along in the carriage with her. "Since Georgiana will stay here while we are in London, I am leaving most of my things behind so that she will not be in a bare room. When we return at Christmas, I will pack the remainder." Hearing a noise behind her, she turned and saw her husband lying upon the bed. "William? Are you unwell? Would you like to rest before we leave?"

"No, I do not wish to rest." He blushed furiously and sat upon the edge of the bed. "I apologize. I should not have presumed... Upon hearing this was your room, I found I could not resist lying in the place that you have slept your whole life."

Elizabeth moved toward William, ran her fingers through his hair, and kissed him gently. "I will spend the remainder of my life sleeping in your arms, my husband."

Though he knew it was not the wisest thing to do in his current state of mind, William pulled his tempting wife into his lap. "I shall thank G-d daily for the privilege of being your husband." William forced his mind away from the way she felt in his arms, redirecting his thoughts to being in her parents' house which was currently full of people. "I think, dearest wife, that we should be on our way home…" He gave her one more peck on the lips.

Elizabeth rose and returned to the dressing table. Glancing at the mirror, she noticed her state of disarray. "You certainly know how to reverse Hannah's excellent work!"

As William watched her attempt to repair her hair, his fingers itched to reverse the improvements she was making. Trying to think of something else, he said, "Are you certain that you do not wish to go somewhere special for a wedding trip, Elizabeth?"

Looking at her husband through the mirror, Elizabeth answered, "I know that years ago we had spoken of Italy, William, but I *am* a rational lady, after all! I understand perfectly well that with the war and the resulting problems at sea, it would not be safe to travel at this time. I intend to live a very long and happy life with you, sir, and do not wish for it to be cut short because I am impatient to see all you have spoken of. We will take our tour of Italy eventually. You have promised me a tour of the Lake District when the weather is warmer as well. I have not been to Pemberley in years and am impatient to see it again. I am certain it can only look beautiful—and special—at any time of year, especially in the winter. There is nowhere else I would rather be right now than at our home."

William moved closer and placed his hands on her shoulders. "Thank you for being the most understanding wife that has ever lived, Elizabeth."

She turned and smiled up at him. "Believe me, my love; as long as we are together I will be very happy—no matter where we are!" He could not resist pulling her up from her seat and kissing her quite thoroughly once again.

Once they had regained their breath, Elizabeth asked, "Shall we bid everyone goodbye?"

William laughed. "Not until *after* you repair the damage I have done to your hair—again!"

Catching her reflection in the mirror she did her best to hold back her mirth and feign annoyance. "I think, sir, we would do better with you waiting in the hall. If this continues, we shall never leave my bedchamber!"

Pulling her into his embrace once more, he looked at her seriously, his eyes shining with love and desire. "I hope you are prepared to spend the majority of our time once we reach London in *our* bedchambers—together—my Elizabeth."

Elizabeth blushed, but said, "I look forward to it with pleasure, William."

Just the beginning...

Epilogue - Part 1

By the time they had been travelling for about two hours, Elizabeth had grown quite concerned. She had asked William several times if something was wrong, and though he denied that there was, she could not help but notice that the longer they drove on, the more reserved her husband became.

When his answers to her inquiries were reduced to mere grunts, Elizabeth could take the suspense no longer. "William, *please*! It frightens me that you are behaving much as you did upon entering Hertfordshire. I do not wish to begin our marriage in this manner!"

William startled. "I apologize, Elizabeth. I was only… I have been thinking about what I should say in regards to a certain subject…" His voice trailed off, and they sat again in silence.

"Please, just *tell* me—what have I done that displeases you so?" Her distress showed plainly on her beautiful face.

He seemed surprised. "Elizabeth, I promise that you have done nothing. I only… you see… your father gave me the books that you had read."

Elizabeth blinked several times in confusion before speaking. "I am certain that this discussion would make a great deal more sense if you shared with me *which* books he has given you. I have read hundreds in my lifetime."

"Two books from the uppermost shelf by the window on the left," he said while feigning interest in the passing scenery.

Elizabeth turned a bright shade of crimson and her eyes opened wide. "My father…!" she gasped. "I must say that I am glad I was not previously aware that he knew I had read them!" She paused for a few moments to regain a bit of composure. "It has upset you to learn that I have read them!"

Since she could not look directly at William, she could not see that he had opened his mouth to speak and she was interrupting him by saying, "Please allow me to explain why I did so! When there were no gentlemen about, at times the matrons would discuss… *that* subject when they *thought* the maidens were far enough away and thus could not hear their salacious conversations. The bits we did overhear were usually frightening to most innocent young ladies!"

She turned her face toward the window, her color deepening. "After what had already happened between *us*… at first I thought that the things I had heard must be falsehoods; maybe the ladies said those things within our hearing purposely so that we would not… so that we would *refrain* until marriage. But then it occurred to me that perhaps there was something wrong with *me*—for when I had been with you, what I had experienced had been so very pleasing that I never wanted you to leave me—but *they* always made it sound as if it were a horrible imposition to be endured and a task to be finished as quickly as possible so that their husbands would leave them to their solitary rest!

"So I decided that before you came for me on my birthday, I should seek out more information from my usual source—my father's books.

"After reading the first, I thought that perhaps all the ladies that I had heard speaking had been… well, going about it in the wrong way… and I felt it would be better if I was well-informed so that the same did not happen to *us*.… so I read another book to see if it corroborated the information in the first. I must say that reading those books did ease my confusion about some of the feelings I had experienced when we had been alone together at Pemberley…" She took a deep breath, and released it slowly.

William looked at his hands as he fidgeted with his ring. "Though I appreciate your explanation—I can assure you that I am happy to hear that what we have shared has pleased you, and I should tell you that I feel the same—I was not truly upset that you had *read* them." He shifted uncomfortably in his seat. "You see, I can only imagine that your father gave them to me to make certain that I would be prepared with the same information that you have…" He stopped speaking for a few moments, and then whispered, "But, I cannot promise that once we are… intimate…" Struggling with his thoughts, he sighed, "Elizabeth! I am sorry, but I do *not* think I will be reflecting on what I have *read* at that time, or that I will be able to readily reproduce it!" He turned to look at her, realizing that his coloring must match hers.

"William, surely you do not think that I would expect everything to happen *exactly* as it does in those books?"

"You do not?"

She met his gaze directly, with just a trace of a smile. "My love, when you are near, the *last* thing on my mind is what I have read in *any* book!" She hesitated, and her expression became one of concern. "Unless—did *you* wish to…?"

"No!" He blurted out, and then collected himself and said, "It was only that I did not want what I do… I did not want you to be disappointed if that is what *you* expected. I think we would do better to allow events to proceed *naturally*…"

The look in her eyes took his breath away as she leaned toward him and, between gentle kisses, whispered, "From what little I have already experienced while in your arms, I do *not* believe it is possible that I shall be disappointed, my husband."

It was advantageous that, before the newly married couple's *lack* of disappointment progressed beyond what was acceptable within view of the public, the carriage began to slow as they approached a scheduled stop outside of London.

~%~

Before they departed the last stop prior to their reaching London, William instructed James to ride ahead of the carriage to Darcy House in order to alert the staff of their impending arrival so that the staff would be assembled to greet their new mistress.

After introductions to the principal staff had been made, and Elizabeth had said a few words to Mrs. Martin and Hanna—her new lady's maid, whom Elizabeth well remembered from Pemberley—William led his new wife to her chambers. Her reaction was a pleasure for her husband to witness! Her eyes sparkled and her face lit up with delight as she inspected the rooms he had commissioned to be decorated for her more than three years earlier.

With a glance at the maid, William asked, "Would you like a light meal after we freshen ourselves, Mrs. Darcy?" He led her through another door and continued, "I can have it set up here in our private sitting room, if you would like… after which perhaps you would enjoy a tour of the house?"

"I find that the basket my mother packed for us and that we partook of in the carriage was sufficient for my appetite. I do not believe a meal is necessary, unless you are hungry, sir." At a shake of his head, Elizabeth suggested, "Perhaps some wine, cold meats and cheeses can be left in the sitting room so that if we do grow hungry *later*, it will be available for us, and we would not have to inconvenience the staff to attend us at that time," after which William could swear he heard, "*much* later" whispered so softly that he knew it was meant for his ears alone.

William's breath caught. "*Could she have meant that she wished to…? No! It is too soon to think of just now!* He reminded himself, *Elizabeth would most likely wish to bathe.*"

His eyes moved down her frame, disappointed as he reasoned that she would change out of this gown after her bath. Earlier, when he had asked her not to change into her travelling clothes, she had probably not even imagined that the plea was made so that he could have the opportunity to remove her wedding gown himself! As often was the case when he was alone with Elizabeth, he had not been thinking clearly when making that request earlier in the day.

William's eyes returned to her lovely face. He could tell she had been watching him closely by the heated expression in her eyes and seductive arch of her brow, causing a stirring within him that quickly became so urgent, that were it not their first night together as man and wife, he would be sorely tempted to suggest they dismiss the servants and…

But it would not be right to expect such a thing. Surely, *she* would think it was too early. He had heard many complaints from men at his club that most ladies would not even begin to entertain the idea of coupling until after dark.

To be safe, he suggested, "Perhaps a tour of the house, then, Mrs. Darcy?" His tone was cool and stiff, but the only thing that Elizabeth noticed was that his ardent regard for her was burning through his eyes to her very soul.

"Perhaps tomorrow would be better for a tour, Mr. Darcy. I find myself… *fatigued.*" Glancing at the door to her bedchamber, the sounds of Hanna unpacking her trunks evident in the background, she raised both eyebrows and the corners of her lips twitched, mirth dancing in her eyes. "I do believe I will retire soon after my bath."

A knock sounded and Hanna appeared and curtsied. "Beggin' your pardon, ma'am. Your bath is ready."

Elizabeth nodded and when Hanna was out of sight, she whispered, "Thirty minutes, then?"

There was no need for words as her husband's gaze answered the question with an ardor unequaled in intensity to date. He stood admiring the grace of her movements as Elizabeth followed Hanna into her bedchamber— turning her bewitching smile upon him as she closed the door between them.

"In the future, I must remember that my Elizabeth is **not** *like most ladies,"* William thought as he grinned and hurried toward his own bedchamber.

~%~

Upon entering his rooms, William did not waste any time before heading to his dressing room to begin his own bath. He hoped that Hughes had thought ahead and made the bath water cooler than usual. He chuckled. Judging by the way he felt at the moment, perhaps *cold* water would be in order!

However, William soon found that a lower water temperature would not be necessary to cool his blood, for when he removed his shirt, he caught sight of himself in the mirror across the room and froze.

Wrapped up so deeply in all that had occurred within the past few weeks— meeting Elizabeth again, regaining her good opinion, worrying about Georgiana, planning the wedding, dealing with all that happened with his aunt and uncle, and going through the wedding itself—he had *almost* forgotten his disfigurement.

Soon after the fire, he had forced himself to refrain from looking into any mirror until he was fully dressed; therefore, it had been many long months since he had seen more than the skin of his arm, which he had avoided examining too closely when circumstances forbade keeping it covered.

Swallowing hard, William walked toward the glass to examine his reflection. He ran his hand over the blemishes on his chest, shoulder, and upper arm; the skin felt so different from his skin elsewhere. The scarring had faded a bit from what he remembered, but not much—certainly not *enough*. Portions of it were still bright red, almost lavender in places… pitted and uneven… ugly…

He clamped his eyes closed as tightly as possible. NO! This was absolutely NOT acceptable!

Being unaware of anything other than the thought *"Elizabeth CANNOT see this!"* his panic only grew worse when he felt two hands take hold of his shoulders and pull him away from the mirror. Opening his eyes, he looked about wildly until he could recognize that it was Hughes steering him toward a chair. Sitting heavily as soon as he was close enough, he slumped over, and with his elbows on his knees, he buried his face in his hands.

A while later, when William's breathing had slowed enough to speak normally, he said, "Hughes… I am sorry that you had to witness that. I thank you for your assistance."

Hughes straightened his form before saying, "I do not know to what you are referring, Mr. Darcy. I have requested additional hot water, and have prepared your clothing for when your bath is complete."

After his bath, while Hughes assisted his master in donning his shirt, William asked, "Perhaps I should dress more formally?" He was dressed in only breeches and a lawn shirt.

"Sir, I believe this will do nicely."

William closed his eyes and said quietly, "I do not know if I can do this, Hughes. She has seen the scars on my lower arm, but the skin there is not as spoiled as it is higher up… and not nearly as bad as my shoulder and chest…"

The room was silent for a few moments until Hughes cleared his throat. "Mr. Darcy, if I may step away from my station for a moment and speak to you as a man…" At William's nod, Hughes continued, "I must say that I am confident you have nothing to fear. It is quite obvious to all that have seen the two of you together that she cares for you, sir, very deeply—equally as much as you care for her.

"Mrs. Darcy sought me out when she was attempting to decide what to give you as a wedding gift. You are well aware that I am very careful with the meaning of the words that I use, sir. I must say that I did not truly understand the meaning of the word 'adore' until I saw the look in Mrs. Darcy's eyes when she spoke of you."

"She deserves more… *better*…"

"That statement would be the greatest falsehood I ever have heard, sir! Pure rubbish! There *are* none better! *And* the lady loves you. Would you insult her judgment by questioning her good opinion of you? All *will* be well."

Even after giving him leave to speak freely, William was so shocked that Hughes had spoken to him in that manner that he began to laugh. "Thank you, Hughes." William straightened his back. "I will not require your services again tonight. Please wait until I ring for you in the morning."

"Yes, Mr. Darcy. Once again, sir, congratulations… to the both of you."

~%~

When he entered the sitting room, William found Elizabeth pacing just outside the door to his bedchamber. As the door opened, she turned toward him, wringing her hands. He was expecting her to smile in greeting, but instead her expression was one of apprehension mixed with alarm. Upon seeing her wretched state, all of his worries were forgotten.

He moved quickly toward her. "Elizabeth! What is the matter?"

"Have I been too forward?" Her eyes were filling with tears as she spoke. "I cannot go back and change the fact that I have read those books if *that* is what displeases you. You know I cannot erase them from my mind."

William took Elizabeth's face between his hands and stroked her cheek with his thumb in an attempt to calm her and ease her obvious distress. "Your behavior does nothing but please me. On the subject of being forward—Elizabeth!" He smiled. "Do you honestly think that I would have fallen in love with you had I disliked that aspect of your character, even a little? Do you remember when I told you years ago that I never wish for you to suppress any thought, feeling, or action when we are alone?" He smiled as she nodded. "I meant it, my love, and I still do. Please tell me, what makes you doubt it?"

"I thought you had changed your mind... that you would not come to me."

"What would make you think such a thing?"

She seemed surprised at his question. "We agreed to thirty minutes, William, but it has been an hour and three quarters since we parted."

"Has it in truth been such a long time?" He turned to look at the clock on the mantelpiece. How long had he been sitting in that chair before his bath?! "I had no notion, my love, that so much time had passed." Turning back to Elizabeth, his troubled expression melted away upon seeing hers. "I apologize. The last thing I meant to do was to cause you any concern. There was a bit of trouble, but I promise you now that if ever I *know* that I am to be late when you are expecting me, I will send word. Truly, dearest, I will."

Elizabeth seemed satisfied, but then cocked her head to the side. "May I know the nature of this trouble?"

William inhaled her calming scent, and his eyes caressed every inch of her beloved face before he answered. "May I tell you tomorrow, my Elizabeth? I would prefer *not* to discuss it now."

His favorite of her smiles slowly dawned across her lips. "Well then, what would you prefer to do? Shall we discuss politics?" The teasing sparkle that he loved so dearly began to dance in her eyes.

"Another time perhaps." He leaned in and gently kissed his wife. "Would you like a glass of wine?"

"Yes, please."

As he turned to hand her the glass, William smiled broadly upon noticing what she was wearing.

"I knew you wished to see me again in this gown, so I had it freshened while I bathed."

"Does she know what it does to me when she looks at me in that way?" William wondered.

It soon became obvious that she did, or at the very least, when she looked at him in *that* manner, her thoughts were similar to his. Elizabeth placed her glass on a table and approached, her eyes never leaving his. Reaching up, her hand caressed his cheek. He turned his head slightly to catch her palm with his lips, and she shivered ever so slightly. Her hands laced through his hair and she pulled his head down to hers, their lips meeting again and again. He was very glad that he had not poured his own wine as of yet so that his both hands were free to pull her against him.

When her kisses began to lessen his control, he moved to claim the creamy skin of her neck, in search of the exact spot which would draw out that delicious sound that she would make when he… *"Ah, yes—there it is!"* He had never dared to continue with these ministrations before, afraid that it would take them too far—but *now* he had every intention on finding out what the result would be when he did so. Her moans threatened to overwhelm him, and so he moved to the other side of her neck to discover if the same noise could be elicited from similar attentions there. He smiled against her pulse when this sound was even more intense.

William's hands found their way to places he had only dreamed of exploring until now. Elizabeth's were wandering as well, and it felt so incredible to have her touch him through only the thin cloth of his shirt. William knew he had found a sensitive spot when she pressed herself against his hips in that same way she had done years before—but *this* time he would not dream of stopping her; instead, he reacted in kind. Her hands moved to the top button of his shirt.

"NO!" William quickly took hold of her hand and pulled away from her. "You cannot!"

For a moment, pained and confused by his response, Elizabeth stood wide-eyed, staring at him—trying to make sense of what had happened. Suddenly, she recognized his tortured expression. Remembering exactly what she had been doing at the moment he pulled away, she understood. *This* look expressed tenfold the agony and fear that he had shown that night in Netherfield's library, when she had pushed up his sleeve to see his scar.

Was *this* the reason he had been delayed in coming to her? He was afraid that she would be disgusted by the sight of his scars?

"*Please*, Elizabeth?" William whispered, begging, between ragged breaths.

She nodded. Blushing, she whispered, "I have wanted to touch you for so long, William. May I touch your back?"

The transformation of William's expression was as instantaneous as it was complete—it was as if the weight of the world had been lifted from him. "Yes... and my left side. You can have no idea how much I want you to touch me, Elizabeth. Almost as much as I want to touch you."

Elizabeth's seductive smile took his breath away as she moved closer to lean herself against him fully. "I would like that very much, my William."

The next morning, Elizabeth smiled as she woke up as she had only once before—to the sound of William's heart beating. Her smile widened when she thought of how *different* the precursor to these two events was. At Pemberley, what happened before was wonderful, but last night had been absolutely *glorious!* She could feel only pity for all those ladies who had complained about their *duties* when she could only hope that William would soon awaken so that she might enjoy more practice in the very pleasurable execution of hers.

It was so dark in the room that she could see nothing for a while and so she concentrated her attention on William's scent, the sound of his heartbeat, and the feel of the rhythm of his breathing.

Elizabeth smiled again when she remembered moving about during the night and waking him with her tossing. She had apologized, but he responded by saying that it was a gift to be awakened to find that she was really there with him—to know that it had not been a dream, as it had been so many nights before—and he said it all had been infinitely better than he had imagined it could be.

It was only when the sun began to rise that she remembered that they had left the bed curtain partially open to allow the candles on the bedside tables to light their new world. She moved slightly to be able to admire her husband's handsome face as the room filled with morning light. It was then that Elizabeth noticed William's shirt; it was not meant to be slept in, and, at some point during the night, the top three buttons had come loose and fallen off. The front of his shirt lay open, exposing part of his scars.

Elizabeth could not help herself; she had to look. Lifting her head very slowly so she would not wake him, she examined his skin with her eyes. Though at Netherfield he had said his scars no longer hurt, they looked so very painful and angry. Her vision blurred with tears. *"Oh, what he has had to endure! I should have been there for him!"*

She would *not* allow him to see her tears, so she put a concerted effort into blinking them away before she would move again. Once she had been successful at quelling her emotions, move she did. Pulling the collar back toward his shoulder, she shifted up onto her elbow and leaned over to gently kiss his scarred skin repeatedly.

Elizabeth knew the moment he woke; she could feel his entire body stiffen and heard him breathe her name in a gasp.

She turned her head towards him and looked into his confused eyes, saying softly, "Do not be upset with me, my love. The buttons fell off during the night, and I awoke to find your shirt open. I am sorry, but I could not stop myself. I only wish that you would allow me to erase all of the memories of pain and replace it with new memories of my touch."

Tears were streaming down William's face as he swallowed several times in an attempt to find his voice. He had been correct; Elizabeth could not be held to his low expectations of the ladies of the *ton*! Her character would never allow it. Why had he ever doubted her? Why had he ever been afraid?

He whispered, "Elizabeth! It is I who should apologize. First I told you not to suppress anything you wished for, yet when you did as I asked, I immediately behaved in a reprehensible manner which I am certain made you feel that I meant the opposite. I am ashamed that I reacted in such a way. It was just that I – I was so frightened… thinking that if you should see me as I am, you would no longer wish me near you. I so wanted you to *wish* to be near me, to desire me as I desire you! And here you are proving me wrong to an infinite degree!

"You are an amazing woman, Elizabeth Darcy. I am the most fortunate man ever to live to have claimed you for my wife, my very own!"

"While I am happy that you think so, the truth is that I am the fortunate one, William. You are the best of men, and I love you so very dearly!"

She opened his shirt wider and settled her bare form completely against his, her hand resting on his scarred skin. With a sort of purr, she said, "Mmmm... I did not think lying beside you could get any better—but *this* certainly is!"

Elizabeth felt her husband sigh deeply, contentedly, and then heard his voice rumble within his chest, "I cannot express how much I love you, Elizabeth. I have not the words."

She moved up onto one elbow and smiled down at him. "Oh, I think you do a wonderful job of expressing your love, my William. As a matter of fact, my first thought upon awakening was 'Glorious!' I should like to see you express your love for me again, my husband."

Surprising Elizabeth, with a single, sweeping movement, and something that sounded a bit like a self-satisfied growl, William managed to situate himself above her. His kisses quieted her laughter; and then he pulled back slightly to look at her, his eyes filled with all of the emotions he was feeling. "Perhaps with *much* practice I can someday come close to showing you just how intense is my love for you, my wife."

"Even if you succeed, I warn you that I shall require frequent reminders."

William smiled and kissed Elizabeth gently. "Oh, it will be an ongoing process, I assure you, for no matter how close I come to success, my physical expression will never be able to match the love I have for you. With every moment that passes, I love you more."

Epilogue – Part 2

Summer 1812

Elizabeth smiled as she stroked the neck of her horse, a recent gift from her husband. "She *is* beautiful, William, thank you."

"Have you finally settled on a name for her?" William asked as he untied the saddle bags attached to Poseidon.

"Yes, Pistis."

William's laughter echoed in the small glade he had chosen for their picnic. "You have named her to dispel any lingering doubts you harbour about riding?"

"Of course! How could I be fearful of riding one who, in Greek mythology, is the personification of good faith, trust and reliability?" Elizabeth answered while detaching the blankets from her saddle.

"A wise choice, my love." He leaned down to kiss her gently and then removed her saddlebags as well. "Are you hungry?"

"Ravenous!" she exclaimed. "Riding certainly increases my appetite. I do believe you have shown me half of Pemberley today!"

William allowed Elizabeth to move off ahead of him to select a location to spread the blankets and was very happy with her choice as it fit perfectly with his own wishes. He chuckled at himself—*of course* she would remember. William took one side and helped her lay it near the circle of stones that, years ago, Elizabeth had gathered to make the fire to warm him after he had been injured and fallen ill. He was pleased the stones were still there, marking the place that they had fallen in love, a memorial of all they had endured.

He began to unpack the food from the saddlebags. "Once we have ridden more of the estate, you will realize we have not toured even a quarter of the grounds as of yet." He waited until the food was laid out and they were both settled comfortably before speaking again. "The day after tomorrow, we will ride south to visit one of the estates along the border of Pemberley's grounds. It has been unused for four years, though the manor house and outbuildings have been kept in very good repair. The owner fell ill and moved to live with his daughter's family at their estate so that she might care for him. The old gentleman recently died, and the family has decided to offer his estate for purchase. I have been inside several times through the years and have been welcome to ride the grounds at will throughout my lifetime. I do believe it may be perfect for the Bingleys."

Elizabeth's bright smile was reward enough for passing on this intelligence. "I knew that their purchasing an estate in Derbyshire was discussed while we were staying at Netherfield in April, but, oh, William! I never dreamed of having Jane and Charles so close by. It would be wonderful indeed!"

"I agree completely. But if they do not approve of it, we will make a purchase offer and hold it as an inheritance for one of our younger children."

"From the information I have seen in your accounts, we would need to have at least ten children to divide up all the 'inheritances' you have amassed, William." Elizabeth bit her lip, and her eyes sparkled in a way that enticed her husband's imagination to run wild.

William leaned over and captured his wife's lips in an ardent kiss. "I believe we can find a way to meet that need, my love." He would have continued had Elizabeth's stomach not chosen that moment to make a rumbling noise reminding him of how hungry she was. They both chuckled as he removed to his side of the blanket, and they began to eat. "Have you heard from Jane recently?"

"Yes, I received a letter from Jane only this morning while you were in your study. They have settled in after their wedding trip, but even Jane is not quite happy with living so close to Mama. I do believe Jane and Charles will enjoy a trip to the north to see the estate. Mama is constantly visiting and pestering my sister to take Kitty and Lydia to London and 'throw them in the way of other rich men' now that she and I have *caught* our own rich men. She says the same to me, but it is easy to fold a letter and put it back into the envelope. It is not as simple for Jane." Elizabeth smiled. "Mary, of course, is not included in these plans since she has caught the eye of my Uncle Philips's new law partner. With the way they were looking at each other in April when we were there for Jane's wedding, I think you would agree that Mama will be planning another wedding very soon. Of all my sisters, I never thought I would feel the need to chaperone *Mary* so diligently!"

William nodded and smiled, more at the amused look on his wife's face than the news she was imparting. "Is all well between Mr. Archer and Mr. Phillips?"

"Yes, apparently they get along splendidly, and his presence has increased my uncle's business. Mr. Phillips is finally comfortable enough to take some time away from his office, making my aunt very happy."

"Very good. While we are on the subject of the residents of Meryton, I heard news from an unlikely source—my cousin Reginald—of Miss King, or should I say, Mrs. Wickham. Since I know you have worried about the lady, I thought it might make you easier to know her fate. She *and* her inheritance are now safe from Wickham. He was killed during a card game after he was caught cheating, but not before Wickham dealt the other man a fatal blow as well. The man he fought with was my uncle's footman, of all people—the same man who helped to blackmail the post worker in Lambton, which is how Reginald came to know of this."

"That is so very…" Elizabeth searched for the proper word, only to find none, and settled for, "odd. Though I am not happy to hear of anyone's death, I am glad to hear that Mrs. Wickham is not tied to that scoundrel for the rest of her life. How do you feel about hearing of his demise, though, William? You did grow up with Wickham…"

"The boy I knew years ago has been long dead, Elizabeth. I cannot feel sorry for the way he died. He could have lived a comfortable, satisfying life if he had been a different sort of man—the sort that both his father and mine had hoped he would be. George Wickham's death was a final reaping of that which he had sowed on the path he had chosen."

They were both quiet for several minutes, but Elizabeth was intent on their picnic not being ruined, and so she searched for another subject on which to speak. "Oh, I almost forgot! Jane had other news—about Caroline Bingley! She has accepted an offer of marriage from a Mr. Benson Scott who owns a large estate in Wales. Do you know him?"

"Yes… yes, I do." William nodded thoughtfully. "They are perfect for one another! He himself is a respectable older gentleman whose wife passed on several years ago. His son was something of a troublemaker, as I recall, gambling away much of the family fortune, but then, through his debaucheries, he become very ill and died, leaving Mr. Scott childless. I believe he began to search for a wife soon after his son's death, to provide his estate with an heir—and with funds. I am certain the reputation of the son had prevented Mr. Scott from easily finding a wife… and since I know for certain that Caroline's *disposition* would have caused many gentlemen to think twice before considering marriage to her, the match would provide them both with what they need most."

Elizabeth nodded, not very impressed with the match, but then Caroline Bingley had never been someone she cared for, and she could not find it within herself to feel too much sympathy. "You have mentioned that in the past, but I cannot help but think they could not be truly happy." She sighed, but was intent on not spoiling this beautiful day with thoughts of this sort either. Changing the subject once again, Elizabeth said, "Lord Hamilton's younger brother seemed quite taken with Georgiana when we met him in London."

William groaned. "Yes, I noticed."

"I was sure that you did. You do know that you frightened the poor boy half to death with your glares. He seemed as shy as you say you were at his age. He is only a year younger than you were when we met at Longbourn as you prepared to attend Cambridge. Think of how you were then—how would you have felt if my father had glared at you in that intimidating manner you have? You would not have been thinking of me in a romantic fashion at that age, and I do not think poor Edwin Hamilton had anything more in mind than you had at Longbourn. Georgiana is older than I was, but still, I believe he wanted only to be friends with her—for now anyway. That does not mean that when they are a little older…"

"Please, Elizabeth; let us speak no more of this subject. I promise to be nicer to him the next time we meet." She gave him an expectant look. "*And* I will attempt not to glare."

She nodded with a satisfied smile, for that was exactly the outcome she desired from the conversation. "Good, as I was thinking of inviting the Hamiltons for Christmas," William opened his mouth to speak, but Elizabeth interrupted while trying to hide her smile, "along with the Leisenheimers. What do you think of including Lord Reginald and Lady Clara on the guest list? I like them immensely." At her husband's nod, she continued, "I also heard from Papa this morning. It seems that the heir to Longbourn, Mr. Collins, has extended an olive branch and requested a visit so that he can choose a wife from among my father's *five* daughters. I suppose he will be disappointed when he hears that there are only two available from which to choose! The letter Papa has described makes me think the gentleman is quite pompous—even ridiculous. He hopes that inviting Mr. Collins will provide an experience resulting in hours of diversion, though he doubts that either Kitty or Lydia would be interested in such a man."

"Knowing your mother's matchmaking tendencies, it should be an *interesting* visit to say the least!" he laughed.

Elizabeth laughed along with him. "I quite agree!" Both finished with their meal, she began to repack the saddlebags, with William's assistance.

"Mr. Collins is a clergyman, is he not?"

"Yes, he is. From what my father says in his letter, he had almost obtained a living at Rosings, of all places, but when Lady Catherine heard the name of the estate he would someday inherit, she had a few choice words for the man, and then ordered her footmen to escort him off her property immediately! He is now a curate in a wealthy parish in Essex."

William sobered quickly. "Speaking of which... I received a letter from Aunt Catherine today…"

She arched an eyebrow. "I can only imagine that it included similar sentiments to the one I received yesterday."

His expression changed to one of concern, then conviction, and he said with a smile, "Elizabeth, if you agree, I believe I will direct our staff to *burn* any letters from my aunt or uncle without delay should either of us, or for that matter Georgiana, receive one in the future! I have no intention of ever reconciling with either of them and feel no remorse at the thought of never reading a word that either of them would care to send to any of us."

Elizabeth smiled, "I agree wholeheartedly, my love!"

William's expression changed to one so full of feeling for his wife, it spilt forth and enveloped her. "They never will accept that their plans were doomed to failure... *nothing* can ever divide us again."

Looking deeply into his eyes, she reached up and caressed his cheek. "Nothing. But really, we have never been divided in the true sense of the word. We may have been separated physically, but our love has been constant." Her eyes sparkled with adoration. "Thank you for bringing me here, my husband."

He closed his eyes and deeply breathed in her scent, reveling in her touch, both of which would never cease to cause the now familiar stirrings within him. Opening his eyes, he found her equally affected, and he proceeded to introduce her once again to the man within him, untamed by the gentleman.

Conceived under the tree his mother had climbed, near the hedge his father had come through, in the beautiful glade where their love had first bloomed... nine months later, the first of seven children, the heir to the Darcy legacy, Bennet Darcy, was born.

Wendi Sotis, the author of two novels and several short stories taking Jane Austen's beloved characters on journeys in new directions, graduated from Adelphi University with a degree in psychology. Sotis resides on Long Island, New York, with her husband, triplets and two guinea pigs.

Also to be released soon:

Dreams and Expectations

by Wendi Sotis

Fitzwilliam Darcy and Elizabeth Bennet quickly recognize their feelings for each other and form a friendship, but misunderstandings, and adventure, blur their path to happiness.